Praise for Foss...

"John Olson's *Fossil Hunter* is a delightful romantic thriller about a female Indiana Jones off on a scientific treasure hunt who finds it easier to cope with desert brigands than with the genteel backstabbing of academic politics. Enjoy the great adventure! I did."
PHILLIP E. JOHNSON, AUTHOR OF *DARWIN ON TRIAL*

"If you like novels that both entertain and make you think, then *Fossil Hunter* is for you. This is one fascinating thrill ride from the fertile imagination of John B. Olson."
JAMES SCOTT BELL, BEST-SELLING AUTHOR OF *TRY DYING* AND *THE WHOLE TRUTH*

"*Fossil Hunter* by John Olson has it all: adventure, romance and an interesting setting. Best of all, it gave me food for thought about Creation. I loved the book and will be recommending it to friends!"
COLLEEN COBLE, AUTHOR OF *ANATHEMA* AND THE ROCK HARBOR SERIES

"*Fossil Hunter* is engaging from page one. I couldn't put it down. A great plot and terrific characters make it a novel you won't want to miss."
RENE GUTTERIDGE, AUTHOR OF *THE SPLITTING STORM*

"John Olson may be the best in the world at writing woman-scientist-in-jeopardy suspense novels. *Fossil Hunter* features nonstop action and solid science, and it also does a terrific job of showing the wretched dilemma that every Christian with a PhD in the hard sciences has faced: You'll face suspicion from your fellow Christians and your fellow scientists. Bravo to John!"
RANDALL INGERMANSON, AUTHOR OF *DOUBLE VISION*

John B. Olson

Fossil Hunter

TYNDALE HOUSE PUBLISHERS, INC.
CAROL STREAM, ILLINOIS

Visit Tyndale's exciting Web site at www.tyndale.com

Check out the latest about John B. Olson at www.litany.com

TYNDALE and Tyndale's quill logo are registered trademarks of Tyndale House Publishers, Inc.

Fossil Hunter

Designed by Stephen Vosloo

Edited by Kathryn S. Olson

Library of Congress Cataloging-in-Publication Data

Olson, John (John B.).
  Fossil hunter / John B. Olson.
    p. cm
  ISBN-13: 978-1-4143-1459-4 (pbk.)
  ISBN-10: 1-4143-1459-0 (pbk.)
  1. Fossil hominids--Fiction. 2. Intelligent design (Teleology)--Fiction. I. Title.
  PS3615.L75F67 2008
  813'.6--dc22   2007038572

Printed in the United States of America

14 13 12 11 10 09 08
7   6   5   4   3   2   1

*To Mom and Dad, who loved me
through this project every step of the way.*

Acknowledgments

If my life were a novel, it would be one of those complicated Russian novels with so many characters a simpleminded reader like me couldn't hope to keep them all straight. So many people helped me with this book I can't begin to list them all. All I can say is, "Thank you, thank you, thank you." You know who you are even if I've temporarily forgotten. And for those of you who don't know who you are, I'd like to thank:

- Jed Macosko, Tim Standish, and Leonard Brand, for great discussions on being men of both faith and science.
- Nick Pyenson, for the guided tour of the UC Museum of Paleontology and for taking the time to show a greenhorn the paleontological ropes.
- Chuck Holton, for insight on what it's like to be an American in Iraq.
- John Simmons, for information on the security and layout of the Iraq Museum International.
- Chris Gowing, Robert Evans, Najmah Shaheen Wilkison, and Tayyab Amjad, for helping with language and culture of the Pakistani and Iraqi people.
- Readers: Jan Collins, Katie Vorreiter, Ellen Graebe, Ronie Kendig, Beth Goddard, Bill Olson, Chris Gowing, Robert Evans, Kathy Marbert, Jenn Doucette, Katie Cushman, Jim Rubart, and Geneva Scharff.
- John Sullivan, Walt Ruloff, Logan Craft, and the rest of the Premise Media gang, for bringing me into this project in the first place.
- Michael Platt, Carl Olsen, Sally Olson, Bill Olson, and Lynne Thompson, for help with plotting and structure.
- Peter Sleeper, Robinette and Steve Laube, for talking me down off the ledge.
- Jan Collins, Donna Fujimoto, Lori Arthur, Ellen Graebe, Judith Guerino, Nancy Hird, Sibley Law, Carl Olsen, Amy Olson, Michael Platt, Jennifer Rempel, Lynne Thompson, and all the other SCUM who helped with this project.
- John Bruce, for wisdom and spiritual guidance.
- Jessica Boulware, for answers to technical questions.
- Peter and Arianna, for being tireless, selfless, encouraging supporters who never fail to bring me joy.
- Amy, for all of the above and a whole lot more.

Whales underwent the most dramatic and complete transformation of any mammal. The early stages were so poorly known fifteen years ago that creationists held up whales as proof that species couldn't possibly have come about through natural selection. Now whales are one of the better examples of evolution.

Hans Thewissen, quoted in *'Evolution of Whales'* by Douglas Chadwick, National Geographic, *November 2001*

Part One

Prologue

*K*ATIE JAMES ran a cold fingertip across the dusty skull. It was so perfect, so . . . beautiful. Her breath drifted above the ancient whale fossil, painting ghostly shadows across its golden brown surface. A dark eyehole stared up through the haze. The whale seemed to be begging, pleading with her to free it from its sandstone tomb.

Stretching out on a worn wool blanket, Katie pulled out her needle pick and pushed it tentatively through the crumbling rock. If she were smart, she would wait until morning. The lantern light was way too dim for such delicate work. But she had to know. Were the nostrils on the top of the skull or closer to the tip of the nose? Was it related to the other whales she had found, or was it closer to the pre-whales Dr. Murad had reported finding in Pakistan? Whatever it was, it was definitely a new species.

And she had found it first.

A sharp clack sounded above the hum of the burning lantern. Katie pushed up onto her knees and stared into the surrounding darkness. Nothing. The Peruvian desert was almost perfectly flat. If there were people out there, she'd be able to see their lights for miles. It was probably just the crackle of her campfire. She lay back down on her blanket and scooted forward on her elbows to get a better look at a dark line in the sandstone.

The snort of a horse brought her to her feet. That didn't sound like any campfire she'd ever heard. "Hello? *Hola?*" Katie called out. Shielding her eyes against the glowing lantern, she turned in a slow circle, searching for pinpoints of reflected light. "Dr. Murad? If you're out there, you might as well introduce yourself. I've already found the whale."

She stood perfectly still, waiting for a reply. Someone was definitely out there. She could hear the stamping of restless horses—at least three of them. "Dr. Murad?" She angled toward her lantern, reached out a hand to extinguish the light. . . .

An explosion slapped into the armpit of her jacket, spinning her around. Katie dove to the ground and rolled as gunshots tore through the night air. Beating hooves charged down on her. Poachers. They were after her whale!

Breathing a quick prayer, she slid into a shallow depression and pressed herself flat against the ground. The mound by her head erupted in a spray of stinging rock. Bullets whizzed over her. Scooting backward, she tried to burrow deeper into the sand. No good. She had to come up with something fast. They'd be on top of her in seconds.

Taking a deep breath, she swept a hand across the shelf above her and came up with a baseball-size rock. *Perfect.* Springing to her knees, she spun toward the lantern and let the rock fly. The crash of breaking glass plunged the campsite into darkness. She dove to the side, rolling over and over across the depression until she hit a rocky ledge.

Katie froze with her ear to the ground. Reverberating gunshots gave way to the clack-clack of horses trotting across sandstone. They seemed to be splitting into two groups—to surround her? If it was the whale they wanted, why not let her escape?

She pushed up onto her feet and started to run, but a volley of gunshots sent her crashing back to the ground. Her campfire! They could see her silhouetted against the coals. She lay motionless for several seconds, pressing herself against the rocks as unseen horsemen circled around her. Finally, just as the two parties drew even with her position, she twisted around and crawled toward the coals. Even if they saw her, they wouldn't be able to shoot—not without hitting the other members of their—

Twang! A bullet whizzed past her ear.

Lunging forward, she grabbed a folded blanket and slammed it down on the bed of coals. Then, rolling to the side, she scrambled toward the shelter of her tent.

More gunshots. Shouting voices. The beam of a flashlight cut through the darkness, sweeping through the campsite. Another beam of light. She ducked inside the tent and pulled out a ten-pound bag of plaster powder. Slitting the side with her knife, she stepped out into the open, spun around in a tight circle, and launched the bag into the air. A white jet arced across the moonless sky and hit the center of camp with a mushroom cloud of hanging powder. Patches of light moved back and forth across the cloud. More voices. They were angry now. This was her chance.

Shutting her eyes, Katie plunged into the shielding cloud. As soon as the rock beneath her feet gave way to sand, she dropped onto her hands and knees and felt her way to the dig site. Her canteen was there somewhere. If she was going to have any chance at all . . . A gunshot tore through the cloud, flattening her to the ground. More shots. A shout to her left.

She scrambled forward, sweeping her arms across the sand. Where was it? Her hand snagged on a canvas strap. *Finally.* Swinging the canteen over her shoulder, she leaped to her feet and ran away from the sweeping lights, away from the shouting voices.

A beam of light flashed across her path, sending her skidding to the right. Horse hooves clacked behind her. She ran faster, plunging blindly into the darkness. Loose rocks turned under her feet. A step down almost tipped her off-balance, but still she managed to keep running. Farther and farther into the night until the shouting had faded into a distant murmur.

Finally she slowed to a walk and turned to look back at the points of sweeping light. Good. They'd given up on her and were searching the camp.

For the whale.

If only she'd taken the time to camouflage it . . . If only she'd thought to cover it with sand, they might have missed it. But now they were sure to find it. She took a step toward the camp and stopped.

There were only three flashlights. Was it possible there were only three of them? She took another step. No . . . she'd heard at least four—maybe as many as six—and they were all armed. She was being ridiculous. They were going to get the whale. End of story. There wasn't a thing she could do about it. She was a bonehead for even considering it.

She stood for several minutes, watching the moving lights. The blanket hadn't started burning yet. Maybe if she hurried . . . If she could get back before it burst into flames . . .

Slipping the canteen off her shoulder, she hefted it in her hand. Almost empty. She unscrewed the top and emptied the water onto the ground. Then, dropping to her knees, she scooped handful after handful of sand into the canteen. When it was full, she screwed the top back on and took off for the camp at a low crouch, circling around to the right as she got closer and closer to the searching men.

With the camp only thirty yards away, she dropped onto her stomach and inched her way toward a protrusion of wind-sculpted sandstone. She heard their voices clearly now. For a second she thought she heard "You check over there," but then she realized they were speaking Quechua or one of the other native languages. She pushed up onto her knees and crawled the last ten feet to the shelter of the rock formation. Peering out from around the rock, she looked past the bobbing flashlights to the dark area where she'd built her campfire. *Come on, burn already. Burst into flames.* . . . What was taking so long?

A loud thwack sliced through the darkness. The ring of metal digging into stone. They were using a pickax? On her whale? She got to her feet. Oh no they weren't.

Something rustled behind her. Katie started to turn, but a heavy shoulder hit her in the back, driving her face-first into the rock.

Chapter 1

*K*ATIE BRACED HER SHOULDER against the ladies' room door. Heavy knocks pounded into her arm, rattling the metal door against its frame.

"Katie, come out right now!" Dietrich Fischer's voice echoed through the tiled bathroom. "Already we are six minutes late. Everyone is now waiting!"

Squinting her eyes against the hard fluorescent light, Katie tried to clear her mind, but the faces wouldn't go away. An old man in a brown suit. Bloodshot, yellowing eyes. A generous dusting of dandruff on his shoulders, more on the left than on the right. The Asian woman standing in the back with the Minolta camera clasped tightly in long, manicured fingers. The fat man in the straining yellow polo. The four undergrads in the front row, whispering and nudging when she poked her head into the room . . .

"So what is it that is wrong? You are being sick?" Dietrich's voice broke through the battery of faces. "Answer me!"

Katie lifted a hand to her cheek. Her skin was cold and moist. Her stomach felt like it was going to boil over. Maybe if she just told him . . .

"Katie?" Dietrich hammered on the door, three piercing blows that buzzed into her brain.

She turned to face the door. "I told you . . . an intimate seminar— just for the department. You promised."

"I did. I invited only the department. They made to put up the flyers, but I told them no."

"But the conference room's almost full. You know I can't . . . We had a deal."

"Katie, listen to me. These people are already liking you. They want to meet this smart, brave fossil hunter they read about in the papers. You should be happy to have such fans. What do you want? To disappoint them?"

"But I . . . you know I can't do this. It's too many people. I'll just make a fool of myself. Maybe if I did a webcast for everyone. I could include pictures and all my data. They'd actually get a much better—"

The door pushed in on her, skidding her ridiculous heels clackety-clack across the tiled floor. Dietrich's jowly face appeared in the doorway, squinty eyes darting around the room before settling on her with a frown.

Pulling herself up straight, Katie stared back at him. She wasn't budging from the ladies' room. If he wanted a confrontation, he was going to get it right here.

"Katie . . ." Dietrich cleared his throat uneasily. "Katie, I know you don't like much the speaking to crowds. But I need you to do this. I and the whole lab. We *need* you."

Katie searched Dietrich's face. Something was wrong. Great beads of sweat were rolling down his expansive cheeks. His pupils were too contracted. "This isn't about the department, is it? Something else is going on."

"Nothing is going on with anything. It is a seminar. That is all. A simple seminar in which Thomas Woodburne just happens to be in the audience. But not to worry about him. He's one of your biggest fans. He told me this himself. Just tell the story of Peru. Show the pictures of the *Pericetus*. You'll be very good."

"Thomas Woodburne? The guy from the Smithsonian? What's he doing here?"

"He's very important in Washington. In the NAS."

"Since when do you care about the National Academy?"

"Since always I care about the Academy. Our grant . . ." Dietrich's face contorted into a scowl. He cocked his head and turned to face the wall. "Grant money does not grow on the trees, you know. This affects your research as much more than mine."

"My research?" Katie stepped toward Dietrich, forcing him to look her in the eye. "You said they'd renewed the grant. You said it wasn't a problem."

Dietrich took a couple of shuffling steps backward until he hit the wall. "It won't be. I'm filing an appeal. Once they find out about your new work . . ."

"So you invited Woodburne without telling me? Who else did you invite? Half of Albuquerque's in there."

Dietrich looked down at his watch. "Eight minutes late! We must go out there now."

"Fine; go ahead. I'm not stopping you." Katie turned to walk away, but a meaty paw pulled her up short.

"Just tell the story of Peru. The capture of the fossil thieves. That is just what they would like to hear."

"But there isn't anything to tell. They destroyed the fossil before I could even look at it."

"Katie, please." His hand tightened around her shoulder. "I need you to do this. Without the grant renewed . . . we'll be out of money by November. I won't be able to pay your salary. Hooman's salary. Wayne's, Peggy's . . . No money, no research."

Katie took a deep breath. The room was *so* crowded. . . .

"You want I should tell Hooman he has to go back?"

"Okay, I get the point. I'm being blackmailed." She resisted the tug on her shoulder.

"Whitemailed only. I'm the good guy boss. Yes?"

Katie couldn't help smiling. She stopped resisting and allowed herself to be led back to the door.

"This will be very easy. You will see." He held the door open for her and guided her through. "They are all your biggest fans."

Katie focused on her adviser's voice as he led her down the hallway. She could do this. It was just like her thesis defense. The number of people didn't matter. Four or four hundred. It was all the same—as long as she didn't look at them.

Dietrich opened the auditorium door and the roar of voices filled her ears. *God, help me. Please . . .* She looked down at the floor, allowing herself to be guided to the front of the room. Her heart pounded in her chest, pulsing through her neck. She couldn't breathe. There was too much pressure.

"Everyone, thank you for being so patient. . . ." Dietrich's voice beat against the roar. Seats squeaked. Desktops clanged into place. Zippers, papers, the shuffling of feet . . .

Katie tightened her grip on Dietrich's arm, leaning against his bulk for balance. One step at a time, she focused on each carpeted stair tread as she climbed higher and higher onto the stage. The murmur of voices assaulted her. She could feel thousands of eyes staring at her. She was naked, exposed, on display for all the world to see.

God, please . . .

". . . earned her PhD in earth and planetary sciences here at the University of New Mexico, where she was the first to discover . . ."

Katie gripped the podium with both hands and pulled herself up straight as Dietrich introduced her. The *Pericetus* whales, the geology of South America . . . She could do this. She didn't have many geology slides, but she could start with her latest findings and use them as a segue into her research on the *Pericetus* fossils. And then maybe, if everything was going okay, she'd tell them about Peru. It was the only thing people seemed to care about these days—even the other paleontologists were more interested in Peru than in her research. Nothing ever changed. Even behind bars the fossil poachers were still stealing her science.

A burst of applause washed through the auditorium. Flashes of blinding light. Katie stared determinedly down at the laptop on the podium. Her ears and cheeks were burning scarlet. Who was taking pictures? She was going to look like a blushing radish.

"Thank you for coming." Her words came out strong and clear. "Before I start talking about ancient whale anatomy, which is, I'm sure, the reason you're all here—" Katie took a calming breath as a ripple of laughter ran through the room—"I'd like to give a brief summary of some recent work I've done on the geology of South America."

The auditorium was perfectly still. Katie relaxed her grip on the podium. She could do this. Piece of cake.

"As you all know, the Tethys Sea, which once covered India, Pakistan, and most of what is now the modern Middle East, was home to the earliest archaeocetes we've uncovered to date: the pakicetids, ambulocetids, protocetids, basilosaurines—"

"Katie, a tiny minute please!" Dietrich called out from the corner of the stage. "For the undergrads and guests . . . Perhaps you must explain the evolutionary significance of these early whales. What is it, the reason of their importance?"

"Okay . . ." Katie closed her eyes and focused on her breathing. She wouldn't let him get to her. Now wasn't the time. "Fifty years ago—" she chose her words carefully—"whales were held up as an argument against the evolutionary model. If modern whales evolved from terrestrial mammals, why didn't we see any evidence in the fossil record? Why didn't we see any intermediary forms?

"Since then, however, paleontologists have uncovered scores of putative intermediary whale forms. The pakicetids, first discovered in Pakistan by Gingerich in 1981, were fleet-footed land animals with very few adaptations for marine life except for a few features of their ears. They lived roughly 50 million years ago during the early Eocene sub-epoch.

"The ambulocetids, or so-called walking whales, also lived during the early Eocene of Pakistan. They too seemed primarily terrestrial and had well-developed limbs and feet.

"The protocetids of the middle Eocene, however, were primarily aquatic. The *Rodhocetus*, for example, swam using elongated, paddle-like hind feet and the side-to-side motion of its powerful tail.

"Later, during the late Eocene, we get the appearance of the basilosaurines and durodontines, which were fully aquatic and swam like modern whales using an up-and-down motion of their tale flukes. These archaeocetes differed from modern whales in that they had very small, almost vestigial, hind limbs. They also lacked blowholes on the tops of their skulls."

Katie glanced over at Dietrich and received a curt nod. *So far so good.* "Okay, as I was saying before, most of the earliest whales have been found in and around the Middle East, but due to certain social and political, um . . . factors, most Western paleontologists haven't been able to get into these areas for a long time. A few privileged scientists have obtained exclusive permits to go into Pakistan, and one scientist in particular, who shall remain nameless, has recently made some pretty amazing discoveries there, but since the fossils aren't allowed outside the country, none of the rest of us have been able to verify them. So those of us who want to study ancient whales are pretty much out of luck. Until now . . .

"It just so happens that the geology of the western South American continent is very similar to that of the Middle East. In theory we should be able to find the same types of whales there that Nick Murad, our unnamed scientist, has found in Pakistan but without all the social and political *factors* that make expeditions to the Tethys region so prohibitive.

"As many of you know, I had the opportunity to explore a middle Eocene plain in Peru and was able to demonstrate the presence of whale fossils there. Unfortunately, the fossil I found was destroyed before I had the chance to study it. The part of the skull I could see looked fairly modern, but until we return to the area and uncover another one, we won't know for sure whether the whale had hind limbs and nostrils at the front of the snout like a *Rodhocetus* or a strong swimming tail and a blowhole on the top of the skull like the more modern *Pericetus* whales we've already found in Peru. The sooner we—"

"Katie, a question." Dietrich called out. "Sorry to be interrupting again, but Dr. Webb has a question."

Katie gripped the podium tighter. She could feel the pressure building in her chest. "Okay . . . Dr. Webb?" She kept her eyes fixed on the laptop keyboard.

"So what makes you question the age of the layer? Was it the appearance of the fossil or the geology of the layer itself?"

"I'm sorry." Katie ran through the question in her mind. "I wasn't questioning the age of the layer. It's definitely middle Eocene. Several other finds confirm the geology report."

"Then how can you question the morphology? If it's middle Eocene, it *has* to be a primitive whale, an *Archaeoceti.*"

"How can I question it?" Katie took a deep breath and let it out slowly. "I question it because it's not known yet. Until we find another fossil, we can't know for sure what it will look like. For all we know, it could have the morphology of Shamu, the killer whale."

A gasp sounded somewhere in the auditorium. So much for her attempt at levity.

"Dr. James," a woman's voice called out from the back of the room, "this whale you're talking about—the one that was destroyed—it was the reason you were attacked by fossil poachers?"

"Yes, I . . ." Katie could feel the blood rushing into her cheeks. "With more and more private collectors buying fossils on the black market, fossil poaching is getting to be a huge problem, especially in impoverished countries where—"

"Could you confirm the report that you single-handedly captured five armed men?" A man's voice.

"I . . ." Katie's face was burning now. "Yes, there were five of them. But I . . ."

"How did you do it?" The woman again. "How did you stop so many men?"

"How did I stop them?" Katie sagged against the podium. Weren't these people listening? "I didn't stop them. I tried, but by the time I got back to camp, they'd already started digging. And then, like an idiot, I let myself get captured. By the time I got back in control of the situation, they'd already powdered the fossil. We think they were looking for teeth. A tooth from a *T. rex* can sell for as much as five thousand dollars."

She hit the Page Down key on the laptop to bring up her first slide. "The whales I typically study, including the *Pericetus* whales I want to talk about now, don't have teeth. They have baleen, which they use to—"

"But how did you do it? How did you get away?"

Katie gripped the podium tighter. "It wasn't a big deal. They weren't paying attention so I . . . whacked them on the head."

A volley of flashes hit Katie in the face as a wave of shouted questions washed over her. She squeezed her eyes shut. Tried to tune out the voices. "Baleen whales—"

"Dr. James! Please! Dr. James!" The woman's shouts rose above the roar, beating the other voices down to a low murmur. "Dr. James, please. How do you expect us to believe you hit five men over their heads?"

"Not all at once. They only had two men guarding—"

"Dr. James!" Webb's bellowing voice. "Back to the subject at hand. You still haven't answered my question!"

Katie looked up from the podium. The Asian woman in the back. Her hand was still raised. A man, freckles and thinning red hair, was holding out a microphone. The man with dandruff. The woman beside him, twisting a finger through her hair. Drooping earlobes with big dangly earrings. Mark Cranley from the White lab. Joe Sayers . . . They were all staring, watching. . . .

Katie's stomach surged. Cold sweat streamed down her face. She felt dizzy. Couldn't breathe. *Please, no . . . not again!*

Pushing away from the podium, she staggered across the stage to the stairs. A shoe twisted beneath her foot, sending her crashing down the steps. She hit the carpeted floor and rolled back onto her feet, running. Up the side aisle. Out the door.

The echoes of clacking footsteps chased her down the hallway and into the bathroom. Through the swinging door, into one of the stalls, she collapsed onto her knees in front of a toilet.

Reporters . . . Dietrich was such a liar. He'd promised intimate, but he'd invited reporters! A shudder convulsed her body. She took a long, deep breath. It would serve him right if she walked into his office right now and quit. Let him find someone else to lead the next Peru expedition.

Katie stood up slowly, bracing herself against the stall partition. The pressure in her stomach was subsiding. She took a few experimental steps.

Of all the childish stunts . . . She tottered over to the counter, pulled out a wad of paper towels, and started dabbing her skin. It'd serve him right if the visas were denied. She leaned against the sink, staring at the drain to avoid the reflection that hovered mockingly in the mirror. All those cameras. Thomas Woodburne. She'd looked like an idiot.

A knock sounded at the door. Katie spun around, bracing herself for another encounter.

"Katie?" It was Hooman, one of the grad students from Dietrich's lab. "Katie, are you all right? Dr. Fischer sent me. He asked me to make sure you're okay."

Great . . . Does he have to yell? Katie took a step toward the door. Why didn't bathroom doors have locks?

"He wants you to come back to the conference room as soon as you feel better, okay? There are some people in the audience who want to meet you."

An unfamiliar voice sounded in the hallway. Another voice, this one female. Katie cast a glance back at the mirror. Tendrils of fine dark hair were plastered to the side of her sweat-beaded face. She was white as a ghost.

"Katie, are you there?"

Katie glanced around the room. A window was partially open. It looked big enough.

Tiptoeing to the back of the room, she slid the frosted glass panel all the way up and stuck her head out. The courtyard was three stories below her, but at least it was empty. And the ledge was more than wide enough. . . .

"Katie?"

Glancing back at the door, Katie kicked off her heels and tossed them through the window. Then, lifting a leg cautiously over the sill, she ducked through the opening and stepped gingerly out onto the pigeon-stained ledge.

An image flashed before her eyes. She was five years old, scaling a rocky cliff on the Navajo reservation. Her father was down below, calling up to her with a ragged voice. A geyser of panic surged through her body, freezing her against the dusty wall. Her father . . . She couldn't lose her job. Not now. Her father needed her.

She swung a knee over the windowsill and ducked her head back inside. If Dietrich didn't get his grant renewed . . . because of her freaking out . . .

Another knock rapped at the bathroom door. The murmur of anxious voices. How many people were out there? It sounded like the whole seminar room.

Katie's head started to throb. What was the point? She took a deep breath and stepped back onto the ledge. Going inside would only make it worse. Throwing up on the reporters wasn't going to get Dietrich's grant renewed.

Gripping the bricks with her fingertips, she inched her way along the ledge, careful not to look down. Heights didn't bother her, but if someone was down there watching her . . . if the crowd from the auditorium . . .

Flashing cameras lit her memory. The man with red hair. Orange-brown freckles framing pale blue eyes. The man with dandruff . . .

Stop it! Katie stared hard at a grainy line of off-white mortar. What had gotten into her? She was acting like a baby.

She worked her way around a projecting windowsill and sidled to the corner of the building in long, determined strides. She swung herself around the corner and looked down at the roof of the adjoining building. Only a ten-foot drop. Piece of cake.

Pushing off the wall, she twisted her body into the shrieking air. Pain stabbed into her feet as she hit and rolled across a sweltering surface of gravel and tar. *Hot!* She hopped from foot to foot across the burning rooftop and flung herself at the edge of the building. Clinging to the blistering cornice work, she swung her legs over the side and climbed down the ladderlike arrangement of ornamental bricks before dropping onto the ground below.

Brilliant. Katie lay on her back, combing her feet through the soothing coolness of the grass. Jumping barefoot onto a blazing-hot rooftop. *Katie James, brilliant fossil hunter.* For her next trick she would jump barefoot into a hot unemployment line.

>>

Nick Murad leaned against an outcropping of rock and wiped his face with the back of his sleeve. The dusty fabric gritted like wet sandpaper. His right eye burned as a drop of sweat rolled across his upper lid. He raised a hand to wipe his face, but his fingers were coated with a paste of sunscreen and dirt. His shirt, his hat, his pants . . . the grit was everywhere. Eating its way like hookworms into every crease and crevice of his body.

He squeezed his eyes shut and shook his head from side to side, flinging away drops of sweat like a big Labrador after a swim. *Beautiful* . . . Now both eyes were burning. What he needed was a shower. A hot shower using nonbiodegradable soap and a towel that wasn't full of sand. He stood slowly, arching his lower back against the Pakistani sunset.

Tomorrow . . . less than twenty hours away. He checked his watch, automatically subtracting nine hours in his mind. It was almost 5 a.m. in New York. Cindy would already be at the airport by now. He could see her standing in line at the flight counter dressed to the nines in an impossibly impractical but totally seductive skirt and blouse. He tried to imagine her carrying twice her limit of suitcases by herself, but his mind's eye kept drifting to her face. Soft, limpid eyes. Full, pouty lips. Her dark sapphire necklace caressing soft, creamy skin.

A hungry ache coiled around Nick's chest, squeezing him until he couldn't breathe. "Okay. Enough." He dropped back to the ground and retrieved his geology hammer from the rocky shelf he'd been working on since noon. He'd see Cindy soon enough. But only a third of the whale vertebra was exposed. If he was going to get it pedestaled before he left, he had to hurry. He grabbed a chisel and started chipping away at the mudstone that encased the fossilized bone. His students wouldn't have time to finish the excavation before their expedition to Iraq, but he at least wanted to know what it was he'd found.

A soft cry drifted up from the valley. Nick stopped chiseling and turned back to stare into the setting sun. The clank of metal on metal. Nick held his breath, listening.

Maaaah, maaaah. The bleating of sheep.

Diving for his pack, Nick pulled a radio out of one of the side pockets.

"Okay, people, we've got sheep!" He threw open the bag and started stuffing it with gear as the static of answering calls filled the air.

"Nick, this is Andy. Annalise is down by the ridge with Ahamed. Waseem, where are you?"

"Karl here. Waseem's with me. We're at the ridge, but Annalise isn't here."

"Annalise, where are you? We've got sheep coming through!"

Nick swung the pack onto his shoulder and ran sliding and skidding down the gravelly slope. When he got to the bottom, he held the radio to his mouth. "Everybody, this is Nick. Get to the camp right away. Karl, tell Waseem I need him to find Annalise now!"

Leaping a clump of polygonaceae shrubs, Nick took off running toward a point just to the right of the ridge excavation. If Annalise had gone off on her own to do some prospecting, she'd probably work her way west along the hills. That's what he'd do.

A bell clanked—just beyond the rise. Nick, already panting for breath, pushed his burning legs to move faster. The bedouin tribes in the north were usually pretty friendly, but this close to the Afghanistan border all bets were off—especially after what happened to the GSP team in western Baluchistan.

A burst of static cut through the radio. "Nick, this is Andy. We've got Annalise. She and Ahamed were already on their way back to camp."

Relief washed through Nick's body, turning his legs to jelly. He slowed to a jog and turned back in the direction of the camp. "Okay, everybody. Stay inside! Have Waseem watch the trucks. . . . I'll be right there."

By the time Nick reached the campsite, only a half mile separated him from the advance guard of the camel-mounted bedouins. He risked another backward glance. Still too far to make out their features. Unless they had binoculars, they couldn't be sure he was a Westerner. Lots of Pakistanis wore baseball caps.

He jogged into the circle of four tents and three vehicles that made up their camp. Karl and Andy were shuttling equipment from one of the transport trucks to the cook tent at the base of a rocky mound. Annalise was rolling up the windows of one of the jeeps.

"Michigan students out of sight now!" Nick leaned over, swept up a pack emblazoned with a big gold *M,* and tossed it into the cook tent. "Waseem, stay with the trucks. Ahamed, you're with me. Make sure you keep your hands out of sight!"

Nick paced the length of the camp, inspecting all of their visible gear. Some pickaxes, a tripod and surveyor's scope, a field laptop wrapped in a sheet of plastic . . . There was a lot of expensive equipment, but nothing to indicate the presence of Westerners. Theft was the least of his concerns. Bedouins weren't generally thieves—even the poorest of them. But with all the anti-American sentiment these days, he couldn't afford to have their whereabouts leak out. Even if they weren't harboring terrorists, bedouins liked to talk. And no news traveled like the news of American scientists prospecting alone and unprotected out in the middle of the Baluchistan desert.

The echo of Pakistani voices carried across the thin desert air. The clomp of heavy hooves. Nick hurried over to his tent and crawled past Ahamed, who was already sitting in the entrance, his right arm extended awkwardly back inside the tent like he was holding a concealed weapon.

"Okay . . . everybody quiet." Nick hissed in a whisper loud enough to carry to all the tents. "I hear one word of English and I'm shipping you back to the States."

"*Jee haan maan.*" Urdu for *Yes, Mommy.* . . . Nick couldn't tell whether it was Andy or Karl. A feminine giggle broke the silence off to the right.

"I'm serious." Nick put a hand to his mouth even though none of his students were there to see his smile. "We'll pack this camp up and leave that *Basilosaurus* behind."

A voice jabbered off to the left. The bedouins were almost even with the camp. Keeping well back from the tent opening, Nick angled forward until he had a clear view of the pass. It was getting darker. The shadow of the tents already stretched most of the way across the camp. If those bedouins didn't hurry up . . .

A pang stabbed through him like a knife. Surely the bedouins wouldn't set up camp so close to their campsite? He had to drive to Quetta in the morning. He needed time to shower and shave and get a haircut. Cindy would be there by noon. If he was going to have any time at all to clean the apartment, he had to leave by 5 a.m. Why hadn't he gone with his instincts and cleaned up before he left?

Come on. Hurry up. Nick's eyes strained into the shadows, willing the bedouins to appear. Maybe they'd already stopped for the night. At least that way the road would be clear for him. As long as they didn't see him leave . . .

Beautiful. Two camel riders plodded into view—not more than a hundred feet from where Nick sat crouched in the shadows of his tent. The bedouins stared back silently at the camp, long rifles still holstered against the sides of their complaining mounts. *Go on. Keep on going.* . . . Nick repeated the words like a prayer as one rider after another passed, guiding a stream of dust-colored sheep.

One of the riders, a tall, lanky, dark-skinned man in a cloak of dusty brown, pulled his mount over to the side and stood facing the tents. He waved with his left hand, keeping his right hand within easy reach of his rifle. Nick crept around the back of the tent until he could see Waseem wave from one of the trucks. Waseem's movements seemed wooden, like he was nervous . . . hiding something. *Of all the stupid mistakes* . . . He should have put Ahamed in the trucks.

He moved back to the right. The bedouin was just sitting there, staring at the camp. Nick shrank even farther into the tent. Of course the guy was staring. They should have been cooking, preparing for the approaching night.

A musical ring tone shattered the silence. Ahamed jumped like he'd been shot. Nick searched frantically about the tent, his eyes finally settling on his nylon pack. Crawling over to the bag, he ripped open the outer compartment and pulled out his satellite phone. Just as he was about to hit the Off switch, he noticed the name glowing on the display. It was Cindy. . . .

The phone rang again.

Had there been another travel advisory? Had they canceled the flight? *Please, no* . . . She wasn't chickening out again. Not now!

He stabbed at the green button and pressed the phone to his ear, turning away from the entrance. "Hello?" he whispered into his cupped hand.

"Hello, Nick? Are you there? I can't hear you." Cindy sounded frantic. Something was wrong. He had to talk to her.

"Hey, Cindy. I really can't talk now. Can you call back in a few minutes?" Nick raised his voice to a hoarse whisper.

"Nick, is that you? I can barely hear you."

"I hear you fine. What's wrong?" His voice sounded like a shout in his ears.

"Must be a bad connection. Anyway, I . . . ." Cindy was about to panic. He could hear it in her voice. "The Middle East is all over the news. New fighting in Iraq. Pakistanis protesting the president's visit. I . . . It just doesn't seem like a good time."

"No . . . it's fine. There's nothing to worry about." Nick knew he was talking too loud, but he had no choice. He couldn't let her back out now. Not after all his plans . . .

"You're sure? They showed a huge crowd on the news. They were yelling and burning American flags."

"That's just for the cameras. Just get on the plane. You'll be safe. I promise. Okay? Just get on the plane. I've got everything planned. I even have a surprise."

"A surprise?" Nick could hear the life coming back into her voice. "What kind of surprise?"

"Just get on the plane, okay? You'll see when you get here."

"You're sure it's safe?"

"I'm positive. I love you, okay?"

"Nick, I . . ."

"I've got to go now. Bye." Nick switched off the phone and turned back to the opening of the tent. The bedouin was still watching their camp, his face lit by the faintest hint of a smile.

Ahamed turned and looked back at Nick, shaking his head and rolling his eyes. "I love you too . . . honey."

Chapter 2

KATIE RACED THROUGH THE GEOLOGY BUILDING, turning first left and then right through the long, empty hallways. A clock on the far wall read 9:07. Dietrich was going to kill her. The note he'd left on her desk said he wanted to meet her at 9:00 a.m. sharp. As if yesterday's seminar wasn't bad enough . . . He was going to fire her first and then kill her.

She turned into an old, deserted lab and wove her way through the clutter to Dietrich's office in the back corner of the room. Light showed faintly under a dark varnished door. The sound of laughter. Katie slid to a stop and listened with her ear to the door. A deep, throaty voice—it sounded like Dr. Nielsen. *Great.* The way the department chairman liked to talk, they could be in there all morning. At least Dietrich couldn't complain about her being late.

She plopped down onto an old lab stool and spun herself in a slow circle. Dietrich was going to be furious, but the seminar wasn't her fault. He knew she couldn't do crowds, but he had invited the reporters anyway—reporters *and* a member of the funding committee. It would serve him right if he didn't get his grant renewed. He'd be getting just what he deserved.

Her gaze wandered to the lab bench beside her. A partially extracted whale skull sat on a nest of supporting sandbags. Unused tools littered the bench: brushes, chisels, the most expensive Dremel set in the entire lab. As far as she could tell, Dietrich hadn't removed a flake of the surrounding matrix in years. At the rate he was going, the layer of dust covering the skull was going to harden and encase the skull, once again, in solid rock.

Sliding off the stool, she wandered over to the desk beside the bench and reread the collection of yellowing comic strips filling the built-in bulletin board. *The Far Side, Calvin and Hobbes, Bloom County* . . . not one of the strips was less than twenty years old. Some of them were older than she was. Her eyes drifted from the comics to the cracked, yellow walls of the lab. Safety posters from the 1980s. Gray slate lab benches, dry and powdery as dust. Old wooden desks covered with a fine filigree of darkening scratches. The whole lab was slowly becoming a fossil. Trapped forever in an earlier age.

The door to the office opened, and Dietrich poked his head into the lab. "Katie, where have you been? We have been waiting already fifteen minutes!"

We? As in Dietrich *and* the chairman? Katie took a deep breath and followed her adviser back into his office. "I'm sorry. . . . I was waiting outside. I didn't want to interrupt—"

"Katie James." Dr. Nielsen rose from a green vinyl chair and shook her hand. "It is good to see you again. I've been reading about your Peru trip in the papers."

Katie lowered her gaze. "Sorry about that. I don't know how the reporters got the story, but it wasn't from me. I promise. I haven't spoken a word to any of them."

"That's quite all right. No harm done. A little free publicity never hurt anyone." He glanced over at Dietrich before turning back to her. "But actually I'm not here about the stories. I've actually . . . received a few complaints about your seminar yesterday."

"Complaints?" Katie looked to Dietrich for help, but he avoided her gaze. "The seminar was supposed to be small and intimate—only a few people from the department were even invited—but then this huge crowd shows up: reporters, photographers, undergrads from other departments . . . It was a circus."

Nielsen nodded. "I understand your dislike of crowds and I sympathize. I really do. But you do realize . . . the department has done everything in its power to make things easier for you. We've dropped our teaching requirements, rescheduled classes, shielded you from crowds at your orals. . . ."

"I know and I really appreciate it, but—"

"Katie, you have to understand what a difficult position this puts us in. Teaching and giving seminars is an integral part of being an academician. You can't just go out into the desert and find things on your own. You have a responsibility to communicate your findings to others—clearly and concisely—in a way that doesn't get twisted into—"

"I understand." Katie looked to Dietrich again. "That's why I wanted to publish my findings first. I was even willing to do a seminar, but when the seminar deteriorated into a feeding-frenzy press conference . . . What good could have come out of that?"

"What good?" Dietrich flung his hands in the air. "Do you hear what it is she is saying? With Thomas Woodburne in the audience, he with the power to renew our grant, and she asks what good?" He turned back to Katie. "There are more things in consideration here than just papers and seminars. Research takes money and good research takes good money!"

"Yes, of course." The chairman held up a restraining hand. "And getting funding requires good communication. It's absolutely essential. The failure to effectively communicate—as we've just seen—can be disastrous."

Katie opened her mouth to argue, but what could she say? She'd run out of the auditorium in front of Thomas Woodburne and a room full of reporters. She watched as the chairman swallowed thoughtfully and settled back in his chair. Whatever it was he wanted to say, she could tell she wasn't going to like it.

"Katie, I know this wasn't your intent, but one of the scientists at the seminar insists you, in your presentation, were calling the process of evolution into question."

"What?" Katie turned a furious look on Dietrich. "That's ridiculous. I went through all the main archaeocete families. I mean, I know I only hit the highlights, but my talk wasn't even about evolution. I wasn't even planning to bring it up."

"I know this obviously wasn't your intent, and I'm sure if he had

had time to ask a few clarifying questions, the whole thing would have gotten sorted out before it ever got to be an issue, but since you had to, uh . . . leave the seminar early, he never had a chance to ask those clarifying questions."

"Okay . . ."

"So he ended up *researching* your background, your beliefs."

Great. A lump rose in Katie's throat. *It's finally happening.*

"Anyway, this scientist came to me yesterday afternoon. He'd discovered your father is a, uh . . . Baptist minister?"

Katie nodded. She could feel her cheeks beginning to tingle.

"And you are a member of his church?"

Katie nodded again and looked him in the eye. "Is that a problem?"

"No, no . . . of course not." He waved the notion aside with a brittle laugh. "It's not a problem at all. I only brought it up because, well . . . people have been talking. A few have even suggested—and I want you to know that I don't believe this for a second—but a few have suggested that you, because of your religious bias, might have fabricated the whole story about the Peruvian fossil poachers. That you yourself destroyed the fossil because it was a further confirmation of whale evolution."

"That's ridiculous!" Katie leaped to her feet. "That's so absurd . . . I don't even know where to begin. Check with the Peruvian police. See if the five men in jail are figments of my imagination. Better yet, check my field notebook. I have pictures!"

"Take it easy. . . . Calm down," the chairman said in a soothing voice. "I already told you: I don't believe them for a second. It's not me you have to convince. But you have to look at it from their point of view. Here in this room, we know how, uh . . . capable you are in the field, but to people who don't know you as well as Dietrich and I do . . . You have to admit, the idea that a lone woman could single-handedly capture a band of armed men is pretty hard to believe."

"That doesn't mean it didn't happen!"

"Of course not. But you can see how people might wonder— especially now that it comes out you're a creationist. You can see—"

"Who says I'm a creationist?" Katie exclaimed. "Just because I'm a Christian doesn't mean I'm a creationist. I know lots of Christians who think God used the process of evolution—"

"Of course, of course—"

"And what do you even mean by *creationist*? Who gets to define the term? The word has way too much baggage."

"Katie, I agree with you," the chairman cut in. "I'm on your side, remember? I'm not labeling you as a creationist. Nobody is. It's just that when you questioned evolution in your seminar—with the press there . . . Of course people are going to talk. It's only natural for the issue of bias to be raised—especially after all the stories about Peru."

"But I never questioned evolution."

"No?" Dietrich cleared his throat and leaned across his desk toward Katie. "I would not wish to disagree, but I remember distinctly you saying *putative*. *Putative* intermediary forms. If this does not call into question evolution, I must wonder what it does."

"But they *are* putative. We don't know for sure *Pakicetus* is on the evolutionary pathway to modern whales. It could have been a side branch, an evolutionary dead end."

"And you saying the whale in Peru could be modern even though its finding was in middle Eocene stratum? What of this? It questions every good principle of integrated biology."

"Not *modern* as in time period," Katie exclaimed. "I said it could have been more modern in form, with the nasal openings on top of the skull rather than at the tip of the nose."

"See?" Dietrich turned to Nielsen with a look of triumph. "She admits it! She expects to find modern forms the same age as four-legged *Rodhocetus*!"

"All I said was we had to reserve judgment until we could look at the actual data. Talk about bias! You're so biased you're condemning me for a lack of bias!"

"So now I am the biased?" Dietrich threw up his hands. "This is outrage!"

"Enough!" Nielsen rose to his feet. "Katie . . . this is all beside the point. I shouldn't have even brought it up. I don't care what you do

or don't believe. It makes absolutely no difference to me *or* Dietrich."
He turned a stern look on her adviser. "But I need you to understand the situation. The fact that you ran out of the seminar without
clarifying your position—the fact that, because of your . . . condition,
you couldn't communicate what you intended to communicate—the
controversy you generated will almost certainly prevent Dietrich from
getting his grant renewed."

Katie sank back down into her chair. They were blaming her for the
loss of the grant? She looked at the floor, automatically assigning ages to
the various crumbs and spills. Finally, after a long, uncomfortable silence,
she looked up at Nielsen. "So what do you want me to do?"

The chairman shrugged and nodded to Dietrich.

"There is grant money only enough to last to November." Dietrich
contorted his face into a look of almost genuine concern. "Not enough
to pay students' salaries to end of semester. Hooman, Wayne, Peggy
. . . they all still take the coursework."

"What if I went without a salary—until we get another grant?"

Dietrich turned to the chairman, who shook his head.

"That's very generous of you to offer, Katie, but I'm afraid I can't
allow it," Nielsen said. "There are rules and regulations concerning
payroll issues."

Katie studied Dietrich's face. He was waiting for her to say something. He actually expected her to quit! The lump in her throat sank
to the pit of her stomach. If she couldn't work for the university, what
would she do? She couldn't move. Her father needed her.

"Perhaps," Dietrich suggested, "if Hooman made to move to a
geology lab. He wanted to study the biology, but . . ."

"That won't be necessary." Numbness spread through her body as
soon as she spoke the words. "I can take a hint. I'm quitting. Effective
immediately. I won't work at a place that doesn't appreciate me."

The bedouin camp lay spread out beneath the early morning stars.
Nick lay stretched out on the ground watching the sleeping camp. No

sentries, no guards, no movement of any kind. He leaned over and whispered to Ahamed, "They're just bedouins. As long as they don't find out we're Americans, we should be fine."

Ragged breathing sounded in his ear. "Not if they hide Al-Qaeda." The Pakistani guide's whisper was so faint Nick could barely make it out.

"If they were Al-Qaeda, wouldn't they at least post sentries?"

"So others may know they hide something?"

"So what are we doing here, then?" Nick hissed. He pushed up onto his hands and knees, but Ahamed pulled him back down.

"Wait . . ."

Nick looked back toward the tents. He couldn't see the road from where he lay, but it had to be at least a hundred feet away from the bedouins' camp. As long as it wasn't blocked by sheep, he would be okay. It was a dark night. Even if the bedouins woke up and managed to get out of their tents in time, they still wouldn't be able to tell he was a Westerner. Not with his headlights on. He'd be fine—just another Pakistani shepherd on his way to the market in Quetta.

He checked his watch: 4:35 a.m. If he didn't leave soon, he wouldn't have time to straighten his apartment. "Stay here if you want. I've got to leave now. Cindy's plane comes in at noon."

Ahamed huffed and rolled his eyes.

"It's okay; they're safe enough. They won't even see me." Nick climbed to his feet and started picking his way back to camp.

Suddenly Ahamed was at his side. "Never safe," the guide whispered at his ear. "If you do not leave before sunrise, you do not leave at all. Even in the dark, you still look of the West."

"My father was born in Peshawar, you know."

"And your mother?"

Nick cast a parting glance at the bedouin camp and hurried to keep up with his friend. His mother was Irish and Lebanese. She could pass for a Pakistani, even up close, if you didn't notice her eyes. Of course, not noticing her eyes was almost impossible. Just like Cindy's eyes—if you could keep your gaze on her eyes long enough to take them in. Everything else about Cindy cried out to be noticed too.

"Not too fast." Ahamed held out an arm. "I think I hear something."

"How could you hear with—" Nick suddenly froze. Three massive shadows appeared out of nowhere. They were carrying guns.

Nick slowed to a stop as the bedouins started barking orders in Urdu. He raised his hands in the air, palms forward, fingers outspread. Ahamed responded with a long jabbering speech. Something about *gora chooras*—white Christians.

One of the men stepped forward and spoke in a slow, solemn voice. He turned and nodded at Nick. The other two bedouins started laughing.

"What's he saying?" Nick hissed.

"Chhh!" Ahamed silenced him with a raised hand and faced the bedouins. He spoke a few more words of Urdu and turned back to Nick. "The bedouins invite us to share their morning meal. You should know the high importance of hospitality our culture values. This is most serious. Very delicate. Think carefully before you give an answer."

"Did you tell them I have to be at the airport in Quetta in a few hours?"

"Under the circumstances, I do not think this is a wise answer."

"Ahamed, I don't have a choice. If I'm not there to meet Cindy as she comes off the plane, she'll turn right back around and fly home to the United States."

"Perhaps this is the best thing."

"Ahamed!"

The guide sighed and turned reluctantly back to the bedouins. After a short, animated speech the men burst out laughing. One of them stepped forward, jabbered something, and slapped Nick on the shoulder.

"What are they saying? What did you tell them?"

"I tell them the fortunate ones in our party are honored to share their meal, but you, to your eternal disappointment, cannot. I say you must meet your spoiled, demanding American woman at the airport and wait on her hand and foot for two weeks of pure, uninterrupted misery."

❯❯

Katie slumped back in her pew. The drone of her father's sermon echoed through the tiny church building, flowing past her like an algae-choked creek. She dug her fingernails into her leg. Her father would want her opinion when they got home. She had to pay attention. Silently she repeated his words over and over in her head. "'Who is this that darkens counsel by words without knowledge?'" *Darkens counsel?* It was no use. The words just weren't sinking in. Her thoughts drifted back to the meeting with the department chairman.

"'Where were you when I laid the foundation of the earth?'" Her father's voice rose to full volume. "'Tell Me, if you have understanding, who set its measurements? Since you know.'"

Katie glanced up at the podium. Her father was looking straight at her, his eyes lit with a mischievous twinkle. *Please, no. Not now . . .*

"These scientists who think they've got the universe all figured out—where were they when God laid the foundation of the earth? Where were they with their careful measurements and observations? Notice it says God 'laid' a foundation. Does that sound like helter-skelter randomness to you?"

Katie shrank down in her seat and stared at the whitening knuckles of her clenched fists. *Calm down.* He was lashing out at Dietrich, not her. The man who had set her up for failure. She wasn't even . . . A lump tightened in her throat. She wasn't even a scientist. Not anymore.

She still couldn't believe it. Dietrich and the chairman had all but fired her. They'd deliberately maneuvered her into quitting. And it didn't take a PhD to figure out why. They'd known about her fear of crowds for years—long before Dietrich had even hired her. But apparently they hadn't known about her faith. Or if they had known, they hadn't cared—not until she'd gotten famous enough for people to start paying attention to what she had to say.

"Turn with me to hymn number 347. . . ."

She pulled a hymnal out of the rack and flipped through the pages. Her father's shaky baritone voice lifted above the wavering tones of the older ladies in the congregation. Katie's lips moved, but she didn't make a sound. "His Eye Is on the Sparrow." It was her father's favorite hymn. What would she tell him? That she was fired because of her faith? That they'd accused her of destroying the fossil because of her perceived bias? He'd be furious. It would just confirm everything he'd always believed about science. She'd never hear the end of it. But what could she say? He'd want to know what happened, and she couldn't lie to him.

And then there was the question of earning a living. There were bills to pay—big bills. And with her father's condition getting worse, the bills were only going to get bigger. She had to get another job soon. If she couldn't work at UNM, she'd have to move to a different university—whether or not she could convince her father to move with her. She couldn't give up paleontology. She just couldn't. . . .

"'. . . and I know He watches me.'" The hymn rose in a final tremulous crescendo. Her father looked out onto his congregation, his face radiant with a triumphant smile. Gripping the back of the pew in front of her, Katie closed her eyes while he led the congregation in one last prayer. What if the chairman was right? If the other scientists were already talking about her, it wouldn't take long for word to spread to other universities. If she didn't clear her name soon, she might never get another job. She had to figure out a way to get back to Peru. If she could find another whale, maybe she could redeem herself in the eyes of her colleagues. Dietrich might even give her her old job back. She had to at least try. She didn't have any other choice.

The prayer ended with a chorus of *amens*, and Miss Agnes launched into a rousing piano rendition of "Shall We Gather at the River." Her father stepped down from the podium and was immediately surrounded by a sea of gray heads. Katie settled back into her pew and watched as the eager Navajo women plied him with questions about his last visit to the doctor. She noticed Miss Ida's tiny hunched figure tiptoeing at the back of the mob. She was patiently working her way through the crowd, clutching a heavy casserole dish to her chest. Her reservation-famous fry bread and corn stew. At least Katie and her father wouldn't starve.

Katie leaned over and riffled through her backpack for something to write on. It would take another twenty minutes for the crowd to clear—an hour if they got her father talking about her seminar yesterday. She pulled out an old field notebook and started working out the details for another expedition. If she sold her collection of *T. rex* teeth to a museum, she might be able to—

Shuffling footsteps approached from the center aisle. Katie looked up. Her father had made his way through the congregation and was heading toward her. Katie's eyes darted to the cluster of women following close behind him. They were all watching her, their faces lit with eager anticipation. *No. Please, no . . .* She grabbed her pack and started for the side aisle.

"Katie." Her father's voice froze her at the end of the pew.

"Dad, please. No more arguments. Not tonight." She turned and faced her father. Pain spread slowly across his face, dissolving his gentle smile. He lowered himself unsteadily onto the cushioned bench and looked up at her with concern-filled eyes.

"Katie, Venita was asking about your group meeting this morning. She wanted to know if Dr. Fischer was mad about the seminar."

"I'm sorry." Katie looked up at the rest of the congregation with an apologetic smile. They had all stopped at the invisible line twenty feet away from her pew. They knew better than to crowd her. "I . . ." She tried to think of something positive to say. Venita was the self-proclaimed prayer warrior of the group. She had obviously been praying about the meeting. "Well . . . he didn't yell or anything. He was actually a lot less grouchy than usual."

"And?" Her father seemed to be expecting good news. Like any good could have come from her botched seminar.

"And . . ." Katie looked up at the semicircle of ladies. Venita was grinning like the coyote that killed the giant. "And I guess I have to redeem myself now. I've decided to go back to Peru to find another whale. But this time I'm not letting anyone else near it."

Chapter 3

*T*HE ROAR OF PELTING ROCKS and sand shook Nick out of his daze. Forcing his eyes open wider, he yanked hard on the steering wheel and guided the rattling truck back onto the rutted dirt road. "Come on, just a few more miles. You can make it." His throat burned with the fine alkaline dust filling the cab. Even with the windows and vents tightly closed, the powdery grit still managed to seep inside, coating everything with a metallic-tasting film.

Bracing his knee against the steering wheel, he unscrewed his canteen and took a sip of warm water. His team would be eating breakfast by now, feasting on mutton and *halva puri*. A heavy weight settled into his stomach. All that sand and grit he'd swallowed must have coalesced into a huge brick. What kind of adviser abandoned his students in the field? For two weeks, no less. He wasn't so worried about the bedouins. They seemed friendly enough. But he'd left Ahamed and his students with the hardest part of the dig: encasing the pedestaled fossils in plaster and toilet paper, hauling them out of the desert, packing up the camp . . . While he ran off on an exotic vacation. What had he been thinking? Who cared how many years it had been since his last vacation? It was ludicrous. How had he let them talk him into it?

A chime rang out, sending Nick into a paroxysm of fluttering limbs. He took a couple of quick breaths and looked at his watch. Who would be calling at . . . 5:50 a.m.? Unless . . . He dug through his pack, pulled out the ringing satellite phone, and switched it on. "Hello, Cindy?"

"Uh . . . nope. Not since last time I checked." A deep voice sounded over the phone—Mike Anderson, his administrative assistant back in Michigan.

"Mike? What are you . . ." He quickly subtracted nine hours. "What's wrong? It's almost nine o'clock there. Are you still at the office?"

"Sorry if I woke you, but this afternoon, while you were still asleep, I got another call from Iraq. This time it was the man himself. What's his name?" The phone clunked. Nick could hear paper crinkling on the other end of the line. "His Excellency Mohammed Saeed Al-Jaza'iri Puffy-pants the fourth."

"Right. The new minister of antiquities . . ."

"Whatever." Mike suddenly sounded serious. "Listen! Puffy-pants said Katie James is going after the whale too. She'll be there in four days. Did you get that? *Katie James.* Four days! You've got to ditch Miss Guccier-Than-Thou and get your team over to Iraq pronto. Dude, I'm telling you, this is your big chance to go head-to-head with her. Mano-a-womano. And dude, I gotta tell you. I looked up her picture on the Internet and all I can say is wuh—mahn—oh!"

"Mike, hold on a second. Slow down," Nick shouted into the phone. "Did he say she's coming for sure? I thought he was giving me an exclusive on this."

"Puffy-pants *is* giving you an exclusive, but apparently she got her claws into another part of the ministry—some sort of terrorist network from the sound of it. She's scheduled to arrive in Baghdad in four days."

Nick took a deep breath. Katie James would get there twelve full days before he was scheduled to arrive. Twelve days! If he went through with this vacation, he might as well cancel the Iraq trip now. She'd clean out every fossil in Iraq. Back in Peru, James had managed to find a whale, start a dig, and become a comic book hero—all in the three days he'd been stranded in Lima with a busted CV joint. She'd gotten in and out of the country before he'd even had a chance to meet her.

"Hello, Nick? I'm going to have to give Puffy-pants an answer. He wants you there right away. What do you want me to tell him?"

"Hold on a second, Mike. Let me think." Nick pressed the phone against his forehead. There had to be a way he could do this. His department already knew about Iraq. If Katie James beat him to the punch again, he'd never hear the end of it. Some of the older members of the department still thought it was a mistake to hire him instead of her. The last thing he wanted was to give them more ammunition to use against him, especially with his tenure review coming up next year.

Maybe if Cindy went with him . . . She could stay the first night at the hotel in Quetta and then caravan with them through Iran to Baghdad. She'd get to see three countries and his grant would pay for everything. It would only be fair; she'd be part of the team. She could help set up the camp, organize the teams, maybe even help with the digging. . . .

Right . . . He smiled at the thought of Cindy with a shovel. She'd never agree to Iraq. She was jumpy enough about Pakistan. Besides, she'd be there in six hours. Everything was already planned. He couldn't bail on her now. He'd made a commitment. He had to stand by his word.

"Hello? Nick?"

"Yeah, I'm still here." Nick sighed. The brick in his stomach was starting to roll over and over in slow, acid-churning somersaults. This whole vacation thing had been a bad idea from the start. What had he been thinking? Cindy had been a great tour guide in New York City, but out in the Pakistani wilderness? He just couldn't see it. "Mike?"

"Yeah?"

"Could you call the minister back and let him know, as much as I wish I could, I have another commitment and can't cut my vacation short? If he still wants me to come in two weeks, I'll be there—whether the fossil's been found or not. But if he wants to cancel, I'll understand. I just can't break my word. Not after she's flown all this way."

"All right, dude, your head in the noose. I'll call him first thing in the morning. Need anything else?"

"No, that's it."

"Okay, later. Have a good one."

"Bye, Mike." Nick switched off the phone and tossed it onto the passenger seat. Katie James . . . She was going to beat him again. If Cindy only knew what he was giving up . . . If only she could understand.

◈

The echo of Katie's footsteps sounded loud and lonely in the dimly lit stairwell. She stopped at the third-floor landing and listened. Silence. The whole geology building was dead. Cracking open the door, she peeked out into the deserted hallway. It was almost eight o'clock. Too late for undergrads and still too early for grad students to be coming back from dinner. She slipped through the door and made her way through the maze of hallways that led to Dietrich's office. He'd called her up while she was still at church, insisting he had to talk to her right away. But what could be so sensitive he couldn't discuss it on the phone? Whatever it was, it had to be pretty important to keep Dietrich at work after six o'clock.

After their meeting that morning, he was probably worried about a lawsuit for wrongful termination. Either that or he was afraid she'd try to go back to Peru. No matter what he said, there was no way he could keep her from going after another whale. The whole department was abuzz with speculation about her resignation. It was only a matter of time before the rumors began to spread to the other universities.

A dim light shone around the door at the far side of Dietrich's lab. Balling her hands into fists, she stormed through the deserted room and rapped sharply on the office door. Just let him try to stop her from going to Peru. She'd sue the university for all it was worth. All that nonsense about communication skills . . . Any judge in the country could see they'd forced her out because of her faith. She stepped back as a chair squeaked. Heavy footsteps creaked across the floor. Hushed voices. The door swung open slowly. Dietrich's florid face appeared in the doorway, framed in a halo of fluorescent light.

"Katie, good! Come inside. I am so happy you should join us."

He reached out with both hands and took her by the arm, eyeing her like a braunschweiger and onion sandwich. "Welcome in. Welcome in!" He guided her into the office, pressing a meaty paw to her shoulder.

Something moved in the corner of the room. Dr. Nielsen was standing by the wall, his teeth bared in a wide, coffee-stained grin. "Hello, Katie. Good to see you again."

Katie tensed as she stepped forward to shake the chairman's hand. Why had Dietrich brought *him* into this? Were they really that afraid of being sued? She stepped back and stood facing the two men. Whatever they wanted, she wasn't about to make it easy for them. This time she had the guns and they had the bows and arrows.

"So . . ." Dietrich finally broke the silence. "I know you may be thinking, what is all this meeting all about?" He glanced at the chairman and then turned to her with a stiff smile. "We want you should know we have very good news! We know a way to pay your salary—and at the same time almost probably get my grant renewed!"

Katie looked from Dietrich to the chairman and back again. "Go on."

"I, because of my reputation in the field, am just being given a great honor for all the university. I am invited to go into a country entirely closed to paleontology before now. A sheepherder there has reported seeing in the desert what is almost certainly a transitional form between *Pakicetus* and *Rodhocetus*, perhaps the earliest species of four-legged whale to live all its life in the waters—a great finding of major evolutionary significance. And they want that I should find it for them!"

"Congratulations." Katie forced a smile. "I'm happy for you, but I fail to see how this can have any impact on me."

"I, of course, am thinking you should join the expedition," Dietrich announced. "It is a once-in-lifetime opportunity, the kind of finding what makes a career for all of time."

"So what happened to your concerns about my faith? You're not afraid I'll destroy the fossil as soon as I find it?"

Dietrich started to answer but Nielsen suddenly stepped forward.

"As we said before . . . we are not now nor have we ever been concerned about such rumors. We simply wanted you to understand what others in the field were saying—to help you appreciate the cost of running out in the middle of a seminar."

"So you're throwing me a bone to keep me from suing the university," Katie said.

"Sue the university?" Nielsen scoffed. "For what? Because Dietrich ran out of money to pay you? Lots of luck with that one."

"So where's the money for another expedition coming from? The fossilized tooth fairy?"

"The UNM Foundation," Nielsen said. "Based on this new opportunity, they've agreed to underwrite the entire trip."

"And my speaking travels too." Dietrich pushed past the chairman, his eyes lit with a strange fire. "The main point what we are saying, Katie, is we want you should join us. I feel personally terrible what they are saying about you. This is your main big opportunity to prove them that they are wrong. Think about it. That your name should be on the discovery of a new species, a new transitional form of whale . . . How can they say you are creationist then, eh?" He flashed her a conspiratorial smile.

Katie searched his face. "And you're not mad about the seminar?"

"Of course not. Is forgotten history."

"And you believe my story about the poachers?"

"Of course so. And the story of Mexico City and the fight in the courtyard. They all say the same thing. Don't forget, I was there for the trouble in Montana. I know what you say is true."

Katie eyed Nielsen warily as she considered Dietrich's offer. If they were telling the truth, if she really did have a shot at a pre-*Rodhocetus,* she'd be set for life. Talk about clearing her name . . . She'd make the cover of *Science* for sure. "So what makes you so sure it's pre-*Rodhocetus*? I assume scientists have already been searching for it. What makes you think you'll be able to find it if they couldn't?"

"First thing: the sheepherders brought back already a vertebra. Just analysis, no searching yet," Dietrich said. "And second thing: it's not I who should find it. I am to be presenting a paper at the South Africa Conference. It's you, Hooman, and Wayne who must be going instead."

"The South Africa Conference? Isn't that next week?"

Dietrich nodded. "August thirteenth through the eighteenth."

"But surely you're not talking about . . ." Katie noticed the tautness of Dietrich's features, the rigidness of his stance. It was all starting to make sense. The urgent phone call, the late-night meeting, the presence of the department chairman . . . "You can't be serious. You want me to put an expedition together . . . in a week and a half? That's impossible!"

"Actually, is very possible. And not at all a week and a half. Three days only. The country's Department of Antiquities has hired already guards and drivers and a translator. My new grant, of course, must pay for everything, but they provide also trucks, weapons, tents—all the equipment."

"Weapons?" Katie studied her former mentor beneath narrowed lids. "Just where is this impossible expedition going?"

Dietrich stared back at her, the faintest hint of a grin playing at the corners of his mouth. "Perhaps it may be too dangerous for you, yes?"

No, you didn't . . . Katie's mouth dropped open. *You did not get us into Pakistan.* "Where is it?" Her voice quavered despite all her attempts at self-control.

"No place you should be caring to go, I think." Dietrich's eyes danced as the suppressed smile broke through. "Anyway. Is a bad time right now. Far too dangerous."

"Dietrich?"

"Only the southwestern desert of Iraq. That is all."

"Iraq?" Katie couldn't believe it. "They're actually willing to let us in? Even with the risk of another war? It doesn't make any sense."

"It makes absolutely the sense. With the new fighting breaking out, the Iraqi ministers fear the fossil to be stolen soon. Every time there is fighting, they lose to looting all kinds of national treasure. I talk to them today myself."

"But three days . . . it's not nearly enough time. This is huge. We can't just rush in without a plan. Fossil hunters haven't been allowed into Iraq for twenty years. We have to gather the geological survey reports, map out a search strategy . . ."

"Of course." Dietrich leaned back against his desk. "If you feel impossible to be prepared, we will find someone else."

"That's not what I'm saying. Three days isn't long enough for anybody. Besides, this is August. Do you have any idea how hot Iraq is now? Why not wait a month for things to cool off?"

"September begins their Ramadan." Dietrich shrugged and looked down at one of the stacks of papers littering his desk. "Even if they would allow us inside their country, I think especially you, being Christian, would not like their times-ten reward for killing infidels during their month of fastings. It might make things even more hotter than just the weather, yes?"

"So we wait until October," Katie said. "It'll be even cooler then. We'll have more time to prepare."

"We leave in three days." Dietrich heaved himself back onto his feet and crossed the office to the door. "Commercial airports are closed. We fly with military transportation from Kuwait directly into Baghdad. I have already the invitational orders. If you cannot be with the team, I am sorry."

"Okay, okay. Three days. I'll be ready." Katie stood her ground. "But I need to talk to Hooman and Wayne. Right now. We have tons of details to work out: geological surveys, plane tickets . . ."

"Yes, yes . . ." Dietrich shuffled his feet uncomfortably. "Wayne is working already on these things."

"*Wayne* is working?" She let the question hang in the air between them.

"You were resigned this morning, remember?" Dietrich shrugged helplessly. "I told Wayne already he would be expedition leader."

"Wayne?" Katie couldn't believe what she was hearing. "He's just a third year. I mean, don't get me wrong, I'm sure one day when he graduates he'll be a very decent biologist, but for such an important project . . . You can't really expect . . ."

"I'm afraid we have no choice." Nielsen stepped forward. "Wayne *will* lead the expedition, and if you wish to join his team, we first need to agree on a few things."

Katie turned a hard stare on the chairman. "What *things?*"

"Well, first of all, I need a guarantee there won't be a repeat of your little seminar fiasco."

"That should be easy enough. Next time I have to give an intimate departmental seminar, don't invite half the newspapers in New Mexico."

"Katie, I'm serious." The chairman's face creased in a glaring frown. "If you find a new transitional species of whale, you'll be under a lot of scrutiny. Remember, you'll be representing a state university. I'm sure I don't need to explain the concept of separation of church and state. I want your word you won't discuss your religious beliefs—not with your team, not with your colleagues, not with reporters. Are we agreed?"

Katie couldn't believe she'd heard him right. "Are you asking me to . . . not talk about my faith? What if it's a personal conversation? What if someone asks a direct question? What am I supposed to do, lie to them?"

"Katie, remember why we ask you this." Dietrich moved to her side. "We want this should be your big chance to save your reputation. Is for your own good we are thinking of."

Nielsen nodded. "Absolutely. You could have a long and brilliant career ahead of you. We're trying to keep you from committing professional suicide."

"So you're just talking about seminars, right? You want me to stick to the topic no matter what I'm asked."

"Right," the chairman said. "And whenever you're talking to journalists or other scientists. Just don't talk about religion. I don't care whether they're calling it scientific creationism or intelligent design or George W. Scientology, it's all religion, and I don't want you going anywhere near it. Just stick to the accepted facts of science and you'll be fine. Do we have your word?"

Katie looked over at Dietrich. He was nodding at her, urging her with his eyes to agree. But how could she? She was a postdoc, for crying out loud. Half her friends were scientists. How would she know when she was off the clock and when she was on? Did eating lunch with her friends count? What about when they were playing dry-ice hockey in the hallways? "I'm sorry, but I can't—"

"Katie, before you answer, you should like to know one more thing." Dietrich paused for a long second. "We are not the only ones who are being invited into Iraq. There is one other team. . . ."

Katie's breath caught in her chest. She waited for Dietrich to say the name, but he just licked his lips and smiled at her, a card shark waiting to throw down his royal flush. *Nick Murad.* He'd already stolen the job at Michigan; now he was going after her career. What else could she do?

Dietrich's face twisted into a grin as he watched her struggle. He had her and he knew it. Murad already had Pakistan. There was no way she could sit quietly by while he built a wall around Iraq.

"The news is better even than you can think." Dietrich's bushy eyebrows twitched like a pair of frightened porcupines. "He is to be taking two weeks vacation in Pakistan starting now. We could find the whale and make partner agreements with Iraq before he even can arrive."

"So what do you say, Katie? Do we have a deal?" Nielsen reached out his hand and left it suspended between them.

Katie stared at the hand. This was her career she was talking about. Her only means of supporting her father. Her only means of clearing her name. She didn't have a choice. "Okay, I'll do it." She reached out and shook the chairman's hand. She felt like she was going to be sick.

"Good, excellent! We knew you'd make the right decision." Nielsen reached behind him and grabbed a book off one of the chairs. "You should read this book. I think it will help. Neurology is a fascinating field. Studies have shown some people have a physiological predisposition to belief in God. The tricks our brains can play on us . . . It's fascinating, really. I'm sure you'll find it very helpful."

"Thanks." Katie reached out and took the book without looking at it, a diseased patient taking a prescription from a doctor. *Why not give me an injection and be done with it?*

Not again! Nick ripped the stapled notices from his apartment door. "Death to America! Death to Zionist Dogs!" He unlocked the door and pushed into the stifling apartment. *Beautiful. This is just perfect.* He wadded up the signs and threw them into the trash. Cindy would be here in less than two hours. What was he supposed to do? Call the plane and tell it to turn around and go back? Crossing the cramped living room in three strides, he threw open the windows and switched on the fans. Then, throwing himself into a big, overstuffed Baluchi chair, he pulled out the newspapers he'd bought at a corner stand and scanned the headlines. It was even worse than he'd thought. An outbreak of fighting in Iraq. A missile attack in Damadola. Protests over the president's visit . . . Of all the times for Cindy's paranoia to be justified . . . Why did it have to be now?

Nick tossed the papers on his desk and hurried back to his bedroom. The protests could last for weeks. Damadola was a long way from Quetta, but once the tribesmen got riled up, it took forever for them to cool back down. He opened his closet and pulled out a long white kurta with hand-stitched embroidery around the collar and a pair of baggy *shalwar* pants. Cindy would be totally weirded out, but he couldn't risk wearing Western clothes. Not with everything that had happened while he was away. Too much was riding on this. Even something as trivial as spitting on the sidewalk would be too much for Cindy. She'd totally freak out.

He carried the clothes to the bathroom and glanced at his dust-covered reflection in the mirror. With his ruddy complexion and dark hair, it was easy enough for him to blend in, but Cindy . . . Her blonde hair and fair skin would be bad enough, but if she wore the kind of clothes she usually wore, she might as well carry a blinking neon sign that flashed "American prostitute." The thought made him smile. He could just see her flouncing through the Quetta market in a tank top and miniskirt. The president himself wouldn't make as big a stir if he were to paint himself blue and juggle live hand grenades. Somehow he had to convince her to wear a *shalwar kameez*. It wasn't going to be easy. He'd rather put panty hose on a cat.

Nick checked his watch: 10:15. He shucked off his shirt and tossed it onto a pile of sand-covered clothes. Buying Cindy clothes would take forever. When was he going to find time to clean his apartment? And with the markets and parks off-limits, what was he going to do with her for two weeks? Take her to his dig? It just wasn't worth it. Maybe he should tell her to turn around and go back home. He and his team would be able to make Iraq. He'd finally get a chance to go head-to-head with Katie James—to prove once and for all the selection committee had made the right choice. A tingle of excitement quickened in his chest. Once he was in Iraq, who knew what would happen? He might even get a chance to meet her.

"No!" Nick spoke out loud, startling himself out of his reverie. Cindy had flown all the way out to Pakistan to visit him. No matter how bad things got, he was going to do his best to show her a good time. He'd given her his word.

Stepping into the bathtub, he pulled the plastic curtain back across the makeshift rod. Two things were certain: If he was going to buy clothes before Cindy's plane arrived, he would have to hurry. And no matter where he went, no matter what he bought her, it would have to be expensive.

Chapter 4

*N*ICK SQUARED HIS SHOULDERS and stood up straighter. No, that wasn't right. He'd look like an English butler. He shifted his weight onto his right leg and leaned casually to the side, gripping the large, gift wrapped box in his left hand. The corner of the package brushed against the cement floor. It was way too big. The whole gift wrapping thing was a bad idea. All it did was accentuate the fact that he was too practical. He should have got her flowers or candy—some sugar to help the *shalwar kameez* go down. Cindy was going to hate it.

An airline worker opened a steel door and a group of men in Western business suits walked into the building. He slid the package behind him and shifted his weight onto his left leg. More passengers filed into the building; these were wearing more traditional dress. He could feel his heart pounding in his ears. It was worse than being onstage. More people disembarked. The line expanded into a milling crowd as the passengers were greeted by friends and family. Where was she? He craned his neck to see around a tall Pakistani in an embroidered silk kurta. Not that there was a chance of missing her. Cindy stood out wherever she went, but here in Pakistan . . . even a blind man would be able to pick her out.

The stream of passengers was starting to thin now. Nick angled toward the door. She was probably seated in the back of the plane. Or maybe she had held back, waiting to make a grand entrance. Minutes passed. The stream had dwindled to a trickle. Finally it stopped altogether. The airline agent moved to the door and lifted the stopper that held it open.

"*Tssst!* Sir? *Maya?*" Nick hurried over to the agent. "Is everyone off the plane?"

The agent held up an index finger and looked back through the door. "One more. There is small delay."

Nick smiled his thanks and moved back to stand by the flight counter. Cindy. It had to be. She would have called if she'd missed the flight. He set the box down by the counter and faked a casual look around the terminal. Not that he was fooling anyone. Anybody looking his way could see the pulse throbbing in his neck. His head felt like one of those inflatable bouncing houses filled with fifteen screaming kids.

A grandmotherly *daadi* draped in a black *chaader* smiled at him as she walked by, pulling a heavy suitcase. He inclined his head and returned her smile. Someone should be helping her with that bag. He looked around the terminal. Ever since the push to modernize Pakistani airports, all the porters had disappeared. And with them the noise and arguments and price-gouging. Maybe she was better off. . . .

"Nick? Is that you?"

Nick swung around at the voice. Cindy had abandoned her carry-on at the door and was running toward him. Nick dropped the present and wrapped her in his arms. The warmth of her skin soaked into him like a summer rain on parched ground. He spun her in a circle, burying his face in the soft scent of her hair. Maybe things weren't going to be so bad after all. . . .

"Oh my gosh, look at you." Cindy pushed herself away and looked him over critically. "You've totally gone native. I almost didn't recognize you."

"And look at you!" He touched the scarf draped around her shoulders. "You're blending in too. Sort of . . ."

"I know! Isn't it horrid?" Cindy pulled the scarf off and held it away from her like it was diseased. "The flight attendant made me wear it. I think she was worried people would think I was a hussy or something."

"*Besharam* and *behaya.*"

"What?"

"Shameless and immoral. It's pretty much their opinion of all Americans. And the more beautiful the woman, the more *besharam* and *behaya*." He put an arm around her and gave her another hug. The scent of her perfume thrilled through him. How long had it been? He pulled back and took a deep breath. "Oh yeah . . . Dressed like that, they'll think you're she-Shaitan herself."

"Satan? I see someone needs to be sent back to flattery school." Cindy pouted and stepped in for a kiss, but Nick put a hand on her shoulder and guided her back toward the gate.

"Not in the airport. This isn't the time. I shouldn't even have hugged you, but it's so good to see you I couldn't help myself."

"I should hope not. We haven't seen each other in three months. And when a man shows up at the airport wearing pajamas . . . what's a girl supposed to think?"

"So . . ." Nick cleared his throat and led her back to the gate door, where the airline attendant stood staring at them with a disapproving frown. "Is this all your luggage?"

Cindy laughed and slipped an arm around his waist. "You're so funny. I'm beginning to remember why I like you." She stepped aside and let him retrieve her suitcase.

"What did you do? Fill it with rocks?" Nick hefted the small case before setting it down and pulling it along behind him. "Pakistan has enough rocks already."

"Wait till you see my luggage. I hope you brought some strong camels."

Nick stole another glance at her and rolled the case over to the counter where he'd left her present. "This is for you." He handed her the masking tape–spotted package. He should have spent more time searching for cellophane tape.

"You shouldn't have." She held the box to her ear and shook it. "Should I open it now?"

"Wait till we get you to your hotel. It'll be easier to carry." Nick started toward the baggage claim area.

"It's pajamas, right?" Cindy pulled his arm around her and leaned against his side. "Matching pajamas to yours."

"Something like that." Nick turned at a loud voice. An old man was yelling at them. Something about American prostitutes and shameful behavior. He pulled away from Cindy.

"What's wrong?" She looked up at him in surprise. "Don't get me wrong. I like your pajamas. They're totally sexy."

"You didn't hear him yelling?" Nick glanced around the airport. Everyone was staring at them. "Public displays of affection are frowned upon here."

"So? Let them frown. We're not hurting anyone."

Blustering men dressed in conservative kurtas were jabbering to each other, hurling angry glances their way.

"We don't want to cause trouble." Nick stepped between Cindy and the men. "Put the scarf back on. Drape it around your neck so it covers your shoulders and um . . . neck." He reached out to take the scarf from her, but she jerked her hand away.

"What's gotten into you? Have you been brainwashed or something?" Her eyes flashed out a warning. One false step and she was going to blow.

"It's okay." He kept his voice soft and soothing. "Believe me, I like what you're wearing. It's just . . . We're just not in America anymore. You know, when in Rome . . ."

"What are you saying? I'm supposed to wear a burka or something? walk twelve feet behind you?"

"No, that's not it at all. Just . . . try to blend in."

"In case you haven't noticed, I'm blonde. No matter what I do, I'm not going to blend in."

"If you put the scarf over your head . . ."

"I . . ." Cindy suddenly pulled away. "So I have to hide now? What happened to it's perfectly safe here?"

"Cindy . . ." Nick stepped toward her. "You don't have to hide, but you do have to use a little common sense. Americans aren't very popular right now. The less you stand out as an American, the less likely we'll run into any problems."

"Problems? Define *problems*." Her voice was getting shrill. He had to get her out of here. They were starting to draw a crowd.

"Come on. Let's get your luggage. We can discuss this in the truck." Nick tried to guide her forward, but she shrugged him off.

"We can discuss this now. What kind of problems?"

"Cindy . . ."

"I'm not taking another step until you answer me. What kind of problems?"

"Okay. Keep your voice down." Nick glanced back at the gathering crowd. "Let's just get to the baggage claim area. We can talk about it on the way."

Cindy stared at him long and hard before allowing him to lead her through the long corridor. The longer they walked, the more she seemed to shrink away from her surroundings. An expression of unveiled disgust was written on her face. Suddenly he was aware of every burned-out light, every flake of peeling paint. The airport had always seemed so modern before. Had they been letting it go? Or had he just not noticed?

"Well?" Cindy finally demanded.

"Okay . . . here's the situation." Nick tried to choose his words carefully. The last thing he wanted was for her to freak out in the airport. "Since you called, I've learned things aren't as safe here as I thought. Apparently fighting has started again in Iraq. That and the president's visit have gotten the Pakistanis really worked up."

"That's what I was trying to tell you." Cindy's eyes flashed. "But would you listen? You wouldn't even talk to me."

"That's because I thought you were just being . . ." Nick hesitated. Way too many land mines in this field. "I couldn't talk because bedouins were passing through our campsite, and I didn't want them to know we were Westerners."

"Because?"

"Because . . . ," Nick continued lamely. "Because there was a very tiny, very remote chance that the bedouins were harboring terrorists. I couldn't take the risk—"

"So you tell me it's perfectly safe here, but you couldn't talk because you were afraid terrorists would overhear?" Cindy demanded.

"That's what I'm trying to explain. Yes, there's a risk to being here, now more than ever. But there's a risk to everything. Flying, driving a car, having a cavity filled . . . But that doesn't mean you have to run away. Especially when there are things you can do to minimize your risks. Like wearing a seat belt or wearing a scarf or not talking on your satellite phone when bedouins are riding through your camp."

"So if I cover my immorally blonde hair with a scarf that clashes with my blouse, that'll make everything okay?"

"Cindy . . ."

"Everybody will automatically think I'm some kind of albino Pakistan person—just because I don't have any fashion sense?"

"That's not what I'm saying. We just don't want to provoke anyone. If you'd just try to blend in. If you could avoid making a scene . . ."

"Like I'm making right now?" Cindy raised her voice to include the whole terminal. "And what happens if I do make a scene? What happens if they notice I'm three shades whiter than anyone else? that I have an American accent—or am I not allowed to talk in public either?"

"Cindy, it's not that bad. If you'd just—"

"No, I'm serious. I really want to know." Cindy's eyes darted around the airport. "I don't see any tents here, and I don't see any bedouins. I want you to look me in the eye and tell me—is it safe here or not? No disguises, no hiding, no costumes. Either it's safe to be an American, or it isn't." She jammed her hands down on her hips and waited, vivid blue eyes boring into his.

Nick glanced around him. One thing about Pakistanis—they didn't have any inhibitions about staring. He turned back to her and looked her in the eye. "After everything that's happened in the news, I'd have to say it's not very safe here right now. Not if you want to go around flaunting the fact that you're an American. But if you're willing to—"

"I can't believe it!" Cindy yanked the carry-on out of his hand and pushed her way through the crowd.

"Cindy, wait!" Nick followed her across the terminal to a row of flight desks. "You just have to take a few precautions. As long as you're careful—"

"All this time you've been telling me how safe you are here.

'Don't worry about me. I'm safer in Pakistan than I'd be in New York.' Well, it's all been a big lie, hasn't it?" A tear rolled down her cheek as she took her place in one of the lines.

"No . . . I'm fine—and my students are fine. But we know how to behave. And we don't take unnecessary chances. Even out in the desert we—"

"Excuse me." Cindy pushed forward to a free spot at the airline counter and handed the attendant a stack of papers. "I need to be on the first flight out of Pakistan. I already have a ticket, but I can't wait two weeks. I can't wait two hours." She turned around and fixed Nick with a cold glare before turning back to the attendant.

Nick let out a long sigh and shuffled over to wait by one of the concrete pillars overlooking the counters. It was his fault. He never should have invited her in the first place. His friends had tried to tell him. Why hadn't he listened?

And now she was leaving him. Probably forever.

A swarm of conflicting emotions buzzed through his brain. He felt terrible. He really did. He'd done everything in his power to make things work out. She just didn't belong in his world. No more than he belonged in hers.

Glancing surreptitiously at the flight desk, he ducked behind the pillar and pulled the satellite phone from his pocket. One more quick look around, and he punched in his office number.

"Murad lab. This is—"

"Hello, Mike? This is Nick." He spoke in a low, barely controlled voice. "Listen, this is important. I need you to call that minister back right away and tell him I'll be there—just as soon as we can pack up camp."

Bill Turner stared out into the darkness through the spotted wind-shield of his ancient Land Rover. All four air-conditioning vents were blasting him with lukewarm air. It seemed a shame to get out now. It had taken the whole trip from Baghdad to finally cool the car to sub-hades temperatures.

"One, two, three." He reached for the key and hesitated one last second, raising his arms to direct the air down the sleeves of his drenched white shirt. "Okay . . . now." Again he hesitated. Daniels would have his whole crew off at the museum meeting. All he had to do was pop over to the dig site and tell the guards he was there to see the supervising archaeologist. There were supposed to be four private security guards—all supplied by the Iraqi Department of Antiquities and Heritage. He could take their pictures and be back to the car in less than fifteen minutes. If he hurried, the car might still be cool when he got back.

"Okay." He turned off the engine and pushed open the door with a groan. A wall of warm air crashed down on him, enflaming the prickling heat rash on his chest and under his arms. He swung his legs out of the car and eased his bulk onto his feet. The camp was a couple hundred yards off the road. He switched on his flashlight and set off in the direction of the ancient mound, stopping every twenty or thirty yards to mop his brow and catch his breath. He wasn't built for such abuse. A man of his size . . . the doctors had told him he couldn't dissipate the heat fast enough. He'd tried to tell his boss at the agency, but Murdock was a moron. What did he know about physics? The way he talked, you'd think Iraq was some sort of supersecret resort. Which maybe it was if you liked living in a dry sauna. It had been dark for two hours, and it was still over ninety degrees. Murdock was going to owe him big-time for this. A summer in Stockholm, maybe. Better yet, a year in the Swiss Alps.

By the time he reached the edge of the camp, he was completely out of breath. He hobbled up to one of the tents and lowered himself into a dusty camp chair. Good, the chair was strong enough. He mopped his face and forehead with a saturated handkerchief and tucked it back into his pocket. Okay . . . he needed to get up and find those guards. *One, two, three* . . . He relaxed back into the chair at a sound coming from the other side of the camp. A metal lockbox opening? The door of a car?

Somewhere in the darkness a truck engine rumbled to life. Great. It was at least a hundred yards away. He wasn't being paid enough for this. He considered yelling for the guards. Yeah right. While he was at it, why not have them pose for pictures with name cards held under their chins? He was supposed to be an archaeologist, an expert in ancient antiquities. Visiting a professor in the middle of the night was straining his cover enough.

He heaved himself out of the chair and waddled toward the sound of the idling truck. In the distance he could see its headlights. Trudging up a steep hill, he cursed Murdock between panting breaths. His chest and arms felt like they were covered in a swarm of stinging hornets. If he keeled over from a heart attack, he was going to sue Murdock for every cent he was worth. He'd gotten signed papers from a doctor. It was an open-and-shut case.

Bill topped the rise and leaned over with his hands on his thighs to support his weight. Below him, parked next to the huge gridded-off dig area, sat a large white pickup truck. Uniformed guards marched back and forth between the truck and a large canvas tent. One of the guards stepped into the light. A tall man with a bushy beard and dark, murderous eyes. It took Bill a second to realize what the guard was carrying: a large stone vase from the dig.

One of the guards looked up and shouted at the other men. Bill froze where he stood, too shocked to move. Then, spinning around with a speed that surprised even him, he plunged down the hill as fast as his legs would carry him. *Nabu and Mithra! This can't be happening.* There was no way he could outrun them—even if he tucked and rolled. He had to do something. Something fast. He could hear them shouting. They were running up the mound.

An erratic beam of light danced and bobbed on the sandy path ahead of him. So that's how they'd spotted him! He reached back and flung the flashlight as far away from him as he could. Then, sliding to a stop at the bottom of the hill, he turned and ran in the opposite direction, dodging and swerving around rocks like an offensive lineman after a fumble recovery. If he could just make it to the tents before they topped the mound . . . If he could just get beyond the range of their lights . . .

A shout sounded just above him. If they saw him, he was dead.

Bill plunged blindly forward, pushing through the darkness on legs suddenly imbued with a life of their own. If his flashlight hadn't broken when it landed, if they searched the path to the left before searching to the right . . . He cast a quick glance over his shoulder and kept on running. One of their lights had disappeared behind a large shadow. A tent from the campsite? Had he made it past the campsite? Angling to the right to keep the tents between him and the searching men, he plodded deeper and deeper into the desert. Ragged, wheezing gasps filled his ears. He wasn't going to make it. Couldn't make it. Couldn't move another step. Finally, his legs buckled beneath him, pitching him forward into the hot sand.

His whole body tingled with burning fire. He rolled over onto his back and lay there, wheezing and gasping, for what seemed an eternity. He had to be quiet. His life depended on him being quiet. Big round breaths. Open the throat all the way. Round, quiet breaths. The dizziness buzzing in his ears finally receded. How long had be been lying there? Ten minutes? Twenty? He held his breath and listened for sounds of pursuit. Nothing but the rumble of a distant truck. Was it the guards? It couldn't be. Surely they would have discovered his Land Rover by now. They had to be out there somewhere—still searching for him.

So what did he do now? He couldn't go back, and he couldn't stay where he was. He wouldn't last two hours once the sun came up.

He pulled the satellite phone from his pocket and punched in his access code. Then, scrolling through the menu, he searched for the military office. Murdock's office, agency fronts in Turkey, Saudi Arabia, Israel . . . There it was—the Iraqi Ministry of Defense. He sent the number and waited for someone to pick up. Surely someone was manning the phones. War wasn't a nine-to-five business—even in Iraq.

"Hello, Baghdad national command. Sergeant Safiya Sharif. Who's calling?"

"This is Dr. Hayden Daniels, field director for the Nippur excavation. I'm three miles to the east of the main mound at Nippur, and I need troops here right away. Insurgent soldiers are raiding our camp right now. If you don't get here soon, they'll carry off some of the most valuable finds dug up in the last three years!"

"Sir, looting is a matter for the Iraqi Police Service. Would you like me to give you the number?"

"You boys are fighting terrorist insurgents, right? So how do you think they're financing their operation? You get out here pronto, and not only will you catch yourself a nice batch of terrorists, you'll set them back millions of dollars worth of bombs."

"I'll relay the message to my superiors, but you should call the IPS. May I have your phone number please?"

Bill swore and hung up the phone. By the time he convinced the IPS to get up off their big bureaucratic backsides, the guards would be long gone—and Daniels's artifacts with them. He rolled onto all fours and pushed himself to his feet with a low moan. His legs felt like overcooked dumplings, but he had to move. It would be hard enough making it back to the road, but if his car wasn't there . . . He'd rather hitch a ride with the terrorists than walk all the way back to the Nippur site. It was almost three miles!

"Are those bombs?" Hooman shouted to be heard over the engines of the C-130 military transport plane. "See those flashes of light? They look like explosions." He leaned back to let Katie see out the small window. Far beneath them a patchwork of dim lights illuminated the outskirts of a sprawling city. A tiny flash of orange lit the darkness below.

"That's not an explosion," Katie shouted into his ear. "It's a rocket firing."

The young graduate student's eyes went suddenly wide, showing like gleaming pearls against milk chocolate skin and silky black hair.

"It's okay." Katie pulled away from the window. "They're too far away to hit us. They're firing at something else."

Hooman nodded uncertainly and turned back to the window. She watched him a few seconds before leaning back in the red nylon mesh seat. The rockets weren't aimed at them. It didn't make sense. The pilot would have taken evasive actions.

If he had seen them.

Glancing up at Hooman, she shut her eyes and silently counted off a hundred seconds. No explosions yet. Just to be sure she counted off sixty more seconds.

"See?" she leaned toward Hooman and shouted. "If they'd been firing at us, we would have heard something by now."

"Good." Hooman didn't look away from the window. "I've seen five more flashes. One of them was almost directly beneath us."

Katie collapsed back in her seat and started counting again. Finally, 120 nerve-racking alligators later, she gave up. If they hit her, they hit her. She was too tired to worry about anything else. Every muscle in her body ached. The roar of the plane twisted and spun around her, tying her limbs into tight, rubber-bandy knots.

She turned to her right and studied Wayne. Incredible. The rangy Texan was slumped over the backpack in his lap, snoring like a hound dog on a sunny day. He'd slept half of the fifteen hours they'd waited for the military flight in Kuwait and most of the eighteen hours it had taken them to get to Kuwait in the first place. How did he do it? She hadn't gotten five seconds of sleep in the last two days.

The passenger across the aisle shifted in his seat. Katie lowered her eyes and tried to concentrate on the sleeping grad student beside her. His rugged, weathered features; sun-bleached hair; polished, just-for-show cowboy boots . . . A cough cut through the roar. A metallic ping.

Katie glanced up and felt as if the weight of a hundred faces were pressing in on her. She shut her eyes and tried to push the faces from her mind. Hundreds of eyes. They were staring at her, sucking the air out of her chest.

"Did you see that? That was an explosion for sure." Hooman's shout sounded through the roar.

Katie turned toward the shout, forced herself to look out the window.

"You okay?" Hooman's voice sounded close to her ear. A hand pressed against her shoulder.

"Fine." She struggled to keep her voice from shaking. "Just trying to relax."

The hand jerked away. "Sorry."

"No! It's okay; I . . ." Katie turned toward the grad student. "Hooman, I . . ." She tried to choke out the words, but her lungs wouldn't respond. What was wrong with her? She should be apologizing. Thanking him for his . . . concern.

His eyes went wide—like he was watching a train wreck. A train wreck named Katie James.

"Hooman, I'm sorry. I'm just . . ." She turned to her right. The man seated across from her looked suddenly away. Her breath caught in her throat. Tension radiated from the man's massive frame. He was wearing a dark, vaguely military-looking uniform, but it didn't have any marks of rank or insignia. The man next to him shifted in his seat. Dark, narrow eyes. A patch of shiny scar tissue enflamed his neck and jaw. Other faces. They were all staring. Looking at her . . .

Katie closed her eyes and tried to force air back into her lungs. It felt like an elephant was sitting on her chest. She had to calm down. Think about the desert. Rocks and sand . . .

The plane tipped suddenly forward, lifting Katie off her seat. Front became down and back became up as the plane fell out of the sky in a steep, spiraling dive. The shell of the plane crackled and groaned as the shrieking wind buffeted them about. With a start, Katie realized she was breathing again. She was still packed like a sardine in a plane full of strangers, but the force of their presence had faded against the shaking of the plane.

She looked over at Hooman. He seemed tense, nervous.

"We're just landing," she shouted over the roar.

"What?" Hooman jerked around to face her.

"Our descent has to be steep—because of the insurgents."

He nodded and cast a quick glance out the window.

"Hooman?" She waited as he turned to face her. "Thanks for all your help. Guiding me through airports like a little old lady can't be easy. You deserve a merit badge."

"Believe me, I don't mind." A boyish grin spread across his face. "You should see the looks I get. People look at me like I'm some kind of rock star."

Katie nodded. Her throat was starting to close up again.

"Seriously. Even the pretty girls. Any time you need an escort, I'm happy to oblige."

Heat prickled at her ears and cheeks. Before she could stop herself, she was nodding again. Up and down like a freak show idiot. She closed her eyes and turned away. The faces were pressing in on her again. Boring into her brain.

The plane shuddered with a loud crash. Katie was thrown forward in her seat. Engines roared as squealing wheels vibrated over the rough runway. The plane swerved sharply to the right and taxied to a rattling stop. Metal clacks sounded over the roar of the still-racing engines. The tail of the plane dropped suddenly away, and beams of bobbing light stabbed through the darkness beyond.

"Everybody out of the plane!" A deep voice boomed beyond the opening. "This is an ERO. Everybody move!"

Katie unbuckled her harness and jumped to her feet. A man in black spun around, swinging a military pack into her face. Men everywhere were donning body armor. Two of them backed into her, shoving her against Hooman's side. Rushing people. Faces everywhere. They crowded against her, crushing the air from her lungs.

"Everybody off! Move, move!"

A wave of nausea washed through Katie's body. Fiery heat prickled at her skin. A dim, twisted figure forced its way into her mind. Her mother's face against an expanding pool of blood. People everywhere. She was shaking now. Couldn't stand.

Grasping hands attacked her from all directions. Grabbing, lifting her onto her feet. Wayne uttered a loud curse inches away from her ear. She felt herself being dragged to the back of the plane. What was happening? Were they under attack?

"Move!"

They stumbled down a broad metal ramp into the sweltering darkness. Hooman and Wayne dragged her after a line of rushing men, but she pulled away from them. Turning her back on the raging crowd, she staggered away from the lights and fell onto her knees. Her stomach tightened spasmodically and she retched onto the hot tarmac. Gradually the agony receded. She wiped a forearm across her mouth and shook off the beads of sweat streaming down her face. *Everything's fine. It's okay.* Gradually, the weight lifted from her chest. Hot, dry air filled her lungs. She rested on her hands and knees, breathing in and out as two days of tension drained out of her like water from a saturated sponge. Everything was okay now. The worst part was over. She'd get to go to the desert soon.

"Here she is. Right this way." She could hear Wayne hurrying across the tarmac. "Don't she look happy to get off the plane?"

Laughter sounded behind her. Katie climbed unsteadily onto her feet and turned to face the voices. Wayne, Hooman, and a group of four Iraqis stood silhouetted against the light.

"Katie, this is Hassan al-Naseri and his men. They're going to be our guides and bodyguards. Gentlemen . . ." He stepped aside with an exaggerated flourish. "This is the third member of my party—the infamous Katie James."

Chapter 5

KATIE SAT IN THE MIDDLE SEAT of a dusty Suburban, sandwiched between two sweating Iraqi bodyguards. Even with the air-conditioning running at full blast, the interior of the car was well over a hundred degrees. It had taken more than an hour and a half to get their paperwork processed at BIOP, the Baghdad International Operations base. Endless lines, squawking PA systems, people rushing this way and that. By the time they'd gotten their invitational orders stamped by the last E6 staff sergeant, the temperature had already climbed to a scorching 116 degrees.

Katie took another swig from the water bottle she'd gotten from one of the refrigerated coolers scattered around the base. The water had been warm when she'd gotten it, but now it was so hot it burned her tongue. She screwed the top back on the bottle and let her gaze drift out the window. A fifteen-foot concrete wall rushed past them. Ever since she'd landed, it had been her only view of Iraq. Dusty asphalt and sand closed in by concrete.

"Don't worry about her; she can share a tent with me and Hooman." Wayne's voice carried from the front of the truck.

Katie frowned and looked up at the guards to see whether they'd been listening. They hadn't spoken two words of English since Wayne's humiliating introduction. When Hassan spoke to Wayne, they seemed to understand well enough, but whenever Katie asked a question or tried to make conversation, they smiled condescendingly and babbled something in Iraqi Arabic. She wondered if they'd respond to Wayne the same way, but so far he'd focused all his attention on Hassan. He hadn't stopped asking questions since they'd arrived—not that he seemed to care so much about the answers. He just wanted to make sure everyone knew he was in charge.

"So, Nasser . . . how old is your daughter?" Katie turned to the heavily bearded guard on her right. "You and your wife must be very proud of her."

The man's eyes went wide. He cast a nervous look at his fellow guardsman but didn't break silence. Katie filed the information away. Either he was surprised she'd gotten his name right or she had gotten lucky and the fine strand of dark hair poking through the sleeve of his faded blue shirt really did belong to his daughter.

"How about you, Kamel?" She turned to the other bodyguard. "Do you and your wife have children?"

The guard to her left tensed and flashed her a cheddar smile before mumbling something that sounded like "My vomit."

Katie nodded and returned the smile. The man seemed pleasant enough, but his whole body radiated tension. She was almost positive she'd gotten his name and marital status right, but he seemed determined not to respond in English. Either he was under strict nonfraternization orders or she was violating some sacred Islamic male-female social interactions taboo. Either way, the reaction of the guards was highly unusual.

Katie turned in her seat and looked back to see how Hooman was getting on with his guard, but the young grad student was angled away from both of them, staring out the window. Katie followed his gaze. The walls had given way to a vast expanse of sand and sand-colored buildings. They drove past a huge pile of rubble and dust that had once been a factory or storage building. A bombed-out tank sat next to the road. The burned carcasses of jeeps and cars were scattered everywhere, silent testaments to the strife that had ravaged the city for more years than anybody cared to count.

The Suburban made a sharp left and then turned right again to take them deeper into the heart of the city. Katie watched as the buildings grew closer and closer together. They passed a small group of rifle-wielding men in white shirts. The men looked up briefly and then started piling into a four-door pickup. She turned and looked out the back window. The pickup still wasn't moving. Apparently, they weren't in any hurry.

Finally, after over a half hour of driving, they pulled up to a huge complex of white buildings and beige walls. Passing through a gate at the front of the complex, they drove around a U-shaped drive and parked in a small lot in front of the nearest building. The guards threw open the doors as soon as the car came to a rest and Katie followed them out into the piercing sun. Heat closed in around her like a bake oven. Superheated air burned down her airways, filling her lungs with fire. She felt like she was being slowly roasted from the inside out. She followed Hassan and Wayne to a covered entrance and was about to follow them inside when Hooman cut in front of her and held the door open.

"Thanks, Hooman." She flashed him a smile and glanced back to see if the others were following. The three guards were still in the parking lot, huddled together in what looked like a heated argument. The guard with the full black beard glanced up and noticed her watching. He whispered something and the other guards fell suddenly silent.

"Are you coming?" Hooman was looking back and forth between Katie and the parking lot.

"Sorry." Katie stepped into the relief of the air-conditioned museum. They were in a large exhibit room filled with statues, pottery, and glass cases. Two uniformed guards stood on either side of the entrance. Each man cradled a military-issue machine gun in his arms.

Katie looked up at an ancient, water-stained sign on the wall:

Please Note the Following Instructions:
Opening Hour of Museum 9:00 a.m. to 1:00 p.m.
Ticket Price:
Iraqis 250 I.d.
Students 150 I.d.
Foreigners 2000 I.d.
The Packages, Cameras, and Guns Must Be Kept into the Reception.

"I don't think we're in Kansas anymore." She pointed out the sign to Hooman.

"I knew we forgot something," he mumbled and glanced back nervously at the armed guards. "You think everybody carries a gun here?"

Katie shrugged and stepped forward to the reception desk, where an attractive Iraqi woman greeted them politely and led them to the hallway at the far end of the exhibit hall.

"Meeting is in newest remodel room." The receptionist smiled shyly and pointed to an open doorway at the end of the hall. "On the side of the left."

"Thank you." Katie waited for the receptionist to leave them before leading Hooman down the dimly lit corridor. Voices emanated from the open room. She slowed her pace. Judging from the tone of the echo, it was an office or small conference room. She could hear two voices besides Wayne's. Neither sounded like their guide. Either Hassan wasn't in the room or he wasn't saying much. Not that he had much of a chance. Wayne was talking loud enough to drown out anyone within a mile radius. She held out a hand and motioned for Hooman to slow down. Another half minute and Wayne's overeager manner would tell the Iraqis everything she needed them to know.

Hooman raised an eyebrow at her and nodded to the door. Katie shook her head and held up a finger. Just a few more seconds. Wayne was babbling on about his last dig in California. With any luck someone would ask him what he'd found.

A low murmur interrupted Wayne's discourse on fossil identification. Footsteps were heading for the door. Katie pulled Hooman forward and almost collided with Hassan as he bustled from the room.

"*Afwan.* My apologies." He stepped back and followed them inside. "I thought you were right behind us, otherwise I never would have—"

"There you are!" Wayne cried out in a loud voice. "We were just startin' to wonder if you'd gotten lost."

Katie stepped into the room and turned to face the polished gentlemen standing on the far side of a large cherrywood conference table. "Minister Khaleed Talibani." She bowed to the shorter and rounder of the two men. "Minister Ameen Hamady." She nodded to the tall, rugged Arab, who seemed awkward and uncomfortable in his gray Italian suit.

"Ministers, this is Katie James, the most senior member of my team." Wayne stepped behind Katie and put a hand on her shoulder. "Katie ain't used to lots of people. Spends most of her time in the desert."

"And this is Hooman Kapoor." Katie pulled out of Wayne's grasp and guided Hooman forward. "Hooman's only a first-year grad student, but he's already one of the best, most patient excavators I've ever known."

"High praise coming from the great Katie James." The short minister stepped around the table and shook Hooman's hand. "Welcome, Mr. Kapoor. And welcome to you, Katie James." He bowed low as he pressed Katie's hand in both of his. For a second Katie thought he was going to kiss it, but finally, after a long pause, he released her hand with an elegant sigh. "I must confess, I've been most eager to meet you. We've heard so many remarkable stories. . . . And your picture doesn't do you justice."

"My picture?" Katie glanced over at Wayne, but he seemed just as confused as she was.

"Please forgive my friend's enthusiasm." The tall minister stepped around the table and gripped Katie's hand in a firm, calloused handshake. "Khaleed is a big fan of your Wild West. I am certain he is disappointed you do not wear boots and hat and a holster full of six-shooters."

"I'm afraid I had to leave my six-shooters at home with my horse." Katie grinned at the short minister, who was scowling up at his friend. "Airport security, you know."

"Then you must allow me to lend you some of mine." The short minister snapped to his full height.

"Khaleed has an impressive collection of pistols from your American West," the tall minister added. "He is a great fan of both the country and the people."

"Perhaps you would like to view my collection? After dinner tonight, *inshallah?*" Khaleed turned and received a nod from his friend. "We would both be honored to share dinner with the great-granddaughter of Jesse James."

"The granddaughter of Jesse what?" Wayne pushed between Katie and the ministers. "She ain't no relative of Jesse James, and she don't have time for dinner either. We've got to pack up and get ready for our trip. We're leaving first thing in the morning."

"I'm sure Hassan and his men will be delighted to assist with your preparations." The short minister nodded to Hassan, who stepped toward the door, motioning for Wayne to follow. "Our assistant, Abdur Rashid, is most efficient. I'm sure he has ordered everything to Dr. James's exact specifications."

Wayne turned and glared at Katie.

"I should probably see to the preparations too." Katie took a tentative step toward the door. "But afterwards I'd love to have dinner with you both. What time should I be ready?"

"Excellent! *Il-hamdu lillaah!*" The short minister rocked back on his heels with a broad smile. "Will 7:30 be too early?"

"7:30 will be perfect. It'll give me a chance to freshen up after my trip."

"Excellent. Check to your supplies, and I'll send Abdur down in a few hours to take you to your rooms, *inshallah.* I'm sure he has you staying at Hotel Ishtar. It's not expensive, but the rooms are very comfortable and the service is excellent, *inshallah.* You will enjoy your stay."

"Thank you so much for everything. We're not used to such pampering."

"I've heard stories of what you're used to." The minister's eyes lit with sudden excitement. "Perhaps we can *rustle up* a gang of gun-slinging fossil thieves to make you feel more at home, yes?"

Katie couldn't help laughing as a disgusted moan sounded from the doorway. Wayne was going to blow a gasket if this kept up much longer. And she was going to have to live with the consequences. "I hate to disappoint, but it sounds like some of those stories you've been hearing may have grown a bit in the retelling."

"Then I'm even more anxious to hear them from you." The short minister bowed and took Katie by the hand. "Until tonight. Abdur will pick you up at 7:15, *inshallah*."

"Okay then." Katie hesitated and then gently withdrew her hand. Hooman caught her eye. He was watching her with a wide, mischievous grin. She had to look down at the floor to keep from laughing. "One more question before we go . . ." She bit her lip to steady her voice. "When is Nick Murad scheduled to arrive?"

"I'm sorry . . . Nick Murad?" The minister looked confused.

"Dr. Nick Murad from the University of Michigan?" Katie turned to the tall minister. "We were told he wouldn't get here for another week and a half."

The two ministers exchanged puzzled glances.

"This Dr. Murad—" the tall minister stepped forward—"he is another member of your team?"

Katie's mouth dropped open as the explanation finally hit her. There was no race with Murad. Dietrich had made the whole thing up—to manipulate her into going on the trip. "I'm sorry. I must have misunderstood Dr. Fischer. I thought one of my competitors was going after the whale too."

A frown creased the short minister's face.

"There *is* a whale, isn't there?" Katie looked from minister to minister. "In the Al Muthanna desert . . . Dr. Fischer said a shepherd had brought back a fossilized vertebra."

"Yes, yes, of course. Our best scientists assure us the fossil must be very ancient indeed. A national treasure waiting to bring scientists from all over the world like a flock of birds to our Baghdad museums, *inshallah*. For such an important find, with all the dangers of the area, we would not have any other scientist—only the best, the great Katie James."

The great Katie James . . . What kind of nonsense has Dietrich been feeding them? "I hope I can live up to your expectations. Dietrich sometimes gets a little carried away with the facts."

"Who?" the short minister asked.

"Dietrich . . . Dietrich Fischer."

"Oh yes." The minister nodded. "Your associate. Yes, he asked to search for the whale by himself, but I insisted. Only Katie James, I said. We need someone who can handle herself in any situation."

Katie nodded and tried to force a smile. The conniving coyote had been using her the whole time.

Bill watched the museum hallway through the back of the glass display case. It looked like his hunch was going to pay off after all. The two Sunni ministers had left the comforts of their air-conditioned offices at the ministry building and driven all the way across the city, enduring crowded streets and blistering morning heat just to meet with a group of foreigners. If that wasn't proof of their guilt, he didn't know what was. They had dirty written all over their grubby little Baathist faces. *Dirty Baathists.* Bill snorted out loud. Sometimes he killed himself.

Footsteps clack-clacked across the floor behind him. A female, light on her feet—the receptionist? He shuffled the pages on his clipboard until the page of pottery sketches was on top and then turned around. The young Iraqi woman stared right past him and kept on walking. Nothing suspicious there. He'd always been invisible to her type. He scribbled a nonsensical note on his pad and turned back to watch the hallway through the back of the glass case.

He'd been shadowing Department of Antiquities officials for days now—ever since he'd stumbled upon the looters at the Nippur excavation. At first he'd been inclined to think they were just looters who had stolen guard uniforms, but the men had barely searched for him at all. They hadn't even bothered to disable his Land Rover. They'd just packed up the truck and driven off, taking only the most expensive artifacts and leaving everything else behind. Thorough, organized, meticulously researched. It reminded him of the 2003 Iraqi museum robbery. The thieves had systematically emptied the museum while American soldiers looked on. The guards at Nippur had displayed the same level of organization, the same brazen arrogance.

Murdock was right about one thing: there was definitely an inside man coordinating the smuggling. And if this meeting was what he thought it was, Murdock's inside man was really two men. Talibani and Hamady. He'd checked up on the Sunni ministers as soon as he'd gotten back from Nippur. Not only had they both been in the Department of Antiquities back in 2003, but they were the ones who had hired the four guards. . . .

A door clacked open at the back of the hallway. The sound of muffled voices. Bill stepped out from behind the display case as three foreigners followed an Iraqi national down the hallway. Apparently the ministers were still inside. He aimed his clipboard at the approaching party and started snapping pictures. The tall, craggy man was almost certainly American, and the younger guy looked Pakistani or Indian, but the woman . . . She was as exotic a number as he'd ever seen. He allowed his eyes to linger on her a moment longer than strictly necessary. No worries about blowing his cover here. He could watch her as long as he liked. It would be more suspicious for him to look away without noticing.

He snapped photos of the woman and her party until they disappeared into the new section of the museum. Whoever they were, they definitely weren't archaeologists. And they weren't antiquities dealers either. He'd been working ancient antiquities for sixteen years and knew everyone in the business by sight—even the university crowd. Up until two years ago, it had been a pretty cushy assignment. Paris, Zurich, Munich, Prague . . . People with enough money to buy 10-million-dollar objets d'art didn't hang out at McDonald's either. But then, after the reorg hit, everything had gone south. Smugglers and black market racketeers were all of a sudden acceptable. If the bad guys didn't have dark skin and pray to Allah, the agency just wasn't interested.

Bill shook his head and turned his attention back to the conference room. The ministers were still inside. They'd probably stay put for quite a while. Whoever these foreigners were, the ministers obviously weren't eager to have their pictures taken with them. He scribbled another nonsensical note in his clipboard and wandered across the main hall, through the new wing to the section at the back of the building. The foreigners were nowhere in sight. Pausing to browse each exhibit, he worked his way slowly to the back corner of the complex. A pair of bored-looking soldiers sat reclining on either side of a metal door. The sign on the door said it was alarmed. Whoever these people were, they certainly had the run of the place.

Glancing at his watch, he hurried back to the entrance. The receptionist smiled at him as he hurried by. "Thank you for your visitation. Please come again." She spoke with a deliciously thick accent.

Bill slowed his pace and returned her smile. "It's going to be hot as blazes outside. Almost worth waiting till the sun goes down." He took a deep breath and pushed his way out into blinding sunlight. The heat crashed down on him like a tidal wave, stabbing needles of pain into his arms, chest, and back. Murdock better be happy. He pulled his car keys from his pocket and took off across the visitors' lot toward the employee parking lot at the corner of the triangular compound. Halfway across the employee lot he stopped and looked around. Muttering to himself about playing hide-and-seek with a car, he turned and followed the access road that led to the back of the complex.

He was halfway to the back parking lot when he saw the trucks. Two white four-door pickups backed up to the loading docks of the museum. *Not again!* His gut turned to ice as he saw a group of blue-shirted men loading packages onto the truck. He forced his feet forward, pretending he hadn't noticed. As long as they weren't interfered with, looters didn't seem to care whether they were seen or not.

He casually turned his clipboard toward the truck and started snapping pictures. There she was—the woman from the museum. She and the tall American were hauling a huge water tank over to the back of one of the trucks. He looked at the packages more carefully. Tents, gasoline tanks, shovels . . . What in the blazes were they up to? A cross-country trip through the desert? They certainly had enough water and gasoline. Maybe that's how they were smuggling the stolen artifacts out of the country. It was just brazen enough to work. To anyone else they were just another team of archaeologists, going out on a dig. It was the perfect cover.

The American stepped back into the shadow of the building and wiped his face with the back of his sleeve. He looked up and eyed Bill suspiciously. Bill casually hit a button on his keychain, praying he was within range of his car. A satisfying chirp sounded from the parking lot around the corner of the building. Adjusting course, he made for the sound, waddling along in his signature bumbling American tourist walk.

He managed to get all the way to his car without passing out. So far so good. Pulling a handkerchief out of his pocket, he mopped it across his forehead and snuck a glance back at the trucks. Most of them were still hauling supplies, but one of the blue shirts had walked to the front of the trucks and was watching him with a wary expression. An electric jolt passed through Bill's frame. The full beard, dark murderous eyes . . . It was the guard from the Nippur looting. The guy that had spotted him first.

Slowly. No sudden moves! He nonchalantly wiped his face and put the handkerchief back in his pocket. *Easy. Slow down.* His hands were shaking as he looked down at the door and inserted the key into the lock. The guy couldn't have recognized him. It had been too dark. All he could have seen was his flashlight. He opened the door casually, waited for some of the heat to escape, and lowered himself into the burning seat. Finally, after closing the door and starting up the car, he allowed himself to glance back at the trucks. The bearded guard was in the back of the pickup, wrestling the water tank to the front of the bed. Good. Now all he had to worry about was heatstroke. If he made it back to the hotel without passing out, it would be a miracle.

"It's beautiful." Katie squinted through the front window of the Suburban as the assistant minister drove by yet another unpronounceable mosque. Her eyes drifted shut. She didn't have time for sightseeing. There were still too many things left to do. Reviewing the geological survey maps, mapping out their stops, requesting new guards . . . A sinking sensation settled in the pit of her stomach.

The guards . . . They'd simpered and smiled and bobbed their heads at her all afternoon, but as soon as she turned her back, their pasted-on smiles dissolved instantly. Several times, out of the corner of her eye, she had caught Blackbeard leering at her, sizing her up like a wolf salivating over its prey. His resentment was almost palpable. It hung in the air like a noxious cloud, dragging the mood of the party into the toilet. Something was seriously wrong. She was positive they understood every word she said, but they refused to acknowledge the fact, despite her best efforts to engage with them.

One thing was certain: her team couldn't spend a month in the desert with that kind of attitude. It would tear the camp apart. Wayne would disagree, but she had to convince the ministers that their team didn't need an armed escort.

". . . There are many beautiful mosques in the city, *hamdu lillaah*. Some of the most beautiful in the world. Would you like to see the Golden Mosque? It is only a little out of our way."

Katie forced her eyes open. "Thanks for offering, Abdur. The city is magnificent. I wish I had a month to explore it, but I wouldn't want to keep the ministers waiting." She managed a weary smile.

"Of course. I forget. You are tired after your long journeys."

Katie nodded. "I haven't slept in over thirty-eight hours. Wayne had us sorting through the supplies all afternoon."

"I take you right away to the museum again." He slowed at an unmarked intersection and turned down a narrow alley. "You leave tomorrow to find the museum's whale?"

"At 7 a.m." Katie rolled her eyes. "I don't suppose you could remind the ministers we've got a long day ahead of us tomorrow."

The assistant nodded and smiled at her. His uneven teeth showed yellow against his sparse black beard. "Knowing Minister Talibani, this will not be easy, but I will personally see to it that the dinner ends before tomorrow morning, *inshallah*—if Allah wills it to be."

"Thanks." Katie started to laugh but caught herself when she noticed he had stopped smiling. She settled back in her seat and stared out the window at the shops and open stalls lining both sides of the street. It wasn't dark yet, but the market area was almost deserted.

Two shrouded grandmothers stood at an open spice market. A half dozen dirty children chased this way and that down a narrow street. If the markets were this empty, maybe the restaurant wouldn't be crowded either. The ministers were important men; maybe they'd have their own private dining room. Perhaps they'd have—

"May I be so bold as to ask a question?"

Katie turned to Abdur with a start.

"When the shepherds brought the bone to us, we sent three teams out into the Al Muthanna desert. How is it you, a foreigner, think to find the whale when we who know the desert could not?"

Katie shrugged and looked out at the road ahead of them, hoping Abdur would do the same. "This is the first I've heard that you've already tried to find it, but assuming none of your teams were led by geologists or paleontologists—"

"How will training make such a difference? The shepherds who found it were uneducated."

"The shepherds stumbled on it. To find it again we'll have to read the geology of the area. Knowing what to look for gives us a huge head start. Who knows? We might not find that whale, but maybe we'll find a different one. Or then again, maybe we won't find anything at all. There are never any guarantees."

"This is not what your Dr. Fischer is saying to us."

"Our Dr. Fischer can be a bit of a used car salesman at times."

"Car salesman?"

"Kind of like a politician."

Abdur nodded and turned his attention back to the road. They drove in silence several minutes. Just as Katie was about to nod off, the car slowed to a stop in the museum parking lot. Abdur got out of the car and hurried around the front to open the door for her.

"Thank you." Katie stepped out of the car and Abdur closed the door behind her like a practiced limo driver—a limo driver who drove a Chevy Suburban with thick metal plates welded helter-skelter all over its exterior. He nodded officiously and led her toward the entrance of the museum.

"So we're meeting the ministers here?"

Abdur nodded. "The ministers thought to eat here at the museum, *inshallah*. With the current detestable situation, they felt safer to arrange a meal brought here instead of restaurant."

"That's perfect!" The weight of her fatigue evaporated like an afternoon shower. No crowds! She could do this. It might even be fun. She followed the assistant up the front steps and paused while he tugged at the door, slipped, and finally managed to wrestle it open for her. Two new soldiers snapped to attention as she stepped into the air-conditioned lobby. A tall, bearded Iraqi stepped out from behind the reception desk and walked up to her. He was wearing a traditional dishdasha robe with a keffiyeh draped loosely over his head. A long, ragged scar stretched from his cheekbone to the base of his ear.

"Minister Al-Jaza'iri!" Abdur hurried around Katie and interposed himself between her and the tall man. "Allow me to introduce Dr. Katie James from the United States University of New Mexico."

"Welcome, Dr. James. *Il-hamdu lillaah!* Allah be praised for the honor of our meeting." Al-Jaza'iri reached around Abdur and took Katie by the hand. "I've heard so much about you. I hope, *inshallah*, you had a pleasant trip?"

"It was very long, actually. . . . We just arrived this morning."

Abdur moved to Katie's side. "Khaleed and Ameen asked that she help with our fossil recovery efforts for the natural history museum."

"The whale fossil, yes. The vertebra the Al Muthanna shepherds brought in." Al-Jaza'iri stepped around the diminutive assistant and guided Katie into the exhibit room. "Dr. James, words can't express how thankful I am for your help in this matter. Every time new fighting breaks out, traitors and thieves use the opportunity to plunder our poor country of its national heritage—the one commonality that unites all Iraqis whether Shiite or Sunni." His eyebrow twitched as he spoke the last word. "My colleagues and I are in your debt."

"Your colleagues?"

"I believe you've already met them—Ministers Talibani and Hamady?"

"So you work for the Department of Antiquities too?"

"I appreciate your confusion. I am but a recent appointment. The coalition government is slowly working to make the department more . . . representative of the cultural diversity of Iraq, *inshallah*. It seems there have been concerns raised about links between certain Sunni-run facilities and some of the so-called looting that is taking place."

Abdur cleared his throat loudly. "Minister Al-Jaza'iri, I'm afraid Dr. James is late for a dinner appointment. If you'll please excuse us."

"With Talibani and Hamady? They are here in the museum?" Al-Jaza'iri led Katie across the exhibit room toward the hallway at the other end. "I did not realize. Please accept my apologies for delaying you." He walked with her to the end of hallway and stopped outside the conference room. "This is where they typically entertain their esteemed guests. If you'll allow me . . ." He opened the door and stepped back for Katie to enter.

"Dr. James, come in. Dinner is just being served." The short minister's smile darkened as he looked past her to the door. "And, Mohammed, what a surprise! I thought you were still in Nippur."

"Only for the single day." Al-Jaza'iri's words were smooth as honey. "I got back late last night."

"Well, well . . . welcome back. Have you met Dr. James?"

"Only briefly. Abdur Rashid introduced us just a few minutes ago."

"Dr. James is here to help us find the whale fossil before it disappears." The tall minister rose to his feet and moved to stand next to his companion. "The Geological Survey of Pakistan has such a whale, and hundreds of scientists flock to Quetta every year just to view it."

Al-Jaza'iri raised an eyebrow.

"Katie here has had great success battling against looters," the short minister said. "Once in Mexico City she was attacked by four armed men and single-handedly brought them to justice. Is this not so, Dr. James?"

"Well, actually . . ." Katie could feel her cheeks starting to flush. "Actually it wasn't that big a deal. It was only two men and both of them were pretty much drunk."

"Such modesty!" The short minister's eyes sparkled. "You must tell us the whole story. *And* the story of Peru. We all, I'm sure, are most

eager to hear it. Dr. Fischer sent us articles from the newspapers but
they gave no details—"

"Perhaps over dinner . . ." The tall minister turned to Al-Jaza'iri.
"We were just about to share a modest meal together. You will, of
course, join us?"

"*Il-hamdu lillaah*. Thank you," Al-Jaza'iri looked down at the elegant table set for three. "But I'm afraid I have a previous commitment.
Perhaps another time, *inshallah*." He turned back to Katie. "It was a
pleasure to meet you, Dr. James. If I can be of any assistance to you,
please don't hesitate to ask."

"Thank you. You've already done so much." She paused, wondering if it would seem ungrateful to mention her concerns about the
guards.

"I see by your eyes there is something else, yes?" Al-Jaza'iri fixed
her in his piercing gaze.

Katie chose her words carefully. "We have everything we *need*. More
than we need, really. For instance, the guards you've supplied. There are
only three of us. I don't see that we need four armed men. . . ."

"This is because you do not know the dangers of Iraq." The
assistant minister, who had been standing at the back of the room,
stepped suddenly forward. "This is not the United States—or even
Peru. . . ."

"But surely . . . if Dr. James feels she can protect her party . . ."
The short minister gestured dramatically to the assistant.

"It is too dangerous! The guards must go," the assistant said. "On
this I will not be swayed."

Katie looked to the tall minister, but he just shrugged and turned
to his companion.

"Abdur, I appreciate your concerns," the short minister said. "But
given the unique circumstances . . ."

"You all know my feelings on this matter," Al-Jaza'iri announced
in a loud voice. "There are many who will oppose this expedition.
Many patriots of Iraq who will not accept this museum or this fantasy
of a whale." He turned to Katie and fixed her with a hard, penetrating
gaze. "Understand this: These are delicate times. When a whole nation

hangs in the balance, even a tiny mustard seed can tip the scales. Allah placed whales in the oceans—on the fifth day. It is a dangerous endeavor, searching for them on dry land. Lying to the Iraqi people, saying such creatures are older than the age of the world—this is very dangerous indeed, even by Iraqi standards."

The tall minister exchanged a dark look with his companion. "Khaleed, now that I understand Al-Jaza'iri's position, I'm afraid I must agree. We must keep the guards. This whale fossil, it seems, may prove to be more dangerous than we at first realized."

Katie turned to the short minister. His dark eyes smoldered beneath a furrowed brow. He glared at Al-Jaza'iri several seconds before finally speaking. "As always, Mohammed is perfectly correct. We would not be good hosts if we offered Dr. James any less than the finest guards available."

I see no good reason why the views given here in this volume should shock the religious feelings of anyone. It is satisfactory, as showing how transient such impressions are, to remember that the greatest discovery ever made by man—namely, the law of the attraction of gravity—was also attacked by Leibnitz, "as subversive of natural, and inferentially of revealed, religion." A celebrated author and divine has written to me that "he has gradually learnt to see that it is just as noble a conception of the Deity to believe that He created a few original forms capable of self-development into other and needful forms, as to believe that He required a fresh act of creation to supply the voids caused by the action of His laws." **Charles Darwin,** The Origin of Species

Part Two

Chapter 6

KATIE PACED BACK AND FORTH across the cement floor of the museum loading dock. What was taking them so long? She looked at her watch again. 10:21 a.m. So much for their early departure time. She leaped down to the parking lot and strode up to one of the guards who was leaning against the back of the lead truck.

"Do you know where Hassan and Wayne went? Did they say anything to you?"

The guard shrugged and mumbled something in Arabic.

"Are you shrugging because you don't understand me or because you don't know where they went?"

A thin smile and another shrug.

"Forget it!" She turned away from the guard, took a running start, and vaulted back onto the loading platform. "Wayne?" Circling around an eight-foot pile of empty cardboard boxes, she marched up to the door at the back of the processing area and gave it a tug. The heavy door swung open with a metallic shriek, bathing her in a wash of cool air. She stepped inside and gasped as a tall guard suddenly moved in front of her.

"It's okay. I'm here at the invitation of Minister Talibani." Katie tried to slip past him, but he blocked her way with his gun. "I'm Katie James. You can call the receptionist and ask her about me."

The big man smiled and shook his head. Either he didn't understand her or he didn't care. Probably both. She was just about to give up and go back around the outside of the building when footsteps sounded around the bend in the hallway. The hiss of hushed voices.

Al-Jaza'iri and Hassan appeared around the corner, followed by the black-bearded guard. Hassan was waving his hands, gesturing wildly. Al-Jaza'iri was nodding, his brow furrowed in a look of pained concentration. His eyes drifted past the guard and went wide as he noticed Katie. "*Hamdu lillaah!* Dr. James!" He waved the guard aside and approached Katie with a formal little nod of the head. "I was just coming to wish Allah's blessings upon you and your team. I wanted to make sure of these men. They will take excellent care for you, *inshallah.*" He bowed and held the door open for her, gesturing for her to walk back out onto the loading dock. "I trust everything is well for your departure?"

"We're all packed and ready to go. Now that Hassan is here, we just need to find Wayne. He may have been . . . delayed in conversation with Minister Talibani."

"Talibani? He is here?" Al-Jaza'iri aimed a fierce look at Hassan.

"I haven't seen him all morning," Katie added quickly. "I just thought maybe . . ."

"Okay, everybody, let's get this show on the road!"

Katie and Al-Jaza'iri turned at Wayne's voice. The drowsy-looking grad student was ambling across the parking lot like he had all the time in the world.

Katie jumped down from the loading dock and rushed over to meet him. "Where have you been?" she whispered. "Al-Jaza'iri's here to see us off. It's almost 10:30!"

"Just picking up a few more supplies." Wayne raised a couple of large plastic bags and grinned. "Where's Hooman?"

"Sleeping in the backseat of the truck. We've been ready for over two hours." Katie took a calming breath and forced a smile before turning back to the loading dock.

Hassan was already in the parking lot checking the tie-downs on the trucks. Al-Jaza'iri stood watching them from the edge of the platform. He raised a hand like a preacher delivering a benediction. "*Ma a s-salaama.* Good-bye. Safe journeys to you all, *inshallah.*"

"Thank you." Katie hurried up to the loading dock. "We appreciate so much your . . ."

Al-Jaza'iri dismissed her with a nod and strode back toward the museum door.

". . . invitation." She exchanged glances with Wayne as the door slammed behind the Shiite minister. "What was that about?"

Wayne shrugged. "I guess he don't hold with long good-byes."

"Okay . . ." She walked to the older of the two pickups and crossed around it to the driver's side. "Hooman and I will take this truck, and you can have the new one." She opened the door and slid behind the wheel.

"Wait up. Hold on just a minute!" Wayne grabbed the door before she could close it. "Hassan don't want us seen. He and his men will drive; we're sitting in the back."

"But what if—," Katie started to object.

"I don't like it either, but that's the way it's gotta be. The less folks here see of our ugly American faces, the less chance there'll be trouble."

Katie shook her head and slid out of the truck. "As soon as we hit desert, I'm driving. I can't work from the backseat—especially not with tinted windows."

Wayne shrugged. "Okay, everybody . . . Load up; we're moving out!"

Hassan fired a volley of Arabic commands at the guards and walked around to the new truck. The youngest guard hopped in the front seat with him while the other two guards climbed into the front seat of Katie's truck. Blackbeard was driving.

Katie pulled the back door open. Hooman lay sprawled across the seat. Damp trails of sweat crisscrossed his dark, cherubic face. "Hooman . . . rise and shine."

Hooman groaned and flopped an arm across his eyes.

"Time to wake and bake. No desert until you've eaten all your vegetables."

"We're leaving now?" Hooman sat up slowly, squinting at her through bleary eyes.

"Finally." She climbed up into the truck and closed the door behind her. The other truck was already waiting at the parking lot exit.

"You guys coming?" Wayne's voice blasted them through a burst of static.

Katie reached over the seat and grabbed the radio as Blackbeard pulled away from the loading dock. She turned down the volume and hit the PTT switch. "Talk to the driver. He won't talk to us."

"No problem. All he has to do is play follow the leader. We've got you." The lead truck pulled out into traffic. Katie sat back and buckled her seat belt as their driver followed. They were over three hours behind schedule. If they drove through lunch, they'd reach the Al Muthanna desert by 3 p.m. It wouldn't be a full day, but they could at least get a good start. She mentally ticked through the items on her checklist. If there weren't any more delays, they'd have time to survey four different points at twenty-five–mile intervals along the road to As Salmon. The next day they could start mapping out a grid by surveying a line through the desert to the west. With any luck . . .

A dust-covered truck sped past them in the opposite direction. Katie pressed her face to the window. Another almost identical truck was right behind it. The truck was loaded with supplies and equipment. They looked like they'd been out on a dig. A third truck flew past. A pile of Western backpacks fluttered in the breeze. One of the packs was emblazoned with a blue and gold *M*.

"Stop the truck! Turn around!" Katie shouted at the driver. "Turn around now!"

Blackbeard jabbered something to his companion and kept on driving.

Katie grabbed the radio. "Hey, Wayne? Stop the truck. We've got to turn around." She waited a few seconds. "Seriously. We need to go back right now."

"What's the matter, Miss James? Forget to pack your six-shooters?"

"Those trucks we just passed—I think it might have been Nick Murad from Michigan."

"So?"

"So Dietrich said he's not supposed to be here for two weeks.

And the ministers told me they hadn't even invited him. Doesn't that
seem a little strange to you?"

"And this affects us how?" The lead truck gradually slowed to a
stop behind a line of backed-up traffic.

"Come on, Wayne. I'm serious. Turn the trucks around. If that
was Murad, he could have found the whale by now."

"Calm down, sweetheart. Cool your guns. Hassan says the
museum sends out all kinds of archaeologists and anthropologists.
Gives them a good deal too. They get to keep all the duplicates they
find."

They were at a standstill now. Even if they wanted to, they
couldn't turn around. There wasn't enough room. "Forget it." Katie
tossed Hooman the radio and flung open the door of the truck.

"Katie, wait!" Hooman called after her. He grabbed at her sleeve,
but she shrugged him off and pushed out into the withering heat.

"Wayne's so smart, tell him to find the whale without me!" She
started jogging back in the direction of the museum. If Wayne wasn't
going to listen to her, there wasn't any point in her going. She slowed
to a walk and swiped an arm across her forehead. The heat was
beating down on her like a heavyweight boxer. She had to be more
careful. Too much exertion and the sun would suck the life right out
of her. She cast a quick glance over her shoulder and kept on walking.
She could see the museum ahead of her. Three trucks were parked
out front in the visitors' lot.

A dark-haired man in a long Indian kurta got out of the first truck
and walked around to the second. She watched as he leaned low over
the window and conversed with his driver. The driver was definitely
a native of the region, but the man . . . there was something oddly
familiar about him. He straightened and looked over at the third
truck. It was Nick Murad.

Katie stopped on the side of the street and stared. Why would
the ministers lie to her? She took another step forward and then
stopped again as several people started getting out of the trucks. Two
darker-skinned drivers and one, two, three . . . young Americans. How
many students did he have? The second driver stayed with the trucks

as the rest of the party headed for the entrance of the building. She hesitated, trying to decide whether to follow or not. A confrontation with the ministers wouldn't accomplish anything. It would only strain a critical relationship. Besides, if the ministers were just as forthcoming with Murad as they were with her . . .

Squealing brakes sounded behind her. The low rumble of an engine.

"What the blazes do you think you're doing?" Wayne shouted at her from the truck window.

Katie turned back to the museum. The Murad team was already inside—everyone but the guard in the truck. "Quick, turn these trucks around," she hissed. "Get us out of here now, before they spot us!" She ran back to the second truck and climbed inside.

"Katie!" Hooman's eyes were wide with confusion. "What's going on? Why did you—?"

"Just a second." She grabbed the radio and held it to her mouth. "Wayne, turn these trucks around right now! You question my judgment one more time, and you and Hooman will be on your own."

"Whoa. Take it easy. In case you don't remember, the boss man put *me* in charge."

"And in case *you* don't remember, the boss man's funding ends in two months. We don't find this whale, and we're all out of jobs. Do you want my help or not? You're in charge; the choice is yours."

The radio was silent for several seconds. Finally the truck ahead of them circled around in a wide U-turn.

Katie pressed the PTT switch. "Good choice. Now listen up. I saw Nick Murad and his team get out of those trucks. If the ministers tell Murad the same lie they told us, then we'll have a huge advantage. We're in a race with someone who doesn't even know he's racing."

Nick leaned over the reception desk, scanning the contents of the museum. Pottery, statuary, stone tools . . . The place seemed more geared to archaeology than natural history. Why had the minister wanted to meet them here? And where was the minister? Except for the guards, the place seemed to be deserted.

He combed a hand through his mop of wet, sticky hair. His face was beginning to feel tight and crusty as the sweat dried on his skin. He wondered if he looked as bad as he felt. He knew he smelled even worse. His truck's air conditioner had given out twenty hours into their thirty-six–hour journey across Pakistan and Iran. It had been a long, hot trip. They'd had to wait over five hours at the Iranian border. Oddly enough, it was Waseem's and Ahamed's visas that held them up. The border officials didn't look twice at their American passports. They'd just stamped them and let them across, forcing them to walk through on foot while a couple of bored Iranian guards inspected the trucks and drove them through the gate.

Ahamed joined Nick at the desk. "You are sure they expect us here?"

Nick shrugged. "Mike talked to the minister himself only an hour ago. He said he'd be here." He looked back at his team. Karl, Andy, and Annalise were sprawled out on the floor of the entryway. Annalise's mouth was hanging open and her eyes were shut. They were all exhausted. Poor kids. He should have dropped them off at a hotel and come back to the museum by himself.

The tap-tap of running footsteps echoed through the exhibit hall. Nick turned as a young Iraqi woman in a black Western-style dress ran up to the desk.

"I am so sorry to make you wait. You must be Dr. Murad." She extended her hand uncertainly.

"I'm pleased to meet you." Nick shook her hand and turned to introduce Ahamed.

"I am so very sorry. Minister Al-Jaza'iri just telephoned. He begs for your forgiveness. He has been delayed at a security checkpoint on Rashid Street. He could not know it would be there. I came on Rashid two hours ago, and it was all good." She looked past Nick and her eyes went suddenly wide. "Please forgive me. You are tired and I make you to wait." She hurried around the desk and grabbed a stack of folders. "Please . . . anything you need and I will get it. There is a conference room with drinks and hospitality. I was just putting them in order when I should have been . . ." She looked up at Nick with an expression that bordered on panic.

"It's okay. We just got here. You didn't keep us waiting at all." He motioned for the students to get up on their feet. "We've been a day and two nights on the road, so we're a little tired; that's all."

A grateful smile spread across the girl's face, and she seemed to relax a little. "Please. Follow me and I will take you to the hospitality." She led them across the exhibit room and down a hallway to a long, narrow room. A ceramic bowl at the center of a large table was filled with ice and drinks. A stack of pastries was on one side and a dish of what looked like lasagna was on the other. "Please, if you need anything at all, I will get it. Anything at all."

"We're fine. Thank you very much. Everything looks wonderful." Nick smiled and the girl's face brightened again.

"I must return to the desk now." She backed toward the door. "If you need anything at all, just let me know."

"Thanks, um . . . *Shukran*." Nick watched her out the door and turned to Ahamed.

"What was that all about?" he whispered to the Pakistani guide.

Ahamed shrugged. "She is obviously nervous to be in your presence. Wanting to make a good impression."

"Right, because I look so good right now."

"I've seen you much worse." Ahamed's face tightened as he fought to suppress the grin that sparkled in his eyes. "She obviously heard that you sent your girlfriend back to America. News of eligible men travels fast in these parts."

"I didn't send her anywhere. She left me. Probably because of all the bad habits I picked up hanging around you."

"That and because she is an undeserving, unprincipled *gora chooras* fool."

A timid knock sounded at the door. Nick turned to see the receptionist standing awkwardly in the doorway. Her eyes flitted back and forth between Nick and something unseen in the hallway to her left. "I am most sorrowful for this interruption, but Minister Mohammed

Saeed Al-Jaza'iri will see you now." She dipped her head and scooted back from the doorway as a tall, powerfully built Iraqi stepped into the room.

"Ah, Dr. Murad. Welcome to Iraq." The minister stepped forward and shook Nick's hand in his crushing grip. "I trust you had a pleasant trip?"

"Yes, thank you . . ."

"Please, call me Mohammed." He turned a curious eye on Ahamed and the rest of Nick's team.

"And call me Nick. This is my associate Ahamed Asif from Pakistan." Al-Jaza'iri shook Ahamed's hand vigorously. "And my graduate students: Annalise Kordell, Karl Werner, and Andy Gill."

Al-Jaza'iri nodded to each of the students. "Thank you for coming on such short notice. Please . . ." He motioned to the chairs around the edges of the room. "Be seated. I can stay only a few minutes, but I understand you've had a long, tiring trip."

Nick took a seat by the back corner of the table and looked up at his host. Al-Jaza'iri seemed more like a battle-scarred soldier than a high-level bureaucrat. The receptionist was standing against the wall just outside the door. Her hands were clasped rigidly in front of her, her fingers white with the tension that ran like an electric current through her petite frame.

"Let me get right to the point. I've asked you here to locate the bones of a giant creature that a group of Al Muthanna shepherds reported finding in the desert. Normally the Department of Antiquities and Cultural Heritage would not take notice of a pile of insignificant bones, but these are troubled times. Our nation hangs in a delicate balance that might at any time be toppled by a seemingly insignificant event: the purchase of aluminum tubes or the publication of a Denmark cartoon or even the discovery of a pile of bones in the desert. The Sunnis in our government, leftovers from the former dictatorial regime, have gone to extraordinary lengths to locate these bones. We can only speculate on their motives, but it is certain they intend to bring about much evil. I have proof of their duplicity."

He turned and surveyed the room with fiery eyes. "The Sunnis have brought in an American team led by Wayne Hubbard. The team left Baghdad—"

"Who?" Nick rose from his chair. "Who's Wayne Hubbard? I thought they were bringing in Katie James."

"The woman Katie James is on the team also, but—"

"So who's this Wayne Hubbard? A geologist?" Nick looked back at Andy, who spread his arms in an exaggerated shrug. Apparently he hadn't heard of him either.

Al-Jaza'iri shook his head. "I do not know all the parties involved, but that is not important. What is important is that the American team left Baghdad only a few hours ago. If you leave now and travel quickly, you should be able to catch up with them. I have sent men to question the Al Muthanna shepherds more closely. I've seen the Sunni map and this—" he held up a folded map of Iraq—"is much more precise. You *will* find the bones before the Sunni team does."

"I appreciate the need for speed," Nick said. "But we haven't slept in two nights. And the air conditioner on one of the trucks is out. We won't be able to leave until it's fixed."

"That is not possible." Al-Jaza'iri's voice rumbled through the room. "You must leave now. I will supply you with a new truck and guards to protect you on the way."

"I've got my own guards."

Al-Jaza'iri scowled. "You will need more. We *must* find the bones before the Sunnis do. Remember well, you are in Iraq now. Nothing is ever easy, and nothing is ever what it seems."

Katie swept her eyes back and forth across the dusty terrain as she picked her way along the rocky floor of the Al Muthanna desert. An unbroken blanket of rocks and powdery dust stretched from horizon to horizon as far as the eye could see. No trees, no water, not the faintest trace of civilization. She pulled the Stetson low over her eyes and scanned the area to the west. A network of faint shadows crisscrossed the plain, valleys, and interconnected wadis. Somewhere out there lay the bones of a 50-million-year-old whale. Maybe she was just fooling herself, but if she were a gambling woman, she'd bet a nickel it was to the north of the center line. She might even go as high as a dime.

"What is she doing? Why is she just standing there?"

Katie turned at Hassan's voice. Wayne and the guards had been following her around the desert like a golf tournament gallery ever since they'd arrived. At least Hooman had the good sense to stay in the truck out of the heat. She motioned for them to back off and headed for an erosion gulley off to her right, purposely dragging her boots across the ground. A fine cloud of dust plumed beneath her feet. Too fine. The soil should be grainier, sandier. She reached down, scooped up a pinch of dirt, and touched it to the tip of her tongue. It tasted smooth and buttery—way too much clay content. The sediment at this level had been laid down during a low-energy period, probably 10 million years ago while the area was still swampy, but well after the Tethys Sea had already receded. She took one more taste and spit the dirt out.

"What is she doing now? Why is she eating the desert?" Hassan's whisper carried across the still air like a shout.

"To figure out how the sediment was formed." Wayne had put on his professor voice. "As paleontologists, we're trained to use all our senses."

Katie wheeled around. "Could you please use your senses somewhere else? I can't hear a word the desert's saying."

"Listen, sweetheart, this is a team survey. I don't tolerate any prima donnas—"

"Then start surveying. You're a paleontologist. Go out and sample the area."

"I was just about to do that, but Hassan here had a few questions."

"Fine. Answer his questions while you're working. You're the team leader; lead the team. Just lead them somewhere else. I'm trying to work." Katie climbed down into the gulley and followed its meandering course for several minutes before turning to look back. Hassan and Wayne were gone. Only Blackbeard remained. Rifle cradled in his arms, he followed along the edge of the gulley about a hundred feet behind her. Great, just what she needed—an armed guard to protect her from the desert. If a giant heatstroke happened to wander her way, maybe he'd scare it away with his big gun.

A piercing chirp made her jump. Swinging the pack off her shoulders, she rummaged through its outer pocket to find her satellite phone.

"Hello?" She raised her voice to be heard over the low-pitched hum emanating from the phone. "Is that you, Dietrich?" She pressed the phone tighter to her ear.

"Hello, is this Dr. James?" A man's voice sounded over the whine. One of Dietrich's cronies? Why would Dietrich give out her number?

"Uh-huh . . ."

"This is Nick Murad. Dietrich Fischer was good enough to give me your number."

Nick Murad? Katie could feel her heart shifting into overdrive. "Nick Murad . . . Hi. . . . How are you doing?" She grimaced as soon as the words were out of her mouth.

"I'm good. Listen, I understand you and I are going after the same fish."

"Could be . . . There are a lot of fish in the ocean. Which one are you after?"

"Same one you're after—the Al Muthanna whale. Word on the street is it's pre-*Rodhocetus.*"

"Okay . . ."

"So I was thinking: why don't we join forces on this one? No point getting tangled up in this Shiite-Sunni rivalry."

"And what rivalry is that?" Katie was suddenly on the alert. Did Nick know something she didn't? If so, then why would he be so eager to share? More likely he was trying to feed her misinformation.

"Iraqi politics. Shiites versus Sunnis. Bad guys versus bad guys. My team versus yours."

"And what makes you think I'm taking sides?"

"Of course you're not taking sides. That's what I'm saying. Neither of us is taking sides, so why not work together?"

"Work together . . . So Michigan has a new faculty position?"

There was a long pause. "Listen, I heard what happened at your candidate seminar, and I don't blame you for being mad. It wasn't fair of them to force you to speak when you were sick. For what it's worth, I'm sorry. I wish it could have been different."

"Someone told you I was sick?"

"Several people, actually. A few professors are still grousing about the decision to hire me. Apparently you made quite an impression."

Katie opened her mouth to reply, but a lump had settled in her throat. Why was he telling her this? "What . . ." She swallowed to clear her throat. "What exactly do you want?"

"Let's team up on this one. Form a collaboration. We're both in the field. Why not work together?"

Katie considered the offer. Murad was so well established that nobody would even notice her contribution. A collaboration with Murad certainly wouldn't help Fischer get his grant renewed. "Actually only one of us is in the field right now. Judging from the background noise, I'd say you're in a truck moving at high speed on a paved road." Katie pictured the map of Iraq in her head. If they were four hours behind them . . . "If I'm reading the vibrations right, I'd say you're heading south on the main highway—about fifteen minutes south of Al Hillah."

"Whoa." There was a long pause. "I heard you were good, but that's ridiculous. Ahamed, did you check our gear for tracking devices? She knows exactly where we are."

An accented voice sounded faintly over the hum. "I tell you already about the receptionist but you would not believe me. News of eligible men travels fast in these parts."

Hearty laughter sounded on the other end of the phone.

Katie shook her head, forcing the smile from her face. She couldn't let her guard down. Her career was at stake—and the careers of every Christian in her field. "So . . . since you're still on the road, and I'm already hot on the trail of the whale, what do you propose to contribute to this partnership?"

"Hot on the trail?" Nick sounded skeptical. "How hot?"

"It's 112 degrees out here. Use your imagination."

A muffled hush damped out the roar coming over the receiver. When the roar returned, Katie could hear laughter in the background. "Okay, about my contribution . . ." Nick paused to catch his breath. "I've got three trucks full of equipment, including a high-resolution CT scanner and a portable laminar flow hood. I also have three seasoned grad students and two Pakistani guides. And I have a map that's supposed to be more accurate than the one you're using."

"More accurate?" Katie stopped dead in her tracks. "I've got geological surveys, satellite photos, military maps . . ."

"Not the maps. The search area. Apparently, after talking again to the shepherds, the Shiites were able to narrow the search area considerably."

"Right, so you'll give me a treasure map with a big *X* in the middle of South America."

"Ah, I see you're on to me. Could I interest you in a map with an *X* on the French Riviera? The whales may be harder to find, but digging for them will be a lot more pleasant."

Katie frowned. The guy was way too confident. But if he really had a more accurate map, why was he so eager to collaborate?

"Seriously," Nick continued. "The minister assured me his map was more precise than the one the Sunnis gave you."

"Which minister was—"

The faintest whisper of a noise sounded behind Katie. She turned and caught Blackbeard creeping stealthily forward only a few yards behind her. He bowed slightly and pointed to a shrub on the other side of the gulley, waving his arm in an undulating motion like a big snake.

"Hello, Dr. James? Are you there?"

Ignoring the voice in her ear, Katie took a running start and powered up the far bank of the gulley. The shrub was too thin to conceal even a small snake and she didn't see any holes. She walked past the bush, increasing her pace to a slow jog.

"You found something, didn't you? Your breathing's speeding up. What'd you find?"

"Nothing of consequence." Katie glanced behind her. Blackbeard was climbing out of the gulley and following her at a quick walk. There was something strange about his gait. He seemed to be favoring his right leg. Had he hurt himself climbing down into the wadi?

"That 'nothing of consequence' sounds like it's got you on the run. Are you sure everything's all right?"

"Everything's fine. I just stumbled onto an ancient sarcophagus and now a mummy is after me."

"That doesn't sound good."

"No problem. I'm used to it. Happens all the time." Katie stopped and pretended to survey the area. The guard was walking slower now. Apparently he just wanted to keep her in sight. "Uh, Nick, I've got to deal with this mummy. Good talking to you. Good luck on your search." She hung up the phone and put it back in her pack, keeping a close watch on the guard out of the corner of her eye. He continued forward a few more steps, then turned to look behind him.

As he turned, she noticed an angular bulge in his front right pocket. It was some type of pistol. A very large pistol. Katie looked immediately away. Why bother to conceal a weapon when he was holding a rifle in plain view?

Chapter 7

NICK KICKED AT A LOOSE STONE until it broke free of the ground and skittered across the sand. He bent over the shadowy depression and ran a finger across the newly exposed sediment. Still too powdery. The area was far too recent. He stood up slowly and stretched his aching lower back. It was starting to get late. Might as well call it a day.

He took a long swig from his canteen and headed back in the direction of the trucks. The sun was low in the sky, but the desert still felt like a bake oven. He plodded across the uneven ground, searching for the truck tracks Ahamed had spotted earlier. After a few minutes he finally found them. Two heavy pickups. It was almost certainly the James party. Who else would be driving cross-country through the middle of the desert?

"Searching for mummy tracks?"

Nick looked up at Ahamed's voice. The guide was making his way back to the campsite along the truck tracks. "I think maybe she managed to escape." Nick smiled as he remembered their conversation. "She doesn't seem like the kind of woman a mummy could slow down."

"Too bad. More competition." Ahamed drew alongside Nick and together they started walking back to the trucks. "So what is the plan going to be?"

"I told Karl we'd set up camp early tonight—to give ourselves some extra time to figure out the new tents."

"Good. It has been a long day. The students are all exhausted."

"They're not the only ones," Nick said. "And we need to be up early tomorrow morning. I was thinking we'd follow the James party a little while. Get an idea what they're up to."

Ahamed grinned at him. "And why would we be chasing after this James woman?"

"Not chasing. Just sizing up the competition."

"I see." A gleam sparkled in Ahamed's eyes. "And after you determine her size . . . you will beg her again for the honor of her hand in collaboration?"

Nick shook his head. "Was I that bad?"

"Not bad, my friend. You are much worse than bad."

"Good." Nick forced a wry smile. "I always like to humiliate myself in front of the competition. Makes them underestimate me."

"A useful strategy. So long as you remember not to *overestimate* her."

"Overestimate Katie James? I don't think so. Everything I've ever heard about her says she's extremely good."

"Maybe so . . . but this extremely good competition searches straight in the wrong direction."

"What?" Nick turned to look at his friend. "Are you sure?"

Ahamed nodded. "I followed the tracks almost two miles. She heads for a point far to the north of the area marked on our map."

Nick walked in silence, giving himself a chance to digest this new piece of information. An uneasy feeling nibbled at the edges of his stomach. "What if our map is wrong?"

"And you have reason to doubt the map?"

Nick shook his head.

"Or reason to believe her course is correct?"

"No, but she might have seen something we missed."

"All things are possible, but far more likely we have something she missed. A more accurate map."

"Maybe." Nick shrugged and turned to walk back in the direction he'd come from. By the time he and Ahamed reached the trucks, Annalise and Andy had already set up two tents and were working on the third. The hum of gasoline generators filled the camp. Minister Al-Jaza'iri had supplied them with three military-issue arctic tents, complete with insulation, built-in air ducts, and portable air-conditioning units. Ever since they'd learned about the new tents, Annalise and Andy had been talking about nothing else. It was all he could do to keep them from pulling over and trying out the tents by the side of the highway.

Nick walked over and helped the grad students with the last tent while Ahamed helped Waseem with dinner. It wasn't until they were all settled around the camp table and eating chicken *qorma* that Nick noticed there were only five people in his party.

"Where's Karl? He's going to miss dinner."

Annalise pointed to the tent closest to the trucks. "He's got another migraine. Want me to take him some food?"

Nick shook his head. Karl wouldn't be able to eat until he was feeling better. He got up from the table and started ladling the thick *qorma* curry onto a clean stainless steel plate. "Tell him there's a plate of food for him in the top food bin." He opened a plastic crate full of onions and set the plate on top. "I've got to figure out a search pattern for tomorrow." He walked back to the table and picked up his plate of stew. As he turned to head for the trucks, Ahamed caught his eye and fixed him with a worried look.

"I'm fine. I just can't shake the feeling we're missing something." Nick grabbed the map box and his pack from the cab of his truck and hauled them to one of the unoccupied tents. "This isn't like Pakistan. Now, all of a sudden, we've got competition, and she's way ahead of us."

"Ahead, yes. But ahead in the wrong direction," Ahamed called after him.

Nick shrugged and balanced his plate on the map box as Andy and Annalise peppered Ahamed with questions. He pulled up on the zipper, and a puff of cool air hit him in the face. He pushed through the narrow opening and dragged his gear into the tent. The tent wasn't exactly cool—it was well above ninety degrees inside—but compared to the temperature outside, it felt almost chilly. He yanked down on the zipper and rummaged through his pack for the lantern. There it was. He flicked it on and pulled the minister's map out of the box. The search area was a wide trapezoid marked in bright red ink. He pulled out his GPS and took a reading. They were already on the northernmost edge of the search area. If Katie James continued to the northwest, it would take her out onto a wide plain, slightly higher in elevation than the area in the marked region.

He laid the map to the side and compared it to the geological survey maps. Based on the surveys, the area she was heading into was too recent for a pre-*Rodhocetus*. She had to know that. What was she doing? Trying to lead him on a wild-goose chase? It didn't make sense. The chance of him running across her tracks was a hundred to one.

The enigmatic Katie James . . . He dug a set of satellite photos out of the box and started arranging them on the floor of the tent. As far as he knew, she never spoke at meetings, never attended workshops, and never even went to any of the major conferences. Certainly not any of the conferences he'd attended. For a while he'd thought she was avoiding him, harboring a grudge for him beating her out of the Michigan spot. But nobody else had ever seen her at a conference either. And it wasn't from lack of looking. For a while a couple of his friends from grad school were almost obsessed with her. James Criswell had gone to UNM once and come back with a stack of all her research papers. He used to joke that he was going to marry her one day and become James James.

Nick chuckled to himself and reached into his pack. If only James could see him now. He pulled out his phone and started flipping through the list of numbers. Criswell's number wasn't on the list. Must be on his cell phone. He continued on through the list and paused at Katie's number. If the search zone on her map included the northern plain, it would certainly answer a lot of questions. He punched the call button and waited, fighting the urge to hang up before she answered.

"Yes . . ." The voice was cautious—she was already going into poker mode.

"Hi, this is Nick Murad." He decided to go for a casual tone. "Did you find that fish yet?"

"Maybe . . . What if I did?"

"Then I'll be the first to congratulate you. Nicely done. I hope I can see it someday."

"Thank you." There was a short pause. Something soft seemed to be tapping on her phone. "So I suppose you'll be going back to Pakistan—now that there's nothing left to find here."

"Oh, I'm in no rush," Nick said. "I think I'll hang around a while longer. It's sunny and warm and the beach is the biggest I've ever seen. Besides, I might just get lucky and find some of your leftovers."

"Sorry to disappoint you, but my father taught me to always clean my plate. Starving fossil hunters in Africa, you know."

Nick chuckled to himself. Slow-witted she was not. She wasn't going to give anything away by mistake. Maybe if he . . . A gentle puff sounded on the other end of the phone. He pressed the phone to his ear. She was breathing hard, like she was climbing a steep hill. She couldn't be still searching. It was way too dark out.

"It sounds like that mummy's still after you," Nick said. "Or are you still out searching for the fish?"

"No, just out for a nice jog. Like you said, the beach is so nice."

"It's already dark. Is everything all right?"

"It's fine. I'm just . . ." She paused for several seconds. He could hear the rush of her breath coming louder over the phone. "Did the DOA provide you with security guards?"

"The DOA?"

"The Iraqi Department of Antiquities . . . How many security guards did they make you take?"

Nick considered an evasive response, but something in her tone made him reconsider. "The minister wanted me to take security guards—he got pretty worked up about it—but I refused. I already had my guards from Pakistan. All I needed was a few more rifles and ammunition."

"And they didn't insist on providing you with guides? translators?"

"One of my men speaks Arabic. There really wasn't the need."

A loud thump sounded over the phone. More breathing.

"Dr. James? Are you okay?"

"How many guards do you have? How many guns?" Katie's voice sounded frantic.

"Two . . . two guards and five guns," Nick shouted into the phone. "What's going on?"

"Where are you right now? If I needed your men, how soon could you get here?"

Nick grabbed the GPS. "What are your coordinates?"

There was a long pause.

"Hello, Dr. James? What are your coordinates?"

A giggle sounded over the receiver. "Hey, no fair; I asked you first."

A boiling fountain bubbled up inside Nick. How could he have been so stupid? Here he was thinking he could pump her for information, but he was the one who'd been pumped. Pumped like a chump. It served him right.

"Nick, are you there?" She was using a sweet, feminine voice now. She almost sounded worried.

"Good-bye, Dr. James. I need to go now." He kept his voice flat and steady.

"No, wait. I need to apologize."

"That's okay. No harm done."

"Let me explain. They really did make us bring four guards, and there really is something funny going on with them. The rest was just . . . I was trying to cover up the information I'd given you, but I crossed the line. I'm sorry."

Nick didn't know what to say. Was she for real or was she still playing him? Loud stomps sounded outside the door of the tent, Ahamed's way of knocking.

"Excuse me a second." He muted the phone and pulled up on the zipper.

Ahamed's head pushed into the tent, hovering in the air like a Pakistani Cheshire cat. His worried expression was softened by the faintest trace of a knowing smile.

"Enough with the looks," Nick said. "It's eleven o'clock in Michigan. I need to talk to Mike before he goes to lunch."

Ahamed's head nodded. "When you finish talking, there's something urgent outside you should see." He started to pull back outside but then popped back inside again and looked up with a grin. "And please tell *Mike* that I too would be honored to take her hand in collaboration."

Nick grabbed a folded map, but Ahamed jerked his head back outside before he could hit him with it. He switched off the mute. "Dr. James, are you there?"

"Yup, still here."

"Sorry about that, but I've got a mummy of my own to attend to. I'll talk to you later, okay?"

"Good. I'm looking forward to it."

Nick hung up the phone and crawled out into the sweltering night. *Good. I'm looking forward to it.* Just what was that supposed to mean? Was she looking forward to talking to him again or tricking him out of more information? Or was she just being sarcastic? Not that it mattered. He wasn't about to risk another call. The flow of information all seemed to be one way.

He spotted Ahamed at the edge of camp and started toward him. Ahamed was looking out into the darkness through a pair of high-powered binoculars. A rifle was slung across his shoulder.

"What's going on?" He walked up and waited several seconds until the Pakistani guide finally lowered the field glasses.

"Look." Ahamed handed him the glasses. "Five miles back, about a half mile to the left of that dark ridge."

Nick trained the glasses on the spot indicated by his friend. He couldn't see anything but shadows. "It's too dark. What am I looking for?"

"A truck. I first saw it this afternoon, but I did not think we had reason to worry."

"You think it's following us?"

"There can be no doubt." Ahamed's words were heavy as bricks. "And the bad part is the color of the truck. Sand-colored and brown."

"You think it's military?"

Ahamed nodded somberly. "There can be no doubt."

Katie lumbered up to the truck and rested the heavy tent on its back bumper, bracing it in place with her thigh. They'd been in the desert four days and every day the tents seemed to get heavier. If they kept this up another couple of weeks, they'd have to get some bigger trucks. She reached around the bulky canvas bag and hoisted it up and over the tailgate. The tent landed with a loud whump, rocking the truck on its suspension. She wiped her forehead with the back of her arm and took a long swig from her canteen. Waiting until after lunch to break camp had been a stupid idea. The water was hot enough to brew tea.

She screwed the cap back on the canteen and started tossing day packs into the back of the truck. She was about to toss her own pack when she remembered the satellite phone. The charge was almost down to zero. Pulling the phone out of the side pocket, she hurried around to the front of the truck and plugged it into the electrical outlet.

"Okay? Everybody ready?" She slammed the door behind her and looked out across the camp. Wayne and Hassan were sitting around a map at the folding camp table while Hooman struggled by himself to get the last tent into its canvas bag. As usual, the three guards were off by themselves talking to each other in hushed Arabic. With each passing day, they had become more surly and uncooperative. It was as if they blamed her personally for the heat and dust. They seemed to blame her for not finding the whale on the very first day.

Not that they were doing anything to help. Katie strode across the camp and crouched down beside Hooman. "Need any help?"

Hooman looked up with a shy smile. "Thanks. These things are heavier than they look."

"It's all the sand we're picking up." Katie stuffed the last fold of material into the bag and helped Hooman zip it. "I think the material is some kind of space-age dust magnet."

Hooman nodded and grabbed the handle on one side of the bag. Katie took the other and the two of them carried it over to the truck and swung it up into the bed.

"Okay, let's go!" Katie called out to Wayne and Hassan. "Fold up the table and chairs. We're wasting daylight!"

The men didn't move. Katie looked over at Hooman with an exasperated growl. She strode up to the camp table and waved a hand between Wayne and the map. "Hello? We're ready to go. Everything but the table's already been loaded."

"Well, that's just the problem, ain't it?" Wayne showed his teeth in a sneering smile. "Where exactly are we going? I was just studying the map, and know what I discovered? We're almost ten miles north of the search zone."

"You're just now figuring that out?" Katie couldn't keep the incredulity out of her voice. "Where have you been? We've been north of the search zone for three days."

"And I suppose you have a reason for this little sightseeing excursion?"

"Yeah. Because that's where the fossil is."

Wayne rolled his eyes at Hassan. "Kind of hard to argue with that logic, ain't it?" He turned back to Katie with a hard look. "Except that the shepherds who actually know the desert say they were further south."

"And they couldn't have made a mistake? They had a GPS device with them and marked the exact location?"

"Ten miles is a pretty big mistake. And the direction you've been taking us puts us even farther away."

"Okay." Katie took a calming breath. "Your advice has been noted. Just let me check out the light-colored patch I saw last night. If we don't find anything there, then we can dip back down to the south and search along the northern edge of the search zone."

"I don't think so." Wayne stood up and started folding the map. "Fischer made me the leader, and I say we don't waste any more time."

Katie glanced at the others. Hooman returned her look with an apologetic shrug. Hassan's face was cold and impassive as stone.

"Come on. It's only a couple of miles farther," Katie urged. "Give me one more day to check it out. If we don't find anything, I promise we'll go back."

Wayne shook his head. "No can do, sweetheart. We've given you four days and all we have to show for it is sunburn and saddle sores. We're going back right now."

"Then you're going back without me. I'm heading north." She turned to leave, but Hassan stepped in front of her and blocked her way.

"As one responsible for your safety, I must insist you work with the team." He turned and shouted something to the guards. After a brief argument, they reluctantly grabbed their guns and headed toward the group.

"What are you going to do? Kidnap me?" Katie slipped the canteen off her shoulder and, with slow, inconspicuous movements, began letting out the strap. "You can't force me to go against my will."

"I feel certain we can come to agreement without force, yes?" Hassan said as the guards stopped in a loose circle around him and Katie.

"Absolutely." Muscles tense, Katie looped the end of the canteen strap around her hand and turned to face the men. "Now that you put it that way, the search zone sounds like a great idea. But let's get the table and chairs loaded fast. We're not going to have time left to search *anywhere* if we don't break camp soon."

She stepped casually toward the men and got no reaction. A few more steps and she was through them. Hassan barked an order in Arabic, and she could hear the sound of folding camp chairs. Good. If Wayne wanted to be a jerk about it, she'd try the search zone. But not before checking out that light-colored streak. She exhaled slowly and wandered over to the lead truck. Carefully opening the front door, she slipped behind the wheel. The keys were in their hiding place beneath the seat. She inserted the key in the ignition and started up the engine.

"Son of a—!" Wayne's voice sounded over the roar of the engine. "Would somebody—?"

Katie stepped on the gas and pulled away with a spray of dust.

She glanced back out the window. Wayne was running for the other truck, but Hassan and his men were just standing there. They hadn't even raised their weapons. One of them seemed to be laughing. The truck hit a low ridge, bouncing Katie's head into the ceiling of the cab. She swerved to the left to avoid another jolt. The terrain was rougher here, more gouged by erosion.

She risked a quick glance at the rearview mirror. So far so good. They hadn't even gotten in the truck yet. She turned her attention back to the desert ahead. There it was. She could just make out a patch of lighter-colored rock. It was only about a mile away. She'd be able to get there, but she wouldn't have much time to explore. And the chances of finding something before Wayne hauled her back to the south were a thousand to one. She didn't even know what she was looking for.

After a bone-crunching ride to the center of the light streak, Katie slammed on the brakes and pulled the keys out of the ignition. Grabbing the satellite phone from the front seat, she ran around to the back of the pickup and retrieved her day pack and an extra jug of water. She could already hear the roar of the other truck. They'd be here any minute. She took off at a quick jog, pounding down the slope to a wide, shallow depression. Following the rocky valley to the west, she searched frantically for a clue to its origin. It was too broad and shallow to be a dry streambed. More likely it was an ancient highway or thoroughfare. Patches of dead plants dotted the area in a sparse, hauntingly familiar pattern. It was almost like being on a cattle ranch. She swept her eyes back and forth across the area, searching for traces of grazing animals.

Nothing Wayne would believe. She pushed on, shaking her head to shed the sweat running down her face. Not far behind her, she heard the growl of skidding tires, the sound of four doors flying open at once. Wayne's voice gushed a stream of orders while Arab voices jabbered in the background. Katie hopped over a dusty shrub and ran up a shallow bank. She bent low, scooped up a small pinch of soil, and touched it to her tongue. Buttered grits—the perfect texture for a shallow sea estuary. Just like the site in Peru.

A faint smudge of golden brown caught her attention. Almost fifty feet to her left. It looked like an old pile of manure.

"Hold it right there!" Wayne called out behind her. "Give me the keys to the truck or so help me, I'll shoot you myself."

Katie slowed to a stop and turned to face the panting grad student. Wayne was bent forward with his hands on his knees. His face was red as a plum. Hooman, Hassan, and the guards were walking up casually behind him. They didn't seem to be in a rush.

"I found it!" Katie shouted loud enough for everyone to hear. "This is where the shepherds came through."

"Sure it is. . . . And just how . . . do you get that?" Wayne asked between breaths.

Hassan walked up to Katie and held out his hand. She gave him the keys and turned back to Wayne. "See those little plants?" She pointed to the tiny sprigs of dead vegetation. "They grew up from goat dung."

"Uh-huh. And here I thought plants came from seeds." Wayne nodded to Hassan. "Come on, let's get back on the trail of that whale. She can stay here with her dead plants if she likes, but we're taking the trucks." He turned and started to walk back in the direction he had come.

"Use your senses, Wayne!" Katie called after him. "I thought I taught you better than that."

Wayne kept on walking.

"Like over there. See that pile of camel dung? Those shepherds came right through here. And have you tested the ground? Shallow estuary—perfect conditions for whale fossils."

Wayne stopped in his tracks. "What camel dung?"

Katie pointed to the smudge in the distance. "I haven't looked at it yet, but I'll bet you a dime it's from a camel."

Wayne strode up to the indicated spot and crouched down beside it.

"Use your senses, Wayne." Katie stepped around the guards and walked up to stand behind him. "Camel dung, goat droppings, sediment from a shallow estuary . . . Put it all together."

"Okay, maybe this is camel dung," he said, "but that doesn't link it to our shepherds. They were here almost eight months ago."

Footsteps sounded behind them. Katie looked up to see Hooman shuffling toward them. She winked at him and nodded down at Wayne. "Remember, a paleontologist has to be observant. You have to use your senses." She crouched down beside Wayne and pressed her index finger into the pile of dung. "Touch it. Take some on your finger." She jutted her chin at him and stared him in the eye.

More footsteps. Hassan and the guards were watching them now.

"Okay." Wayne glanced up at the guards and then back down at Katie to return her stare. He reached out his finger and stabbed it into the dung.

"Now lick your finger." Katie didn't take her eyes off Wayne as she raised her hand to her mouth and licked the tip of her finger.

Wayne didn't flinch. He raised his finger to his mouth and licked it. "So?"

"So . . ." Katie fought to keep a straight face. "Remember how paleontologists are supposed to be observant? Well, I stuck my index finger in the dung, but I licked my middle finger."

A burst of laughter sounded behind them. Katie looked up. Hassan was staring furiously at the three guards. All traces of mirth instantly vanished from their faces as they assumed their masks of cold, hard stone once again. But the masks couldn't conceal their uneasiness. Something had changed. She could sense a burning animosity smoldering right below the surface. Blackbeard cast a sly look at Hassan, who tipped his head in a barely perceptible nod. The guard reached slowly toward his pocket.

Chapter 8

WHAT'S SO FUNNY?" Wayne turned a red-faced scowl at the assembled team. "I know what I'm doing. I grew up in ranch country." He stuck his finger in the camel manure and licked it again, slowly staring at each person in turn. "Taste it yourself. It's not fresh. It's close to a year old."

Katie braced herself for action. Blackbeard's hand was in his pocket. Through the thin material of his baggy pants she could see the hard outline of a pistol.

"Katie's right. I'm man enough to admit it," Wayne continued. "There's a good chance those shepherds *did* come through here, and if that's true, then there's a good chance the whale fossil is somewhere close by."

Keeping her eyes locked on the guards, Katie slowly ran her fingers over the ground until they closed upon a small rock. She hefted it in her hand. It wasn't very heavy, but it would have to do. She'd only get one shot.

"So what are you waiting for?" Wayne bellowed. "Get off your tails and hunt for that whale! The sooner we find it, the sooner we can get out of this hellhole."

The guards didn't move. Finally Hassan nodded and said something in Arabic. They seemed to relax a little. Blackbeard drew his hand out of his pocket. It was empty.

"What are you waiting for, sweetheart?" Wayne reached down and yanked Katie to her feet. "An engraved invitation?" He pulled her closer and stared down into her face.

Katie tensed. Her grasp tightened around the rock. "If you'd just—" She broke off as the guards started moving away from the group. They were talking in low voices together. She thought she heard her name. She leaned in close to Wayne's ear and whispered, "We need to talk sometime."

Wayne's eyes widened.

"Not now. Later, after everyone's asleep." Katie pulled away and looked over at Hooman to see if he had overheard.

"All right, then. Now we're talking," Wayne mumbled under his breath. A wolfish grin slowly spread across his face. "Okay, everybody, listen up!" He called out. "Katie and I will search the area to the east. Hooman, you and Hassan take the west."

"Actually, I'm heading west," Katie said.

"Like I said . . . ," Wayne continued without missing a beat. "Hooman and Hassan are searching east, and Katie and I will take the west!" He flashed a saccharine smile at Katie and strolled self-confidently away in the direction of the late-afternoon sun.

Hooman looked at Katie and screwed up his face in an incredulous grimace. "Would someone explain to me what just happened?"

Katie responded with an exaggerated shrug. The guards were still watching her. She'd have to talk to Hooman tonight. Reluctantly she turned away and followed after Wayne. At least he'd given in and allowed them to search the area. They were getting close. Electric excitement was already prickling at her skin. But what would happen when they found the whale? Hassan and the guards were as keyed up as mustangs before a big hunt. Maybe they were just ready to get out of the desert and get back home to their families, but she doubted it. Since when did thinking of home make people reach for concealed weapons?

She scanned the area ahead of her, searching for the telltale sheen of fossilized bone. The spoor of the shepherds and their goats had faded, but she was almost positive she was still on the right trail. Traces from the goats would be more spread out when they were on the move. The shepherds had obviously camped for the night back at the spot where she'd found the camel manure.

The scrape of stealthy footsteps broke through Katie's thoughts. Right behind her, almost fifty feet away. The hairs at the back of her neck prickled at the sinister presence. It was old Blackbeard; it had to be. She forced herself to look straight ahead. She had to keep going, act like she hadn't noticed. If the guard was going to shoot her, she'd already be dead. He was biding his time, waiting for something.

Waiting for them to find the whale? The realization hit her like a two-ton pickup. This was Peru all over again. Everything fit—the guns, the subterfuge, the nervous anticipation . . . The footsteps were getting closer. Katie stopped and casually scanned the horizon, shielding her eyes with her forearm. It was Blackbeard all right. Behind her and to the left. He didn't seem to be paying any attention to her. He had turned and was looking off to the south. Katie followed his gaze and saw Wayne stooped over, examining something on the ground. The whale fossil? A jolt of adrenaline shot through her. *Please, God, no. Not yet.* She needed more time. Time to work out a plan, to force their hand while she still had bargaining power—while they still needed her to find the whale.

She kicked at a rock. "Look at that!" she cried out and veered away from Wayne at a slow jog. *Come on, Blackbeard. Follow the leader! Forget about Wayne. Remember who ate the camel poop!* She reached into her pack and pulled out her satellite phone. Lately, every time she touched the thing, the guards went into a frenzy of nervousness. She pretended to punch in a number. That should get him. She stopped and held the phone to her ear, listening for sounds of pursuit. If only she'd asked Nick for his phone number, she'd be able to call him for real. If only she hadn't given him such a hard time . . .

"Hi, Nick. This is Katie. . . . Where are you right now? . . . Wow, that's really close." She paused to listen. No footsteps so far. She risked a quick glance back at the guard. *Great.* He wasn't even paying attention. Wayne was digging in the sand with his geology hammer. Blackbeard was almost on top of him.

"Sorry, gotta go." She stuffed the phone back in her pack and took off in pursuit. The guard was only a few yards away from Wayne. She wasn't going to make it. Katie pulled the canteen off her shoulder and ran harder. He was right behind him now. Looking over his shoulder . . .

"Hey, Wayne!" Katie called out in a loud voice. "Need any help?"

The guard spun around, swinging his rifle to point straight at her chest.

"I don't know." Wayne didn't look up. "What do you make of this?"

Ignoring the menacing weapon, Katie slowed to a jog and plodded over to where Wayne crouched. There was still time. Maybe she could convince Blackbeard it wasn't a whale after all. She leaned over Wayne's shoulder and looked down at a large, dark gray rock. She almost laughed out loud. It definitely wasn't a fossil.

"So where do you think this came from?" Wayne asked. "It's the only black rock I've seen since we got here."

Katie crouched by the grad student and studied the pitted stone. She could feel Blackbeard pressing in close behind her. Now was her chance. She might not get another. "Wayne . . ." She channeled all her nervousness into her voice. "Do you have any idea what this is?"

"Some kind of volcanic basalt?"

She swung the pack off her back and spilled her tools out onto the ground. Reaching out with a trembling brush, she started whisking away the dust and sand.

"What? What do you think it is?"

"Holy cow. Look at that!" Katie dropped the brush and started digging around the rock with her hands. "It's way bigger than LA 001. How big would you say it is?"

"What is it?" Wayne scooted to the other side of the rock and started helping her dig. "Remember, I'm the one that found it."

"And I'm the one who led us here." Katie let a touch of anger creep into her voice. "We're working together. It belongs to the whole team."

"Okay, okay. But what is it?"

"See those ripples on its sides? the band of white across the center?"

"Yeah."

"And look how pitted the surface is. You can see where it was melted from the heat of entry."

"What . . . you're saying it's a meteor?"

"A meteor*ite.*" Katie nodded like an idiot. "And not just any meteorite—a huge, larger-than-twenty-pounds meteorite. Do you have any idea how rare these are?"

Wayne shook his head.

"Really rare. If it was a steak, it'd still be walking around eating grass."

Wayne screwed up his face. "You're joking, right?"

"I'm serious. *Dead* serious." Katie caught his eye for a second and then let her eyes drift over to her left to where the listening guard was standing.

Wayne didn't take his eyes off of her. "So what do we do with it? What's one of these things worth?"

Katie breathed an internal sigh of relief. Good, he was playing along. "Last one I heard about was called LA 001. It sold for almost a million dollars—and it wasn't anywhere near as big as this one."

Wayne shook his head and looked down at the rock. "And you're seriously serious?"

Katie nodded and took a reading from her GPS unit. "Come on! Let's go get Hooman. We're going to need help loading this baby onto the truck."

She rose to her feet and turned to walk to the trucks, but Blackbeard moved in front of her to block her way. Katie pretended not to notice and took a step forward. His rifle was hanging crosswise in front of his stomach. If she could just get a little closer, he wouldn't be able to bring it to bear on them. She took another step. The guard hesitated. His eyes were flitting back and forth between her and Wayne, who was coming up on her right. Finally he stepped aside to let them pass.

"You two go on." Katie stopped before Blackbeard could get behind her. "I've got to pack up my tools."

Wayne turned suddenly. "Don't you go poaching my meteorite."

"Right." Katie grinned. "I'm going to smuggle it back to camp in my pocket."

He nodded and set off for the trucks at a brisk pace. For a second Katie thought Blackbeard was going to follow him, but he seemed to change his mind and turned back around to face the rock. Katie watched Wayne walk across the desert until he disappeared over a low rise. Turning her back on the guard, she started gathering her tools. He wouldn't shoot her now. Not after giving Wayne such a big head start. If Wayne made it to the trucks and managed to drive off with Hooman, the Iraqis were as good as dead. Surely he had to realize that.

Sweat trickled down her back as she shoved her tools back into her pack. Things were moving way too fast. She needed more time to think. If the guards fell for the meteorite, she needed to be ready for them. What would the guards do if they thought the rock was valuable? Would they strike now or wait for them to find the whale?

A rustling noise sounded behind her. She could feel the guard's eyes playing across her body. They were boring holes into the back of her neck. He was right behind her, raising his rifle to his shoulder. Katie took a deep breath and slowly unwrapped the canteen from around her waist. Once she turned, she would only have a fraction of a second.

A strange noise broke the silence. The sound of splashing water. Well away from her—off to her right. Katie turned slowly and froze. The guard was standing with his back to her about thirty yards away. Now was her chance—while he was still watering the rocks. She rose to her feet and silently crept toward him. She hefted the canteen in her hand. It was almost full. All she had to do was connect with his head. . . .

Her stomach felt suddenly heavy. She took another step forward and stopped. The guards had never hurt them. Sure they understood English, but since when was that a crime? Maybe they had a very good reason for not wanting to speak English. Maybe they were supposed to be spying on the Americans. Making sure they didn't steal anything that rightfully belonged to the country of

Iraq. Katie quietly coiled the canteen back around her waist. Now that she thought of it, the whole notion that the guards could be some kind of desperado band was absurd. How had she gotten to be so paranoid?

"Ready to get going?" She called out to the guard and started walking back to camp.

The guard whirled around at her voice. His eyes were wild. The rifle was clasped tight in his hands.

Okay, so the man was jumpy, but that wasn't any reason to bash his brains in. If she was wrong, she was wrong, but she wasn't going to hurt anyone until she was 100 percent sure of her facts. She turned away from the guard without a second glance and headed back in the direction of the trucks. Her elongated shadow led her up the rocky slope. It would be dark soon. If nothing happened as a result of the fake meteorite, she'd talk to Wayne and call off the witch hunt. They all had to get a grip before somebody got hurt.

When she arrived back at their makeshift camp, Wayne was nowhere to be seen. Surely he couldn't have gotten lost. The other two guards were lounging in camp chairs in the shade of the lead truck.

"Wayne?" Katie shrugged off her backpack and dropped it on the ground by the chairs. "Hooman? Hassan?"

"Over here!"

Katie walked around to the other side of the trucks. Wayne was approaching the camp from the south. With him, smiling and laughing like they'd made the discovery of the century, were Hooman and Hassan.

"It took me a while to find them." Wayne explained as he got closer to Katie. "Unlike *some* people, I didn't want to drive a truck off without telling everyone."

Katie ignored the jab. She looked over at Hooman for the nod or wink that would tell her Wayne had talked to him.

"So is it really a meteorite?" Hooman was all smiles. Apparently Wayne hadn't gotten a chance. Maybe it was just as well. Acting wasn't a required course for biology students.

"It's huge." She tried to match Hooman's smile. "You're not going to believe it. I'm still not sure I believe it." She looked back at the truck to check on Blackbeard. Sure enough, he was jabbering away with his buddies. Even if they were poachers, which wasn't very likely, they wouldn't make a move without a go-ahead from their leader.

"Hassan." She intercepted the guide before he could talk to his men. "Could you help me get the wheelbarrow out of the truck?"

He studied her face for a second, then nodded and followed her over to the second truck.

"I'm thinking if we can just get a wheelbarrow and a couple of pickaxes over to the dig site—" she lowered the tailgate and climbed up into the back of the truck—"we should be able to get that rock out of the ground before it gets too dark."

"Good idea."

Something in the tone of his voice made her look back. The Iraqi guide was aiming a pistol right at her face. She turned to the lead truck. Hooman and Wayne had their hands in the air. The rifles of the two youngest guards were in their backs.

"You're making a big mistake." Katie turned back to Hassan. "You won't be able to find the whale without us."

"Thanks to my good friend Wayne, we don't need the whale any-more." Hassan turned a smile on the fuming grad student. He barked an Arabic order at Blackbeard, who ran around to the other side of Katie's truck, covering her with his rifle the whole time.

"Sorry to disappoint you fellows, but the meteorite isn't real," Katie said. "It's just a lump of worthless basalt."

"Of course I believe you." Hassan's smile turned suddenly to a fierce scowl. "Get down from the truck now! One bad move and I shoot you right here. I shoot everyone!"

Bill pushed into his hotel room and groaned. He'd already complained to the hotel manager three times, but the maids had turned the air conditioner down again. He shuffled across the room and checked the setting of the big floor unit. Sure enough, it was set on medium cool. He cranked it up as high as it would go and leaned over the vents, sighing as they blasted his burning skin with cool air.

So much for getting to sleep early. It would take forever to cool the room back down. Maybe if he pushed the bed against the AC unit, he could cover the vents and bed with one of his sheets and make an air-conditioned tent. Or maybe he could hop a plane back to Switzerland. He rested his hands on the window and allowed the jets of air to bombard the grease fires raging out of control under his armpits. Murdock would be waiting for his call by now, but he'd just have to wait. If the agency wanted to waste the skills of their best agent by sending him to put out forest fires in the darkest corner of hell, then they'd just have to live with a few communication delays.

He leaned over the air conditioner until his feet and lower back started to complain louder than his heat rash. One more blast under the arms and he walked over and collapsed onto the bed. Now for Murdock. He dug his phone out of his pocket and punched in the fifteen-digit code that unlocked the phone. Scrolling down the menu, he selected in his boss's office number.

Murdock answered on the first ring.

"Hi, Allen, this is Bill."

"Turner . . . what's going on? You were supposed to check in two hours ago."

"Sorry about that. I had to take a pit stop—medical emergency. Things are really starting to heat up around here."

"So what's going on? Did you get anything on those two ministers?"

"Nothing new. I'm recommending we call off the stakeout and go with what we already have. If I stop by the government building for one more drink of water, I'm going to blow my cover. I've already seen every exhibit at the museum twenty times."

"So back off to standard street surveillance."

"Like I said, things have gotten way too hot for that."

"I talked to Washington, and we need something concrete. We can't go to the Iraqis with a secret meeting at one of their museums. They'll laugh us out of the country."

"A meeting with three foreigners and a confirmed antiquities thief!"

"Identified by an unnamed agent at a distance of fifty yards in the dark."

"I know what I saw," Bill said angrily, "and I'm telling you it's a solid link. The ministers are behind the looting. And I'm almost positive they're using the proceeds to fund the insurgency."

"Which is another problem. Eugene and his boys aren't buying the terrorism angle. With Iran pumping bajillions into the country to fund the insurgents, why bother with antiquities smuggling? It's a lot of work for money they could get a lot easier elsewhere."

"But . . ." Bill swallowed back his retort. "Okay. If you don't think there's a link, then pull me out. This wasn't my idea. You're the one who sent me."

"I'm just letting you know what they're saying in Washington. If I didn't think you were on to something, you wouldn't be there. But I need a smoking gun. I need incontrovertible proof."

"Such as . . . ?"

"For all we know, the people in those photos are German tourists. Get me some IDs. Get me some photos of the ministers with real, genuine bad guys."

Bill swore under his breath. "I never signed up to be a cop. I'm a trained archaeologist."

"I know, I know. . . . Just a few more weeks." Murdock had switched to his den mother voice. "Get me one more thing and we can nail the lid on this one. I promise, as soon as you give me something I can use, it's back to Switzerland with you. You'll be back at the museum in no time."

"I'd better be. Because if I drop dead from heatstroke, you're the only name on my pallbearer list."

"Yeah, yeah . . ."

"We're talking a lead-lined coffin here. A nice big one with gold-plated accents and a blue velvet lining."

"Just get me the proof!"

Chapter 9

*K*ATIE SQUINTED INTO THE GLARING LIGHT as one of the Iraqi guards stepped between her and the lantern. *"Seer, seer!"* He motioned with his rifle. Apparently she was supposed to move closer to the others.

"Sorry." Katie raised her hands and shuffled submissively over to stand next to Hooman. Now wasn't the time for defiance. The more docile she appeared now, the less they would expect trouble later.

The guard stepped out of the light and stood next to his companion. The barrels of their rifles were drooping lower and lower to the ground. They seemed to be getting bored. Katie angled her arm into the light and checked her watch. 8:45 p.m. Time to get things moving. Blackbeard and Hassan had already been gone ten minutes. They'd taken a pickax and wheelbarrow from the truck and gone out to retrieve the black rock while their compatriots stayed behind to guard the prisoners.

She brushed against Hooman's arm and nodded. With an almost imperceptible shuffling of her feet, she scooted another six inches back toward the lead truck. Hooman kept almost perfectly even with her and Wayne followed right behind. There. That would have to be good enough. The truck was almost ten feet away. Any closer and the guards would start getting nervous.

Her arms dropped to her sides. Slowly, with one hand, she worked loose the canvas strap that secured the canteen to her waist.

"Wayne, talk to me in a calm, even voice." Katie kept her tone low and conversational.

"What do you want me to say?" He sounded stiffer than a voice recognition system.

"It doesn't matter. They can't understand you anyway," Katie said.

Hooman turned toward her, but she grabbed him by the wrist and dug in with her fingernails.

"I have a gun hidden under the other truck." She smiled benignly as she spoke. "When I give the signal, Wayne, I want you to make a dash for it. Not this truck but the other one. It's up against the rear left wheel. Hooman and I will try to distract the guards."

"Where'd you get a gun?" Hooman's voice had just the right amount of vibrato.

Katie smiled again. "Minister Talibani loaned it to me. It's a Colt .45 from his collection."

One of the guards jabbered something in Arabic. He pulled out a flashlight and switched it on. Katie forced her eyes to go wide as he walked over toward the other truck. *One alligator, two alligators, three alligators, four* . . . He should have reached it by now. A few more seconds for him to get down on the ground . . .

"How did he know?" Katie leaped forward, whipping the canteen around her in a wide, sweeping arc. The heavy metal canister whistled through the air, smashing the guard in the temple with a sickening smack. She'd snapped the canteen back into her hand and was running to her friends before the guard hit the ground.

"Quick!" She hissed. "Under the truck." She darted over to the nearest pickup and pushed Hooman and Wayne to the ground. Then, reaching over the partially open door, she vaulted up onto the roof of the cab.

A voice shouted out in Arabic. The sound of running footsteps, the splash of bobbing light.

Katie backed as far away from the lantern as she could, but she couldn't get low enough. She could still see the top of the lantern. If the guard looked up, he'd be able to see most of her face.

The guard stooped by his fallen comrade, sweeping his gun back and forth to cover the night. He grabbed his friend's rifle and slung it over his shoulder. Then, creeping forward at a low crouch, he approached Katie's hiding place. His eyes were locked onto the shadows beneath the truck. Could he see Wayne and Hooman? A soft scrape sounded beneath her. The guard raised the rifle to his shoulder, pointed it in the direction of the noise.

Katie leaped forward and swung the canteen down on the guard with all her might. *Crack!* If he'd been a golf ball, she would have won the Masters. She leaped off the truck and retrieved the fallen guards' rifles. "Hooman? Wayne?" Keeping an eye on the prostrate men, she crouched down beside the truck. "Are you guys all right?"

"Where are the guards?" A hoarse whisper came from the other side of the truck.

"It's okay. They're right here. I've got their weapons." She jumped up and looked at her watch in the light of the lantern. "Come on! It's been twelve minutes! Blackbeard and Hassan will be back soon."

"Blackbeard?" Hooman and Wayne came out from behind the truck and stared incredulously at the fallen guards.

"Take this." She thrust a rifle into Wayne's hands. "Make sure these guys don't make any noise. I'm going after the others."

"Want me to come with you?" Hooman's voice was still shaking.

Katie shook her head. "I can move faster alone." She leaned her rifle against the pickup and fastened the canteen around her waist. "Turn off the lantern as soon as you get these guys settled. It'll make you harder to find."

She grabbed the rifle and headed out into the night. Blobs of streaking light trailed from the lantern, dancing before her eyes. Her foot caught on a rock and she almost went down, but she caught herself and kept on running. With the lantern behind her, she was a huge backlit target. No time for her eyes to adjust. She had to get out of there. She stumbled forward, lifting her feet high to clear any rocks lurking in the shadows. All around her the darkness bristled with unseen rifles. A black phantom shifted just in front of her. A click sounded off to her right. She put her head down and ran, leaping and bounding to escape the pursuing light.

Suddenly everything went dark. The guys had finally turned off the lantern. She dropped to the ground and waited for her eyes to adjust to the darkness. The moon was still below the horizon, but the desert stars shined above her, bright and vivid as jewels in a velvet display case. The rocky terrain gradually came into focus. She swept her eyes slowly over the slope ahead of her. As long as she was careful, she'd be able to see them coming. Dark shadows against the dim light of the lower stars. They, however, wouldn't be expecting her. She'd be practically invisible until she was right on top of them. She might not even need the rifle.

She picked herself up off the ground and crept up the slope, stopping every few seconds to scan the top of the rise for moving shadows. Gradually she began to veer to her left. They might not be expecting her, but they'd be even more surprised if she came at them from behind. Angling further to her left, she crouched lower and lower until she was pressed flat against the ground. Finally she peered over the top of the hill. The murmur of Arabic voices drifted through the valley. A soft squeak seemed to sound from several directions at once.

Katie slung the rifle over her shoulder and inched her way silently forward, barely holding herself off the ground with her forearms, knees, and toes. Five feet, ten feet, fifteen feet . . . She rose up onto her hands and knees. Thirty feet, forty feet . . . The voices suddenly stopped. She dropped to the ground and searched the surrounding darkness. Waiting. Listening. Seconds turned into minutes, minutes into more minutes. Where were they? She should be able to see them by now. She carefully pulled the rifle over her head and cradled it in her arms. Rising slowly to a crouch, she continued the circle to her right. The valley was silent as a tomb. They were out there somewhere, waiting for her to strike. Somehow they'd managed to see her coming.

She lowered herself back to the ground and sighted along the rifle, slowly scanning the length of the valley. A dark shadow almost forty yards away arrested her attention. A pile of dirt next to a small hole. A pickax was lying right next to it. She systematically searched the surrounding area. They were hiding somewhere. They . . .

Where was the wheelbarrow? Katie leaped to her feet and started running back to the trucks. Somehow she'd missed them. Somehow . . .

A volley of gunshots sounded on the other side of the rise. Two shots, three. Two more! She raced up the slope, pumping her arms and legs as fast as they would go. A bobbing light met her eyes as soon as she crested the hill. A man was running with a flashlight. She pounded down the hill after him. He was dragging something, shoving it into the truck. A roar sounded over the rush of her breath. The camp area suddenly lit up with blinding light. Headlights from the truck! More headlights. The trucks were starting to move.

Katie skidded to a stop and raised the rifle to her shoulder. Aiming for the tires of the lead truck, she squeezed off a shot. One more try. She fired another shot and another, but the trucks didn't slow down.

"Hooman! Wayne!" She started running. "Hooman?" Her shouts echoed through the darkness. "Hooman!"

A dark shape showed black against the desert floor. Off in the distance, close to where the trucks had been. Katie stopped, watching for signs of movement. Her insides turned slowly to ice. It was the unconscious guards, it had to be. Hassan and Blackbeard had left without them. That had to be it. The stars tilted and rocked. She felt dizzy, sick to her stomach, like the darkness was a milling crowd. She couldn't look. Not now. Too much was happening all at once.

She forced one foot in front of the other. They could still be alive. They needed her. She shuffled forward in a slow, wooden jog. The shadow wasn't moving. It was too balled up. It didn't even seem human. She gasped as the shadow resolved itself into the shape of an inverted wheelbarrow. "Hooman? Wayne?" She called out at the top of her lungs and raced around the clearing. Her backpack, a broken lantern, tire tracks, two camp chairs tipped over on their sides . . . Where were Hooman and Wayne? The unconscious guards were missing too. It didn't make sense. "Wayne! Hooman!"

"Katie!" A voice called out through the darkness. "If you're alone, shout out the suborder of whales you study."

"Hooman!" Katie started running toward the voice.

"Stop!"

Katie skidded to a halt and ducked behind a large rock. "Hooman, what's going on?"

"If you're alone, shout out the suborder of whales you study."

"*Archaeoceti*? What's wrong? Did one of the guards stay behind?"

Two figures gradually emerged from the shadows and walked toward her position. One of them was carrying a rifle. Squinting into the darkness, Katie raised the rifle to her shoulder. "Tell me what's happening, Hooman."

"It's okay!" One of the figures waved his arms in the air. "Don't shoot!

"We just had to make sure you weren't bait for a trap." Wayne's voice.

Katie jumped up and ran over to her friends. "When you didn't answer, I thought you . . ." She launched herself at Hooman, throwing her arms around his neck and squeezing him until he started to struggle.

"When Hassan and the guard started shooting, I tried to shoot back, but the gun didn't work." Wayne's voice sounded like it would break any second. "We had no choice but to run."

"I thought you were dead." Katie pulled away from Hooman and wrapped her arms around Wayne.

"We *are* dead." Wayne shrugged her off and kept on walking.

"What are you talking about?" Katie hurried after him. "We're fine."

"They took the trucks, didn't they?"

"Yeah."

"With all our water?"

"I've still got my canteen—and a satellite phone. We can call someone. Murad's in the area. If we can't get anyone else, we can call him."

Wayne stopped and spun around. "So what are you waiting for? Call the police. They stole my meteor!"

"Your meteor?"

"Whatever—*our* meteor."

Katie studied his face. It was too dark to tell for sure, but he seemed to be serious. "You didn't really think . . . You know it wasn't a real meteorite, right?"

Wayne shifted his stance. His eyes were narrow slits.

"I was just . . . pretending. I thought you knew. The guards had been acting so strange. . . . I wanted to see what they'd do if we found something."

The night grew suddenly quiet. Wayne seemed to have stopped breathing. Finally, after several tense seconds, his face contorted into a fierce scowl.

"So you're telling me we almost got killed . . . over a worthless rock?"

"I thought if we—"

"Because *you* decided to play war games with a bunch of armed soldiers?"

"I—"

"I can't believe it!" Wayne spun around and stomped off into the darkness. "Of all the stupid—"

"Stop it!" Hooman called out after Wayne. "Stop it right now!"

Wayne turned slowly around and faced down the younger student.

"It's not Katie's fault," Hooman said. "They would have done the same thing as soon as we found the whale."

"*If* we found the whale."

"What's wrong with you?" Hooman took a step toward Wayne. "Katie saved our lives. You should be thanking her."

"Guys . . ." Katie stepped between them. "Guys! This isn't help-ing. We only have one canteen between the three of us. If we don't get Murad on the phone soon, we're not going to last half a day." She pushed past Wayne and headed back to the area where they'd parked the trucks.

"Look for my pack," she called out behind her. "I left it some-where. . . . There it is." She jogged over to the khaki bag and rum-maged through its outer pocket. "I was beginning to wonder if they'd taken it." She pulled the phone out of the bag and held it out to show the guys.

Hooman and Wayne pressed in around her as she turned the phone on and started searching through the menu. "Oh no." The low-battery icon flashed out a warning. "I didn't recharge it long enough!"

"Quick, call Murad!" Wayne shouted in her face.

"I don't have his number!"

"Information is 411 back home," Hooman said.

Katie punched in the country code and the number. "It's ringing. . . ."

"City and state, please . . ." A loud beep sounded in her ear. The phone was running out of juice.

"Ann Arbor, Michigan! Hurry. This is an emergency."

"And the name of the party you're trying to reach?"

"Nick Murad's office at the University of Michigan. Department of Geological Sciences."

Click. For a sickening second Katie thought the phone had died, but then a recorded voice came on with the number. Katie called out each digit as she heard it. Another beep sounded. No time for the message to repeat. She terminated the connection and punched in the new number, repeating it over and over in her head while the phone rang.

"Murad lab. This is Mike."

"This is an emergency. I need to speak with Nick Murad. My phone is running out of batteries, and I'm stranded in the middle of the desert," Katie blurted into the phone. "I need the number of his satellite phone."

"I'm sorry, who is this calling?"

"Please . . . just give me his satellite number. This is Katie James—in the Fischer lab."

"Katie James? *The* Katie James?"

"Please, if you don't give me the number right now, three people—" *Beep!*—"are going to die."

"Katie James . . ." There was a long pause. "I'm not supposed to give this out, but if this is an emergency . . ."

"Please, my phone's running out of batteries."

"Okay, I guess he won't mind." *Beep!* "It's 734-555-1200."

She repeated the number back to him.

"Right, so tell me again, what's the emergency—?"

Katie hung up and punched in Nick's satellite number. "It's ringing!" she called out to the others. "Come on, pick up; come on . . ."

"Hello?"

"Nick, this is Katie James. Listen very carefully. This is an emergency. My phone's almost out of batteries. We don't have much time," Katie shouted into the phone. "Do you have something to write with?"

"So what's it this time? That mummy still giving you trouble?"

"Nick, this is serious." Katie forced herself to calm down. "Our guards attacked us and left us stranded in the desert without any water. I need you to write down our coordinates."

"Whoa, slow down. Your guards attacked you?"

"Nick, please. Just write it down." *Beep!* "Our coordinates are . . ." Katie paused, mentally subtracting a few miles from the position of the shepherds' trail. "Our coordinates are North 30 degrees 27 minutes, East 45 degrees 25 minutes. Got that? N 30 degrees 27 minutes, E 45 degrees 25 minutes."

"Uh-huh . . . And those are the coordinates to that big *X* in the middle of South America we talked about, right?"

"Nick, I'm serious. Did you write the coordinates down? We only have one canteen of water between the three of us."

"I thought you said you—" *Beep!* "—have any water."

"Practically no water. One small canteen!"

"And these guards, they just—"

"Nick, please. N 30, 27; E 45, 25. Write it down!"

"Not until you answer my questions. First, why would the guards do something like that?"

"Because they're poachers. They stole a . . ." Katie sighed. She didn't have time for explanations. "They stole a rock one of my students found."

"What, the whale? You found the whale?"

"No . . . a piece of basalt. I didn't trust them, so I made them think it was valuable, okay?"

"Uh-huh . . . And then—" *Beep!* "—guards tried to kill you."

Katie took a deep breath and spoke in her calmest, most professional voice. "N 30, 27; E 45, 25. Did you write it down?"

"N 30, 27; E 45, 25."

"Correct." She breathed a sigh of relief. "Yeah. Two of the guards held us at gunpoint while the other two took a wheelbarrow to dig up the rock. I knocked the first two out and tried to intercept the others, but I must have missed them in the dark. They attacked my students and took off in our trucks before I could even make it back."

Beep! "—expect me to believe you knocked out two armed guards—"

"I had a canteen! They forgot to take it away from me."

Silence sounded on the other end of the phone.

"Nick? Hello? Are you there?"

"That was pretty good. You almost had me going there."

"Nick, I'm serious. It really happened. We need you to pick us up. Tomorrow morning. As early as possible. We won't make it until the end . . ." She paused to listen. When had the sound of static disappeared? "Hello? Nick? Are you still there?"

She held her breath as she waited for an answer. "Nick?" She looked at the phone. The light had gone off. She switched the phone off and switched it back on again. Still no light.

"What did he say?" Wayne asked. "Is he coming?"

Katie tried the phone again and shook her head. "I don't know. I don't think he believed me."

Chapter 10

NICK STARED AT THE PHONE and dropped it onto his sleeping bag. "She hung up on me."

Ahamed was watching him from across the tent. He nodded and regarded Nick with an I-told-you-so look. "What does she say about her guards? They are trying to kill her now?" His voice was dripping with incredulity.

Nick nodded. "She says they abandoned her team in the desert. She wants us to go . . . rescue them."

"You surely do not believe her."

Nick shrugged. "She sounded really, I don't know, frantic."

"Ah . . . frantic. That makes all the difference. More frantic, I assume, than she sounded when she called last? When she asked for our coordinates?"

Nick looked down at the coordinates he'd scribbled on the back of his hand. "I know what it sounds like, but some of the things she was saying . . . Why make up such a ridiculous story?"

"Such as stories of mummies chasing her through the desert?"

"I know. . . ." Nick pulled out a map and located the coordinates Katie had given him.

"Where is it?" Ahamed scooted across the tent and leaned over to see. "Is it even on the map?"

"About four miles to the north of the search zone." Nick pointed to the spot on the map. "You said those tire tracks were headed to the north. Couldn't they have—?"

"The tracks were here." Ahamed ran a finger along the map. "If she followed true to her course, she should be somewhere here." He drew a big circle well to the north of the coordinates.

"They could have headed south. That at least puts them in the same general area."

Ahamed shook his head. "I think where it puts them is exactly right here." He pointed to the center of the search zone. "Four or five miles east of *our* location."

"What?"

"You don't think it strange our competitor in this race calls tonight, right after we see the military trucks this afternoon?"

Nick didn't get the connection. They'd caught sight of the military trucks several times since the first time Ahamed had spotted them.

"And the last time she called, I also just saw the trucks."

"So?" Nick didn't like what Ahamed was implying.

"So who are these people following us? If they are terrorists, why have they not attacked? The same if they are thieves. And if they are Iraqi soldiers, why do we still live?"

"So you're saying the James team is following us?" Nick tried to wrap his mind around the idea. "It doesn't make any sense."

Ahamed nodded. "Obviously we are getting close to the whale or she would not try all these tricks."

"So what happened to your theory there's another team of paleontologists in the game?"

"The minister would have warned us of such a team." Ahamed looked down at the map and shook his head. "Why blame your neighbor's goat if yours likes to climb its fence? We already know Katie James likes to play with us these games of cat and mouse."

A musical ring tone suddenly went off, making him jump. "It's her!" He scooped up the phone. "Hello?"

"Hey, Nick, this is Mike."

"Mike?" It took a second for him to change gears. "Hi. . . . What's up?"

"This is probably nothing, but I thought you should know. . . ."

Katie James called and asked for your satellite number. I know I'm not supposed to give it out, but she made it sound like it was an emergency. I hope it's okay."

"When did she call? Did she say what the emergency was?"

"Just a few minutes ago. I asked her what was happening, but we were cut off before she could answer. I think the batteries on her phone went dead."

"The batteries went dead. . . . Are you sure?"

"Yeah, she said they were about to run out."

Nick looked away to avoid Ahamed's gaze. "And she didn't mention anything about guards attacking her or abandoning her?"

"Nope. Just that she was stranded in the desert. I thought you'd want to know right away. It'll probably take a while for her batteries to charge."

"Okay. Thanks, Mike."

"Sure thing. Bye."

Nick tossed the phone into his pack. The batteries dying, the guards stealing a rock, Katie knocking out not one but two men—with a canteen? It didn't add up. Nick looked down and stared at the back of his hand. He'd seen pictures of Katie James; he'd heard so many stories. . . . She was supposed to have the best eyes in the business. He couldn't imagine her resorting to such a dirty trick. But then again, he couldn't imagine her running from mummies or trying to intercept armed desperados in the dark either. And nobody had ever said she wasn't competitive. The world of paleontology was overflowing with dirty tricks and bitter rivalries. It came with the Jurassic-size egos. He plopped back down onto his sleeping bag and covered his eyes with his hands. Suddenly he felt weary and all alone. Aside from his own wishful thinking, he'd never had any reason to assume she was different from any of the others, but still he was disappointed. On the phone she'd seemed so clever. So . . . refreshing.

"So . . ." Nick sighed. "What do we do now?"

"We go to sleep."

"And in the morning?" Nick rolled his head to the side and looked over at his friend.

"In the morning we wake early and do what we came here to do. We find the fossil whale before our enemy, Katie James."

Nick nodded and shut his eyes. He knew he wasn't being rational, but he couldn't decide which was more disappointing: having Katie James turn out to be a scheming trickster or not having a chance to finally meet her.

Squeak, squeak . . . The sound of the rolling wheelbarrow echoed against the walls of the dark gulley. Katie readjusted her grip on the wooden handles. Her hands felt like raw hamburger. By the time they arrived at the rendezvous site, she'd have a wicked set of blisters—if she had any fluid left in her to fill them. The wheelbarrow bounced over a rock, jostling their gear in its sandy bed. All they had were two camp chairs, a pair of rifles, a pickax, and a broken lantern. The others had wanted to leave the stuff behind, but Katie had insisted on bringing it. If Nick was delayed, they'd need it to build a shelter. The extra materials could mean the difference between surviving half a day or half a week. If Nick didn't show up, it would be weeks before the ministers thought to send a rescue party—assuming they bothered to send one at all.

A rock turned under her foot and Katie almost let the wheelbarrow tip over. One more spill and Wayne would blow a gasket. He was still furious about the fake meteorite. Not that she blamed him. How could she have been so stupid? She scanned the left bank of the gulley, searching for a spot smooth enough to push the wheelbarrow up. They'd already gone too far west. She needed to get them going south again.

"How much farther?" Hooman's weary voice broke the silence. "It feels like we've been walking all night."

Katie paused for a second and checked their position on the GPS. "Just a little bit farther. You can do it. We're almost there."

"If she hadn't screwed up the coordinates, we wouldn't be walking at all," Wayne growled. "You're batting a thousand tonight, sweetheart."

Katie kept her mouth shut. She'd already apologized a dozen times. It had been a snap decision. There hadn't been time to consider the consequences—or to work out the math. She'd only meant to be off by a mile or so—not six. "At least Murad won't find the shepherds' trail when he picks us up."

"A heap of good that'll do us if we're dead."

"Nobody's going to die," Katie snapped. "Come on. It's just a few more miles."

"What if he doesn't come?" Hooman's voice was so soft Katie could barely hear him. "What if he didn't believe you?"

"He'll be there," Katie said. "I know he will. What would you do if the situation were reversed? You wouldn't leave Murad to die—not if there was even the tiniest chance he was telling the truth."

"But what if he's already there?" Hooman asked. "What if he searches the area and leaves before we can even get there?"

"I told him to wait till morning. I . . ." Katie stopped dead in her tracks. Had Nick actually heard the last part about waiting until morning? When had the batteries run out? "Surely he wouldn't go out searching in the dark. . . ."

"Wouldn't you?" Hooman asked. "If he told you what you told him?"

Katie dropped the wheelbarrow. Oh no! What had she done?

"See? See what I've been saying?" Wayne stepped up to the wheelbarrow and kicked it over, wrenching it out of Katie's grasp.

The night seemed to spin around her. She didn't have time for this. She had to hurry. If she ran, she'd lose too much moisture. But if Nick beat them to the site . . .

"I'm running ahead!" Katie called back over her shoulder as she charged up the bank of the gulley. "You guys conserve your energy. You may need it tomorrow!"

Nick rolled over onto his back and stared up into the darkness. He could just make out Ahamed's rhythmic snoring over the rumble of the gasoline-powered generators. He rolled back onto his stomach and buried his face in his pillow. Still no good.

"Ahamed, are you awake?"

The snores ended with a gasp. A long, breathy sigh faded into the sound of moving air, and then, after a long pause, the snoring started up again.

"Ahamed!"

A throaty gasp. Then silence.

"I know she likes to play games, and I know we're in a race, but what if she's telling the truth?"

A rustling sound came from Ahamed's side of the tent.

"You didn't hear her. She really sounded, I don't know, scared. What if she was injured? What if there really was a fight?"

"You will not let this goat sleep, will you?" Ahamed's drowsy voice sounded over the zipping of a zipper.

"I'm just saying . . . I've heard when she goes into South America, she goes by herself. Into some very hostile situations. What if she really did overpower her guards? People are capable of almost anything when they're desperate."

"So you are going to talk about her all night?"

Lantern light suddenly filled the tent. Nick sat up on his bedroll and blinked. Ahamed was already dressed. He was sitting on the floor of the tent, lacing up his boots. "I am thinking you did not wash your hand?"

Nick flipped his hand over and breathed a sigh of relief. "It's a little fuzzy, but I can still read it."

"Good. Tell me when you finish staring all night into the mirror. I will prepare the truck with gasoline."

"I . . ." Nick shook his head. It wasn't worth it. "I'll be ready in a second." He waited for Ahamed to crawl out of the tent before stealing a peek at himself in his shaving mirror. *Beautiful.* He looked like a homeless mud wrestler. He'd been planning to shave in the morning; it would only take a few extra minutes. . . . He reached for his shaving kit and then hesitated. If Katie James was really in trouble . . . he'd already wasted too much time. Besides, if he shaved now, Ahamed would never let him hear the end of it.

He threw on some clothes and hurried outside. Ripping a page from his field notebook, he scribbled a hasty note of explanation and slipped it under the plastic cover of the duty roster. By the time he reached the truck, Ahamed had already filled the tank and was sitting patiently in the passenger seat. Nick checked his GPS unit and slid behind the wheel.

"Thanks for doing this." He looked over at his friend and started the truck. "I know you don't think she'll be there."

"Neither do you." Ahamed grinned mischievously. "If you really believed the lady would be there, you would have washed the desert off your pretty face."

Nick flipped the headlights on and pulled away from the sleeping camp. "All right. It's the middle of the night. Remind me, so why am I driving out halfway across the desert?"

"Because you like so much the talking to Ahamed."

"Oh yeah. I almost forgot. . . ."

"Is true. If I did not come, you would talk the whole night about this woman. 'Ahamed, what if she got bit by a mummy? What if the guard's head dented her canteen?'"

Nick shook his head and swerved to avoid a low, rocky ridge. "Ahamed, what if you stopped talking and made yourself useful?" He tossed the GPS unit to the Pakistani guide. "We need to get to N 30 degrees 27 minutes, E 45 degrees 25 minutes. With all these formations in our way, it's going to be a long, bumpy ride."

Nick strained forward, searching the terrain ahead. Erosion gulleys, jagged rocks, shifting sand dunes . . . Finally, after almost an hour and a half of circuitous driving, they reached the indicated coordinates.

"Okay, this should be it." Nick stopped the truck and compared the terrain to the markings on the geology map. "What are our readings?"

"N 30 degrees 27 minutes 3.14 seconds, E 45 degrees 24 minutes 58.19 seconds," Ahamed read off the coordinates from the GPS. "I do not see any thirsty ladies."

Nick got out of the truck and looked around. "It's too dark. They could be anywhere." He cupped his hands to his mouth. "Hello? Anybody out here? Katie James? Anybody?" He pulled a flashlight out of his pack and flipped it on.

Ahamed got out and walked around the truck to stand by Nick. "Maybe she hides from the mummy?"

"Or maybe we're in the wrong place. She only gave us coordinates to the nearest minute. I'll search to the south; you take the north. Try a ten-by-ten search grid—increments of fifty meters. We don't have to see them. They just have to hear us shout."

Nick waited for Ahamed's nod and took off across the desert. "Hello? Katie?" he called out every thirty or forty meters.

Nobody.

He walked almost half a mile to the south before zigzagging back and forth from east to west to east again. No signal rocks, no tents, no truck tracks or even scuff marks in the sand. The longer he searched, the more angry he became. Even if they'd been trying to hide, he would have found them. They simply weren't here.

Ahamed was waiting for him when he finally arrived back at the truck. "Did you find them?" Nick knew the answer before he even asked.

"I did search. A very large grid. Larger than five hundred meters."

Nick stared down at the back of his hand. "I could have gotten the coordinates wrong."

"Yes, of course . . ." Ahamed rolled his eyes. "This is so much more better an idea than Katie James playing games. Her imagined face is very much too beautiful for that."

"But why?" Nick yanked the door of the truck open and climbed behind the wheel.

Wordlessly, Ahamed walked around the truck and got in beside him.

"It doesn't make sense." Nick started up the truck and stomped on the gas, spinning the truck around in a tight half circle to head back to their camp. "It was annoying, but it didn't cost us any real time."

"I know you do not wish to believe this, but I think it must now be certain that the James team is following us. It is they who drive the military trucks we are seeing."

"But why? Why send us out on a wild-goose chase? She had to know I'd go out and check."

"Perhaps she wished us away from the camp?" Ahamed said. "Perhaps we will realize the answer when we return."

Nick shot a look at his friend. "You don't think? No . . . she wouldn't." He leaned forward in his seat and pressed harder on the gas. "She'd never do anything like that. Sabotage is way over the line."

Ahamed shrugged. "It is good you know this lady so well. Of course, I was happy also to know she would never—what do you say?—send us on a wild goat's cheese."

Katie slowed to a jog and plodded out onto a moonlit plateau. Almost there and still no sign of Murad. She braced her hands on her hips and walked in a tight circle, searching the surrounding desert for any signs of life. Nothing. Not only had she wasted her breath, but she'd wasted a lot of sweat. She pulled the GPS from her pack and angled it toward the moon until its soft light reflected off the LCD display. A few hundred yards to the southeast and she was there. If Nick had been there searching for her, she would have seen him by now.

She put the GPS away and wandered in a vaguely southeastern direction, scanning the barren plain for materials she could use to build a shelter. Climbing into a broad wadi, she searched for sticks, dead plants, washed-up boards—anything to block the sun. Without a shelter, they'd be roasted alive. She'd be lucky to last through the morning—especially after all the running she'd just done. She should have told Wayne and Hooman to bring the wheelbarrow. They could have inverted it over a wadi and used the rifles and chairs as poles to support a covering of rocks and sand.

She climbed out of the wadi and searched the top of the plateau. Nothing. Not even a decent flat rock. Pulling out the GPS unit, she followed it to the exact position she had given Murad. The area was flat and rocky—the perfect spot for signaling a plane or satellite. Where were the guys? She looked at her watch. They should have been here a long time ago.

"Wayne—" She coughed as she tried to shout the name. Her throat and lungs felt like she'd been drinking battery acid. She reached up and tightened her bandanna over her mouth and nose. The alkaline dust was so fine, it managed to get through even the tiniest of gaps. She cleared her throat and tried again. "Wayne! Hooman!"

No response.

Great. How hard could it be to follow a star? They should have been here twenty minutes ago. Maybe they were bringing the wheelbarrow after all. She waited a few minutes and called out again. "Wayne? Hooman?"

An answering cry rang out from across the plateau. *Finally* . . .

"Over here!" She ran over to the edge of a wadi and waved her arms in the air. "Do you hear me?"

Another answering cry. They were getting a little closer.

She moved back to the meeting point and started clearing the area of rocks, piling them in a long curving line. She was almost finished with the first *S* in her SOS signal when Wayne and Hooman came walking up. They hadn't brought the wheelbarrow or anything else with them.

"Nick's not here yet." Katie dropped the rock she was carrying and arched her back to stretch out her complaining muscles. "What took you guys so long?"

"You had all the water," Wayne croaked. "We need a drink."

Katie shook her head. "We don't know when Nick will show up. I haven't had any water since this afternoon."

"It's been even longer for us. I'm about to pass out." Wayne reached for the canteen at Katie's waist.

Katie pulled away. "Nobody drinks unless we all agree." She looked hard at Wayne and uncoiled the canteen strap from around her waist. "This isn't about comfort and convenience anymore. This is survival. Understood?"

Hooman nodded. Wayne's eyes never left the canteen.

"We don't know how long it's going to take for them to find us. Murad could come this morning or he could come five days from now. We need to prepare for the worst."

"Who made you keeper of the canteen?" Wayne took another step closer. "Don't we need to agree on that too?"

Katie looped the strap around her hand. "Hooman, who do you think should keep the water?"

"It's your canteen. . . ." His shy smile seemed to glow in the moonlight. "After what happened tonight, I think it's safest right where it is."

Katie looked to Wayne.

"Hey, I never said I wanted it. I just want some water. One little sip. What's it going to hurt?"

Katie shook her head. "Just think how much more you'll appreciate that sip tomorrow when the desert floor is 140 degrees. We only have a couple more hours of darkness to prepare. If you two finish this SOS, I'll go out and start working on a shelter."

"I'll help you with that shelter." Wayne looked back at Hooman. "You're doing the SOS, right?"

The young grad student nodded.

"Just let me know if you need help with the spelling." Wayne flashed him a smile and strode out of the clearing.

Katie reached out and squeezed Hooman's hand. "Thanks," she whispered and turned to follow Wayne.

"Wayne?" She hurried to catch up with him. "We need to find a deep wadi with steep sides, okay? One with a really steep north-facing slope would be perfect, but if you find one that's narrow enough, we can make do even if it's running north-south."

Wayne stopped suddenly and stumbled backward. A look of pain creased his face.

"What's wrong?"

Wayne lifted his hand and pointed to a sandy patch to their left. A set of tracks cut through the sand. Jagged black shadows against a moonlit plane. Katie moved in for a closer look, but she could already tell they were fresh. The wavy treads were still visible. They probably were less than an hour old, three or four hours at the most. Nick Murad had already come and gone.

Chapter 11

NICK JUMPED OUT OF THE TRUCK and ran across the camp to his tent. Yanking up on the zipper, he thrust his head and flashlight inside. Everything seemed to be in order. His pack lay on the floor against the left wall of the tent. The map box was in the back corner—just like he'd left it. He crawled inside and opened up the box. Nothing seemed to be missing. One of the satellite photos was facing the wrong direction, but he could have done that earlier when searching for the geology map.

He turned and looked at the maps spread out on the floor at the back of the tent. The minister's map was on top. Had he left it like that? He tried to remember. They were about to go to sleep and he'd tossed them to the back of the tent. Which one had been on top then?

Ahamed poked his head inside the tent. "The water supply is good. I checked the trucks, the tents, the generators. Everything seems good."

Nick nodded. "I'm pretty sure everything is good here, too."

"Pretty sure? Your face says not so good."

"I'm just trying to remember which map was on top of the stack. I usually keep the search map on top, but last night . . ."

"This explains everything!" Ahamed's eyes blazed. "You told her our map was better. I heard you say it. That is the reason she called. She had to get us out of this tent!"

Nick shook his head. "I offered to share the map and she wasn't interested."

"They trust little who are little to be trusted. She would not believe a map freely offered—only one stolen in secret."

"But . . ." Nick looked doubtfully at the map. "But why didn't she just wait until we were all out in the field? Why make up such a ridiculous story?"

"That is, I think, the wrong question." Ahamed looked him in the eye. "The question I want to know is why you always refuse to see what is right before your eyes? You only believe what you want to believe—especially when concerning a woman."

"This has nothing to do with . . ." Nick couldn't finish the sentence. The wounded look in Cindy's eyes stabbed through his memories like a knife. She'd been right about the danger. Why hadn't he believed her? Or had he believed her too much? Had he only seen what he wanted to see? How could he even tell the difference?

"I am sorry." Ahamed's expression softened. "It was wrong for me to say. I only want that you are not fooled again. The New York woman, the *gora choora*, she was not what she pretended to be. Neither is our new competition."

"Okay . . ." Nick tossed the maps back on the floor. "So what do we do now?"

"We talk to the woman in her camp. Make her understand that we are not to be fooled."

"Right now?"

Ahamed nodded solemnly. "I'll get Waseem and Andy. Karl, I think, should not be trusted with a rifle." He turned to leave the tent.

"No rifles. We're just going to talk. Just the two of us. Let Waseem sleep."

Nick followed Ahamed out into the camp and left another note for his team. Then, jumping once again behind the wheel of the truck, he looped around the camp and turned to face the graying eastern sky.

Ahamed's expression was grim. Despite Nick's urging to the contrary, he had insisted on bringing an assault rifle.

"You know you're not going to need that." Nick looked over at his friend as they bounced along the rutted ground.

"The only rifle not needed is the one strapped to your back."

Nick shrugged and turned his concentration back to the terrain ahead. They drove in silence for two miles before Ahamed finally spoke. "They are there! To the left side."

Nick turned in the indicated direction. About a mile ahead of them, almost lost in the shadow of a broad erosion gulley, were two military trucks and a scattering of low-lying camouflaged tents. Nick made for the small camp while Ahamed raised the binoculars to his eyes.

"See anybody?"

"Most likely they still sleep."

A deep wadi blocked their way, forcing them southward until it was shallow enough to cross. Nick plunged into the gulley and drove up the other side. Then he angled back toward the small camp. Still no signs of life.

"Wait! I see a guard," Ahamed announced. "Definitely Iraqi. He wears a uniform."

Nick leaned forward. It was just light enough for him to make out the lettering on the crates in the back of the trucks.

"He sees us. He wakes the others."

A stream of shadowy figures emerged from the tents. Khaki uniforms, checkered keffiyehs, automatic weapons . . . These guys weren't guards. They were real soldiers!

"*Rokna!* Stop!" Ahamed shouted. "Turn around! *Jaldi!*"

This wasn't Katie's camp. It couldn't be. Nick swung the truck in a tight U-turn and stepped on the gas. The truck rattled and bounced across the rocky terrain, sending their cargo flying. Rocks pelted the undercarriage in a continuous barrage of bangs and clangs.

"Are they following us?" Nick cast a quick look back.

"Not yet. They may be too busy shooting!"

They sped across the desert plain, weaving back and forth to avoid the larger obstacles. Nick shot another glance at the rearview mirror. All he could see was billowing dust. The men would be able to see their trail for miles. He veered to his left, but then reconsidered and turned back in the direction of their camp. The men in the truck already knew where they were camped—whether he led them there or not.

"When we get back, I need you to wake everybody up and have them pile everything onto the trucks," Nick shouted over the clattering din. "We need to be packed up and out of there in five minutes."

"Where are we going?"

"They'll expect us to continue west, so I'm thinking north. If they know about the search zone, they might not think to search outside it."

Ahamed shot him a look. "Where we searched for Katie James?"

"Remember all the wadis we saw on the way? We'll hide in one of the deeper ones. If we stick to the rocky ground, we should be harder to track."

"And if they find us first?"

"Then we may have to fight. Everybody gets a gun—even Karl."

"Katie, do you hear me?" A distant voice pounded into Katie's aching head. "Are you all right?" It sounded like Hooman's voice—only different. More like Hooman as an old man.

She cracked open her eyes, but all she could see was blinding white light. She tried to move her head, but the attempt sent pulses of shimmering pain through her brain.

"Katie, answer me."

"I . . ." The word burned in her throat. She tried to swallow, but her mouth was dry as cotton. "I . . ."

Paper crinkled all around her. "Katie, listen. We're in the sun. We need to move to the other side of the wadi."

"Okay." She finally managed to croak the word out. She sounded like a frog. A big green frog on a lily pad surrounded by deep green water. An icy cold stream, crystal clear and gurgling like rustling papers . . .

Grasping hands tugged at her arms and shoulders. Loud voices. Grunts and sighs. A wave of nausea washed through her body as she was hoisted onto her feet. She tried to take a step but her legs buckled beneath her. She was falling.

"Easy. I got her!" Another pair of hands buoyed her up.

"Get her over to the ledge!"

"I can walk," Katie whispered. Ignoring the pain that throbbed in her head, she forced one foot in front of the other. "I can't see. What's wrong with my eyes?"

A faint shadow passed in front of her face and a layer of white paper was peeled back from her eyes. The toilet paper. She'd almost forgotten. They'd wrapped themselves in toilet paper to hold in the moisture and protect them from the sun.

Hot, prickling pain tingled into her legs. Her dizziness seemed to be receding. "I'm good. I think I can walk."

A tissue-wrapped face leaned in close. Hooman's concerned eyes peered into hers. The hands guided her across an uneven bed of jagged rocks. She was lowered into the shadow of a rocky bank, but the hot sand burned through her clothes. "Too hot." She pushed back onto her feet. "Where's my pack?" She looked around. Wayne, arms and head wrapped in toilet paper, was holding an unfolded map over his head. He staggered back across the dry streambed and returned with her pack. Gritting her teeth against the throbbing in her head, she dug in the bag for her geology hammer and started digging in the pile of loose scree at the bottom of the slope.

"What are you doing?" Wayne's voice croaked in her ear.

"Don't talk. Breathe through your nose," Katie whispered. "The surface is still hot. Ten inches down will be much cooler."

Hooman knelt beside her and helped her clear the dirt with his arms and hands. Ten inches was way too much digging, but even the few inches they were able to scrape from the top made a big difference. She had the others lean back against the slope and helped them arrange the unfolded maps over their heads before collapsing between them.

"Here . . . two more sips of water. Two small sips. There's not much left." She held the canteen out to Hooman, who unscrewed the cap and tipped the metal canister to his mouth. When he was finished, she passed the canteen over to Wayne. She watched his throat as he drank. Only two small sips. Maybe she'd misjudged him. It wasn't his fault Fischer had put him in charge.

"Guys . . ." She turned and leaned back against the slope. "I'm sorry. It's all my fault. If I hadn't given Murad the wrong coordinates—"

"It was an honest mistake," Hooman jumped in. "If it weren't for you . . ."

"Shhh . . . Breathe through your nose," Katie said. "It *was* my fault. I was so focused on beating Murad, I . . . ." The guilt that had been crushing down on her for the last twelve hours took away her breath. If they died because of her . . . How could she say it? What would they think? "I'm so sorry. But I . . . gave him the wrong coordinates on purpose. I don't know what got into me. All I could think about was not putting him onto the shepherds' trail."

A heavy silence filled the air. It closed around her like a fiery oven, smothering her with its intensity.

"I know I don't deserve it, but please . . . please forgive me. I wasn't thinking. I'm doing everything I can to make it right."

"Murad ain't coming." Wayne's voice was dull and flat. "There's nothing any of us can do."

"We can . . ." Katie stopped midsentence. The gag rule. She'd given her word she wouldn't say anything. Besides . . . the timing was terrible. She'd just admitted to lying. They were all going to die because she was a selfish, competitive, arrogant liar. To talk about prayer now, after she'd been quiet for so long. They'd think she'd betrayed them. She *had* betrayed them.

"Guys, we can . . . pray." Katie closed her eyes and waited for it to begin. *Go ahead. Laugh; get angry. I deserve it.*

Silence.

Her heart pounded in her head until she thought it would explode. What was she supposed to do now? He couldn't expect her to do it out loud. They'd think she was crazy. That she was trying to push her beliefs off on them. Katie waited for them to say something. A long minute passed. Two more minutes. Crud! Now she'd waited too long. It was way too late now. The moment had passed.

"God . . ." Her voice broke the silence like a gunshot. "God, I'm sorry I've been so competitive. I'm sorry I've been thinking so much about myself. Please help Nick Murad to find us. Make him come back." Katie hesitated, suddenly unsure of what more she should say. "Amen."

More silence. Katie took a long breath in through her nose.

"Thanks, Katie." Hooman's voice broke the silence. "Thanks for everything. We wouldn't be alive now if it weren't for you."

"It's not your fault." Wayne's voice sounded from the other side.

An aching lump formed in Katie's throat. Her stomach tightened and her eyes burned. A sense of relief and thankfulness and joy washed through her. *No. Please . . . No tears. Not now.* She breathed through her nose and forced herself to relax. "Thanks, Wayne," she finally managed to say. The worst was over now. It didn't matter whether she died or not.

"You didn't drink." Hooman was leaning over her. "I watched you and you never took a drink."

Katie remained silent.

"You haven't been taking your share of the water, have you?" He took the canteen from her side, unscrewed the cap and held it up to her face.

Katie leaned forward and pressed the canteen to her cracked lips. She tilted the canteen back until the water touched her mouth and pretended to swallow. It was her fault Hooman and Wayne were in this mess. The water was all for them.

Nick paced back and forth as Andy, Karl, and Annalise worked to set up the last tent. Muffled clacks, scrapes, and thuds sounded all around him. No laughter, no joking around, nobody was even talking. Just whispers and movement. Fast, efficient, silent.

He walked over to the trucks and checked to see if there was something left to haul. Nothing but the generators and AC units. It would be a long, uncomfortable night, but they'd all decided it would be best to do without lights and power. In the thin desert air, the roar of the generators could be heard for miles.

He climbed up into the bed of the lead truck and turned to survey their new camp. They were at the bottom of a long wadi. Even if the soldiers drove into the mouth of the winding canyon, they wouldn't see them until they'd driven all the way around the last bend. Waseem and Ahamed had erased every trace of their passage. As long as they hadn't been followed, they'd be perfectly safe. He'd done all he could possibly do.

Nick jumped down from the truck and walked up the canyon to inspect the placement of the tents. Karl and Andy's tent had a long rip on its side from when they'd loaded it into the truck. They'd been so sure the soldiers were right behind them that they'd pulled the tents up and dumped them in the trucks without folding them. They hadn't even bothered taking their gear out. But the soldiers hadn't shown up. They'd had time to drive west, out onto a hard-packed, rocky plain before turning north. Ahamed watched their backs the whole way, but he never caught even a glimpse of the military trucks.

Nick couldn't understand it. Why let them get away so easily? Were they that confident they could find them again? And what did they want? What were they waiting for?

The satellite phone went off like a siren. Nick grabbed it and jabbed at the connect button. The camp was completely silent. Everyone stood frozen in place, scanning the rim of the canyon. Annalise, hand over her chest, glared at him and sank into a camp chair. Nick shrugged and held the phone to his ear.

"Nick Murad." He spoke in his normal voice. If the soldiers were close enough to hear him, it was already too late for caution.

"Nick, this is Mike. Listen . . . I finally got hold of that minister guy—Mohammed Saeed Al-Whatsamajigger. Get this: when I told him you were being chased by soldiers, he said not to worry. That he had sent them for your protection."

"What?" Nick tried to process this new information. It didn't make sense. Two trucks full of soldiers? Protecting him from what?

"I know. Makes you feel better, doesn't it? Knowing they were shooting at you for your own protection."

Nick thought back to that morning. "I suppose the bangs we heard could have been rocks hitting the undercarriage. . . ." He looked up at the rim of the canyon, where Ahamed was keeping watch. "What else did he say? Did he say anything about the James team?"

"No. I even asked him. He said he hadn't heard anything about them being attacked. He seemed interested though. Asked a ton of questions."

"Okay . . ." Nick replayed the telephone call with Katie in his mind. The ministry had supplied her with soldiers too. She'd sounded so . . . frantic.

"Hello? You still there?"

"Yeah, I'm here. Did the minister, uh . . . How did he act when you told him about Katie's team? Did he seem . . . worried, outraged, sad?"

"That's the weird part. He didn't seem that surprised. He didn't ask any of the questions I would have asked, like 'Is this chick a head case?' or 'Is she doing hard drugs?' Instead he wanted to know what was stolen, what time it happened, stuff like that. He sounded almost happy about it. Like his team was winning the race."

"Okay . . . Thanks, Mike. That helps a lot." Nick walked to the base of the canyon wall and started climbing up to the top. "I'll keep in touch, but right now I have to do something. Talk to you later."

"Later."

Nick dropped the phone into his pocket and scrambled up the steep wall. Ahamed was crouching at the top, scanning the area with a pair of high-powered field binoculars.

"See anything?" Nick kept his voice to a loud whisper.

"Nothing. I think we lost them." Ahamed handed Nick the binoculars to let him see for himself. "What did Mike say?"

"Al-Jaza'iri claims he sent the soldiers for our protection." Nick scanned the area with the binoculars and handed them back to Ahamed. "Mike says the minister didn't seem that surprised when he told him about Dr. James's phone call. He said the minister believed the story right away."

Ahamed shrugged. "He might have sent them, and he might even have sent them to protect us, but they are Iraqi soldiers. What they want and what he wants may not be the same thing."

"But what about Katie James? If the minister believes her story . . ."

"Does the minister know of her other calls? of the mummy? how she tries always to trick you?" Ahamed waved the concern aside. "Did he know the story of her hitting her guards all on the head?"

"But what if the minister's soldiers are working with Dr. James's guards?"

"Maybe they are—if both were hired by the ministry for our protection. Maybe that explains why the soldiers do not give us chase."

"Or maybe the soldiers are waiting for us to find the whale. Then they'll attack. There's only one road out of here. They could be waiting by the road for us to return with the whale. Just like Katie James's guards were waiting for her to find something."

Ahamed looked at him and shook his head. The trace of a knowing smile touched his lips.

"Would you just listen for a second?" Nick growled. "This is serious."

"I did not say a thing." Ahamed's eyes were wide with wounded innocence.

"In case you didn't notice, Dr. James wasn't at that camp," Nick said angrily. "She couldn't have had any other motive for making that call."

"Ah, finally it comes out what you have not said all afternoon." Ahamed's smile broadened. "But remember. We searched for her already. Her team was not there."

Nick studied the back of his hand, then turned to look down on their camp. "We took so long to get there. What if they were hiding in a wadi?"

"Hiding from their rescue?"

"Taking shelter from the sun. That's what I would have done. They might have been asleep. We should have searched a wider area. They might have walked miles to find a suitable shelter."

Ahamed shook his head. "There were no footprints. No tracks from their trucks. Nothing to show—"

"So what will it hurt to check again? It's only a few miles away. If the soldiers are there to protect us, why bother to hide?" Nick stood suddenly and started climbing back down the slope.

"But if the soldiers don't mean to protect us . . ." Sand and rocks rained down on Nick as Ahamed scrambled after him.

"Then there's a good chance Katie James's guards weren't there to protect her either." Nick reached the bottom of the ravine and headed for the trucks. "Either way I have to go."

"Then either way I go with you." Ahamed fell into step beside Nick.

"No. I need you here." Nick reached the last truck and threw open the door. "If anything happens while I'm gone . . ."

"If the soldiers attack, my remaining will make no difference. I will go with you. You cannot say no."

Nick climbed into the cab and shut the door while Ahamed planted himself firmly in front of the truck, rifle grasped tightly in his hand.

"Okay, okay. You can come. But first tell the others where we're going." He called out the window, "And give Karl a rifle. He's in charge until we get back."

Ahamed shot him a nasty look and jogged off to relay the information to the others. Nick started the truck and positioned the AC vents for maximum effectiveness. If he was wrong and the soldiers found the camp . . . how would he ever be able to live with himself? But if he was right . . . he couldn't just sit by and let a whole team die in the desert. He could still hear the desperation ringing in Katie's voice. Why hadn't he searched harder?

"Okay." Ahamed jumped in the truck beside Nick. "Karl is in charge. If the soldiers don't shoot our team, Karl will."

Nick nodded and pulled the truck forward. Right or wrong, at least he was doing something. Hiding out in the wadi with nothing to do but worry for twenty-four hours would have killed him faster than the soldiers.

The hum of the engine reverberated off the canyon walls. Nick slowed the truck to a crawl as they reached the mouth of the ravine. He waited until Ahamed had a chance to scan the area with the binoculars.

"See anything?"

"Nothing yet."

Nick angled the truck to the northeast and drove slowly over the rocky ground. "If I'm right, we'll have to hide our tracks again."

"As we must do even if you are wrong." Ahamed didn't look up from the binoculars. "We are in the desert now. Thinking is no excuse for not thinking."

Nick turned his attention back to the treacherous terrain. He was forced again and again to detour around rock formations and wadis. The heat beat down on them relentlessly, overwhelming the capacity of the truck's air conditioner.

By the time they finally reached Katie's coordinates, he was exhausted. It was almost dark and it suddenly occurred to him that he hadn't eaten anything since yesterday.

He opened the door and slid out of the truck. He was so tense, his shoulders felt like they were growing out of his ears.

"Over here!"

Ahamed's shout galvanized him to action. Nick darted around the truck and ran up beside the guide, who was standing at the edge of a wide clearing. A strange pile of rocks stretched from one side of the clearing to the . . . SOS! The letters hit him like a punch to the stomach.

"How could we have missed this?" Nick was too stunned to move.

"Come. They are here somewhere." Ahamed ran across the clearing and disappeared into a shallow wadi.

Nick started to follow and then turned to search a different quadrant. "Hello? Dr. James?" He shouted at the top of his lungs. "Hello!" He ran back across the plateau. A twisting, turning shadow snaked its way through the rocks. Distances were so hard to judge in the desert. The wadi seemed to be only a couple hundred feet away, but that could easily mean two or three hundred yards. He ran for what seemed like forever. Finally he was standing at the top of a narrow gulley, panting and gasping for breath. "Hello? Dr. James?"

No answer. He slid down the steep gravelly bank into the shadow of the western wall. The change in temperature was dramatic. She had to be here. It was the perfect shelter from the sun. He turned to his left and ran along the bottom of the wadi at a slow jog. "Hello? Dr. James?" he called out every thirty or forty feet. How far should he go? He still needed to check the gulley to his right.

He was just about to take a GPS reading when he saw them. Three people wrapped up in white.

"Ahamed!" he shouted. "I found them!" He ran over and knelt by the recumbent figures.

The one on the right stirred. "Please . . ." The dark-skinned man waved the canteen away when Nick tried to pour water on his face. "She needs it more than I do."

Nick turned to the still figure in the middle of the group. Katie James. Silky dark hair spilled out from under the bands of toilet paper, moon-kissed swells in an ink black sea. He leaned over her and gently tore the wrapping from her face. His breath caught in his throat at the sight. Full red lips, cracked and bleeding. Her eyes were creased in pain. He ran a finger across her skin. It was dry and hot to the touch. Not good at all. Gently he raised her head and poured water across her neck and face. Then he soaked her clothes and arms, fanning her with his hands to cool her off.

"Ahamed!" he shouted again. "Over here. Quick, I found them!"

"Hey, doc. She going to be okay?"

Nick jumped. He'd forgotten all about the guy on the left. He gave the man some water and turned back to the unconscious woman. "Ahamed!" He poured more water on her face, let a few drops dribble into her mouth. What else was he supposed to do? He tried massaging her arms and hands. "Ahamed!"

An answering cry sounded from across the plain.

"Over here. I found them!" He poured more water across Katie's arms and face and went back to massaging her hands.

"Nick Murad?" A soft voice whispered his name.

He looked down into dark oval eyes. "Katie James!" He was so relieved he almost laughed aloud. "It's good to finally meet you."

A soft smile touched her features for a breathless second before twisting to a grimace of pain. She was trying to sit up. "Hooman? Wayne?"

"They're fine." He eased her back onto the ground. "Rest. Drink some water." He held the canteen to her lips and tilted her head up so she could drink. "We'll get the three of you into a nice air-conditioned truck. You'll all be good as new."

Footsteps crunched behind him. Nick turned to find Ahamed staring with wide eyes at the team of bandaged scientists. "I can't believe it," he said after a long pause. "Mummies and everything. I take everything back what I said before."

Chapter 12

*K*ATIE TOOK A FEW MORE SIPS of water and leaned her head back against the ground. Hot waves of pain throbbed through her brain as a cascade of words tumbled over her. Her stomach was twisted up in knots. She couldn't drink any more. She turned her head to the side as another water bottle was pressed to her lips.

"Katie . . . ," the voices repeated over and over. "Katie, can you hear me?"

She couldn't answer. It hurt too much to shake her head.

"Katie, you need to drink this." Water ran down her face. Hands were sliding across her forehead, forcing her to turn her head.

"No!" Katie lashed out with her arms and twisted herself away. She opened her eyes to a crowd of pressing faces and reaching hands. Squeezing her eyes shut, she rolled onto her hands and knees. Her stomach tightened. It was happening again. She was going to be sick.

"Everybody get back!" Hooman's voice cut through her panic. "Can't you see she's scared?"

A jumble of voices. Crunching footsteps. They were getting farther away.

"Katie?" Hooman's voice soothed. "It's okay. Everybody's leaving you alone now. Can you hear me?"

She nodded slowly. Nick Murad was watching. Of all the humiliating . . . She pressed her forehead into the dirt as a raging wall of fire burned through her brain.

"Here's some water." She heard the thump of a plastic container being set down next to her ear. "You need to drink it. We'll give you some space." The footsteps receded. She could hear whispers off in the distance. Wayne's rumbling voice. She caught the phrases: "called demophobia," "always freaks out."

Great. Katie's face prickled with heat. Another wonderful introduction. She took a couple of deep breaths and pushed herself up onto her feet. Nauseating pain expanded inside her head until her brain felt like it was going to explode. Her vision dimmed and the world tilted around her. She took a couple of steps forward, two steps to the side.

A strong arm encircled her. She felt herself being lifted off her feet. "I'm okay. . . ." She started to resist, but the throbbing in her head squelched her efforts. She eased open her eyes. Curly dark hair, soft brown eyes, a strong, rugged jaw . . . Nick Murad was looking down at her, his face etched with concern. She shut her eyes as his arm jolted beneath her head. He was carrying her up the side of the wadi, out across the open plain.

"The truck's a couple hundred yards away." He spoke between heavy breaths. "You're going to be fine. We just need to get you cooled off. Get some water in you."

Katie nodded and turned to rest her throbbing forehead against his shoulder. "Thank you for coming," she said in a quiet voice. "I was afraid you wouldn't believe me."

Nick's arms tightened around her. Katie waited several seconds, but he didn't say anything.

"Wayne probably told you it was all my fault." She squeezed her eyes shut tighter. "He's right. I almost got the team killed."

"He said you saved their lives."

"After almost getting them killed."

There was a long silence. Katie could hear the voices following somewhere behind them. Nick stopped and shifted her weight in his arms.

"Put me down. I'm too heavy." She straightened her body in an effort to slide onto her feet.

A laugh sounded above her. "You'd be fine if you'd quit squirming." Nick transferred her into one arm. "Just put an arm around my shoulder."

Katie opened her eyes at the metallic squawk of a door. She twisted out of his grasp and slid onto her feet. Her legs started to buckle, but Nick's arm was around her in an instant.

"I'm fine. I've got it." She tried to sound annoyed.

"Right . . . you look fine. Hold on a second." He reached inside the truck and turned the key. The sound of the rumbling engine was almost drowned out by the roar of the AC. "It will take a few minutes before the truck's cool enough. Here . . ." He handed her a bottle of water from the truck. "Take a few sips while we're waiting."

Katie started to unscrew the top but an arm caught her behind her knees and lifted her off her feet. "I said I'm okay—"

"It's called heatstroke. Ever hear of it?" Nick growled. "People are always fine until they're dead."

"Okay, okay . . ." Katie stopped squirming and leaned back against his arm. "You can rescue me. Satisfied?"

"Yes." A wide grin spread across his face. "Thank you."

"You're welcome." Katie shot him an exasperated look and took a sip of hot water from the water bottle.

Nick sucked in his breath. His eyes were wide. He was staring at her like he was watching some kind of freak.

"What?"

"You really *did* knock out those guards. . . ."

Great. Not this guy too. Katie looked down at the water bottle and pretended to read the label. She never should have said anything.

"You are waiting, I assume, for the whole desert to be cold?"

Katie turned at the strange voice. An older Indian-looking man was standing with Hooman and Wayne about twenty feet away from the truck. Wayne nudged Hooman and whispered something in his ear. Katie felt like an idiot. She was perfectly capable of standing on her own.

"We're waiting for the truck to cool down," Nick said. "It's 150 in there."

"I see the reason exactly." The Indian's eyes were smiling as he nodded. "Go ahead, then. Cool off the desert all you like."

Nick rolled his eyes and closed the door of the truck. "That's Ahamed Asif, my right-hand man," he told her under his breath. "He's from Pakistan. Whatever you do, don't listen to a word he says."

"Okay . . . Ahamed." Katie stole another glance at the Pakistani. He and Hooman were laughing like they'd known each other for years.

Nick carried Katie around to the other side of the truck and set her gently on her feet. "You still okay?" He kept one arm protectively around her as he opened the front passenger-side door.

"Much better, thank you." Her vision blurred as he lifted her into the truck. Throbbing, cranium-splitting pain. She fought to stay upright as an arm reached around her and buckled her in.

"Okay, everybody pile in."

Clambering footsteps. The squawks and clanks of slamming doors. Katie pressed her hands to her temples as the truck shuddered and bounced beneath her. It was too much. She was going to be sick.

"These two men say the guards attacked right after the finding of something valuable." The Pakistani's shout sounded next to her ear. "They were hired by the antiquities department for sure—just as with the soldiers." He was leaning forward over the seat, watching Nick expectantly.

"Okay, I'll be careful," Nick called back behind him. "Keep a sharp lookout."

"A lookout for what? What soldiers?" Katie scooted sideways in her seat. "What's going on?"

"Military trucks have been following us for days." Nick glanced back over his shoulder. "Minister Al-Jaza'iri said he hired them for our protection, but something doesn't feel right. Were your guards hired by Al-Jaza'iri or the Sunnis?"

"What?"

"Your guards. Did the Sunni ministers hire them?"

"You mean Talibani and Hamady? I always assumed so, but I don't know for sure."

Nick nodded. "We should probably assume the worst." The truck bounced and tipped as he stepped on the accelerator.

Katie's head rang like a pounding war drum. A cloud of electric blue lights drifted across her field of vision.

"Katie? Are you okay?"

"I'm fine." She managed a weak nod. "It's just that . . . we don't have any tents. They stole the trucks and all our equipment."

"Don't worry. You can join forces with us. We're outfitted for at least two months. We have plenty of food and water, and Waseem is a great cook."

"That's . . . really generous, but it's not necessary. . . ."

"Seriously. Let's search for the whale together. You can share a tent with Annalise. She'll be happy for the company."

"Thanks for the offer. . . ." Katie buried her face in her hands. She should do it. She should just say yes. But Dietrich would never go for it. Not with his grant in trouble. Not in a million years. "I'm sorry, but we can't. Please. Just drop us off at the nearest town, and we'll be fine."

Nick tiptoed up to Annalise's tent and hesitated. It wasn't even 10 p.m. yet. Katie had been asleep less than three hours. What if he woke her?

He turned around and drifted back toward the halo of light surrounding the camp table. Karl's animated voice sounded above a murmur of subdued voices. He was telling the story of their breakfast with the bedouins—how he'd walked into the wrong tent at the wrong time. A howl of laughter rose up from the group. Karl's voice rose in volume and pitch. There was no stopping him now. Next would come the goats in the airport, then maybe the whale with *T. rex* teeth.

Nick turned and looked back at the dim outlines of the tent. Katie hadn't stirred since he'd carried her to the cot. He'd doused her with water, massaged her arms and legs, given her plenty to drink.

What else could he do? He walked back to the tent and crouched down to unzip the flaps. Her temperature was normal. Moisture had seeped back into her skin. She was fine. What she needed was rest.

"I thought I should find you here."

"Shhh!" Nick jumped to his feet and swung around. "She's still asleep."

Ahamed's shadowy figure nodded. "And you think to wake her maybe? In the manner traditional for sleeping princesses?"

"Don't you think we should check her again? What if she develops a fever?"

"In the last ten minutes? She is not the one, I think, to have a fever, my friend. Come. We should sleep now. Tomorrow is a busy day."

"I'll be there in a second. I need to discuss a few things with the James team before they turn in."

Ahamed nodded. "Give her my apologies for being woken."

"I'm not . . ." Nick shook his head and headed for the camp table. Ahamed wouldn't be happy until Nick had made a complete fool of himself, which, judging from past experiences, wouldn't take very long. He stood at the end of the table waiting for Karl to finish the airport story. Hooman was locked in conversation with Annalise while the tall Texan—was his name Wayne?—seemed half asleep.

Nick cleared his throat, but Karl kept on talking. He cleared his throat again. "Sorry, Karl, but we need to discuss our plans for tomorrow." He waited until he had the James team's attention. "I know Dr. James wants to continue looking for the whale on her own, but given our current situation with the soldiers, I don't think a trip to the nearest town is an option. I hope we'll be able to agree on a collaboration. My team is willing to take a backseat on the first publication to come out of it." He looked to Karl and Annalise and received two nods of approval.

"Why're you worried about what she thinks? I'm the leader of this expedition." Wayne opened his arms in a long, languorous stretch and leaned back in his chair to stare up at Nick.

"I mean . . . when she wakes up. We're going to need to talk her into—"

"No, we're not. I'm still the leader. I speak for the whole team."

Nick studied the grad student's face, waiting for him to break a smile.

"Seriously. Dietrich put me in charge. He don't trust Katie anymore. Don't get me wrong. She's a good finder. The question is whether she's a keeper."

"What are you talking about?"

"Haven't you heard? Everybody's talking about it. They think she destroyed that last whale she found in Peru. Chopped it to bits with a pickax. Didn't want to put another feather in the old evolutionary cap."

Nick shot a look at Hooman. "What is he talking about?"

The Indian grad student shook his head.

"Seriously. Call Dr. Webb at UNM. He'll tell you. Katie's a born-again creationist. Just as soon convert you as look at you."

Nick looked around the table. Nobody else was buying it either. "Look, I really think we need to focus on the issue—"

"Ask Hooman; he'll tell you." Wayne rose from his seat and put a hand on Hooman's shoulder. "What did she do while we were out in the desert? Tell them what she did."

All eyes turned to Hooman.

"What do you mean, *what she did*? She saved our lives." Hooman rose to his full height and squared off against Wayne. "Or have you already forgotten the way she handled the guards? She went without water so we could have more."

"And she prayed a fancy little prayer too. Out loud so we'd be sure to hear."

"We were rescued, weren't we?"

"See?" Wayne turned on Nick with a triumphant smile. "Like I said, she's a born-again creationist. Dietrich made me the leader. That's why I speak for the whole team."

"Katie, are you okay? Can you hear me?"

Katie cracked open her eyes. A shadowy hand was reaching

toward her face. She scooted back, pulling a sheet up around her shoulders.

The man stumbled backward, looking frantically toward a half-open tent flap. "I'm sorry. Annalise . . . she was supposed to be right behind me."

"Dr. Murad?" Katie checked her clothes before sitting up on the rickety cot. "What are you doing here? Where are we?" She scanned the interior of what looked like an arctic dome tent. A blanket and pillow were laid out on the floor. A stack of women's clothing was laid out on a worn pack.

"We're at my camp. You fell asleep while we were trying to cool you off." He stepped toward her, awkwardly extending a bottle of water. "You've been asleep for over sixteen hours. . . . I was worried you'd dehydrate again."

Katie accepted the offered bottle and took a long drink. *Delicious. Like the first rain after a long, dusty summer.* She drained the bottle and handed it back to Nick. "Where are Hooman and Wayne?"

"They're fine. Hooman's on lookout with Karl, and Wayne's trying to strong-arm Ahamed into driving him back to Baghdad. Somehow, he has this strange delusion he's in charge of your expedition."

"Actually, he kind of is."

Nick raised an eyebrow.

"It's a long story, but when Dietrich was first invited over here, I wasn't working for him at the time."

"Okay . . ." Nick cocked his head to the side. For a few seconds he seemed to be lost in some internal debate. Finally he looked back at her. "What happened?"

"Nothing really. I just—" She stopped midsentence. What could she tell him without breaking her word to Dietrich and Nielsen? "I'm not . . . Actually, I don't think I'm allowed to talk about it."

"Not allowed to talk about it?" He looked at her like she'd just announced she was an Easter egg. "Says who?"

"Our department chairman. I gave him my word."

"Okay, if it's none of my business . . ." He shifted his weight toward the opening of the tent.

"It's not that." Katie's words came out in a rush. "I'm really not allowed to talk about it. You know, department politics. Big egos, tiny budgets. Things getting blown way out of proportion . . ."

Nick faced her with a disapproving frown. "Political infighting at a state university? Impossible." The frown melted into a grin. "Kinda makes you appreciate being out here in the desert, doesn't it?"

Katie returned his smile. "When people come at you with guns and knives, at least you get a chance to defend yourself."

"Tell me about it." He sank down onto the edge of the cot. "There's a reason I spend so much time in Pakistan. And it isn't the students, either."

Katie nodded uncertainly. What was he saying? She glanced down at his left hand. No ring . . . She looked up and caught him smiling. Had he noticed her looking at his hand? "I . . ." She could feel warmth rushing to her cheeks. "I appreciate all the help you've given us. I really do. You saved our lives. Literally."

"No problem. I'm just sorry we didn't get there sooner."

"The timing was perfect. Just in the nick . . ." She looked down at her hands. Now she really sounded like an idiot.

"So . . ." He shifted on the cot. "I'm still interested in working out a collaboration. Why not look for the whale together?"

"It's not that I don't want to." Katie chose her words carefully. "Please don't take this wrong. I really appreciate the offer—especially after all you've done for us—but I'm not sure my boss will go for it."

"I take it you don't mean Wayne."

Katie laughed. "Dietrich Fischer. He needs this find to get our grant renewed. With your name on the paper I'm afraid nobody will even notice his."

"Tell him he can take the lead. I'm okay with being listed as a collaborator. Heck, I'm okay with not being listed at all."

"You can't be serious." Katie studied Nick's face. How could he even offer such a thing? "It's *your* equipment, *your* people, your everything. . . ." She shook her head. "It wouldn't be fair. Just take us to the nearest city. Better yet, lend us a truck. We'll bring it right back—just as soon as we get reoutfitted."

"You're forgetting about the soldiers chasing us. They've probably joined forces with your guards and are waiting for us by the access road."

"If we dip down to the south and cut across to the freeway . . ."

"Not going to happen." Nick shook his head. "I'm not letting you drive into an ambush. They're probably combing the desert for us right now."

"You'll have to drive out eventually."

"True, but the longer we wait, the more likely the soldiers will give up and look for an easier target."

Katie searched his eyes. He seemed to be perfectly serious. If he absolutely refused to drive them out, Dietrich wouldn't have a choice. He'd be forced to agree to a collaboration. "All right. Dietrich's speaking at the South Africa Conference tonight. I'll call him as soon as he gets out."

"Good." A wide smile lit Nick's face. "I want you to know, I'm being totally selfish about this. I've heard you're brilliant in the field. It'll give my students a chance to learn from someone new. They're sick to death of all my stories."

"That's quite a buildup. I hope you're not disappointed."

"I don't think there's much chance of that."

Katie looked away. When had he gotten so close? "So . . ." She stood up and took a step toward the entrance. "We should probably get to work. My satellite phone needs charging and you probably need to—"

"Before you go . . ." A hand brushed her sleeve, freezing her where she stood. "There's something I need to ask you."

She turned warily and studied his face. Way too serious.

"Last night Wayne said some pretty strange stuff."

"Like what?" she asked cautiously. With Wayne it could be almost anything.

"I don't know. It was kind of weird. He said you were a . . . creationist. That that was the reason Dietrich put him in charge of the expedition."

"What else did he say?"

"A lot of nonsense mainly—mostly about Peru." Nick frowned disapprovingly. "The fossil you beat us to—he said you destroyed it. Because you didn't want it to give more credence to evolution?"

"That's insane!" Katie reached for the tent flaps. "Don't tell me you actually believed him!"

"Of course not. Anybody who's read one of your papers can see you're not one of *them.*"

One of them. Katie stopped in the entranceway. "Why? Because I write from an evolutionary perspective?"

"Because you write about real science. Because you can write at all."

"So what are you saying?" Katie turned to face him. "You're saying creationists are illiterate?"

"No, I'm just saying . . ." Nick stopped and stared at her with wondering eyes. "You never answered my question. *Are* you a creationist?"

"What do you mean by *creationist?*"

"What do you mean, *what do I mean*? A creationist. Someone who believes in God or an Intelligent Designer or whatever they're calling it these days."

"Those aren't the same. They're not even close."

"What aren't the same? Why can't you just answer a simple question?"

"Because it's not simple. It's not even clear what *creationist* means anymore. It's become a rhetorical device, a way to label people so you don't have to listen to them."

"So call it intelligent design. I really don't care."

"Intelligent design isn't even supposed to be a label. It's just the suggestion that certain scientific observations seem to imply life was designed. The idea that there's too much complexity in nature for purely materialistic explanations to account for."

"I know; I've heard the drill. Bacterial flagella, irreproducible complexity, yada yada yada . . . The question is, do you believe it?"

Katie fought down her irritation. "Do I have a naturalistic explanation for how ten different proteins coded by ten different genes could have evolved by a stepwise process when all ten of them are needed to make one working flagellum? Can I think of any possible way life could have come about in the first place? The answer is no. Can you?"

"So you think God—excuse me—an *Intelligent Designer* did it all?"

"It depends on what you mean by *did it.*"

Nick let out an exasperated sigh. "What is it with you people! It's like talking to a lobotomized cat!"

"What is it with *us people*?" Katie whirled around. "It's not *my people* that are the problem! Did you even consider that maybe I'm not *allowed* to answer your questions? Ever think that maybe I'll lose my job if I say the wrong thing? That I had to accept a gag rule in order to even come on this expedition? No, wait. I'm sorry. You're not one of *my* people, are you? You get to say anything you want. Academic freedom, the open and free flow of ideas—all that nonsense. Well, welcome to my world!" Katie yanked up on the zippered flaps and ducked through the opening.

"Katie, wait! I didn't mean it that way." The sound of billowing canvas. Nick was right behind her. "I'm sorry, I just wanted—"

"Sorry, illegal subject!" She held up her hand to cut him off. "Now you're the one who's not allowed to speak. I'm through with this conversation."

Chapter 13

*T*HE HUM OF GASOLINE GENERATORS drifted on the sluggish night air. Katie stood at the edge of the ravine, looking down on the sleeping camp. A rectangular table, dark tent-sized patches, the glint of soft starlight on windshields . . . Everything was perfectly still.

Swinging her pack over her shoulder, she felt her way down the rocky slope. She'd been such a jerk—throwing a tantrum like a six-year-old brat. . . . It wasn't his fault she couldn't defend herself. He hadn't stuffed a gag in her mouth. He'd just been trying to give her a friendly heads-up on Wayne. Maybe if she apologized . . . Maybe if she explained her situation from the beginning . . .

She skidded down a pile of scree at the bottom of the slope and made her way through the dark camp. Tiptoeing past Nick's tent, she crept over to his truck and eased the door open. Her satellite phone was sitting on the front seat, still plugged into the lighter outlet. She popped the cord out and slid inside the truck, pulling the door closed behind her. After all Nick had done for them, she owed him another chance. Anyone willing to give away credit for a major publication couldn't be that shallow. She thumbed through the phone's menu and selected Dietrich's cell number. Nick she could deal with. Dietrich, on the other hand . . . She ran through her arguments as the phone rang.

"Hello." Dietrich sounded exhausted.

"Hi, Dietrich, this is Katie. I hope I didn't wake you."

"No, this is good. You have, I hope, good news?"

"I'm afraid not." She hesitated. There was no easy way to say it. "We're okay, but the Iraqi guards turned on us. They stole our trucks and supplies."

"What?" Dietrich shouted. "How is it every time I send you out, you get things stolen? What do you do to these people? Are you so eager to always getting in a fight?"

"*I* didn't do *anything*." Katie tried to keep her voice calm. "We found something and the guards tried to steal it. They were going to kill us!"

"Always people are trying to kill you. It is not believable! Why do I even spend the money?"

Katie took a calming breath. "Dietrich, just listen. Nick Murad picked us up, and I think he's willing to collaborate with us—at least he was willing this morning. He can provide the trucks, equipment, and supplies—everything that was stolen."

"Absolutely no! No collaborations. For us to renew our grant, we must find the whale first. That is what the committee is saying."

"He's offered to let you be the lead on the paper. I don't know if the offer still holds, but he even mentioned not having his name on the paper at all."

"And you believe this?"

"He seems to want to help."

"Why? What is it he knows?" There was a long pause. "How close are you to finding the whale?"

Katie considered the question. How much could she tell him? "I'm almost positive we found the shepherds' camp. And the geology there seems—"

"The camp. Murad knows it as well?"

"Not yet, but without trucks and supplies it's only a matter of time—"

"What is it you are waiting for? Go out there and search. I want you finding the whale right now!"

"But our trucks are gone. Murad won't drive us out to get new supplies. We have to—"

"No collaborations! This conference ends before two days. After that I will get for you the supplies myself. But now I want you search-ing. I want you finding the whale tonight!"

"But—"

"This is your job depending on it. I need you finding that whale!"

A sharp click sounded and the connection went dead. Katie low-ered the phone to her lap and stared at the backlit screen. He couldn't be serious. Find the whale tonight? The shepherds' camp was miles away. The screen of the phone went black, leaving her in total darkness. She sat for a long minute, considering and reconsidering her options.

Finally she opened the door and slid outside. She hadn't flown halfway around the world to make excuses. She'd come to find the whale—before Nick Murad found it.

Keeping to the shadows near the edge of the canyon, she fol-lowed the line of trucks to the supply truck and climbed inside its cluttered bed. Rice, dried lentils, sacks of onions . . . She searched through the food supplies until she found what she was looking for—the box of emergency food rations. Every expedition packed them, but nobody she'd ever heard of had actually been desperate enough to eat one. She dropped four of them into her pack. It looked like she'd finally get to see what desperation tasted like. Probably a lot like working for Dietrich.

Swinging herself over the tailgate, she hurried over to the lead pickup. A dozen or so plastic water jugs were lined up in the back. She lifted four of them out of the bed and looped them through her belt, distributing the weight as evenly as possible around her hips. Taking a tentative step, she grimaced in pain as the heavy plastic containers cut into her waist. If she was having trouble walking now, how would she ever make it to the wheelbarrow? And then, even if she made it that far, she'd still have to push the wheelbarrow another four miles after that. Could she make do with less water? She started to unbuckle her belt, but then decided against it. She had no idea how long it would take to find the whale. Compared to heatstroke, her pinching belt was almost pleasant.

Finally, after checking and rechecking all her equipment, she snuck over to the camp table and scribbled a note on the duty roster.

*Gone searching for the whale. Dietrich's orders. Sorry we couldn't
collaborate.*
Katie

Taking one last look around at the sleeping camp, she turned
away and walked out into the desert night.

Nick jammed down on the brakes, sending the truck skidding to a
halt. There it was. The SOS signal. If she wasn't here, he didn't know
where else to look. He pushed the door open and climbed outside.

"I'll take the west; you take the east," he called back to Ahamed
and jogged over to the spot where he'd first discovered her party.
"Katie!" He searched the rocky shadows at the bottom of the narrow
wadi. It was just steep enough to be dangerous. If she had fallen and
hit her head . . .

"Katie!" He walked the length of the wadi, shouting her name
every three to five minutes. His voice was a ragged mess. He'd been
searching all afternoon. First he'd tried the area around the camp;
then he and Ahamed had tried to track her across the desert, but
apparently she hadn't wanted to be followed. Not that he blamed
her. He'd been such a jerk. Accusing her like a common criminal.
Attacking her when she was already down.

"You think it's close by?" Ahamed's voice sounded by Nick, making him jump.

"What? Katie?"

"The whale. You think it is here?"

"It's a lot closer than where we were searching yesterday," Nick
said. "I should have known."

"Does it not concern you we are out of the search zone?"

Nick shook his head. "I don't know how she knew, but I think
Katie was right all along."

"Then you think as I do—we should return back to searching for
the whale?"

"And leave her out here all by herself?"

"Her students say she is nothing to worry about. She does this searching alone all the time. If you believe only half the stories what they are saying, she is some sort of comic book woman."

Nick eyed the guide cautiously. It was sometimes hard to tell whether Ahamed was teasing or not. "Maybe you're right. Hooman and Wayne both confirmed her story about the guards, right? I mean a woman like that . . . she's not going to let a little heat and sand get in her way. She probably found the whale and totally lost track of the time. She's probably working on the extraction right now."

"Let us hope not."

Nick shot him a dark look. "You don't mean that."

"And why should I not? You should not forget: she is the competition. The enemy we must defeat."

"This isn't a war. She's a fellow scientist, a colleague. We're both trying to accomplish the same goal. If you think of it that way, we're actually on the same team."

"I see." Ahamed nodded. "And it makes no difference to you she is a beautiful woman?"

"No difference at all."

"And if you were searching for the whale, she would stop everything and drive all day to search for you? Because she is on the same team?"

"Sure."

Ahamed stared back at him with dark, inscrutable eyes.

"Maybe . . . if I'd just had sunstroke."

The guide's expression didn't change.

"Fine. We'll check back at the camp." Nick turned his back on the setting sun and started toward the truck. "But if she's not there, we're going right back out after her."

By the time they got back to camp, it was almost midnight. Nick slammed the door of the truck and called out to the group assembled around the camp table. "Is she back yet?"

Long faces. Empty stares.

Annalise shook her head. "Hooman says she sometimes keeps searching—even after dark."

Nick turned a hard look on the Indian grad student. "So you think she's okay? She's just wandering around the desert without food and water, hoping to get lucky?"

"Essentially, yes. Only with Katie James, luck rarely has anything to do with it." Hooman smiled and exchanged a quick glance with Wayne.

"You know where she is!" Nick stalked around the table to face the two students. "You've been letting us search all this time, but you know, don't you?"

"Sorry," Wayne drawled. "I don't *know* anything."

"But you suspect. . . . Where is she?"

"Searching for the whale."

"Where?"

Wayne shrugged. "Pretty close to where the guards attacked us, I'm guessing."

"But we went there. We searched the entire area."

"You might have gone back to where you picked us up, but that wasn't anywhere close to where we were attacked."

"So where was that?" Nick asked. "Could you take us there?"

"I could . . . if I knew where it was. But we walked the whole way in the dark. Seems to me Katie was pretty careful not to mention any directions. I'm guessing she didn't want us to be able to answer these kinds of questions."

"So you've known the whole time what she was up to? And you just let us keep on searching?"

"Hold up just one second." Wayne pushed up from the table and took a step toward Nick. "The note told you what she was up to. And we've said all along she was fine, so what are you so worked up about? You afraid she's in trouble? Or are you just mad because we can't draw you a map to the whale?"

Nick stared back at Wayne. "I haven't even considered the whale."

"Well, maybe you should. Isn't that what the taxpayers are funding here?"

Nick turned back to Hooman. "Could you at least tell us when you think she'll be back?"

"I think not for some time yet." The Indian student shrugged apologetically. "I cannot be sure, but it is my guess, from all the walking we did, that our original campsite must be miles and miles away."

Katie collapsed on the ground and rolled over onto her back. A billion silent stars pressed down on her, pinning her to the ground. Sharp rocks jabbed into her shoulder blades and spine, but she was too exhausted to move. She'd have to get up soon enough. The sun would be out in less than two hours, and she still had another mile to search before she could rest. She really had to get moving. If she got caught out in the sun, she was dead.

Groaning softly, she pushed herself up into a sitting position and slung the canteen off her shoulder. A hollow plink sounded inside the metal container. She shook the canteen. Only a few sips were left. She'd better save them for later. No telling how long she'd have to make her water supply last. Dietrich might not show up for days—if he showed up at all.

"Here goes." She climbed unsteadily to her feet and set out along the rock-covered floor of a narrow canyon. The clop-clop of her footsteps sounded like gunshots against the silence of the night. No generators, no insects, no noise of any kind. She was completely and utterly alone.

Feeling along her belt, she pulled the satellite phone from the case at her waist. Maybe if she called and apologized. It was Dietrich's fault she had to leave. Nick would understand. She switched on the phone and checked the battery level. But what if he asked where she was? What could she tell him? He would insist on picking her up.

Katie punched in a series of numbers from memory and stopped to listen as the phone rang.

"Hello?" Her father's unsteady voice made her shiver.

"Hi, Daddy."

"Katie! Where are you? Why haven't you called?"

"I'm fine. We're still out in the desert. I'm calling from Dietrich's satellite phone."

"The satellite phone? What's wrong?"

"Daddy, I need to ask a favor. Are you in the kitchen? Do you have something to write with?"

"Just a second." She smiled at the squeak of an opening drawer. She could almost see him riffling through pencils in the old Christmas card box. "Okay. Got it."

"Write down these numbers." She read off her coordinates and listened as he read them back to her. Then, locating Nick's entry on her phone, she read off his number.

"Okay. What do you want me to do with these?"

"That's Nick Murad's phone number. He's my . . . friend. If you don't hear back from me in five days, I want you to call him and give him those coordinates. He'll know what to do with them."

"Katie, what's wrong? Have you been caught in the fighting? Iraq's all over the news. You've got to get out of there now."

"Daddy, I'm fine. We're not anywhere near the fighting."

"So what is it? Did the truck break down again? Tell that penny-pinching boss of yours—"

"It's not the trucks. Really. Everything is fine."

"None of that. I didn't raise you twenty-eight years to have you say nothing's wrong. What's that man doing to you now?"

"Nothing. It's just . . . he wouldn't agree to a collaboration, even though it would have saved us days of pain and effort. He's being a real jerk."

"So walk away. Get out of there. This is your life we're talking about. It's not worth it."

"But it could be a new species. We're so close."

"Katie, I know you want to see things for yourself, and I've tried to be patient, I really have, but eventually you're going to have to learn you can take God at his word. We're called to walk by faith, not by sight."

"Daddy, please . . . don't start. Not now. This isn't about faith. It isn't even about God. I'm just trying to figure out how he made things."

"God already told us! If you're going to have faith, you have to take him at his word. He said he created the world in six days."

"Dad!" Katie took a calming breath. "Look . . . we've already been through this. It's just not that simple. Genesis wasn't meant to be a science textbook. It wasn't even written as history. . . ."

"None of that liberal mumbo jumbo. Can't you see what they're doing to you? Next thing they'll have you believing up is down and right is wrong. Katie, you've got to—"

"Would you just stop?" Katie fought to control her anger, but sometimes he made her so furious. "First of all, nobody's doing anything to me. Believe what you want, but *I'm* taking my cues from the passage. Can't you see how structured it is? The first three days he creates the containers, the next three days he fills them? In the Hebrew it's full of poetic language, plays on words, puns. . . . *Adam* is the Hebrew word for mankind. *Adamah*, the word for ground. *'Et-haadam aphar min-haadamah.* Mankind of dust from the ground.' What does that sound like to you?"

"Like somebody's trying to explain their way out of the simple meaning of the passage."

"The simple meaning? Who said it has to be simple? The rest of the Pentateuch isn't written that way. Why do you insist on interpreting everything the same?"

"But where does it stop? Are we supposed to interpret Jesus' miracles as figurative too? What about the Resurrection?"

"You know as well as I do those passages are a completely different genre. Firsthand historical accounts. Of course we have to interpret them differently. But Genesis 1 is so structured and figurative, we can't know for sure how to take some of the details. It could have been seven days or seven ages. There's evidence for both interpretations. Why are we only allowed to choose one?"

"Why do you always have to make things so complicated? God said seven days because that's what he meant."

"You think God is simple? Is that it? He's so far above our comprehension he can't even describe himself to us without using metaphors. So why do we think we could even begin to understand how he created the universe?"

"Katie, I know you don't think I know anything about science, and compared to you, maybe I don't, but I've been reading this book and the author blows your four-billion-year-old earth out of the water. The whole system scientists use to measure ages—it's filled with logical errors. Take that radiometric dating technique. The author says—"

"Is the author a geologist? Has he spent his whole career working on radiometric dating?"

"He's looked at the technique himself. He—"

"Do you have any idea how arrogant that is? Hundreds of scientists have spent hundreds of thousands of hours working on this. Did you ever consider that maybe they might have a clue what they're doing? The idea that some—"

"These people have an agenda! You know that."

"And you don't?"

"Of course I have an agenda. I'm trying to save people. There's more at stake here than just a few chapters in a textbook. This is salvation we're talking about. People's lives! How can you say you believe in the doctrine of original sin if you don't take Genesis literally? if you don't believe in a literal Adam and Eve?"

"I'm not talking about Adam and Eve. I'm talking about the creation leading up to—"

"How can you claim to be a Christian and even consider evolution?"

Her father's words hit her like a slap across the face. "What are you saying? You don't think . . ." She tried to squeak out the words, but her voice had swollen shut. "Bye, Daddy. Love you. But I . . . gotta go." Switching off the phone, she collapsed into a heap on the ground. The night dissolved around her in a hazy mist as she buried her face in her hands.

"No! No crying!" Her voice echoed off the canyon walls. She couldn't break down. Not now. She didn't have enough water left for tears.

Chapter 14

BILL STALKED ALONG THE SWELTERING SIDEWALK, swinging his legs from side to side like a cowboy after a hundred-mile ride. The blasted heat rash was killing him. The only thing that kept him going was the thought of strangling Murdock with his own two rash-free hands. He was finished with watching the museum. He was finished with the whole febrile assignment! The agency could fire him if they didn't like it, but he was going to march into the antiquities office and demand to see the records for every guard the department had ever hired. He'd tell Murdock what he could do with his cover. He'd tell him what to do with the whole flaming country.

Bill stepped up to the gap in the concrete barricades surrounding the ministry building and handed his papers to the soldiers at the gate.

"Orders, please." A swarthy Iraqi soldier stepped forward, speaking in a heavily accented voice.

Bill pointed to the name on his ID and thrust the stack of papers back to the soldier. Murdock had given him blanket orders from the prime minister himself, but he wasn't about to dig them out for a lowly barrier guard. Besides, what would a Swiss museum curator be doing with orders from the prime minister? He might as well print *SPOOK* on his forehead in big, bold letters.

"You may go now." The soldier handed him his papers while the other two quickly patted him down.

Bill nodded and trudged through the gate. Twenty yards, an eternity of chafing stairs, and then paradise. Pure, air-conditioned bliss.

A uniformed officer rushed past him and ran up the stairs, taking them three steps at a time. Bill grimaced. Already the insides of his thighs were on fire. Maybe if he went around to the back . . .

The officer turned as he pulled open the door. The full black beard, dark cruel eyes . . . It was the guard from the museum!

Bill swung his legs faster. He couldn't afford to lose him now. The guard was his "get out of hades free" card. Gritting his teeth against the pain, he limped up the steps and swung open the door in time to see the guard turn left at the end of the hallway. Pushing past the soldiers at the door, he pounded down the hall after the bearded guard. He was almost running now. If the guard saw him, his cover would be blown for sure.

When he finally reached the end of the hallway, he swung around the corner. *Great; another hallway.* The guard was nowhere in sight. His panting breath roared in his ears, a rasping siren sure to give him away before he was even close. He slowed to a stiff-legged limp and checked all the doors opening into the corridor, but the guard had disappeared. Up the stairs? Probably. The offices of the Sunni ministers were on the second floor.

Cursing under his breath, Bill swung a foot onto the first step and froze. Footsteps were approaching him from above. Two men speaking in Arabic. Their voices sounded familiar. He backed around the corner and ducked into the dimly lit alcove leading to the men's room. Whipping a damp handkerchief from his pocket, he was pretending to dry his hands when the two men walked past. What a coincidence! Khaleed Talibani and Ameen Hamady, his two favorite antiquities ministers.

He stuffed the handkerchief back in his pocket and followed the men down the hall. The short minister was talking rapidly. He kept up a running stream of conversation until they reached the front doors and pushed their way outside. Bill took a deep breath and followed them out into the heat. By the time he made it down the stairs, they were half a block ahead of him. He forced himself to move faster. The skin on his legs would grow back eventually. This was his only chance.

Finally the men stopped suddenly—right in front of his parked Land Rover. Bill staggered to his right and pressed his backside into the recessed doorway of a sand-colored office building. It wasn't a very good hiding place. Three full feet of him was sticking out into the sidewalk, but fortunately the men didn't look back. They didn't even seem to be looking at his car. At the first break in the traffic, they crossed the street and disappeared into a canopied shop. It looked like some kind of café. He looked at his watch. 4:30—Iraqi tea time.

Dusty rocks gritted under Nick's feet as he strode through the widening gulley. The late-afternoon sun was brutal. The temperature had been over 115 degrees since midmorning. He adjusted the keffiyeh he wore under his baseball cap and wrapped it around his face to shield his sun-scorched skin.

Two days of intense heat and dry winds. Minimal water, physical exertion, no shelter . . . He kicked at a heavy rock. Pain was his only lifeline now. He tried to focus on his foot, the heat, his tired, aching muscles, but he couldn't escape the dark cloud of dread rising up inside of him. She would have had to walk miles. How could anyone hope to survive?

And it was all his fault. How could he have been such an insensitive brute? She'd just woken up after passing out from heatstroke. He hadn't even given her a chance to get out of bed before he'd lit into her. What had he been thinking?

"Katie James!" Ahamed's distant voice broke through the turmoil of Nick's thoughts. He'd been calling out her name all afternoon. Did he still think there was a chance she'd answer? The Pakistani knew the dangers of the desert better than anybody. If *he* could still hope, maybe there was still a chance. . . .

His satellite phone rang out like an alarm. Nick pulled it out of his pocket and jabbed at the green button with fumbling fingers. "Hello?"

The voice was too faint to make out.

"Hello? Is this Katie?"

"Nick, this is Katie. Can you hear me?" The voice was a little louder now. It sounded like she was crying.

He pressed the phone to his ear. "I can barely hear you. Where are you?"

"Still searching for the whale. How about you?" The voice was suddenly much clearer.

"What do you mean, still searching?" Nick shouted. "Do you have any idea how worried we've been? We've been looking all over for you."

"Looking for me? I'm fine. Didn't you see my note?"

"Your note?" Nick's voice caught in his throat. "I can't believe . . . I've had my whole team out searching for you for the last two days. We thought you were dead. How could you be so . . . irresponsible?"

"Irresponsible? For doing what my boss told me to do?"

"For leaving without telling anyone. For not checking in with us."

"I left a note."

"Right. A note. No explanations, no mention of how long you'd be gone."

"I didn't know how long it would take. I still don't."

"I'm just saying . . . if you had talked to me first, I could have helped you. I . . ."

"So you wouldn't have tried to follow me? You wouldn't have insisted on knowing where I was going?"

"No!" he shouted into the phone. *Not unless I thought it was too dangerous.* "I would have offered to help. I could have driven you . . ."

"Exactly! See? I didn't have a choice. You wouldn't take us to get reoutfitted, and my boss won't let me work with you."

"Listen, all I'm saying is you should have called. We've been worried sick."

"What do you think I'm doing now? And who was worried? Wayne and Hooman? They know I can take care of myself. I do this all the time."

"Okay, I admit it. *I* was worried. I don't like it when my people take unnecessary chances, especially when—"

"Well, I'm not one of your people. I'm your competition, remember? I'm the one you beat to get your current job."

"Okay . . . you want to play it that way? Fine. But don't expect me to wait around in one spot while you search for the whale. Once I pull up camp, you're not going to have a base to return to. You can't expect the whole world to stop just because—"

"Fine. I wasn't planning on going back anyway." A click sounded over the line. The sound of dead air.

"Katie!" Nick shouted into the receiver. "Katie, wait, I was just kidding!"

He fumbled with the phone, jabbing at the buttons with shaky fingers. "Come on!" He flipped through the phone list: John Campbell, Karl Werner, Katie James! He dialed the number and pressed the phone back to his ear.

"Hi, this is Fischer team. Please leave a message. . . ."

Nick sank down onto a sweltering bed of rocks and sand. What had he just done?

Bill limped up the street. He was an absolute idiot. The Sunni ministers' offices weren't anywhere near the stairs. They must have already been on their way out of the building when the bearded guard got there. There wouldn't have been time for a meeting. There wouldn't even have been time for a handoff.

But if the guard hadn't gone there to meet with the Sunni ministers, whom was he meeting? The Shiite? He huffed and puffed his way back to the concrete barrier and waved his papers at the guards. The soldiers glanced at the documents, patted him down again, and let him through. He waddled over to the stairs and paused to catch his breath. He couldn't keep doing this. What good would he be to the agency if he were dead? Besides, the building was way too big for him to search by himself. By the time he got halfway up the stairs, the guard would be long gone.

The squeal of an opening door sounded above him. He shot a look up the stairs. A thin, sparsely bearded Iraqi in a rumpled, eighties-style business suit had paused outside the door and was eyeing him curiously. Bill scowled and looked down at his watch. The man was one of the ministers' assistants. He recognized him from his files. What was his name? Abdul something? Abdur?

He dabbed his face with his handkerchief as the assistant padded down the stairs and passed by on his left. Now was the critical time. Without even a look in the assistant's direction, he cast an anxious glance back at the top of the stairs and checked his watch again. He couldn't tell for sure, but the assistant's footsteps seemed to miss a beat. Had he paused to look back at him? Maybe he had been the bad guy all along. Nobody ever said it had to be one of the dogs at the top. Bill waited until the sound of his footsteps had faded in the distance and hurried back through the barrier. There he was, only half a block down the street. He was getting into a white Toyota pickup.

Bill charged down the sidewalk and squeezed into his Land Rover. By the time he got the beast going, the pickup was almost out of sight. Revving the engine, he pulled out into traffic, dodging into the oncoming lane to get around a slow sedan. Where was the pickup? He gunned the engine to get to the intersection before a mob of running boys. There it was, caught behind a line of cars in the left lane. He slumped down in his seat and maneuvered around a clot of double-parked cars to pull up behind the waiting pickup. That was his man. He slapped his steering wheel and let out a volley of oaths. One of the benefits of his size was that people almost never recognized him when they saw just his face. Behind the wheel of his Land Rover, he was just another obnoxious American. He leaned on his horn and waved his hands in a show of frustration. There . . . Now he was practically invisible.

The pickup finally turned left and worked its way through the heavy afternoon traffic. It took over forty-five minutes to reach the outskirts of the city. Bill dropped farther and farther behind until he was almost three blocks away. Wherever he was going, the assistant didn't seem to be in much of a hurry. He slowed to a crawl at every intersection, as if he was searching for an unfamiliar street. Either that or the assistant had made him. Bill cursed under his breath. He was just about to slow down and look for a place to pull over when the pickup's brake lights came on and the assistant pulled to a stop outside an old, bombed-out shell of a building.

Bill slammed on his brakes and pulled to the side of the road behind the skeleton of an old Chevy Suburban. He watched through the Suburban's broken-out windshield as the assistant took a set of keys out of his pocket and unlocked a weathered door set into the back wall of the ruined building. Fifteen seconds later he was walking back through the door, staggering beneath the weight of a large burlap sack. Picking his way through the scattered rubble, the man arched his back in an attempt to hoist the bag over the side of his truck. The bag was clearly too heavy for him. He had to set it down on the ground and lower the tailgate in order to get it into the truck. A Sumerian marble perhaps? Maybe one of those alabaster vases? Whatever it was, it was plenty heavy.

Bill reached for his phone and punched in his security code. Once it beeped, he pulled up the menu, scrolled to Baghdad Imports, and selected the number. The call connected and there was a long period of silence.

"Hello," he finally said. "Is this Charlie Burnpaw?"

"Go, Turnpike."

"I need a running random checkpoint set up immediately. Cursory vehicle inspection—untargeted. Keep it boring and routine."

Bill pounded his palms against the steering wheel. What was taking them so long? How long did it take to search the bed of a pickup? He leaned to the left and right, trying to see around the line of cars clogging the road ahead. They'd managed to get the checkpoint set up four cars ahead of the assistant. He would have preferred a little more lead time, but that was the best they could do on such short notice. The assistant hadn't stayed on any of the city streets long enough to get a roadblock set up. They'd been forced to wait until he left the city.

A uniformed police officer walked back along the long line of cars and stopped next to Bill's Land Rover. *Nabu and Mithra!* What did the idiot think he was doing? The officer leaned over and motioned for Bill to roll down the window. *Oh, great! Let's all draw attention to the undercover agent.* He gritted his teeth as he rolled down the window.

"What's going on?" he yelled. "I've been sitting in this traffic forever!"

"My commander tell me to say . . . Charlie Turnpike?"

"What is it?" Bill hissed. Heads were going to roll for this. Somebody had screwed up big time!

"We find large bag inside truck, just what we are told. But inside the bag is only worthless rock."

Bill huffed. *A worthless rock. Right! This is how they train their security forces?* "Did it ever occur to you the *worthless rock* in question might actually be a priceless archaeological artifact?"

"Of course. Just this we tell to our chief. He tell me to say Charlie Turnpike."

"And I suppose the driver was listening to this long conversation? I suppose he's watching us right now?"

"No, sir. His papers look suspicious. We take him inside our van for more questions."

"Great . . . and you never even considered bringing this worthless *rock* to me? You're going to make me get out and walk in all this heat."

"I am sorry. I did not—"

Bill sighed wearily and pushed his door open. He heaved himself out of the car and followed the officer along the line of slowly overheating cars. "I don't suppose he happened to mention why he was carrying a bag with a worthless rock in it?"

"He brings it to museum to use for a . . . decoration. His commander ordered he should bring it."

"His commander?"

"He works for Department of Antiquities. His commander is Mohammed Al-Jaza'iri. We work now to confirm this."

Al-Jaza'iri? Suddenly everything made a lot more sense. Al-Jaza'iri had been a freedom fighter before his appointment to minister. Maybe his days of freedom fighting weren't over yet. "I bet you a million dollars this *worthless* rock of yours is part of a priceless ancient Sumerian relief sculpture." Heat rash all but forgotten, he practically ran past the line of cars. "An ancient Sumerian relief sculpture; what do you want to bet?"

The officer shrugged and led him to the back of the pickup. Bill leaned over the tailgate and pulled the burlap sack open. Inside the bag was a large, dark gray rock—a lump of basalt from the looks of it. He stared at the worthless rock, shaking his head in disgust. So much for his brilliant detective work. He was officially back to square one.

Katie lay on her back, staring up into the darkness. Her legs and feet were almost completely numb. She'd have to get up soon and walk some feeling back into them. She might as well do a little more prospecting while she was at it—even if it cost her some moisture. The daylight would give her a whole new perspective on things. Now that her flashlight was dead, she could walk right past the whale and never even notice it.

She pushed up onto her elbows and pulled her legs back through the eighteen-inch-deep trench she had dug her first night alone. Finally, she was able to sit up with her head beneath the bed of the inverted wheelbarrow. She touched the crusty metal surface with her fingers. It wasn't cool anymore, but it wasn't hot either. She'd buried the wheelbarrow under over a foot of sand, so even during the hottest parts of the day, it never got more than a little warm to the touch.

Katie took a few swallows from one of the water jugs and flipped over onto her hands and knees to worm her way out through the foot of the trench. A trickle of sand drizzled into her hair as she pushed on the folded camp chair lying across the top of the hole. Bright sunlight filtered through a cascade of falling grit as she slid the sand-covered chair forward. She rolled over onto her back and pulled herself up through the narrow opening. As soon as she was out, she slid the chair back into place and shoveled more sand on top of it. After walking around in the heat, she'd need a nice cool hole to return to. Without Nick there for backup, she had to make every drop of sweat count. Her life depended on it.

Katie dug a white scarf out of her pack and wrapped it around her head and face. A tiny collapsible umbrella provided even more shade. Then, following the direction indicated by her compass, she set off to survey the area she'd discovered during the night.

It took her twenty minutes to reach the rocky erosion plain. She stooped and tested the dirt on her tongue. Hot buttered grits. It was as good a starting point as any. She walked in a gradually widening spiral, sweeping her eyes from side to side with the rhythm of her steps. A small glimmer of sorrel—no, it was only a feldspar deposit. Another patch of sorrel, the tip of a shiny brown shaft—some sort of *Nursallia* fish? Her spiral grew wider and wider until she was almost a quarter mile from her starting point. She wiped a sleeve across her face and patted herself down to check her clothes. They were already damp. She was losing way too much water. She'd have to go back. It just wasn't worth the risk.

Katie pulled out her GPS unit and took a reading. Her shelter was a little less than a mile to the southeast. If she swung first to the south and then headed east, she could follow the . . .

A low-lying rock off in the distance glistened reddish brown in the setting sun.

"No . . . way . . ." She stumbled forward, leaped over a patch of rocks. Then she was running, faster and faster until her umbrella caught the wind and flipped itself inside out. "No way!" She slowed to a walk as she approached the partially exposed whale skull. A line of vertebrae peeked out above the rock behind the skull. The first seven vertebrae minus C4, which had already been dug out by the shepherds.

Katie circled around her find, appraising it from every direction. Finally, after so much time and effort . . . It didn't seem real. She stared at it a long time before snapping back to her senses. "Time—" she checked her watch—"6:39 p.m., 18 August." She pulled the field book out of her pack and started taking notes. Orientation, landmarks, GPS coordinates . . . Then, digging in her backpack, she pulled out a Sharpie and a strip of yellow marker tape. She wrote her name and the date of discovery on the plastic flag, looped it through a metal piton, and drove it into the ground next to the skull. She had officially beaten Nick Murad.

Now if she could just stay alive long enough to brag about it. She pulled out her phone and punched in Dietrich's number.

"Hello?" He sounded even crankier than last time.

"Hello, Dietrich? This is Katie." She paused to give him a chance to ask the inevitable question.

"Where have you been? I have been telephoning to you for the last two days."

"Wrong question." Katie swallowed back her annoyance. "But I'm fine, thank you. As well as can be expected after living in a hole for two days—after recovering from heatstroke—after being left for dead by the guards *you* hired for us."

"Katie, I'm sorry. But this conference . . . I wish you could hear the nonsense these people are saying. They don't appreciate like you and me the importance of the work we are making progress in. Even the members of the funding committee . . ."

"Dietrich, I found it."

Silence.

"Did you hear me? I said I found it."

"The whale? Without the collaboration of Murad?"

"Without the collaboration of Nick Murad. But I need you to send trucks and supplies right away. I'm running out of water. If they don't get here by tomorrow at the latest, they're going to find *two* fossils."

"Yes, tomorrow, of course. I should be calling the ministry now."

"Wait, not yet!" Katie shouted. "I need to give you my coordinates. Do you have something to write with?"

Katie waited until he said he had found a pen and gave him the coordinates of her shelter—not the fossil. It would be just like Dietrich to rescue the whale and leave her behind.

"Okay, tomorrow afternoon. I'll be waiting. Bye." She switched off the phone and dropped it into her pack.

Tomorrow afternoon. She could probably afford to waste a little more sweat . . . She pulled out a whisk brush and started brushing the loose sand away from the skull. There was a lot more exposed than she thought. She got all the way down to the rostrum and froze. The nostrils were way too far back on the skull. She grabbed her pick and started chipping away at the surrounding matrix. This couldn't be right. It couldn't be . . . She stepped back from the fossil and studied it again. How could she have been so blind? The size, the shape of the skull—it was all wrong. She'd found the whale the shepherds had reported, but it wasn't pre-*Rodhocetus* at all. It wasn't even pre-*Dorudon*.

All that wasted effort, not just one team but two . . . How could they have been so wrong? The scientists at the museum, the ministers, Dietrich . . . Katie reached for the phone. She had to catch him before he humiliated her in front of every scientist at the conference. Punching in his number, she paced back and forth in front of the mocking fossil. "Come on, pick up!"

"Hello?"

"Dietrich, this is Katie. I just cleared away some of the matrix and the whale isn't what we thought. It's much more recent. Much more akin to *Basilosaurus* than *Rodhocetus*."

"Impossible. You are making some mistake."

"No, a good part of the skull was already exposed. The position of the nostrils, the size—it's all wrong."

"I don't believe it. Abu Feiraz—he looked at the vertebra himself. He assured me it was pre-*Rodhocetus*."

"Dietrich, I'm looking at the skull right now, and I'm telling you, it's one of the *Basilosauridae*—one of the later *Basilosauridae*. It's not going to give us anything new on whale evolution."

There was a long silence. She could hear the murmur of voices in the background.

"Dietrich, are you okay?"

More silence.

"Hello?"

"Katie, listen to me." Dietrich's voice rang with an edge of desperation. "I'm needing you to keep searching. You must find something else. Yes? Anything else. There's no hope left for us here. I'll fly myself there to join you. Don't waste any more time extracting the whale. I'm needing you to find a bigger discovery. Understand?"

"Sure, but the whale is still a good specimen . . ."

"I'll worry about the whale. You keep searching. I'll fly, not tomorrow, but the day after. I want to see results!"

"But I don't have enough water to . . ." A click terminated the call.

"Hello?" Katie's brain buzzed in the sudden silence. If Dietrich didn't fly out until the day after tomorrow, he wouldn't get to her until the next day. She tried calling him again but was transferred to his voice mail. *Great.* She left a message and started walking back to her shelter. If Dietrich didn't send supplies tomorrow, she was going to be in big trouble.

Who is this that darkens counsel by words without knowledge? Now gird up your loins like a man, and I will ask you, and you instruct Me! Where were you when I laid the foundation of the earth? Tell Me, if you have understanding, who set its measurements? Since you know. Or who stretched the line on it? On what were its bases sunk? Or who laid its cornerstone, when the morning stars sang together and all the sons of God shouted for joy?
Job 38:2-7, NASB

"Surely there can be no subject so interesting to man as why he has appeared on earth. . . . Much of evolution looks as if it had been planned to result in man, and in other animals and plants to make the world a suitable place for him to dwell in."
Robert Broom, The Coming of Man: Was it Accident or Design?
(H. F. & B. Witherby, London, 1933, p. 10, p. 220)

Part Three

Chapter 15

*N*ICK LEANED FORWARD OVER THE STEERING WHEEL. There they were again. Thin, wispy stems reflecting silver and white in the head-lights of the truck. The patches of shadow were thicker here. This could be the spot they'd been searching for.

"Hey, guys . . ."

A dark band appeared suddenly in front of them. Nick yanked the steering wheel hard to the right as the truck plunged down into the darkness. They hit the bottom of the gulley with a grinding crash and bounced forward to stop at the base of the far slope.

"Sorry about that." Nick looked over at Ahamed and called to the passengers in the backseat. "I totally didn't see that one. Everybody all right?"

"I'm okay." Hooman's voice sounded a little shaky.

"The back of my head left a pretty good dent in the roof," Wayne growled. "Next time give us a heads-up before you give us a heads-up."

"Sorry." Nick heard the metallic snap of a seat belt being buckled behind him. He flipped the dome light on and turned in his seat. Wayne glared back at him with a dark look. It probably wasn't the time for a lecture on seat belts. "So . . . you guys still think we're close?"

Wayne shrugged.

"It's too dark now for any more searching." Ahamed checked the GPS and wrote a note on the map. "We should go back to the camp. The others will worry."

"Hooman?" Nick looked to the other student.

"The plants and rocks were just starting to look familiar," Hooman said. "She may be very close."

"Okay, a little farther, then." Nick backed up the truck and pulled it around to follow the dry streambed. "Thirty more minutes and then we—"

His satellite phone went off with a loud chime.

Nick stopped the truck and grabbed the phone. "Hello?" His heart was pounding so hard he could barely hear.

"Hello, Nick?"

"Katie? Thank God! Are you okay?"

"I'm fine." Her voice was a scratchy whisper. She sounded terrible.

"Where are you? We've got water and food. We can bring it over right away."

"I'm fine, really. I just . . ." There was a long pause.

"Katie? Are you okay? Listen, about what I said—I'm really sorry. I'd never move the camp. You have to believe me. We've been searching for you ever since you called." He paused and waited for a response. "Katie, are you there? Just tell me where you are, and I'll pick you up. I'll take you to a city, wait until you get supplies . . . I won't even look for the whale until you get back. Okay? Katie?"

"Hooman and Wayne are still all right?"

"They're fine." He turned to check the backseat. "In fact, they're right here. Want to talk to them?"

There was another long silence.

"Katie, what's wrong? Let me help you."

"I found the whale."

"What?" He couldn't have heard her right. She sounded like she was at the point of tears. "You found it already? That's fantastic! Congratulations."

"It's not what we were hoping for. Probably a *Basilosauridae.* Maybe even more recent than that."

"Still, that's a great find! You should be thrilled."

"Dietrich isn't." Her voice was dead. "He told me to keep looking until I find something . . . grant-worthy."

"Katie, listen. Please don't think I was prying, but Hooman told me about your father's condition. You can't let Fischer do this to you. He's going to get you killed."

"He's not *doing* anything. . . ."

"Please, just tell me where you are. If you don't want to come back to camp with us, fine. But at least let us bring you food and water. Please."

"I'm at N 30 degrees, 26 minutes; E 45 degrees, 19 minutes."

Nick repeated the coordinates for Ahamed and watched as he marked her position on the map. She was only a couple of miles away. "We're almost there now!" Nick took his foot off the brake and stepped on the gas. "Stay right where you are. We'll be there in less than ten minutes."

"Nick?"

"I'm still here." He raised his voice to be heard over the sound of the straining engine.

"Thank you."

Nick's eyes started burning and a lump formed in his throat. She sounded so tired, so . . . vulnerable. "You're welcome, Katie. Don't worry about anything else. I'll be right there."

"Okay. . . . See you."

"Wait . . . ," Nick blurted into the phone but the connection had already gone dead. He looked at the phone and started to call her back, but what more could he say? He'd just start blathering like an idiot again. Besides, if they didn't fall into any more canyons, he'd be talking to her in person in just a few minutes.

He drove up a steep, rocky slope and swung the truck back around toward Katie's position. He'd promised he would just leave food and water, but he had to figure out a way to get her to go back to camp with him. Being alone out in the desert wasn't safe. Especially as hot as it was now. If she started to suffer from heat exhaustion, someone had to be there to treat her. He couldn't just sit by and do nothing while Fischer worked her into the ground.

It only took them eight minutes to reach Katie's coordinates. Nick slowed down and wove the truck back and forth in long snaking curves to throw his high beams on as much ground as possible. Ahamed was the first to see her. She was leaning on a large pickax in front of a shallow dig site. Nick pulled the truck right up to where she was standing. She looked like a ghost. Her clothes, her skin, even her hair were completely covered with dust. She squinted into the lights with a weary smile. Maybe she was a little thinner, but she seemed healthy enough. Nick grabbed a water bottle and jumped out of the cab. Hooman and Wayne were right behind him.

"Glad you could make it." Her dust-coated face lit with a dazzling smile.

Nick slowed to an uneasy walk. He'd spent an eternity rehearsing his apology, but suddenly he was at a loss for words. "Thirsty?" He handed her the bottle and watched as she took a few sips.

"Thanks." She handed the water back and turned to face the dig. "Want to see it?"

A whoop sounded in Nick's ear. Suddenly everybody was talking at once. Hooman and Wayne charged forward and pressed around Katie. Hooman lifted her off the ground, swinging her in a tight circle. Wayne pounded her on the back until a huge cloud of dust hung in front of the truck's lights. Nick hung back and let them enjoy their moment. They had won the race. They had a right to celebrate. He nodded and tried to smile as she pointed out some of the fossil's features, but his heart just wasn't in it. He couldn't stop thinking about the first time he had seen her, about carrying her in his arms, giving her water, massaging her hands. But this time . . . He looked up at the celebrating team. What was wrong with him? After all they'd been through, he should be happy for them. What was his problem?

Katie glanced over at him and her smile suddenly faded. "I'm sorry. I didn't mean to . . ." She took a step toward him and hesitated, eyes flitting back and forth across his face. "We wouldn't have found this if it weren't for you. We wouldn't even be alive. I don't care what Dietrich says; this was a collaboration."

"No." Now he really felt like a jerk. "You found it. Please . . . I just wanted to help. I still want to help." He gestured awkwardly with his hands, grasping for the right words. "We don't need to be on any of the papers, but at least let us help with the dig. We drove all the way out here—it seems a shame to go back now without the students getting a chance to do any work."

Katie's forehead wrinkled. "Okay . . . if that's what you want."

"Thanks." Nick felt like a huge weight had been lifted off his shoulders. "Let's get back to the camp. After a good night's sleep, we'll pack everything up and move out here in the morning." He shot a worried glance at Katie. "You will come back to the camp with us?"

"Sure . . . if it's okay." She studied him again with those bright, probing eyes. "I could ride in the back if you're worried about getting the seats dirty."

Nick laughed—probably a little too long and a little too hard, but he didn't care. He herded everyone back to the truck. Wayne and Hooman climbed into the backseat and Katie was about to follow when Ahamed stepped in front of her and ducked inside.

Katie turned and regarded Nick with a suspicious look before walking around the truck and climbing inside. Nick shook his head—as if he had any control at all over what Ahamed did. He slid behind the wheel and glared up at the rearview mirror. Ahamed's reflection stared back at him with a self-satisfied grin.

Katie slipped her pack over her shoulder and ducked out of the air-conditioned tent. A burst of laughter sounded from the dig site. She stopped and listened to the commingled voices of the students from both labs. When was the last time Fischer's team had laughed like that? It just didn't happen. Fischer's personality had set the tone for the whole group. But Nick's team . . . Not only was it fun, but they'd all been so kind, so generous. . . . Her hand drifted to the lump of fabric gathered at her waist. Annalise had lent her shorts, T-shirts, a scarf . . . she'd even given her some of her underwear. It was almost too much. They all genuinely seemed to want to help—especially Nick. He'd been the perfect host. Almost too perfect.

She walked over to the dig area and watched as Nick showed

Hooman and Annalise how to wrap a pedestaled section of vertebrae in toilet paper and burlap-reinforced plaster. Hooman had done it a hundred times before and from the look of things, so had Annalise, but they were both hanging on Nick's every word.

". . . and then," Nick said, "after I'd poured the whole concoction over my sister's doll, I realized why paleontologists use plaster instead of oatmeal. My neighbor's two Labradors trotted up and gobbled up the whole sticky mess—Baby Boo-boo and all."

Hooman and Annalise laughed while Ahamed rolled his eyes. The Pakistani guide jerked his head at Nick, who turned suddenly and jumped to his feet.

"Katie, good morning." His smile looked nervous, almost forced. "We were just . . . finishing up C3 and 5."

"Sounds like fun." She glanced over at the partially exposed skeleton. "You know, I don't have to go out prospecting right now—if you need some help . . ."

"We're fine. Karl will be done with the dishes soon and Wayne will be right out. You go ahead and make history."

"Right . . ." Katie wasn't so sure she wanted to make history. Working on the whale seemed a lot more . . . interesting. Besides, it wasn't fair for Fischer to get all the credit while Nick's team did all the work. She started toward the skull, but Nick's expression brought her up short.

He stepped ominously toward her and spoke in a soft whisper. "Can we talk?"

Katie nodded, taken aback. Nick's guide was watching her with the strangest expression on his face. What was going on now?

She followed Nick across their new camp, waiting for the atomic bomb to drop. He stopped near the lead truck and stood scanning the distant horizon. Silence beat down on them with the intensity of the afternoon sun. After what seemed forever, he finally cleared his throat. "Ever since we picked you up, I've been hoping for a chance to talk with you. It's been crazy. For a person who doesn't like crowds, crowds sure seem to like you."

Katie risked a smile. "So what did you want to talk about?"

"I wanted to apologize. Our argument the other day, all those things I said while you were still recovering—I can't even think of it without hating myself."

"The stuff Wayne told you? That wasn't *your* fault."

"Yes, it was. I shouldn't have pushed so hard. And I certainly shouldn't have lost my temper. I don't know what got into me. I'm not normally like that. I'm totally open to the idea of God."

"That's big of you."

"I'm not trying to be condescending; I'm just trying to figure things out." Nick fell silent and studied her with a wary expression.

"Figure what out?"

"Don't take this wrong. I'm not criticizing. I'm just trying to understand. You're a paleontologist, right? So how do you account for the fossil record? Like the *Basilosaurus* you just found—how do you account for the tiny hind limbs?"

"Well, I believe there was a primitive whale called *Basilosaurus* that had tiny, perhaps vestigial, hind limbs." Katie shrugged. "What's so hard to understand about that?"

"But how does it fit into your, you know, worldview?"

"You mean, do I think it evolved into modern whales?" Katie looked him in the eye. "Maybe . . . Maybe not. I'm pretty open to either possibility."

"So you're saying you're an agnostic?"

"Not on the issue of God. I know from experience he exists. But just because we've found a ton of extinct ancient whales, it doesn't necessarily mean they're part of an evolutionary pathway leading to modern whales. Look at the ajolote, the worm lizard from Baja. If we found a 50-million-year-old fossilized ajolote, wouldn't we be tempted to classify it as an evolutionary intermediate between snakes and lizards?"

"But look at the middle ear bones in the whale fossils, the movement of the nasal openings . . ."

"The use of the word *movement* is an interpretation, but I know what you mean, and I agree with you. The evidence for an evolutionary mechanism is pretty compelling. Especially the time line. The fact that the older whales had more and more terrestrial features. The fact that modern whales didn't appear until much later . . . Maybe God did use a process of evolution. I don't know. That's why I'm a paleontologist. I'm trying to figure the whole thing out. The thing that gets to me is that everyone else already seems to have made up their minds. And then they have the gall to say *I'm* the one who's biased."

"That's not what I was saying. . . ."

"You want to talk about bias, look at the pressure we have to get funding. Everyone wants to find a new reference species. Everyone wants their fossil to be a key intermediate in a major evolutionary pathway. And now that the science popularizers are squaring off against the intelligent design people, it's getting worse—on both sides of the debate. The whole thing has become political. It's a pitched battle for the minds of America's youth. And just like it did in politics, the battle has created a false dichotomy. Nobody's allowed to take a position in the middle. You're either for us or against us. Friend or foe. Republican or Democrat. Who says you can't believe in God *and* science?"

"I certainly don't." Nick broke into a dopey grin. "I don't have a problem with anything you said."

"And that surprises you?"

"I just don't get it. Why would your boss have a problem with that?"

"Not just my boss, the department chairman too. He said he was trying to protect my career. He even gave me a book to help me deal with my little *God problem.*"

"Are you sure you're not just misinterpreting what he was saying? Just because someone disagrees with you doesn't mean he's trying to suppress your voice."

"It does when he fires you as part of the disagreement. I know exactly what he was doing. I was there, remember?"

"Okay." Nick flung up his hands. "I didn't mean anything by it. It's just that it doesn't make any sense. I can't imagine anyone . . . not wanting to hear what you have to say."

"That's because . . ." The words froze on Katie's lips as she looked up into his eyes. Her chest was starting to tighten. Not now. Her ears were beginning to ring with an all-too-familiar buzz. She couldn't be having an attack. He was only one person.

She looked down at the ground, focusing on the individual grains that made up a small pile of sand. She took a long, deep breath. One more . . .

"Katie, I'm sorry." Nick's voice sounded right above her head. She felt a gentle touch on her shoulder. "I didn't mean it that way. I don't know why, but everything I say lately seems to come out wrong."

Katie risked an upward glance. "It's not you. You're fine. I'm the one that . . ." She inched away from Nick and took another deep breath. "I've never been good with people. I'm not making excuses; it's just the way I am."

Nick opened his mouth to say something, but then he closed it again. Apparently he was going to make her keep going.

"You know I don't like crowds," she said. "It's called demophobia. I've had it almost as long as I can remember. That's what happened at the Michigan candidate seminar. I freaked out in front of the selection committee. I actually threw up on the steps leading to the stage."

"I'm sorry. If I had known, I would have . . ."

"No," Katie spoke up with more force than she'd intended. "The right man got the job. I realize that now. I wasn't ready for teaching. I'll probably never be ready for teaching."

"I don't believe that. I've been watching you with the students—"

"Please," Katie said. "Let me finish. I know I tend to be distant and standoffish. Heck, I've even been known to run away from camp in the middle of the night. But I want you to know that it doesn't have anything to do with you. You've been perfectly . . . perfect in all of this. I'm the one who's messed up. Okay?"

"No more than the rest of us." Nick shook his head. "That's not right. What I meant to say is I don't think you're messed up at all. I think you're one of the most amazing women I've ever met."

The words buzzed in Katie's ears. Nick's eyes were boring into her like diamond-tipped drills. It was happening again. She stared at the ground, tried to lose herself in the weathered grain of the exposed rock. She wouldn't run. She'd throw up in front of him if it came to that, but this time she wouldn't run away.

"Katie, are you okay?" Nick's voice came to her from what sounded like a long distance away. "I'm sorry. I didn't mean to . . . What do you want me to do?"

"I'm fine," Katie managed to gasp. "I told you I was messed up."

A soft laugh sounded by her side. "You have no idea about messed up. Let me tell you about my old girlfriend. She flew all the way out to visit me in Pakistan and then turned right back around because she wasn't willing to wear a scarf that didn't match her blouse. That's messed up."

Katie felt her muscles starting to relax. The brick in her throat was starting to sublimate.

"Once she wouldn't speak to me for a week because I said I thought Gucci purses were ugly."

Katie smiled and peeked up at Nick. He was doing a good job of hiding it, but she could tell he was worried. His eyes gave him away.

"Are you going to be okay?"

She nodded and looked back down. "I think I'm good."

"Want me to leave you alone?"

She took a deep breath. It would never work. She was insane for even considering it. "Not unless you want to."

"Good. Want to get back to the dig now?"

"Actually, the dig might be a bit much. Let me go try to make history for Dietrich, and then when I get back, maybe we could . . . talk some more?"

"I'd like that."

She looked up into Nick's eyes and was actually able to return his smile.

Nick pushed a needle pick through the loose sand. Katie had been gone over two hours. What if something had happened to her? Heat exhaustion, snakebite, Iraqi soldiers . . . This business of prospecting alone out in the desert was ridiculous. He should have gone with her. He should have insisted.

The thought brought a smile to his face. Yeah, forcing her to do something she didn't want to do, he'd have to try that some-time—sometime when she wasn't carrying that stainless steel canteen of hers. If he could believe even half of what Hooman had told him about the night they were attacked, Katie was some kind of Navajo ninja goddess, dropping people right and left with a big drink of water. He looked up from the pattern of concentric squiggles he'd been tracing in the sand. Hooman and Annalise were working side by side on the T4 and T5 vertebrae. They'd been spending a lot of time together. It was obvious she had a crush on him. He hoped the feeling was mutual. For a while he'd thought Hooman's affections tended in another direction.

"Hooman, listen . . ." The words were out of Nick's mouth before he could stop himself. "This condition Katie has—the demophobia—does it keep her from being able to, you know, make friends?"

Hooman shot him a knowing look and lowered his eyes back to the vertebrae. "She makes *very* good friends. She just doesn't make many. Meeting new people is painful for her—especially lots of people at once."

"I suppose my motley crew must have come as a pretty big shock to her, then."

"Not too bad actually." A mysterious smile twinkled in Hooman's eyes. "I've been kind of surprised."

"Surprised? In what way?"

"Quiet!" Ahamed jumped to his feet and raised a hand in the air. A faint humming noise drifted toward them on the breeze. An echo from their generators?

"Everybody to the rifles!" Ahamed shouted and started running for the camp. "Get behind the trucks. They approach this way!"

"Come on!" Nick shouted at the frozen students. "Everybody move! We're going to have company."

Andy and Karl were already running. Nick cut behind Hooman

and Annalise and urged them toward the trucks. Ahamed was already in the back of the tent truck, handing out rifles. He jumped down as soon as Nick arrived and thrust a rifle into his hands. A cloud of dust was making its way toward the camp. Two, maybe three, white pickup trucks.

"Everybody takes a rifle!" Ahamed called out to the group. "Hold it like you mean to use it—even if you don't know how!"

They stood in a line behind the trucks, soundlessly raising their rifles as two pickups drove up to the edge of camp. The trucks stopped in front of the whale excavation. A door opened and an overweight man stepped out into the swirling dust. He was dressed all in white and wore a fifties-style pith helmet.

"Dr. Fischer!" Wayne shouted and stepped out from behind the truck. "We thought you weren't coming until tomorrow."

Dietrich Fischer. Nick recognized him from the Evo-Devo conference in Chicago. He stepped out from behind the lead truck and headed back to the dig site to introduce himself.

"What is all of this?" Fischer called out to Wayne and Hooman from across the dig area. "Katie told to me all your tents were stolen!"

"Whoa . . . calm down, hoss." Wayne stopped just across the excavation from his boss. "This is Dr. Murad's stuff. He's been helping us out some while we were waiting for you to get here."

Nick walked around the trench and extended his hand. "Dr. Fischer. I'm Nick Murad. It's good to finally meet you in person."

Fischer eyed Nick suspiciously and then shook his hand. "The pleasure is all mine." He turned back to Wayne and Hooman. "I thought I made myself clear. We cannot afford to a collaboration."

"They were just helping us," Hooman spoke up. "If it wasn't for them, we'd all be dead right now."

"Katie explained your situation." Nick stepped forward and turned to guide the big man to their camp. "We're happy to help out—any way we can. We don't expect to be included on any of the papers."

Fischer's brow furrowed. "Since you realize already our situation,

I'm sure you understand why we cannot accept. Thank you, but you should be going now. We have now all the equipment we need."

Nick took a deep breath and waited for the burning tide in his gut to subside. "Listen, why don't we get out of the sun and discuss this. I'm sure we can come to some kind of agreement."

"Do you deny Katie James found the fossil first?" Fischer's face was dotted with patches of livid red.

"No, of course not. I'm not trying to—"

"Yet you force your way into our dig, knowing without shelter and water my people are helpless to deny you."

"Nobody forced anything on anybody!" Nick snapped. "We offered to help out of kindness—something you obviously don't understand."

"I understand well enough what I've seen before and before," Fischer bellowed. "At first it's always goodness-of-the-heart helping— until it becomes extortion and stab-in-the-back robbery."

"Okay, forget it, then!" Nick turned and started to walk away. "Forget I even offered!"

"I want you and all your team gone from here in thirty minutes!" Fischer's voice lashed out at Nick's back.

"Thirty minutes?" Nick swung around. "That's crazy. We're not going to touch the fossil. What difference can it make where we're camped?"

"Thirty minutes!" Fischer shouted. "This is our find. I want your camp gone from here."

Katie . . . Nick turned to search the western horizon. She wouldn't be back for hours. He couldn't leave now. He was just starting to break through. "Listen . . ." Nick swallowed hard. "Let's just calm down. You have my word; I'm not trying to horn in on your discovery. I don't want any credit for anything we may have done to help. But we can't just pack up and leave. We need a little time."

Fischer looked back at his trucks and signaled with a raised hand. The doors opened and five Iraqi men got out. They were all carrying guns.

"This is ridiculous." Nick looked back at the grad students and guides who had silently gathered behind him. "See? Look around. Everyone knows this is ridiculous."

Hooman stepped forward. "He's right. All they've done is help. Why not let them stay?"

"For what reason?" Fischer demanded. "They'll be better off to be away. They'll have a chance to find their own whale." Fischer turned back to Nick. "Dr. Murad, my team and I appreciate all the help already you have given. We are happy to help you pack."

"But . . ."

One of the Iraqi guards stepped forward, flipping one of the switches on his rifle. Was he taking the safety off or putting it back on?

"Okay . . . thank you," Nick finally said. He turned to the rest of the team. "Dr. Fischer is right. It would be best for us to leave now."

Chapter 16

THE DESERT ROCKS GLOWED golden in the purpling gloom. Katie turned reluctantly to the west. The sun, now a huge disk of shimmering fire, was sinking into a soft bed of reds and oranges. Soon it would be too dark to see. With so little moisture in the air to diffract the light, night always came quickly in the desert. She turned back toward the camp and hesitated. Fifteen minutes. She had at least fifteen minutes of light left. She looked back across the wide plain she'd been prospecting. Fifteen minutes wouldn't make any difference. Besides, she was hungry. She'd already skipped lunch. She couldn't skip dinner too. Sooner or later she was going to have to face him. She couldn't put it off any longer.

Turning back to the camp, she forced one foot in front of the other. It wasn't as if anything was going to come of it. She was just going to humiliate herself in front of the others. First she'd freeze up, and then she'd run. She could already feel icy fingers closing around her heart. It wasn't worth it. Besides, this was a terrible time—for anything. With her reputation in tatters and Dietrich's grant expiring . . . Why was she even considering . . . talking to a guy like Nick? She didn't know a thing about him.

Katie opened her canteen and drained it. There . . . that was the last of her water. She had to go back now. She started walking faster. The quicker she got it over with, the better.

It had been dark for over an hour by the time she reached the outskirts of camp. She stopped next to the dig site and listened to the

sounds of the night. Something was wrong. The sound of the generators, the positions of the tents, the trucks . . . everything was different.
The camp was ominously quiet. It felt like a graveyard. She let out
the strap of her canteen and crept silently through the loose semicircle of tents. Hooman was sitting alone at the camp table, his face
glowing eerily in the lantern light. She stopped and watched him for
several minutes. He was just sitting there, turning a manila envelope
over and over in his hands. He seemed a little down, but nothing to
be alarmed about. Maybe he and Annalise had had a fight. They'd
been spending an awful lot of time together. Something was bound
to happen sooner or later.

Katie watched him another couple minutes and then slipped
quietly into camp. Hooman rose to his feet when he saw her. He
definitely wasn't happy.

"What's going on?" Her voice was a hoarse whisper.

"Dietrich's here," Hooman said. "He came this afternoon and
made the Murad team leave."

"They're gone?" Katie turned to the empty spot where Nick and
Ahamed's tent had been. "All of them?"

Hooman nodded glumly.

"But why? Why would he . . . ?"

Hooman handed her the envelope. Her name was written in
bold, indelible letters across the front. She tore it open and shook a
single sheet of paper out onto the table.

Katie:

*I wish we had gotten a chance to work together. I meant every word I said
about wanting to help, but your Dr. Fischer has some severe trust issues.
He's making us leave right away—very much against our will. I'm sorry we
never got a chance to finish our talk. Maybe at the next SVP conference?
I'd love to get to know you better. Any time you're in Michigan or Pakistan
or anywhere else your boss doesn't happen to be, please give me a call.*
Nick

Katie slid the letter back into the envelope and looked up at Hooman. He was watching her with wide, concern-filled eyes.

"What?" she snapped. "He just said he was sorry he wasn't going to have a chance to work with us. He suggested we chat at the next SVP conference." She started for her tent and stopped. She didn't even know which tent was hers. Dietrich was here now. Ahamed and Karl and Annalise and Andy and Waseem were all gone.

"Yours is the middle tent." Hooman's whisper sounded right behind her. "I'll be in the next one over if you want to talk."

Katie nodded and hurried over to her new tent. She yanked up on the zipper and plunged inside. As she crawled back into the shielding darkness, her hand brushed against something soft. She pulled out her flashlight and flipped it on. There, sitting in the middle of the floor, was a neat stack of Annalise's clothes. Katie fumbled with the switch of the flashlight as warm tears flooded her eyes.

Nick shoveled down his *halva puri* breakfast without pausing long enough to taste it. They had a ton of prospecting to do, and the day was heating up rapidly. He looked around the camp table at the circle of long faces surrounding him. Annalise hadn't touched her breakfast. Even Waseem seemed to be down. He'd never seen them like this. They were usually full of jokes and mischief—even early in the morning. Maybe they missed her too.

"So . . . want us to pack up the tents after dishes?" Karl asked through a mouthful of curry.

"What?" Nick looked back at his senior grad student.

"Want us to pack up the tents?"

"No, didn't I mention it?" Nick looked across the table at Ahamed. "We're going to look around for a while. Who knows when we'll get another chance to search in Iraq again."

"And we should not forget the soldiers," Ahamed added. "The more time we delay, the less likely they are still to be waiting for us.

Right, Nick?" He nodded back at Nick with that annoying half smile of his.

Nick shrugged and carried his dishes over to the dishpan. "We'll go out on the first run in half an hour. Make sure you have plenty of water." He walked back to his tent and ducked inside. Finally, a chance for a little privacy. He zipped the door up and pulled the phone out of his pack. Punching in Katie's number from memory, he scooted to the back of the tent and listened as it rang.

"Hello?" Dietrich Fischer's gruff voice sounded over the phone, making him jump.

Fischer? Nick tried to think of a legitimate excuse for calling Katie. Something that wouldn't get her in trouble with her boss.

"Hello? This is Dietrich Fischer."

"Hi, Dietrich, this is Nick Murad."

Silence.

"Listen, I was hoping to talk to Dr. James about some . . . equipment one of my students loaned her."

"Katie has your equipment?"

"Not mine. One of my students'. May I speak to her?"

"She already is out in the field. What is the equipment, and I will tell her?"

"I'd rather discuss it with her in private."

"What, so now it is private equipment?"

"Just tell her I called, okay? She can call me back on my satellite phone. She has my number."

"I'll tell her," Dietrich said. "But she is very nervous talking to strangers. I doubt very much she'll talk to you—even if you should call to her again."

"I'm sure if you tell her—"

The connection ended with a click.

Beautiful. Nick tossed the phone at his pack. Now if he called again, Dietrich could just say Katie didn't want to talk to him. He'd already established his excuse. Something told him Dietrich was the kind of professor who enjoyed making life miserable for his students.

❯❯

"This is insane!" Katie slammed her pack down on the camp table. "We already found what we were looking for. We're not going to find anything else!"

"All I ask is you should go out and try. This is asking so much?" Dietrich raised his arms in an awkward shrug. "After I pay all this money for you to be here, now you do not like to search anymore?" His mouth dropped open. He actually looked hurt.

Katie softened her tone. "I searched all yesterday and all the day before. I found a *Nursallia* and a *Paleobalistum* fish, but you keep saying they're not good enough. You're not going to be happy with anything short of a miracle."

"And this is why you quit now?" Dietrich shook his head. "After our discussion with Nielsen, I thought maybe you believe in these miracles. Or did you consider maybe his book is right?"

Katie caught her breath. This wasn't the time. "I'm just saying . . . maybe you need to accept the fact that the grant isn't going to be renewed. There will be other grants. You've got plenty of time."

"Of course I have time!" Dietrich barked. "You are the one what doesn't have the time. I have always my professor chair, but you . . ." He spread his hands wide. "If I have no money to pay you and Hooman, what can I do? Especially if you refuse to work even to save yourself."

"Okay, okay . . ." Katie grabbed her backpack and slung it over her shoulder. "I'm going already. But don't be disappointed if I don't come back with the find of the century. Paleontology just doesn't work that way."

"Make sure to look to the deepest strata," Dietrich called after her. "We want an older whale. More transitional."

"You want fries with that?" Katie muttered under her breath as she stalked out into the desert. Dietrich could be so infuriating. She was almost looking forward to him not getting his grant renewed—even if it meant never being able to work in paleontology again. Even Ronald McDonald would be a better boss than Dietrich. At least Ronald was *supposed* to be a clown.

She marched across the sand and headed for the outlet of a deep channel cut into the rock by centuries of winter storms. Maybe if she went back to Nick and explained her situation . . . Even being an eternal postdoc would be better than flipping burgers. Especially being a postdoc for Nick.

Nick Murad . . . The heaviness in her chest became a knot in the pit of her stomach. He'd been gone three days, and he hadn't even bothered to call—not that she'd expected a prolonged good-bye or anything, but still, would an explanation have hurt him so much? She sank down onto a rock in the shade of the wadi's southern wall. He was probably already back in Pakistan, working on his next find, flirting with the next paleontologist to come across his path. He'd probably forgotten all about her. She was his competitor, after all. Of course he was going to feign an interest in her. Anything to give him an advantage. It was telling that they'd talked more on the phone while they were racing to find the whale than they had since she'd found it. It was the whale he'd been interested in, not her.

Katie let out a sigh and slumped over to rest her forehead on the palms of her hands. *Okay, God. What now? My life feels like one huge dead end. How long am I supposed to keep on looking?* She pushed herself to her feet and pulled one of the water bottles out of her pack.

Then she noticed it. A pale gray rock right in the middle of a bed of smooth rocks. It was a different shade than all the other rocks. It must have been washed down from higher up in the . . .

A light brown spot caught her eye. It couldn't be. Her heart froze in her chest. She dropped onto her knees and lifted the large chunk of rock with trembling hands. It was part of a tooth—and a mandible! Her pulse beat and pounded against her brain. *The curve of the jaw . . . Reduced molars . . . Too big to be human . . .* The dry streambed around her rocked and tipped like it was still full of running water. She sank to the ground, cradling the rock in both arms. Could it really be possible? It was way older than *Homo sapiens*; it had to be. But an ancient hominid—in Iraq? It was too amazing to believe.

Katie sat up and set the rock carefully back on the ground. She shouldn't have touched it. Not without a video camera to record it.

She jumped to her feet, took a step toward camp, and then turned around again. What was she thinking? She dumped the contents of her pack out on the ground. A GPS reading, the time, orientation, surroundings . . . Her hands were shaking so badly she could barely write in her notebook. A hominid fossil! She was a *finder* now. Like Donald Johanson, Richard Leakey, Raymond Dart . . . Her name would make the textbooks. They'd write about her expedition. About what she was doing right now! Suddenly self-conscious, she misspelled her own name on the yellow tape marker. Katie Jams—the name said it all. She staked the tape into the ground without correcting it. It would just add to the story. Her story.

Dumping everything back into her pack, she stepped away from her find to take in its surroundings. No more gray rocks in sight. Maybe further up the wadi? She turned and started to walk toward the side of the gulley, but she couldn't force herself to leave the fossil. She couldn't even stand to turn her back on it. What if someone stumbled across it while she wasn't looking? Or worse, what if Dietrich's new guards turned out to be just like the last guards? She cast a quick glance behind her and knelt down in front of the small gray stone. *Easy* . . . She lifted it gently from the ground. Then, hugging it to her chest, she made her way cautiously back to the camp.

Hooman and Wayne were hard at work on the whale extraction when she arrived. She made a wide circle around them, searching all the while for the guards. They were probably napping in their tent. She couldn't see Dietrich either. Maybe he was having a slumber party with the guards.

She crept across the compound, tiptoed over to her tent, and gently set the fossil inside. Then, running back across the camp, she searched the trucks for weapons. Good, the guards were as sloppy as they were lazy. She found two assault rifles, one on the backseat and one on the front. She hid one of the rifles in the bed of the supply truck and checked the other for ammunition. Twenty-four rounds. Hopefully that would be two dozen more than she needed.

Okay . . . Katie's heart was pounding again. One, two, three . . . "Wah-hooooo!" She shouted at the top of her lungs and ran up to

Dietrich's tent. "Everybody, get out here quick! I found something!" Her excitement felt forced and artificial. It would have been much easier to pretend she was excited if she hadn't been so excited for real. It was her big find. Why did she even have to pretend?

Dietrich and the guards came clambering out of their tents. Dietrich's thinning hair was standing out all over his head in long cottony whips. "Katie, what is this? What is going on?"

"I found something. Something huge!" Katie shouted and pointed in the direction of the canyon with her rifle. "Over there at the mouth of the big wadi. I can't believe it. We were sitting practically on top of it!"

Either the guards were all excellent actors or they really weren't interested. Three of them turned drowsily and crawled back into their tent. The other two stumbled over to the camp table and started foraging for food. They didn't even notice she was holding one of their rifles.

"Big? How big? What is it?" Dietrich stammered. "No, you must show me, of course. But how far is it? Is it a whale? A very much older whale?"

"Much better than a whale." Katie beamed. "I can't tell for sure yet, but it could be really big. Lucy big! The Taung child big!"

Dietrich just stood there, staring off into space like a shined deer.

"Dietrich, did you hear me?" Katie pushed on his shoulder. "Forget about saving your puny little grant. This is big enough to get a real grant. Real money!"

"Hey, what's the big fuss?" Wayne came jogging up with Hooman close behind. "Find another meteorite?"

"Come here!" Katie led the group to her tent and handed Wayne the rifle. "Careful. It's loaded." She stooped and unzipped the tent. Then, holding her breath, she reached inside. For a brief, heart-freezing second, she didn't see the rock against the gray canvas floor. Then it was there, in all its understated glory.

She pulled it out and turned the fossil toward the group with a flourish. At first there were only looks of confusion, concentration.

Then Wayne's mouth dropped open. "That ain't . . . You don't seriously believe . . ." He looked up at Katie. "Is that what I think it is?"

Katie turned to Dietrich. Still the deer-in-the-headlights stare. "Hooman?"

"It's part of a jawbone, right?"

Katie nodded. "Note the size of the molar, the angular curve of the jaw . . ."

"A . . . *human* jawbone?"

"Depends on your definition of human."

"Woo-hoo!" Hooman grabbed Wayne and started jumping up and down.

Katie's hands started shaking. She turned and set the fossil back in the tent as convulsive laughter came bubbling out of her. Tears streamed down her face. Then Hooman was jumping up and down with her. Wayne and Hooman were hugging her. Everybody was hugging everybody. It was finally real now. She'd finally found something big.

Meaty arms closed around her and pulled her into a smelly embrace. Dietrich's face leaned in close to hers. "I told you to keep searching. Didn't I told you? I knew if you just kept looking with those excellent kaleidoscope eyes . . . I knew it!"

Katie stiffened and pulled suddenly away. The guards! They'd left the camp table. She should have known it was too good to be true. She took the rifle from Wayne and made for the guards' tent at a low crouch. Reaching out with her left hand, she slowly lifted up on the zipper. One inch, two inches . . . She dropped onto the hot sand and peered in through the tiny gap. The five men were stretched out on the floor—sleeping like babies.

A laugh sounded from the team. Katie picked herself up off the ground and brushed the sand off her clothes before walking back to join the group.

"Is okay, Katie. These guards are safe." Dietrich was still laughing. "I am not so stupid as maybe you think. I hired them this time from the *other* minister."

Katie nodded uncertainly.

"So, boss, what do we do now?" Hooman was looking to her.

"We get busy," Katie said. "We have to be out of here in twenty-two days. And now, in addition to finishing the whale extraction, we have to search for the rest of that hominid. I found the mandible in the middle of a dry streambed. Flash floods could have carried it miles away from its point of origin. And who knows how many pieces the rock might have broken into during the process?"

"I am sure when the ministers hear our amazing discovery, they will extend to us a long time in Iraq to study our find," Dietrich said as he walked over to his tent. "You will call to them, Katie? I understand the ministers are most exciting to be talking to you." He laughed again as he lowered himself awkwardly to the ground and crawled inside his tent. "Lucy and the sky with diamonds!" He bellowed above the roar of the generators. "Lucy and the sky with diamonds. Oooh. Oooh."

Katie and Hooman exchanged amused smiles. Dietrich singing? She'd never seen him so happy. And for him to sing the song Johanson's team had played after discovering Lucy—that had to mean he agreed with her. She'd found something big. Something huge!

". . . da-da-da da da-da da past the flowers that grow so incredibly high . . ." Dietrich finally crawled back out of his tent and heaved himself onto his feet. "Here, call to the ministers." He held the satellite phone out to her. "Tell them we need a lab at Baghdad University. Many months to study the find."

Katie took the phone and dialed the ministers' number. A man with a gravelly voice answered in Arabic.

"Hello," Katie said. "Do you speak English?"

"Yes," the man rumbled in a heavy Iraqi accent. "This is Department of Antiquities and Heritage. Ministers' office. Who would you like to speak?"

"Hi, this is Dr. Katie James. I need to talk to either Khaleed Talibani or Ameen Hamady, please. It's very important."

"The ministers are meeting now. You would like to take a message?"

"How about Minister Al-Jaza'iri? Is he free?"

"Al-Jaza'iri is meeting with Hamady and Talibani."

"Could you just tell them Katie James is calling? I'm sure they'll want to talk to me."

There was a long delay.

"Hello, Katie James! I am happy to talk again to you." The short minister sounded like he was in the middle of a big cave.

"Hi, Minister Talibani. It's good to talk to you, too. I wanted to let you know we found something."

"The whale, yes. Dr. Fischer already has informed us. You will bring it back to our museum soon?"

"Yes, we should have it out within the next five days. But I wanted to let you know we found something else as well—something even bigger."

"Bigger than a whale?" The voice was Hamady's.

"Hello, Minister Hamady. I should have said more important. We found an extremely old hominid fossil. Its location alone makes it an important find, but if it's as old as I think it is, it could be one of the biggest discoveries of the century."

"A hominid fossil?" Talibani asked. "That would be a fossil of a . . . human?"

"A prehuman."

"No! This will not be tolerated!" An angry voice echoed on the other end of the phone. "Absolutely not!"

"I'm sorry," Katie faltered. "Who is this?"

"A whale was bad enough—but a human! I will not allow this materialist propaganda inside our museum!"

"Hello . . . Is Minister Talibani still there?" Katie asked.

"This is Khaleed. I'm sorry, Katie, but your announcement is a big surprise to Minister Al-Jaza'iri. A big surprise to us all. An extinct whale harms nobody, but we were not expecting you to bring back . . . human remains. Surely you understand, given the current situation of our country, why this would not be a good thing—"

"Not a good thing?" Al-Jaza'iri's shout drowned out Talibani. "It is disaster! Every museum in the country will be bombed. The whole country will be in flames!"

The short minister said something in Arabic. Al-Jaza'iri yelled something back and then the phone was buzzing with angry Arabic voices.

"Hello!" Katie shouted over the voices. "I'm still here. May I make a suggestion?"

It took several seconds for the argument to die down. "Yes, Katie, please. What is your suggestion?"

"This is a very important find. The analysis will take months— years. Why don't you let us take the fossil back to the United States? By the time we're finished studying it, maybe things here will have settled down a little."

"Impossible! Absolutely not!"

"I'm sorry, Katie." The short minister's voice was solemn. "But this time I have to agree with Minister Al-Jaza'iri. What's found in Iraq must stay in Iraq. How can we stand against the smuggling and looting if we ourselves allow artifacts to be taken secretly out of the country?"

"Then you'll have to give us more time. We can't characterize the fossil in only twenty-two days. Give us at least a semester. We could do the work at Baghdad University."

"I'm sorry. My colleagues and I will discuss this, but I'm afraid more time is out of the question. Once Ramadan starts, we will no longer be in a position to guarantee your safety."

"But you have to at least . . ."

"I'm sorry, Katie," the short minister interrupted. "I understand how you would like to study this unexpected fossil, but perhaps it would be best to focus your attention on the whale."

"But the whale isn't nearly as important as the hominid—"

"Don't worry. We will discuss this. Perhaps you can study this new fossil another time. Thank you for calling with this new information. We must talk now. Good-bye."

"Wait!" Katie shouted as the connection went dead. She punched in the ministers' number again and spoke to the receptionist, but this time he wouldn't let her through.

"The ministers are meeting now. They will call you when they are agreed." He spoke slowly as if reading a cue card and then hung up.

Katie looked up at the others. Dietrich was pacing back and forth behind her; his face was red. Veins bulged at his temples. He looked like he was about to have a heart attack.

"I take it you heard?" Katie asked.

"They can't do this," the big man sputtered. "It's our fossil! We can do with it whatever we want!"

"As long as we don't want to study it or take it out of the country," Katie murmured.

"Maybe we can sneak it out?" Wayne suggested.

"That's fine as long as you don't ever want to do another dig outside the United States."

"So? We just wait until next year to study it," Hooman said. "What's the big deal?"

Everyone stared at the young grad student. Finally Katie voiced what everyone had to be thinking. "If they don't want the fossil at a government museum or university, I doubt very much a mosque will take it. Even if they allow us to come back next year, we may find there's no fossil left to be studied."

Chapter 17

*B*ILL CHECKED HIS WATCH AND GROANED. 5:10. Ten minutes after quitting time. Time for him to get started. Grabbing the metal bars on either side of the handicapped restroom stall, he hoisted himself to his feet with a groan loud enough to be heard all the way down the hallway of the ministry building. He threw in a contented sigh for good measure and flushed the toilet. One more flush just to add to the mystique. People expected big things from big men. If there were any chuckling guards out in the hallway, he didn't want to disappoint.

He snapped back the lock of the stall door and pushed it open with a satisfying squeak. Then, washing his hands, he splashed cold water on his face and hair and checked his reflection in the mirror. Perfect. He looked almost as sick as he felt. He moved painfully to the bathroom door and pushed out into the hallway. A briefcase-toting Iraqi man stared at him as he walked by. Two uniformed guards were laughing. Bill ignored them and started limping toward the stairs. He was the elephant on the coffee table. As long as he didn't surprise anyone, he'd be completely invisible.

The guards jabbered something at him in Arabic. He shrugged at them and started up the stairs, pausing to catch his breath at each step. The guards were behind him now. He could hear the hesitation in their voices. He wasn't going anywhere fast. They had plenty of time to decide what to do. To get used to him. To rationalize their way out of reacting. Bill grinned as they gave up and walked back down the hallway. He was a master of not being worth the trouble.

He wheezed and groaned his way painfully up the stairs. Minister Al-Jaza'iri would be long gone by now. He'd been watching the ministry building for over a week, and Al-Jaza'iri had never once stayed past quitting time. Usually he was out of the building by 4 p.m.

After telling Murdock about the bearded guard's visit to the ministry building, his boss had finally relented and given him permission to bug the offices of the three ministers. "Permission to pursue a course of electronic surveillance" was the official phrase—just ambiguous enough for him to claim he'd thought he'd been given permission and still leave Murdock with enough wiggle room to claim he'd expected proper procedures to be followed.

By the time he reached the top of the stairs, Bill was no longer *pretending* to be out of breath. He leaned against the wall a few minutes before limping down the hallway that led to the offices of the three ministers. Fortunately the ministers' assistant wasn't at his desk. Bill squeezed past the sixties-style, battleship-gray desk and made for Al-Jaza'iri's door. This was the tricky part. He pulled his wallet out of his pocket and removed two slender picks with adjustable hinged tips. Aside from playing around last night with the lock on his hotel door, he hadn't done this in the field since . . . okay, he'd never actually done it in the field. And even back in the days when they'd forced him to practice, he'd never been any good at it. He inserted the pick in the lock and scraped it across the internal mechanism. Yup. It sounded scrapey inside. How the blazes was that supposed to tell him anything?

He jabbed the pick deep into the keyhole and yanked hard on the doorknob. The knob turned smoothly and the door swung open. Had he actually done it, or had the door been unlocked to begin with? He scooted inside and shut the door behind him. Whether he'd done it or not, his official report was going to say the door was already unlocked. No point giving Murdock any more stupid ideas.

Bill crossed the cluttered office and squeezed behind the antique mission-style desk to look for a good hiding place. He pulled a ziplock Baggie out of his pocket and removed one of the tiny microtransmitters. Russia, vintage late nineties. They didn't have anywhere near the range or clarity of the American transmitters, but they had one huge advantage: it didn't matter whether they were discovered or not. The last thing he wanted was to have to climb up all those stairs just to retrieve the little jobbers.

Supporting himself with a hand on the chair, he picked up the trash can and set it on the desk. The plastic liner looked like it hadn't been changed in forever. He pulled it out and inspected the inside of the metal can. Not nearly as nasty as he would have liked. He pulled out a Baggie full of brown, fuzzy, sugary crud and squeezed some into the inside corner of the can. Then, pressing one of the bugs into the sticky mess, he tied the trash bag into place and set the can back in its spot next to the desk. Perfect. Eventually some overachieving janitor would clean out the can and nobody would ever be the wiser.

Footsteps sounded in the outer office. Bill froze. The steps were heading his way. Had Al-Jaza'iri forgotten something? He scanned the room frantically. No place to hide. No place but . . .

A ring of keys jangled outside the door. He pulled the chair away from the desk and dropped onto his hands and knees. The door opened with a squeak as he crawled under the desk. His forehead hit the back of the leg space way too soon. What was he thinking? He hadn't been able to fit under a desk since he was three.

Tap, tap, tap . . . The footsteps were in the office now. The rattle and snap of something metal. A gun? Bill angled his head to the side and tried to crawl another few inches under the desk, but it was no use. The biggest, least attractive part of him was jutting way out into the room. He had to think of something, some kind of excuse. Earthquake? Taking cover from bomb blasts? Maybe he could wet his pants and pretend to be terrified people would notice.

The footsteps crossed the room and came to an abrupt stop. Behind him and to the right. Another metallic clank. Great. That about took care of the pants-wetting bit. How many inches of fat and muscle could a bullet penetrate? Why didn't the agency ever teach anything useful?

Suddenly the room was filled with an ear-shattering roar. Bill jumped, hitting his head hard against the top of the desk. This was nuts! He was an American! He didn't have to hide—not from any-body. He backed out from under the desk and staggered to his feet. "'Scuze me . . ." He did his best drunk American imitation. "Cud'ju tell me where . . ." He turned in a sloppy circle.

A man in a janitor's uniform stood there staring at him. In his hand was the handle of a seventies-style vacuum cleaner.

Nick hoisted a generator into the back of the truck and swiped an arm across his forehead. "Okay, everybody!" He pulled Karl's pack out of the supply truck and held it up for everyone to see. "All your packs and personal belongings go in the *lead* truck. We'll be driving straight to the airport. I'm not unpacking all three trucks."

He handed the pack to the grinning grad student and hurried back to the equipment truck to help Ahamed secure the last tent. Ahamed was humming a Pakistanized Elvis tune to himself.

"Happy to finally be going home, are we?"

Ahamed winched down the last cargo strap and looked up at his friend. "Of course I am happy. I have my wife and children waiting. But you . . ." Ahamed's brow furrowed. "Why do you not go back to USA with your students? What will be in Pakistan for you now?"

"Getting those whales out of the ground was the easy part," Nick said. "I still have the papers to finish."

"And what of the two weeks vacation you were to take?"

"I'm afraid this was it. Lucky for me I like camping." Nick forced a smile.

Ahamed shook his head. "You should call her."

"Who? Cindy?"

Ahamed just glared at him.

"Katie? I already did—three times. Dietrich Fischer keeps answering the phone. He's not going to let me talk to her."

"Even to say good-bye?"

Nick shrugged. "You know, he might be telling the truth. Did you ever think Katie might not want to talk to me?"

Another glare. This time his friend actually looked angry.

"Okay, okay. You don't believe me; I'll prove it to you." He walked back to the lead truck and climbed inside. Unplugging the phone from the charger, he punched in Katie's number.

The phone picked up on the first ring.

"Hello, Khaleed? What did he say?" It was Katie's voice.

"Katie!" Nick blurted into the phone. "This is Nick. I didn't think Dietrich was ever going to let me through to you."

"Um . . . yes, sir. Right. Just a minute. Let me get away from these generators."

"Katie?" Nick could hear movement on the other end of the phone. "Katie?"

"Hi, Nick. Sorry about that." Katie spoke in a hushed voice. "Too many oversize ears lazing about the camp. What did you mean—that part about Dietrich letting you through?"

"Your Dr. Fischer is worse than my mom. I assume he didn't tell you I called?"

"You called? When?" Nick couldn't tell whether she was incredulous or just angry.

"Three times actually—right after Dietrich kicked us out of our camp. Listen, I want to apologize for that. I waited as long as I could for you to come back, but Fischer's guards were so worked up I was afraid of what might happen if I stayed a second longer."

There was a brief pause. "So you called . . . and got Dietrich? You told him you wanted to talk to me?"

"At first he said you weren't there. Then he said you didn't want to talk to me."

"He lied." Now Katie really sounded angry. "He never even mentioned you'd called. All this time I thought you . . ."

Nick's brain buzzed at the emotion in her voice. There was a long silence as he waited for her to finish the thought.

"Nick . . ." Her voice was suddenly tight and controlled. "I just found something new—and I could really use your help."

"Sure. What did you find?"

"A hominid fossil. Four teeth and almost half of the lower jaw. We haven't run any tests, but I'm guessing it's 4 or 5 million years old."

"You're kidding me, right? An *Australopithecus* in Iraq?"

"Do I sound like I'm kidding?"

Nick hesitated. She wasn't laughing. "You're serious? You actually found an *Australopithecus*?"

Katie laughed. "It gets even better. It actually has a band of volcanic ash running through the matrix. We'll finally be able to get an accurate date!"

Nick heard what she was saying, but something wasn't right. "So what's the problem? Why aren't you screaming your head off?"

He could hear her breath catch. "The problem is the Iraqis. They don't want a hominid fossil at their university, and they won't give us time to study it. They want us out of here in twenty days, and I have a feeling the fossil won't be around if and when we're ever allowed to come back."

"But why? What about the Baghdad Natural History Museum? Surely they want it."

"The ministers wouldn't let them—even if the museum was willing to risk it. They're afraid it would touch off more rioting—more suicide bombings."

Nick considered this for a second. "They're probably right. But I don't see what I could do to help. The problem is religious not scientific."

"The problem is political," Katie said. "If we can get enough of the international scientific community behind us, we might be able to pressure the Iraqi government into letting us take the fossil out of the country. Dietrich wants us to do an accelerated letter with an initial characterization, but we only have twenty days and we don't have any equipment. He's trying to have a portable CT scanner flown in from France, but you already have one here; plus you're used to doing these characterizations. I read your first *Pakicetus* paper—it was the best analytical write-up I've ever seen."

"So you want to borrow my equipment?"

"No, I want you to help us. This time it will be a formal collaboration; you'll actually get credit."

"And Fischer is okay with this?"

"Not yet, but he will be. I promise you that. I'm the one who found the hominid fossil, and it's small enough I could easily unfind it."

Nick grinned. He'd love to be a fly on the wall for that confrontation.

"So what do you say? Can you help us?"

"Just a second." Nick poked his head out of the truck. "Ahamed!" He jumped out and ran over to where the guide was cinching down the last of the equipment. "Ahamed, an emergency has just come up. Can you take the kids to the airport and make sure they get on the plane okay?"

"What kind of an emergency?" The guide's eyes narrowed.

"I have the opportunity to analyze what could be a 4-million-year-old *Australopithecus.*"

Ahamed frowned and shook his head.

"I'd be working side by side with Katie!"

"And why should this make a difference?" His lips were pressed together in a tight line. He shook his head no, but his eyes danced with a resounding yes.

Katie chipped away at the sedimentary rock encasing the jawbone. "There you go, Eve. That feel better?" She whispered encouragement to her fossilized new best friend. "It looks much better."

A few more chips and she had exposed the whole top surface of the second premolar. It was unbelievably worn down. Even assuming a lot of sand in her diet, Eve must have lived to a considerable age. Katie tipped the rock toward the tripod-mounted video camera and angled the electric light to illuminate the top of the tooth. There; so much for posterity. She laid Eve back down on the table and started chipping away again.

"Katie!" Dietrich poked his head in through the entrance of her tent. "I talked already to Thomas Woodburne. He is agreeing to hold for us a spot in the next issue of *Science*—but we must send to him the article in nine days. Nine days, understand that? That's millions of scientists all around the world what will be reading it. The ministry will be impossible to destroying the fossil now!"

"That's great news."

"I'm calling next the president of the NAS! Thomas gave to me his private number. He used to teach with him at Princeton!" Dietrich pulled back out of the doorway, leaving the tent flaps hanging open.

"Lucy and the sky with diamonds. Lucy and the sky . . ." She listened as Dietrich bellowed his way across the camp. At least someone was happy. She wondered how happy he'd be in twenty days, when it was time to hand the fossil over to the ministers. The thought of anyone destroying such a valuable find made her physically ill. People got upset about the Taliban blowing up two-thousand-year-old Buddha statues, but it wasn't like the statues held the key to the mystery of man's origins. How could the ministers even consider "losing" such an important find?

"Katie, I got him!" Hooman pushed his way into the tent and froze in front of the video camera. "Sorry."

"It's okay." Katie suppressed a smile. "Who'd you get?"

"I finally found someone at the Baghdad University who's willing to talk to us. An American molecular biologist—he's there on sabbatical."

"And he didn't leave when the fighting started?" Katie was surprised. Apparently they weren't the only ones who didn't have any sense.

"He said he'd check around to see if anyone there can do radiometric dating for us." Hooman didn't look up from the camera as he talked. "He said he'd call me right back if he found anyone."

"Good. Let me know as soon as he calls. I've already got a couple of cinder samples ready to go."

"Okay." Hooman turned and ran back out of the tent.

"Make sure you close the . . ." She was too late. He was already halfway across the camp. Not that it made much difference. People had been popping in and out of the tent all morning. Either they had one more piece of news that couldn't wait or they just wanted to check on her progress. Dietrich was the worst. He'd hovered over her shoulder for a long, nerve-racking hour, groaning at every chip of sediment she'd removed, until she finally convinced him to start generating support for Eve's cause back in the U.S.

"He's here!" Hooman came skipping back into the tent. "Nick Murad is coming with his equipment!"

Katie turned off the light and video camera and followed Hooman outside. A white truck was tearing across the desert floor, bouncing and jostling at every bump.

"What does he think he's doing?" Katie spoke the question aloud. The other two trucks were way behind the first truck. Was it some kind of one-sided race?

The truck skidded to a halt at the edge of the camp. Nick flung the door open and leaped out into the heat, a rifle clutched in his right hand.

"Hey, Nick." Katie stepped forward self-consciously. "Thank you so much for coming. I can't tell you how much I . . ."

Nick turned his back on her—without so much as a nod or a token "how's it going?" Katie could feel her temper beginning to flare. If he was going to be such a jerk about it . . .

"They're coming!" He called back to her without taking his eyes off the trucks. "Alert your guards. We're going to need every gun you've got."

"Who's coming?" Katie scanned the area behind the other two trucks. "The rest of your team?"

"Those trucks aren't mine. They're full of Iraqi soldiers. My team's on its way to the airport."

"Wake up the guards!" Katie shouted to Hooman and ran to her tent to retrieve her rifle. By the time she got back to Nick, the trucks were less than two hundred yards away. At first she thought they'd slowed down, but then she realized they weren't moving at all.

"What are they doing?" She glanced up at Nick. He looked just as confused as she was.

"I don't know. I guess they're watching us. Waiting for us to make the first move."

"And what move is that?"

"I don't know."

Hooman came running up with five disheveled guards. "What's happening? Should I go get Wayne?"

"Just wait." Katie held up her hand to silence the guards as they took up positions behind Nick's truck. She turned back to Nick. "So where did they come from?"

"Out of a wadi about a mile and a half east of here. I think they've been watching your camp for some time now."

Katie considered this. She'd searched the area to the east the day before she found the fossil. She would have seen them for sure if they'd been there. But ever since then she'd been preoccupied with their new find. They could have parked right outside her tent and she wouldn't have noticed.

"Here we go," Nick called out in a hushed voice. The trucks were starting to move. Katie raised the rifle to her shoulder as the trucks slowly approached them. Finally they turned around in a wide, looping U-turn.

Katie followed them with her rifle until they disappeared out of sight. "Okay . . . That was weird." She lowered the rifle and looked up at Nick.

He nodded his agreement and smiled back at her. "So . . . thanks for the invitation. It's not every day I get to show up at a party with a full military escort."

"You're welcome."

They stood in silence for several awkward moments.

"So . . ." Katie forced an upbeat tone. "Are you ready to meet Eve?"

He quirked an eyebrow at her.

"Your date for the party." She started leading him back toward her tent. "I think you're really going to like her. She has the most amazing smile." She held back the flap of her tent for Nick to enter.

"Dr. Murad!" Dietrich's voice rang out from across the camp. "I didn't hear your arrival. Please. I must speak with you." Dietrich, red in the face and soaked with sweat, came huffing up to Nick. He held out his hand.

Nick glanced questioningly at Katie before shaking it.

"Before you visit our discovery, I must speak with you in private, please."

Katie shot a warning look at her adviser as he guided Nick over to the entrance of his tent. They'd made a deal! He'd already agreed to the collaboration. She paced furiously up and down in front of her tent. He'd been planning something all along. She should have realized it when he'd been so quick to agree. This was it! The pickax that broke the *Camposaurus*'s back. If he went back on his word now, she'd quit—just as soon as she finished up her work on Eve.

By the time Nick finally emerged from Dietrich's tent, Katie had worked herself up into a rage.

"I'm so sorry." She took him by the arm and pulled him into her tent. "I promise you: he agreed to the collaboration when I talked to him. He said your name would add credibility."

"It's okay. Dietrich was fine." Nick sounded dazed. "He just apologized for being so overprotective. Said he thought I was trying to steal away his star postdoc."

Katie stared at him, waiting for the real story. He was kidding, right? He had to be kidding. Oh, great. Now she'd paused too long. She had to say something. Anything. "And you're saying you weren't trying to steal me away?" She stuck out her lower lip in what she hoped would look like a childish pout.

Nick didn't respond. His jaw sagged open. His eyes looked glassy.

Great, now she'd crossed the line. "Nick, I'm sorry. I was just kidding." Katie stepped toward him, but he wouldn't look her in the eye.

"Nick?"

He leaned to the side and stared over her shoulder with wide eyes.

"It's *her*, isn't it?" she demanded in a petulant voice. "You guys are all alike. I get all dressed up in my nicest borrowed clothes and all you can do is stare at *her*. Okay, I'll introduce you!" She led him over to the makeshift lab bench. "Dr. Murad—" she flipped on the light—"I'd like you to meet Eve."

»

Something tickled at Nick's neck, sending shivers up and down his spine. Katie was leaning over his shoulder again. The soft perfume of her hair licked at his mind, distracting him from the plastic-encased Tablet PC in front of him.

The last three days working with her had been among the happiest of his life. The heat, the long hours, even the ubiquitous sand and grit—it had all felt like some kind of fairy-tale vacation. The fossil was truly an amazing find. The results from the CT scan they'd done had been breathtaking. So much fine detail—it was almost like working with a real bone. And the teeth . . . Two of the molars still seemed to be made of the original enamel! It boggled the mind—that the materials of the teeth could actually escape being replaced by all those minerals washing through the soil . . .

"What's wrong?" Katie's soft voice sounded in his ear. "You still don't like the wording of the discussion section?"

"What?" Nick turned and her hair brushed across his face. She pulled away and squatted down next to his chair. Her eyes were droopy, but even under the weight of all her fatigue, her face still seemed to glow. It was mesmerizing. Like some kind of powerful magnet, reaching down deep into his soul.

"Nick, wake up!"

Nick jerked back awake. "I'm okay. You ready to send off the paper now?"

Katie shook her head. "We should get some sleep. We can send it in the morning. It's almost 3 a.m."

"It won't be any better in the morning. We're still not going to have a date."

"I know. It's so frustrating!" Katie banged her forehead against an imaginary wall. "The first time in my life I've had a sample with a band of igneous rock in it, and I still can't get a date."

"Tell me about it." Nick grinned. "It's the story of my life."

"Yeah, right." Katie reached for one of the sealed Eppendorf tubes on the table and held it up to the light. The sample of compressed volcanic ash showed black in the translucent tip of the bullet-shaped tube. "We're so close. If only there were a radiometric dating lab in Baghdad."

"Wait a minute." Nick reached for the other tube. "I have a friend at Berkeley who would be happy to analyze the samples. Who says we can't overnight them?"

"The Iraqi government says. Two trucks full of soldiers—"

"But the only time the soldiers ever bother us is when we start up one of the trucks, right?"

"So what are you suggesting?" Katie asked. "We smuggle the samples out of the country? We walk all the way to Berkeley?"

"Why not?" Nick unplugged the satellite phone from his PC and started punching in numbers. "Only why walk when we can get Ahamed to pick us up halfway?"

Chapter 18

"*HELLO, THIS IS DR. KATIE JAMES.* I want to speak with Minister Khaleed Talibani please." Katie paced the length of the tent while the administrative assistant transferred her call.

"Hello, Katie. It is a pleasure to hear from you. How are you?" The short minister's voice sounded genuine enough, but he was a politician, after all. He could probably hold a pleasant conversation about slitting your throat with a knife.

"Khaleed, I need to know the truth. Did you send a group of soldiers to watch after us?"

"The guards Al-Jaza'iri sent with Dr. Fischer? What happened? Al-Jaza'iri selected them himself. He assured us they could be trusted completely."

"Not the guards. A group of soldiers riding in military trucks. They've surrounded our camp and won't let us out to do any more searching."

"The whale is in danger? They try to steal the whale?"

"I don't think so. They seem more interested in us than in our dig."

"I don't understand."

"So you're saying you don't know anything about the soldiers?" Katie demanded.

"Nothing at all. I assure you."

"Okay, I'm going to trust you. . . ." Katie didn't trust him, but if he'd sent the soldiers, she wouldn't be telling him anything he didn't already know. "The soldiers seem to be there to prevent us from leaving the camp."

"It is as I feared, then. Word has somehow leaked out about the human bones. Someone is afraid you will try to make it into another Denmark cartoon situation."

"Khaleed, listen to me. The fossil is an extremely important find. It *has* to be studied. It could add a lot to our understanding of human origins."

"But is it worth the stability of an entire country? Is it worth the risk to your life? Please, Katie, follow my advice and leave the fossil alone. Give it into the hands of the museum, and we will take care of it. It is the best idea for everybody."

Katie started to argue but decided against it. She now knew where the minister stood. There wasn't any point telegraphing her next move. "Thanks, Khaleed. You may be right. I'll let you know if anything else comes up."

She said good-bye and hung up the phone.

"Well? What'd he say?" Nick looked up from Eve's workbench.

"We've got to move fast." Katie strode out the door of the tent and jogged over to Nick's equipment truck. She could hear Nick following close behind.

"What? You think he sent the soldiers?"

"He said he didn't, but that doesn't mean much." She lifted a portable glove box out of the truck and checked it for damage. "Whether he sent them or not, he made his position on the fossil perfectly clear. As soon as we turn Eve in to the museum, he's going to have her destroyed."

Nick let out a long sigh. "So what do we do now?"

"We stick with the plan. We meet Ahamed tonight and find an overnighting service to mail the samples to Berkeley." Katie carried the glove box back to her tent and set it down next to the worktable.

Nick trailed alongside her. "And until then?"

"We study the heck out of Eve. Remember how you were joking about filling one of Eve's cavities?"

"You're actually considering drilling a tooth?" Nick looked around the tent in amazement. "This isn't exactly a sterile environment. You're not worried about damage, contamination?"

"When the fossil's going to be destroyed anyway?" Katie grabbed a spray bottle of ethanol and started spritzing the box. "I say we go for it. If Mary Schweitzer could find soft tissue in a 65-million-year-old *T. rex*, who knows what we'll find in a 3- to 5-million-year-old hominid tooth?"

"Okay. . . . It's your tooth. I'll see if we still have any EDTA." Nick ran back out of the tent.

Katie put on a pair of vinyl gloves and rinsed them off with ethanol. She'd just bent over to lift the glove box onto the table when she heard footsteps behind her. "Do we have enough?"

"Dr. James?" A heavily accented voice sounded at the entrance.

Katie whirled around. Two of their guards were standing in the opening to the tent. Both were carrying rifles. "Yes?" She glanced across the room. Her rifle was lying on the floor in the corner, right next to her canteen and backpack.

"The assistant minister of the government called to us right now. We are ordered to guard this rock." The men stepped into the tent and assumed positions on either side of the doorway.

"Great." Katie forced a smile. "I'm glad somebody is thinking about these things." The men eyed her suspiciously as she approached the worktable. "It's okay that we're studying it, right?"

"To study is okay. Just so the rock stays inside this tent."

Katie nodded. Ahamed would be waiting for them tonight. Their simple plan had suddenly become a lot more complicated.

Nick adjusted a knob on the microscope, focusing on another branched translucent tube. "Katie, look at this! This one has red blood cells in it! You can actually see them!" He shifted over to another cluster of tubules. More red blood cells. They were all over the place! Tiny, red, lozenge-shaped disks.

"Nick, come on! We're going to be late for our meeting!" Katie called to him from the back of the tent.

"We can't go now. This is soft tissue. *Real* soft tissue—not just elastic microfossils. Do you know what that means? There could be DNA. We could get a sequence!"

Footsteps came up behind him. He felt a hand on his shoulder, Katie's lips close to his ear. "Collect some tissue samples. We can take them with us too. But we can't miss our meeting with Ahamed."

Nick forced his eyes away from the microscope. "I know, but this is so huge. . . ." He caught a glimpse of one of the guards who had moved away from the entrance of the tent and was watching them with narrowed eyes. "Dietrich won't mind if we're late for our meeting." He spoke just loud enough for the guard to overhear. "It will be his fault anyway—for scheduling the meeting so late. This is ridiculous."

"Okay, take some samples, then!" Katie stepped away from him and opened a bag of sterile tubes. "But if Dietrich blows a gasket, don't blame me."

The guards seemed to relax a little. One of them moved back against the wall of the tent and sank down onto his haunches. Nick reached his hands back into the gloves of the glove box and started setting up to collect a sample. "Didn't Hooman say there was an American molecular biologist on sabbatical at Baggins University back in the States?" He caught Katie's eye and motioned toward the entrance of the tent.

"Yeah . . . I think he did mention something about that. . . ."

"If I had a question about PCR and automated sequencing work, do you think Hooman could put me in touch with him?"

"Maybe . . ." Katie gave a slight nod and headed for the tent exit. "But if I were you, I'd worry about being on time for our meeting with Dietrich."

"Tell him I'll be there in five minutes!" Nick shouted after her and turned his attention back to the glove box. Fingerprints, sweat, tiny droplets of saliva discharged into the air . . . human DNA was everywhere. No matter how careful he was, he'd never be able to avoid claims of contamination—especially when working under these primitive conditions. But if Katie was right, if they were really going to destroy the fossil, he had no choice but to try.

Even working as fast as he could, it took over an hour for him to collect two samples and seal them in sterile tubes. He cleaned up the worktable slowly, waiting for Katie to appear at the doorway for the twentieth time.

"You about done?"

Quickly, while the guards were distracted, Nick dropped the samples into his pants pocket. "All finished. Are they still meeting?" He stepped toward Katie, but one of the guards blocked his way. Nick tried to look unconcerned as the other guard walked over to the table and checked the fossil. He said something in Arabic. Apparently he was satisfied, because the guard at the entrance stepped aside and let Nick follow Katie outside.

"Did you get them?" she whispered to him as soon as they'd gotten a few yards away.

Nick nodded and tapped his pocket. "And you've got the number of the guy at Baghdad University?"

Katie led him over to the supply truck and pulled out a plastic thermos bottle. "I got the number, but if we're going to wait around long enough to give him the samples, we won't be getting back until late tomorrow afternoon. We'll need a cover story; otherwise the guards might sound the alarm."

"Leave a note for Fischer. Tell him we're going out on an expedition to find more pieces of Eve—"

"Why don't you tell him in person?" Dietrich's voice sounded behind the supply truck.

Nick spun around. A shadowy figure stepped out from behind the truck. He was carrying a roll of toilet paper.

"Dietrich!" Katie hurried over to her boss. "We need you to tell everyone we'll be out all tomorrow on another search."

"And where will you really be?"

"We'll be—" Katie looked back at Nick— "mailing cinder samples back to the States for radiometric dating."

Nick nodded. "Plus we'll be taking two other samples to Baghdad for analysis. Today we tried Schweitzer's demineralization technique and found soft tissue—after only ten hours exposure to EDTA. If we can get a sequence—"

"Soft tissue! Are you sure?" Dietrich was practically jumping up and down. "I knew it. I knew it was special. If we could get sequence . . . Maybe even the president will intervene for us!"

"Whoa. . . . Calm down," Katie said. "First we have to get the samples past the soldiers. We need you to tell everyone we're off searching for more fossils."

"Wayne can say that." Fischer waved aside Katie's suggestion. "I must go to Baghdad with you. I have important connections—"

"It's too dangerous," Nick interrupted. "We'll have to crawl on our bellies past armed soldiers. We need you here."

"Nonsense. I am used to crawling on my belly. I write grant applications every year."

"This isn't a joke!" Nick looked to Katie. Maybe she could talk some sense into him.

"Dietrich . . ." Katie put a hand on his shoulder. "Nick's right. We need you to stay here. The guards would never believe the three of us would leave Wayne and Hooman alone while we—"

"No more talk," Dietrich said. "I am going to Baghdad. On this my mind cannot be moved. Either I go, or nobody goes."

Dietrich's wheezing gasps broke the stillness of the cool desert night. He sounded like an asthmatic walrus clomping across a rocky beach. No matter how clear the area was, he always managed to find a hole to stumble over or a rock to kick.

"Quiet!" Katie whispered back at him. "We're in the danger zone." She stopped and made them all sit down to give Dietrich a chance to catch his breath. If their footprints were any indication, the soldiers had been confining their patrol to an area between three hundred and eight hundred yards away from camp. If a soldier came anywhere near them, he'd be able to hear Dietrich's breathing—whether he could see them or not.

Nick leaned in close to her. "Shouldn't we keep moving?"

"You want to carry him if he passes out?" she whispered.

He shook his head slowly, the pale moonlight sparkling in his eyes.

Katie rose to her knees and searched the floor of the desert in every direction. As far as she could see, everything looked clear. There was a wadi about a hundred yards ahead of them, however. Almost anything could be waiting for them there.

"Okay, let's keep going." Katie stood up and helped Nick hoist Dietrich onto his feet. "Only a mile and a half to go." She turned and started picking her way across a strip of hard-packed sand, angling as far to the left of the wadi as she could afford to go. The closer she got to the wadi, the louder Dietrich's breathing sounded.

What was that? She angled farther away from the wadi. Dietrich's breathing was a raging storm. She walked faster. They needed to put more distance between themselves and the—

Smack! Dietrich swore under his breath as he tripped over another rock. Katie pressed a hand over his mouth. A noise sounded over by the wadi. She pulled Dietrich down onto the ground. "Quiet," she murmured into his ear. "Someone's coming. Don't even breathe!"

She scanned the area. There he was—a darker shadow moving against the stippled night sky. Flattening herself to the ground, Katie reached a hand back to her waist and unclipped the strap of her canteen. The figure was moving straight toward them now. Running at a low crouch. The jutting outline of a long rifle barrel swept across the stars with every step he took.

Slowly, careful not to make the tiniest scrape of sound, Katie pushed herself onto her hands and knees and uncoiled the canteen from around her waist. He was only twenty yards away. He had to see them. If he started shooting now, there'd be nothing she could do.

She crawled stealthily forward to meet him, dragging the trailing canteen across the ground. The man slowed to a walk. He was aiming his rifle straight at her. One more step, another one, almost in striking distance . . .

"Ahamed?" Nick's whisper sounded behind her. "Katie, no!"

Katie hesitated as the man lowered his gun.

"*Accha!* Nick, is that you?" Relief washed through Katie as she recognized the Pakistani's voice. "I thought they capture you. And you are here all this time? Sleeping in the middle of the desert?"

"Sorry we're late." Katie climbed onto her feet. "I couldn't drag your friend here away from Eve."

"Now another woman?" Ahamed let out an exasperated sigh. "The man is *paagal* crazy, sick in the head for women!"

Chapter 19

*L*IGHT FROM THE RISING SUN glinted on the truck's windshield. Nick shifted in his seat to face away from the piercing light. They'd driven all through the night and he was exhausted. It had taken only five hours to get to Baghdad, but then they'd had to find the university, then the College of Sciences building. . . . If he was going to get any sleep before their 8 a.m. meeting with the molecular biologist, he was going to have to get it now.

"That may be the professor." Ahamed's voice roused him just as he was starting to get settled. Nick straightened in his seat. An older man in a green polo shirt and khaki pants was walking across the parking lot with a laptop computer bag. There was something distinctly American about the way the man moved. He was almost certainly their man.

"Okay, nap time's over!" Nick called to the backseat. Katie was slumped against her door, a lock of dark hair protruding from the corner of her mouth. She looked so serene, so innocent and carefree. . . . He hated to wake her. "Katie . . ." He spoke in a soft voice. "Dr. Littman is here. Time to get up." He watched her until she started stirring and then turned quickly away.

"What's going on? Is it time?" She sounded like a little girl.

"We walked too far last night!" Dietrich announced from the back. A foot or a knee shoved against the seat and into Nick's back. "My shoes are no longer fitting on my feet."

"Come on." Nick reached for the door. "Let's go. The sooner we get this over with, the sooner we can get back to the fossil. I don't like the idea of leaving it with the ministers' guards any longer than we have to."

"You don't have it with you?" Ahamed turned on Nick in surprise. "I thought the whole reason of coming was to learn a date for the fossil."

"We brought two different samples." Nick checked the backseat to make sure they still had the thermos with four Eppendorf tubes. "Volcanic ash from the rock and soft tissue from inside a tooth."

"And this soft tissue allows you to date the fossil? This is why we never did this radiometric dating on our whales?"

"We didn't get dates for our whales because there wasn't any nearby volcanic ash," Nick said. "Fossils can't be dated directly, nor can sedimentary rock. Age has to be inferred based on the strata they're found in."

Ahamed nodded uncertainly.

"The matrix around Eve contains a small band of volcanic ash. By measuring the ratios of isotopes such as uranium and lead or potassium and argon in the cinders, my friend at Berkeley should be able to tell us how long ago that volcano erupted."

Nick got out of the truck and stretched the burning pain out of his lower back. Katie had gotten extremely lucky. The odds that such a small sample would contain a band of volcanic ash were already in the range of a billion to one, but to find soft tissue as well? The odds were completely off the charts. Now that he stopped to think about it, the probability that they'd be able to get a DNA sequence was off the charts as well. DNA degraded far too quickly—especially if exposed to radiation from the sun. But then so was the probability of finding intact red blood cells in a 3-million-year-old hominid fossil. Or, for that matter, finding red blood cells in a 65-million-year-old *T. rex* fossil. When Mary Schweitzer made that discovery, someone had asked her why nobody had found soft tissue in dinosaur fossils before. She'd said nobody thought they would find anything, so they never bothered to look.

If they did manage to get a partial sequence . . . It was too staggering to even imagine. A 3-million-year-old DNA sequence! It would be *Jurassic Park* all over again. Even better, since mutations occurred at a known, fixed rate, they could compare Eve's DNA sequence with the modern *Homo sapiens* sequence and, based on the number of mutations that had occurred, calculate the age of the fossil—completely independent of the radiometric dating! As far as he knew, it was the only fossil ever discovered that had the possibility of being dated in two different ways. Its importance to science couldn't be exaggerated.

Dietrich finally opened the door of the truck and stepped gingerly out onto the pavement on feet that strained the limits of his already loosened shoelaces.

"Okay, let's hurry or we'll be late." Nick led the group across the parking lot to the rambling, two-story sciences building. It looked more like a parking garage than a modern research facility. Nick wondered whether Dr. Littman would even have a PCR instrument, much less one of the new, high-speed automatic sequencing machines. He pictured a group of bedouins cycling through the PCR temperature steps manually, using a crude water bath. If Littman didn't have the right equipment, they'd just have to send the soft tissue samples along with the volcanic ash to Brian Gibson at Berkeley. Even if Littman *did* have the right equipment, it was probably a good idea to send one of the soft tissue samples to the States. People were going to be skeptical if they got a sequence. Independent corroboration would be expected.

The entrance to the biology department was halfway around the back of the building. Above the official blue and white Dept. of Biology sign, a crude *apatosaurus* was hand-painted in white against the weathered concrete. At least the Iraqis were willing to admit dinosaurs had existed. For a long time fundamentalist Muslims in Pakistan had taught that dinosaurs were lies perpetrated by the evil materialist West. Now they just thought the dinosaurs had lived at the same time as man and were destroyed in some kind of Noah's-ark-type flood.

"Listen," Nick called to the trailing group, "we have to get back to camp, so let's make this as quick as possible. We'll check out their facilities. If they have decent equipment, we'll leave them one of the soft tissue samples; otherwise we'll send both to Berkeley along with the volcanic ash. Okay? Quick in and quick out."

"We can't leave without using the bathroom," Katie said. "Think of it. Running water. I have to at least wash my hair."

Nick shook his head. "It's too risky. What will it look like if we go back to camp with clean hair? They'll never believe we were out on a survey."

"I'll wear a hat. The guards won't even notice."

"So you're willing to risk the find of the century just to have clean hair?"

Katie's brow furrowed for a few seconds. "Absolutely. We've been in the desert three weeks. For a shower I'd risk just about anything."

Nick smiled. "Okay, we check out the equipment, wash up, and *then* hit the road." He led them up a flight of open-air stairs just outside the biology department entrance.

The man in the green polo shirt was waiting for them just inside the door. "Welcome!" He threw the door open, beaming at them with an impossibly wide smile. "Come in, come in!" He ushered them into a cool, air-conditioned hallway. "Nick Murad!" He wrapped Nick's hand in both of his and pumped it up and down. "It's so good to meet you."

"It's good to—"

"And you must be Katie James!" The man turned to Katie and eagerly took her hand. "I've been reading about you on the Internet. Amazing stories, simply amazing. Oh! And Dietrich Fischer! I can't tell you what a privilege it is to meet you all. I'm so glad you could come." He shook Dietrich's hand and turned to Ahamed. "I'm Jerry Littman. . . ."

"I'm sorry. This is my associate Ahamed Asif." Nick stepped to Ahamed's side as Littman shook his hand.

"Asif—you're from Pakistan? *Accha!* Excellent! It's an honor to meet you. *Aap ko mil kar bahut khushi hooee hae.* Thank you so much for coming." Littman led them down a cluttered hallway and into a well-lit lab. The bench tops along the walls were filled with instruments—almost all of them brand-new. Some of them were still inside their boxes.

"Please forgive the mess." Littman swept a hand to take in the large room. "The university is so eager to catch up with the biotechnology revolution, we can't keep up with all the equipment they're buying. It's a nice problem to have, but I keep telling them the problem is training. There just aren't enough of us to go around. Isn't that right, Yassin?"

The young Iraqi who was sitting behind the computer monitor of a UV-VIS instrument stood up and nodded to the visitors with a shy grin. His eyes lingered on Katie for several seconds before turning back to his adviser.

"Yassin is studying single-nucleotide polymorphism in mice." The young grad student's face lit up as Littman put a hand on his shoulder. "He has one of the sharpest and most intuitive minds I've ever encountered. And Nabon is here somewhere." Littman looked quickly around the large lab. "He's just gotten back the most interesting results." He said something to Yassin in Arabic.

The student responded with something that sounded like "computer camera" and ran out of the room. Nick listened as the sound of his footsteps disappeared down the hallway. He'd never seen such an enthusiastic student—especially not in the Middle East. Littman's energy seemed to have rubbed off on him.

"Yassin will get him. In the meantime, I could show you some of the projects one of my other students is working on. . . ."

"Actually, we're in a big hurry. We . . ." Nick looked back at Katie, but her attention was focused on a modern PCR cycler in the corner. "We're actually in a bit of trouble." Nick decided he had to trust Littman. "Our sample—" he pointed to the thermos in Katie's hand—"comes from an extremely old hominid fossil. The ministers in the Department of Antiquities aren't too happy about our find, and we're practically under house arrest out in the middle of the Al Muthanna desert. We had to slip away from our guards in order to drive up here, and if we're not back soon, it could cause trouble."

"Of course." Littman nodded understandingly. "Is there anything I can do for you? Besides trying to get a sequence, which of course I'm delighted to do."

"We're fine, thank you." Katie opened the thermos and handed him one of the soft tissue samples.

"We just need to get back as soon as possible," Nick added.

"But surely you must eat something first!" Littman hurried across the lab and placed the sample in a foam bucket full of ice. "My wife . . . she would never forgive me if I let you get away without an invitation to lunch. A late breakfast perhaps? I'll call her right now and she can have it all ready by the time we get there."

"Thanks for the invitation, but we really don't have time." Nick stepped toward Littman.

"We've got two bathrooms. You could wash up while you were waiting."

A hand clamped around Nick's arm like a vise. "Breakfast *and* a shower?" Katie glanced at him with wide, plaintive eyes. "Dr. Littman, that would be . . . I can't even tell you how much we'd appreciate that. Thank you."

"Excellent!" Littman beamed. "I'll call my wife. She'll be so happy to have guests!"

Nick followed him to the office at the corner of the lab. "Actually, your offer is very generous, but we really can't take the time—"

"Of course we can!" Dietrich's voice sounded right behind him. "Anyway, I must overnight mail the samples at government offices. I can drive the truck, Dr. Littman, if you will take to your house the rest of the team?"

"No problem at all." Littman scribbled something down on a sheet of paper and handed it to Dietrich. "My apartment is right on the edge of campus. It's a large, red-tinted adobe on Anter Street, right off Anter Square. Apartment number five. You can't miss it."

"Wait a second. Slow down!" Nick rubbed his temples with the heels of his hands. "Listen, I want a shower as much as anyone else, but we really have to consider the guards. What will they do if they realize we're gone? Destroy the fossil? Take the grad students hostage?"

"Oh my . . . I didn't realize your situation," Littman said. "You're right to be concerned, of course."

Nick turned to get Dietrich's opinion, but he was gone. He hurried out into the lab and almost ran into Katie and Ahamed. "Where's Dietrich?"

"He's gone to mail the samples," Ahamed said. "I just gave him the keys to the truck."

Nick groaned. "What if he gets lost or attacked by insurgents? Did anybody even think about that? What if the guards discover we're gone and hold Hooman and Wayne responsible?"

Katie's expression clouded. She turned suddenly away.

"Katie, no . . ." Nick stepped toward her and stopped. "I'm sorry. I didn't mean it that way." He reached out to touch her shoulder but hesitated. His hand dropped helplessly to his side. "Hooman and Wayne will be fine. We just need to hurry back."

"You're right. We never should have come here in the first place. I wasn't thinking about Hooman and Wayne."

Heaven! Sheer heaven! Bill rotated slowly back and forth in front of his new twelve thousand Btu air-conditioning unit. He held open the sleeves of his T-shirt, letting the blast of arctic air numb his prickling skin. He should have thought of this weeks ago. How much agony had he endured watching the ministry building from his sweatbox of a car? Its air conditioner was a joke.

Movement outside on the far side of the street caught his attention. He craned his neck to see over the top of the mammoth window unit. False alarm. Just another Iraqi businessman making his way through the security barriers.

Voices sounded over the roar of the big AC unit. He glanced back at the pair of low-frequency receivers sitting on the floor of the otherwise empty office. The voices sounded like they were coming from the bug in Al-Jaza'iri's office. The Shiite was always jabbering away about something. Nothing Bill would ever be able to understand, though. He turned back to the AC unit and funneled a blast of cold air into his right sleeve. So far he'd only managed to bug two of the ministers' offices: Al-Jaza'iri and Talibani. The other guy, Hamady, was going to be tricky. He had this stupid thing about always locking his door—almost made you wonder if maybe he had something to hide. . . .

". . . the person what found the whale!" The shouted words carried above the roar of the air conditioner.

English? Who's he talking to? Bill hurried over to Al-Jaza'iri's receiver and turned up the volume. A man's voice. His accent sounded German. ". . . the whale . . . digging . . . best eyes in the business . . ." He could only make out a few of the words. Sighing, Bill ran back across the room and reached a reluctant hand to the air conditioner's power switch. Cold air blasted his chest and arm, soothing the rash that covered his skin. One more second . . . He held his sleeves open and channeled the air under his arm. The other arm . . . *No!* With a soul-rending effort, he turned off the unit and hobbled back to the receiver.

The German was still talking. ". . . he is of course good. What I am saying is Katie is much the better. The race for finding the whale proves this beyond shadow of doubt. With myself managing to organize the digs, we will find even more greater discoveries for your museum. And with the exclusive agreement between us in place, digs will be much better organized. No more fighting between teams. No more valuable finds getting lost in confusion."

"Thank you, Dr. Fischer." Al-Jaza'iri's smooth voice buzzed over the speakers. What was he doing? Sticking his head in the trash can? "I will discuss your generous offer with the other ministers, but I must ask why you are not at the dig site. Why drive all this way to Baghdad to see me when we can talk on the phone? You do not plan to leave the country before your team is finished with the dig?"

"Of course not." The German's voice was louder now. He must have moved closer to the bug. "I was to be already in Baghdad, so of course my desire was to take the opportunity to meet with you in person."

"Of course. But what brought you to the city? Surely you have gone to a great deal of trouble."

"I had to mail off a sample to be analyzed, so of course I thought—"

"Out of the country!" Al-Jaza'iri thundered. "You mailed a sample out of the country? Out of the question! Our laws forbid it!"

"*Nein*, no . . . not an artifact. Of course you misunderstand. . . ." The German was clearly rattled. "Dirt only. Three samples for the radiometric dating. Taken from the matrix, the surrounding dirt . . . The dirt surrounding the . . . whale."

"Where was it mailed? When?"

"I did not mailed it anything yet. I have it still. Of course I want to ask permission from you first before sending anything out of the country." There was a rustling sound, the sound of scraping footsteps. "See? A few grains of dirt only. Some black powder and a little mud. Just like already I said."

"And this is everything? You have nothing else to mail?"

"Of course not. To mail anything else will be illegal. I know this. I am on many digs all over the world."

"Please accept my humble apologies then. Allow me and I will mail these for you." There was a dull thumping noise followed by the sound of heavy footsteps. "I will personally make sure they get mailed this afternoon, but I caution you. You are to go immediately back to your camp and are not to leave again without first informing me. And if you want this exclusive arrangement with our museum, you will not mail anything else. You will not even go near a post office! Do you understand me?"

"Of course. I am doing this for more than thirty years. Never am I questioned for integrity reasons. But Murad . . . Already I understand he has brought back many finds to the United States. Me, I have nothing!"

"Yes, yes, of course. I do not question your honor. We brought you here because we have the highest respect for you and your team. You just surprised me. That is all. Thank you, Dr. Fischer."

A loud clang rang through the speakers, making Bill jerk his head away. There was a soft clicking noise. The sound of papers rattling, people moving around. What were they doing? Writing notes to each other? Did Al-Jaza'iri realize he was being bugged? Bill leaned in closer to the speakers. He thought he could hear them whispering. Or was it just breathing? He listened for several minutes, going through every German archaeologist he could think of. None of them were named Fischer. There was that underwater archaeologist from Southern California—the guy who worked on sunken ships—but he wasn't German. He talked like a surfer dude. And what was this whale they were talking about? A Babylonian amulet of some kind? He'd never heard of such a thing.

A faint Arabic voice sounded over the speakers. Bill leaned in closer. This was different. Had he been there all the time? Suddenly, Al-Jaza'iri yelled something that sounded like "artichokes." Then the two Arabs were jabbering back and forth in rapid-fire Arabic. What had happened to the German? Bill pushed himself onto his feet and staggered over to the window. A big man in a wide-brimmed hat was walking out of the ministry building compound. His off-white shirt and pants were dust-stained and worn. He'd obviously been working at a dig.

Bill spun around and started for the door, but then stopped with a curse. His stupid car was five blocks away. He'd never make it in time. Returning to the window, he watched helplessly as the German got into a white four-passenger pickup truck and drove off. No destination, no license plate numbers, not even a good look at his face. He'd just let the best lead he was likely to ever have slip right through his little calamine-lotioned fingers.

Nick drained his glass of milk and sighed with contentment. "Mrs. Littman, those were the best pancakes I've ever eaten." He leaned back in his chair as a drowsy calm settled over him like a warm blanket. After a hot shower and a huge breakfast of pancakes and eggs, he felt like a new man. As much as he'd eaten, he probably looked like two new men.

"I've got four more ready. They won't be as good if you let them get cold." The professor's wife bustled toward Nick with a skillet and spatula.

"No, thank you," Nick protested. "They're wonderful, but I really shouldn't."

"Of course you should." She plopped a tall stack of blueberry pancakes on his plate. "Listen to Ahamed. You're not going to get blueberries out camping in the desert. Would you like more eggs? How about you, Ahamed dear?"

"No, thank you. Really . . ." Nick groaned as Mrs. Littman hurried back to the kitchen.

Ahamed let out a hearty laugh. He grinned at Nick over the top of a half-eaten stack of pancakes. "Just think to yourself," he said. "Tomorrow is back to Waseem's burned *halva puri*. Makes the syrup taste sweeter, *jee haan*?"

Nick shook his head. "Now you're just being mean." He poured syrup over his pancakes and took a big bite.

"Why don't you stay the night with us?" Dr. Littman wasn't giving up. He'd been trying to tempt them to stay longer all morning. "Some university students are coming over for dinner, and I'd love you to meet them."

Nick swallowed the pancakes and was just looking at his empty glass when Mrs. Littman came up behind him and refilled it. "I wish we could." He washed the pancakes down with a sip of milk. "But we really have to get back to camp. Maybe another time? On our way back up through Baghdad?"

"Absolutely. This has been so rushed. We'd love to get a chance to really visit. You still haven't told me anything about the whale you found—or your work back in Pakistan."

Nick glanced down at his watch and frowned. It was almost noon and Dietrich still wasn't back. If he didn't turn up by the time Katie got out of the shower, they were going to have to go out looking for him.

"Don't worry. I'm sure Dr. Fischer is fine." Littman seemed to read his mind. "I wrote down our address. If he has any problems finding us, he can always stop and ask someone."

A door squeaked and soft footsteps sounded from the hallway. "Sorry that took so long. I just couldn't force myself to turn off the water."

Nick turned at Katie's voice. She stood framed in the doorway, her burnished skin glowing warmly against the pale greens and soft blues of Mrs. Littman's silky dress. A lustrous cascade of dark hair tumbled over her left shoulder. Soft eyes, glistening lips . . .

"I . . ." Nick's tongue felt thick and clumsy in his mouth. "I think the guards are going to notice."

"I should say so!" Mrs. Littman walked up to Katie and took her by the hands, holding her arms out to admire the fit of the dress. "You look absolutely stunning, dear. You must keep the dress. I'll never be able to wear it again—not now that I know its potential. Just look at her, Jerry. Isn't she stunning?" She stepped aside and regarded her husband.

Dr. Littman chuckled. "Sorry, dear, but she's exceeded my ability to safely comment."

"And what's that supposed to mean?"

At that moment there came a heavy knock on the door. Nick jumped up from his seat and followed Dr. Littman into the foyer. The knock sounded again, harder this time.

"Just a second." Littman opened the door and stood back to let Fischer storm inside. "Dr. Fischer. I hope my directions—"

"We must leave now. There is no time being wasted!" Fischer's face was red and streaming with sweat. His hair was plastered to his head in a wild, Medusa-like coil.

"What took you so long?" Nick demanded. "Did you get word from camp? What's wrong?"

"Nothing is the matter." Fischer's eyes darted about the room. "Where is Katie? We must go now. Already we may be too late."

"What's going on, Dietrich?" Katie stepped into the foyer. Nick glanced at Fischer to get his reaction, but he didn't even blink. Surely this wasn't the way she *always* looked?

"Somebody followed behind me from mailing the sample," Dietrich said. "A big white truck. I had to drove all around the city to lose them."

"You're sure you lost them?" Katie asked.

"Of course I lost them. You think I would lead them back to here? This is just what takes me so long!"

Nick exchanged glances with Dr. Littman. "I'm afraid we'd better get going." He hurried back to the dining room, where Ahamed was stuffing the last bite of pancakes into his mouth. The professor's wife was stacking a tower of pancakes on a clean plate.

"Mrs. Littman, thank you for a wonderful meal, but we really have to go. Dietrich says he may have been followed, and it would be best if whoever it was didn't find us here."

"But your clothes aren't even dry yet. I just hung them out on the line a few minutes ago."

"Then we'll just have to wear them wet. As much as things are heating up outside, it shouldn't take them long to dry."

Chapter 20

*K*ATIE LUGGED THE GLOVE BOX out to Nick's equipment truck and heaved it over the tailgate as one of the soldiers' camouflaged trucks passed slowly by. They'd been circling the camp in tighter and tighter circles ever since four days ago, when she, Dietrich, Nick, and Ahamed had snuck back into camp. Apparently the soldiers had been alerted to their escape, although how they learned about it wasn't clear. She and the others had hidden Nick's truck in a deep wadi almost three miles away from the camp. She thought they'd snuck back into the camp without being seen, but apparently she was wrong. Hooman had assured her the guards had been oblivious to their absence. When the five men weren't standing guard over the fossil, they were sleeping or eating in their tent. They hadn't even noticed Ahamed's presence yet. Or if they had, they certainly didn't give any indication they cared.

She grabbed a telescoping tripod and walked back to Eve's tent. Unzipping the flaps, she ducked through the opening and pushed past the guards. Nick was hunched over his field laptop. He claimed he was revising the paper they'd sent Thomas Woodburne, but they both knew it was just an excuse to stay connected to e-mail. His laptop had been plugged into his satellite phone all morning. If Littman didn't send the results soon, Nick's phone bill was going to exceed the national debt.

"Any word yet?" Katie already knew the answer, but she couldn't help asking.

"No." Nick looked up from the computer. His eyes were bleary. Lines of fatigue were etched into his face. He hadn't shaved since their return from Baghdad. "Maybe we should call him again. Even if we got the results *now*, it's going to take time to write them up."

"He knows our deadline. I've already called him twice this morning."

"So make it three times. Tell him if he doesn't give us what he has now, we'll go to someone else. It's our sample. Where does he get off keeping the results from us?"

Katie shrugged. They'd been through this a dozen times already. Littman had called them yesterday and told them he'd gotten a sequence for one of the markers, but he'd refused to say anything else until his team had a chance to repeat the experiment. *Repeat the experiment!* It had to be something really huge or he wouldn't have gone all cloak-and-dagger on them. He'd promised he'd send the results by the end of the day, but time was running out. Nick was right. It was going to take every second they had left to analyze the results—whatever they turned out to be. Maybe if they promised not to publish anything until he'd gotten back to them with confirmation . . .

A loud chirp spun Katie around. Her satellite phone! She thrust a hand into her pocket and came out with the ringing phone. Jabbing at the connect button, she pressed it to her ear.

"Hello?" she shouted into the mouthpiece. "Hello!"

"Katie. Good; I'm glad I reached you." Dr. Littman's voice. "I've been trying to reach Nick, but his phone is busy."

"You said you were sending e-mail. We've been waiting all morning."

"Yes, of course. Well—"

"Did you repeat the experiment? Do you have the results?"

Nick sidled up to her and leaned in close, pressing his ear to the phone. His arm circled around her. Her shoulder was completely engulfed in his hand.

"Yes, well . . . About the results . . . I'm afraid I have disappointing news."

"Disappointing news? You didn't get a sequence?"

"No, I got a partial sequence for one of the markers, and it's definitely not *Homo sapiens*—at least not modern *Homo sapiens* anyway—but it doesn't look to be anything near as old as *Australopithecus*. We did the analysis twice and got identical sequences. . . ."

"So what is it?"

"I don't exactly know. We of course compared it to the Neanderthal sequences, so we know it isn't Neanderthal. About the best we can say is, based on the computer models we use to generate phylogenetic trees, the number of mutations away from modern *Homo sapiens* puts the age of our sample at just over a hundred thousand years. Nothing close to the 3 million years you'd prepared me to believe."

"Okay . . ." Katie felt like she'd been kicked in the stomach. "A hundred thousand years . . ." Was that going to be important enough to save Dietrich's funding? Was it even good enough to save the fossil from the Iraqis?

"Katie? Are you still there?"

"Yeah . . . I'm here."

"I'm sending the sequence now—as well as the results from the computer modeling. And Yassan has taken the liberty of writing up an experimental and results section for you. Feel free to use it however you want."

Katie nodded absently. What would she say to her father? Moving would kill him.

"Katie?"

"What?" She snapped back to the present and rapidly played back Littman's words in her mind. "Oh yeah. Thanks, Dr. Littman. Thanks for everything. Make sure you send the names of everybody who helped. We'll let you know how it goes."

"Okay, that'll be fine. Sorry it wasn't better news."

"It is what it is. Can't do better than that. And please tell your wife thank you for the dress and for the meal. She's very sweet."

"Okay, I'll tell her. I'm sending the data right now."

"Thanks." Katie hung up the phone and looked up at Nick. His face was slack. His eyes a million miles away.

"So it's not *Australopithecus*." His smile looked forced. "At least it's a new species! We've got ourselves a reference fossil!"

"Maybe . . ." Katie wasn't so sure. "Depends on how different the sequence is from *Homo sapiens*. Littman made it sound pretty close. A hundred thousand years is practically within the error bars for a date estimated by sequence homology. Natural variation within the current human population would probably give you an estimate of close to fifty thousand."

"So do we include the sequence information in the paper or not? Woodburne's already accepted the paper without it. Maybe we shouldn't rock the boat."

"We have to at least tell him. He'll probably . . . Oh no!" What was she going to tell Dietrich? After the disappointment with the whale fossil, he was going to hit the roof. He'd been talking up his new "*Australopithecus*" find for days. The funding committee was going to laugh him right out of the Academy. And she knew him well enough to know who he was going to take it out on. She could already hear him. *Go already right back in the desert and don't return to camp without you find for me a* real Australopithecus!

"What's wrong? Are you okay?" Nick was searching her face, his brow furrowed in concern. He stepped in closer and lifted a hesitant hand to her shoulder.

"I'll live." She sighed. "Until Dietrich kills me. You go ahead and call Woodburne. I'll give Dietrich the bad news. We'll really have to scramble if Woodburne wants us to mention the sequence."

"Okay . . . if you're sure." Nick turned slowly back to his laptop and unplugged it from the phone.

"Tell him we have some great new pictures for the article." Katie shuffled over to the door, stepping between the half-sleeping guards. "And remind him it's still the oldest sequence on record."

She pushed through the flaps of the door and stepped outside into the lung-deflating heat. *Whew!* It had to be at least 120 degrees. "Dietrich!" she called out and jogged over to the tent he was now sharing with Nick and Ahamed. "Dietrich! Are you in there?"

"Wait for a minute!" he called from inside the tent. "One minute!"

"We just got a call from Littman," she shouted through the side of the tent. "He has a sequence, but it's pretty close to *Homo sapiens*. Probably just over a hundred thousand years old."

"What?" The tent shook violently as Dietrich's head and shoulders thrust through the door. "I didn't hear you. How old did he say?"

"Just over a hundred thousand."

"Impossible!" He crawled out of the tent and heaved himself to his feet. "He's not looking at the fossil itself. It is 3 million years at the least!"

"Not according to the DNA sequence."

"Then he is making great big mistake!" He slashed his forearm against his reddening face. "You talk to him. He has sequencing contamination! You check and you will see!"

"He ran the sequencer twice and came up with the same thing. Unless Nick is a closet Neanderthal, there are too many mutations for it to be anything but genuine."

"The fossil is genuine 3 million years old. Just look at it! It is plain as the day. . . ."

A faint musical tone sounded behind her. Katie held up a hand to silence Dietrich's tantrum. Nick was still in Eve's tent. She could barely make out his voice as he answered the phone. "Hello . . . Brian? Great!"

It was Brian Gibson, Nick's friend at Berkeley. Ignoring Dietrich's bellowed protests, Katie ran back to the tent and plunged inside.

Nick was pacing back and forth across the tent. His face was screwed up in an incredulous frown. "What do you mean contaminated? That sounds like they got the same sequence we got over here." He looked over at Katie and shook his head. "So how do you know it's the soft tissue? Maybe the cinders were contaminated. Maybe you made a mistake with the radiometric dating." He stalked over to his computer and tapped a few keys. "Okay. . . . Go ahead and send it. But send the sequence too. I want to at least compare it to what we got here. . . . All right. . . . Okay, thanks, Brian." He set the phone on the table and swiveled on the stool to face Katie.

"Well?"

"When it rains, it pours." He shook his head and stared at the wall a few seconds. "I've got good news and bad news."

"And the good news is . . . ?"

"Thomas Woodburne was okay with putting the sequence in the paper. In fact, he was more than okay. He thinks it will make the paper a lot stronger."

"And Brian Gibson had bad news?"

"More bizarre than anything. He gave the tissue sample to a mo-bio friend of his. It sounds like he got the same sequence Littman got—just over a hundred thousand years away from *Homo sapiens.*"

"And this is bad because . . ."

"He says the sample was definitely volcanic. The results of the radiometric dating were conclusive."

Katie waited for the last nail in her coffin.

"He's putting the date at 3.4 million years."

"What?" She studied Nick's expression. He wasn't kidding. But 3.4 million years? How could that be possible? Her entire history with the fossil flashed before her eyes. What had they done wrong? She went through every detail of the extraction process, every detail of the sample collection, the sterilization of her tools. The sequence was so unusual. It couldn't have been contamination. There was no way they could have made a mistake.

"So what do we do now?" Nick looked completely deflated.

"What choice do we have? We report the data."

"You know anyone else would just sit on the new data until after the paper came out. Especially as important as it is for the paper to come out right away."

Katie nodded. "But which data would we sit on? We have no way of knowing which data set is wrong—or even if any of them are wrong. What if the sequence and date are both right? Maybe the computer models are wrong."

"Do you hear what you're saying?" Nick shook his head. "For a sequence *that* close to *Homo sapiens* to be *that* old, the whole evolutionary model would have to be wrong. It would mean that human

DNA hardly changed at all over the course of 3.4 million years. You can't believe that."

"I don't know what to believe! What do you want me to do? Lie about our results? Pretend we never got the phone call from your friend?"

"That's not what I'm saying! I just . . ." He turned on his heel and started pacing the length of the tent. "I know we have to report the data, but it's just so . . . weird. You know they're going to reject the paper. You know that."

Katie took a deep breath and looked down at the floor. "I know."

Nick hung up the phone and checked another name off his list. Sixty-five scientists down, only 2,285 to go. He closed his eyes and pressed his palms to his temples as Katie said good-bye to one scientist and started punching in the number for another. He and Katie had been talking nonstop to National Academy of Sciences members for three days—ever since they'd turned in the final draft of their paper. It had taken some quick talking on Katie's part, but in the end Thomas Woodburne had agreed to accept the inclusion of the sequence *and* radiometric data.

They'd admitted in the paper that they didn't know how to resolve the apparent contradiction, and they'd highlighted the need for further study, but even though it was enough for Woodburne, it wasn't enough for some of their colleagues. The next issue of *Science* wouldn't come out for another week, but he and Katie had already sent out over five hundred preprints of their paper. If nothing else, it was generating lots of discussion. And discussion was good. Right now all they could do was talk to as many scientists as possible and urge them to put pressure on the Iraqi ministers to send the fossil back to the United States for further testing.

"Thanks. I appreciate it. . . . All right. You too. . . . Bye." Katie hung up the phone and checked another name off her list. She was an indefatigable dynamo. He didn't know where she got all her energy. If it had been up to him, he would have given up days ago.

She turned and caught him staring. He lowered his gaze to the list of names on the table and tried to think of something to say. Maybe she'd like to go out for a walk or something? Even dodging armed soldiers would be better than making more phone calls.

His phone rang—again. Nick shrugged apologetically and answered the phone. "Hello, this is Nick."

"Nick? This is Brian. We've got to talk."

"Okay. What's up? Change your mind about that date?"

Katie's head snapped around and she stared a question at him. Nick shook his head and waved her back to the list of names.

"*My* date stands." Brian's voice sounded ominous. "But I think you should know I just got off the phone with Max Weimmer, and he's livid."

"The president of the NAS?"

"Nick, listen to me. Max is convinced you're perpetrating some kind of a scam—Son of Piltdown, he's calling it."

"That's ridiculous. Just because the sequence doesn't match the date?"

"It's not just the date. It's the whole 'Iraq is going to destroy the fossil' thing. He thinks you're deliberately holding the Academy hostage—forcing us to endorse your findings or face the consequences—even though we all know it can't be right."

"Brian, that's . . . You know me. I don't like this any more than you do, but what can I do? The Iraqi ministers really may destroy the fossil. Am I supposed to just turn it over to them without a fight?"

"I know that's what you think, but has it ever occurred to you you're being set up?"

"Set up? By whom?"

"Katie James. Max says he has information linking her to those intelligent design people. He has hard proof she's already perpetrated another hoax."

"What? That's ridiculous! She . . ." Nick glanced over at Katie. She was hanging on his every word. "Listen, tell him he doesn't know what he's talking about. That's the most ridiculous thing I've ever heard." He stood up from the table and moved closer to the tent entrance.

"Hey, I know she's pretty. That's probably why they chose her for this, but she's a creationist, Nick. She's setting you up. She's setting us all up."

Nick unzipped the tent and stepped out into blinding sunlight. "Listen, I know she's a Christian, but that doesn't make her a creationist—not like you're talking about. She told me herself—she's totally open to evolutionary theory."

"And you believed her?"

"Sure, but even if I didn't, even assuming what you say is true—and I'm still not at all convinced—there's no way she could have done it. I'm the one that collected the samples. I did the work myself."

"And there's no way she could have switched them? You had them in your possession the whole time?"

"But where could she have gotten the DNA? We're out in the middle of the desert. And don't tell me she brought it with her. We weren't even looking for hominids. We were looking for a pre-*Rodhocetus*."

"Didn't you say the fossil was embedded in a chunk of sandstone? And that sandstone was loose in a dry riverbed?"

Brian's words slithered their way into Nick's mind, making him feel immediately guilty. "No. I refuse to believe it. I know her! She wouldn't do such a thing!" He stalked away from the tent.

"Nick, listen to me. You have to distance yourself from this woman. Take your name off the paper. Tell them you had no idea what she was doing. What she *was*. You have a good reputation in the field. People will believe you."

"But what if you're wrong? What if she didn't do anything?"

"So you're saying you believe in a 3.4-million-year-old *Homo sapiens*?"

"I don't know what to believe yet. All we have are the data. The data and the fossil. And we won't be able to reanalyze the fossil if the Iraqis conveniently lose it. We'll never know the truth."

"Come off it! You know the truth as well as I do. The woman is a creationist. You're just too emotionally involved to see straight. That's always been your problem—ever since our time at UCLA."

Nick's stomach swirled like a witch's cauldron.

"Look. Do what you're going to do, but take my name off the paper. I don't want to have anything to do with it."

"But we've already turned it in!"

"So unturn it in. Sorry, Nick. If this goes bad for you, don't say I didn't try to warn you."

The connection went dead.

Nick stared at the phone, trying to figure out what to make of the call. If it had been anybody else, he would have said they were crazy, but Brian Gibson . . . Brian was one of the most levelheaded guys he knew. He wouldn't let himself get caught up in witch-hunt hysteria.

But Katie James setting him up? It just wasn't possible. There was no way she could have done it. And even if she *could* have, she *wouldn't*. He knew her. She'd never do such a thing, never in 3.4 million years—especially not to him.

He turned slowly and started walking back to the tent. What was he worried about? Katie wasn't guilty. He'd just talk to her, explain the whole misunderstanding. They'd work it out together. It would make for a good laugh. She needed the break.

Brian was probably exaggerating anyway. Max Weimmer was just taking his paranoia out for a little stroll. Nobody listened to Max anyway. He was more political than the U.S. Congress. As soon as Woodburne took Brian's name off the paper, Brian would be crawling back to him begging to have it put back on.

He scrolled through the phone's menu and selected Woodburne's office number.

"Hello?" A woman answered the phone.

"Hi, this is Nick Murad. I'm trying to reach Thomas Woodburne."

"I'm sorry. Dr. Woodburne no longer works here."

"I'm sorry. You misunderstood. Thomas *Woodburne*—the paleontologist."

"Yes, sir. Thomas Woodburne no longer works here."

"But I just talked to him two days ago. He just accepted a paper for accelerated publication. He never mentioned anything about leaving."

"Sorry for the inconvenience, sir, but Dr. Woodburne left unexpectedly. If you're calling with regard to a *Science* paper, his responsibilities have temporarily been reassigned to one of the other editors. I'll take your name and you'll be contacted by the new editor within the next couple of days."

Nick's head felt like a hive of buzzing bees. Woodburne left *unexpectedly?* This couldn't be happening. "Do you know why he left? Did it have anything to do with a paper he'd just accepted?"

"I'm sorry, sir—"

"Ma'am, I'm the author of the paper. I need to know if that's the reason he was fired."

"I'm sorry, sir. All I'm allowed to say is that he left unexpectedly."

"All you're *allowed* to say? Thanks. That's all I needed to know." He hung up and scrolled through the phone's menu. "Come on, come on!" He stopped at the listing for his Michigan office and jabbed at the select key. Things had gotten way out of control. He had no choice but to pull out. Katie would understand. As a postdoc, she could weather the storm, but he . . .

"Take a number!"

Beautiful. Mike was in one of his moods. "Mike, listen. . . . I need you to get on the phone and call up—"

"Nick! Where have you been? I've been calling you all night. Don't you ever check your voice mail?"

"Mike, listen to me. I need you to call the AAAS office and have them delay publishing the paper we just submitted. Tell them I need to figure out what's wrong with the data first, okay? Make sure they know I think something's wrong with it."

"You're talking about the paper with Katie James, right?"

"Right."

"Well, lucky you. I just got a call this afternoon—make that yesterday afternoon—saying the paper was rejected."

Nick nodded. He should have realized this would happen. "Okay. Then I need you to get me the phone number of the president of the NAS. His name is Max Weimmer."

"Nick . . ."

Nick didn't like the tone of Mike's voice. "What's wrong?"

"You got a letter from the department yesterday."

"Okay . . ."

"They said you didn't make tenure."

"What are you talking about? I'm not even up for review—not until next year!"

"I'm just telling you what the letter said."

"Just because I sent out a few preprints? That's ridiculous. They can't do this!"

There was a long pause. "I'm sorry. I don't know what else to say."

"That's okay, Mike." Nick could barely speak above a whisper. "I'll figure something out. Don't worry. I'll figure out something."

He hung up the phone and dropped it into his pocket. Ahead of him, the row of trucks rippled and shimmered in the radiating heat. The whole camp looked like a mirage, like none of it really existed. The fossil, the sequence, the radiometric dating . . . the whole thing was just a huge never-ending nightmare. Even Katie . . .

Nick swallowed against the film of dust that coated his throat and plodded toward Eve's tent. Things were deadly serious now. He didn't have time for any more games. He had a lot of questions, and he intended to get some answers.

Chapter 21

*O*F ALL THE ARROGANT ... Katie gritted her teeth and hung up the phone halfway through the scientist's tirade. She drew a line through his name—a thick black line that cut deep into the paper. What did he expect her to do? Change the data? It's not like she could control the outcome of the analysis. She hadn't even done the sequencing work!

She pushed the list away from her and rested her forehead on the table. A few of the scientists were supportive, but most of them just wanted to get on with their work. Several of them were downright hostile. Maybe she and Nick needed to try a different approach. She was starting to get the feeling they were generating more resistance than support. One of the scientists had even said he'd been warned she would call. As if she were some kind of severe weather condition . . .

The metallic buzz of the tent zipper ripped her back into the moment. Nick appeared in the doorway, dark eyes overshadowed by a furrowed brow. Roiling emotions played like a storm across his face.

"Hey, what's wrong?" She jumped to her feet and walked over to meet him. "That was your friend at Berkeley, right? Did he have more bad news about the analysis?"

Nick just stared at her.

"It's okay. I can take it," she said. "Just tell me."

"Woodburne isn't there anymore. He's been fired."

"What? Because of our paper?"

"What makes you say a thing like that?" He eyed her suspiciously. "Did you know this would happen?"

"No!" Katie took a step toward him. "I mean, I knew they wouldn't like it, but I had no idea—"

"Who wouldn't like it? Define *they*."

"You know . . . the powers that be. The scientific establishment."

"Evolutionists, you mean? Your enemies in this big battle you keep talking about?"

"Evolutionists aren't my enemies. I already told you—"

"Brian told me different. He just got off the phone with Max Weimmer from the NAS. Weimmer is convinced this whole thing is a forgery. He has proof you perpetrated another hoax just like it."

"And you believe him?" Katie sputtered. "That's the most ridiculous thing I've ever heard."

"I don't know what to believe anymore."

"Can't you see what's happening here? He's too biased to accept the data. He *has* to believe it's a forgery."

"Is that what you think? The whole world is biased against you? First it's your department; then it's the Iraqi ministers; now it's the president of the NAS? I'm beginning to see a pattern here."

"Not biased against me personally. Biased against the data. He's defending his cause, trying to discredit us before we can convince anyone."

"Defending his *cause*? You really are fighting a battle!" He spun around and pushed through the door.

"Nick, wait!" Katie ducked through the tent flaps and followed him out across the camp. "Would you just listen to me?"

Nick's strides lengthened. Katie had to trot to keep up with him.

"Okay, fine! Walk away." Katie flung the words after him. "Treat me like a criminal. While we're on our witch hunt, why don't you burn me at the stake too?"

Nick spun around and glared at her with heaving chest and clenched fists. "I just lost my job because of you. Because I was stupid enough to trust you!"

"You lost your job?" She stepped toward him. "How? Why?"

"Because you set me up!"

"First of all—" Katie fought to control her voice—"I didn't set anybody up. You're the one who discovered the soft tissue, and it was *your* friend we sent it to."

"But you're the one who found the fossil, remember? Conveniently sitting out in the open—in the first place you happened to look. I should have seen it from the start, from the first time we talked on the phone!"

Nick woke with a start. *What was that?* He sat up and searched the darkness of the tent. He could just make out the still outlines of Ahamed and Fischer. They seemed to be asleep, but with the hum of the generators drowning out their breathing, it was hard to tell for sure. He scooted onto his hands and knees and crawled to the entrance of the tent. Tugging gently on the zipper, he wormed his way out into the chill desert night and climbed onto his bare feet.

Nobody was at the camp table. The whole area was perfectly still. A million stars blazed down on him, pulsing with silent intensity. The roar of the generators only seemed to intensify the silence, the isolation. He was completely alone. No direction, no position, nobody who really cared. He circled the table. Walked around it again and again and again. A deep, aching emptiness was gnawing at his gut. He could feel it eating away at him, devouring him alive from the inside out. He'd lost his job; he'd made a fool of himself in front of his colleagues. Everything he'd worked for was gone, yet none of those things seemed to matter now. All he could think about was his fight with Katie. Why couldn't he get her out of his mind? They'd accomplished so much, working together side by side. He'd trusted her, cared for her. And she had seemed to care for him.

His accusations played over and over in his mind. He'd been so angry, so unfair. What if she'd been telling the truth? Even if she'd planted the fossil, how would she have known there was soft tissue inside the tooth? He'd drilled it himself, prepared the sample. It just didn't make sense. None of it made any sense!

Nick crept across the compound and yanked up on the zipper of Eve's tent. Both guards were sound asleep, sprawled on either side of the entrance. Pushing into the blackness, he felt his way with outstretched hands. The table was right in front of him. He reached out a hand, snagged the cord of the electric work light, and followed it up to the switch. Switching the light on, he shielded his eyes with his left hand.

The guards were starting to stir. He squinted into the light, searching back and forth across the surface of the table.

The fossil was gone!

"What's going on?" He turned to face the squinting guards. "Where's the fossil?"

One of the guards sat up and looked around the tent. The other grabbed his rifle and leaped to his feet.

"Where's the fossil?" Nick demanded.

"Is not here?" The guard stumbled over to the table. His eyes went wide with surprise. *"Dunya!"* He shouted something else in Arabic and the other guard seized Nick from behind, running his hands up and down Nick's body.

"I don't have it! It was gone when I came in! I . . ." *Katie!* He jerked free of the guard and stalked out of the tent. Right after their big confrontation. Right after she'd practically admitted she was in a war with the establishment. It couldn't be a coincidence.

He headed over to her tent and yanked up on the zipper. "Okay, where is it?" He plunged his head inside. "What'd you do with the fossil?"

"What?" Katie croaked. Her shadowy form was sitting up on her bedroll.

"Did you take the fossil?" He moderated his tone. Suddenly he wasn't so sure anymore.

"Eve? Is something wrong?" She sprang to her feet and pushed him back out of the opening.

"It's missing." Nick followed her to Eve's tent. "I just checked the tent, and the fossil isn't there."

Katie slipped through the opening. Her throaty gasp could just be heard above the roar of the generators.

"Hey!" Wayne's voice called out through the dark. "Would you love-birds mind turning the volume down? Some of us are trying to sleep."

"What is it? What's going on?" Dietrich was stumbling toward him with Ahamed right behind. "More business from soldiers?"

"Get everybody up!" Katie appeared at the entrance of the tent, backlit by a corona of electric light. Her eyes were smoldering coals, burning through the shadows that painted her face. "Make sure nobody leaves. We have to search the camp now. Somebody stole the fossil!"

A camouflaged truck crested a distant hill, windshield flashing orange in the setting sun. Katie lowered the binoculars. This was it. It was headed straight for them. She turned and started jogging back to camp. She wanted to be there when Nick had to eat his words. He'd called her a liar and a fraud in front of everybody. He'd actually accused her of taking the fossil—just because she was a Christian. As if her belief that stealing was wrong automatically made her a thief.

They'd spent the entire day searching for the fossil—in her pack, her tent, under her tent . . . Of course they hadn't found it. The soldiers had it. It was the only thing that made any sense. Nobody in their group would have taken it. What would their motive be? It had to be the soldiers, but who did they work for? Minister Al-Jaza'iri? The two Sunni ministers?

Katie slowed to a walk as soon as she passed the semicircle of tents. The others were all sitting around the camp table. She crossed the compound and sat down at the opposite end of the table from Nick. She could feel his eyes on her, but she didn't so much as glance his way. Nobody was talking. Maybe they were mad at him too.

"So . . ." She finally broke the silence. "The soldiers are heading this way. Looks like they're finally going to let us know what's going on."

The table erupted in an explosion of questions.

"They're coming from the east. Should be here any minute." She remained in her seat while the others got up and headed across the camp. A few minutes later she could hear the truck's engine. She had been right. They were stopping. Pushing up from the table, she sauntered over to stand with the rest of the group.

The truck rolled to a stop at the edge of camp. Three uniformed men with holstered weapons got out first. Something was wrong. They weren't dressed like soldiers.

The front passenger door opened and Al-Jaza'iri stepped out into the fading light. "Katie James, Nick Murad, Dr. Fischer," he called out to the assembled group. "*Hamdu lillaah!* It is so good to see you!"

"Minister Al-Jaza'iri," Katie said. "What are you doing here?"

"I just received . . . some distressing information. Most distressing, I am sorry to say."

"You heard—"

Katie jabbed Nick in the side with her elbow. "You heard . . . what kind of information?"

"I am sorry to say, Dr. Murad, but my information says you are planning to smuggle the human fossil out of the country. I have come to escort it back to Baghdad."

"That's crazy!" Nick stepped forward. "I didn't have anything to do with it."

The uniformed men drew their guns. Their uniforms . . . They weren't soldiers. They were the police!

"Minister Al-Jaza'iri—" Katie pushed in front of Nick—"the fossil's right inside the tent. Would you like to see it?" She planted the heel of her boot down on Nick's toe.

Al-Jaza'iri didn't even glance at her. He was watching Nick, sizing him up. Either he was a very good actor or he didn't know about the theft. Which meant . . . someone was trying to frame Nick. But why? An Iraqi jail would be a death sentence for an American—even for one night.

"Come on. I'll show you." She pulled Nick toward Eve's tent. Ahamed started to follow, but she waved him off. The last thing she needed was for someone *else* to do something stupid. They were in enough trouble as it was.

"Stay close," she whispered to Nick before reaching down to unzip the tent. Then, turning back to Al-Jaza'iri and the three police officers, she smiled and raised her voice to be heard over the generators. "Okay. . . . Watch your step. Things have been hectic lately. We haven't had much of a chance to straighten up."

Her heart slammed into high gear as she stepped inside the dark tent. Good. The two guards weren't there. Apparently they no longer felt the need to guard an empty tent.

"It's a little dark in here. Let me get the light." She felt for the light's electric cord and yanked it out of the socket. She could hear Al-Jaza'iri moving right behind her. The police officers were still outside. "Sorry, it's not working. Here . . ." She reached into a crate on the floor and came up with a small, plaster-encased whale bone. "Be extremely careful with it. It's fragile." She handed the bone to Al-Jaza'iri.

"So this is the cause of so much trouble. I understand how you feel, doctors, and I'm terribly sorry, but a small little bone is not worth the stability of an entire nation." He turned and moved toward the entrance.

"Please, if you could just give us more time . . ." Katie edged closer to the worktable. "Just a few more weeks." Sliding her fingertips across the cluttered surface, she picked out a scalpel and slipped it behind her back. Nick's eyes went wide. He started to reach for her hand, but she pulled away from him.

"I am afraid I have given you too much time already." Al-Jaza'iri glanced back at them, freezing Nick with his gaze. "Your colleagues from the United States are already making the situation quite difficult." Finally he turned and ducked through the entrance.

Katie sprang away from Nick and stabbed the scalpel through the back wall of the tent. Slashing through the thick canvas panel, she ripped it halfway to the ground. Then, grabbing Nick by the forearm, she squirmed through the narrow gash, pulling him after her.

An Arabic shout sounded on the other side of the tent. Al-Jaza'iri had gotten a good look at the bone.

Katie yanked Nick to the side and pulled him toward the neighboring tent. Gunshots rang out behind them. The twang of ricocheting bullets.

Running from tent to tent, she led Nick along the back of the camp. More gunshots. Shouting voices ahead of them. The sound of distant trucks. They were calling in the soldiers!

She pulled Nick behind the last tent and threw herself on the ground. Lifting up the bottom edge of the tent, she thrust her head beneath the heavy canvas and wriggled her way under the tent's heavy floor. Nick was grunting and squirming right beside her. "Roll over on your back," she hissed. "Spread your arms and legs. Try to keep the floor above us as smooth as possible."

"What happens . . . if they go . . . inside?" Nick's whisper sounded between panting breaths.

The jabber of Arabic voices. Running footsteps. They were heading their way.

Suddenly the tent shuddered. The metallic rip of an opening zipper. Katie held her breath as a beam of light lit up the canvas floor above her. She could see the dark outline of a sleeping bag. It covered her legs and right arm, but the whole left side of her body was exposed. *God, please . . . don't let them see. . . .* She held her breath until her pounding chest felt like it was going to explode. What were they saying? Did they see her? The light swept across the floor again.

Something brushed her ankle. Something else tickled at her neck. She bit her lip as long, hairy legs brushed across her cheek. Camel spiders—ten-inch creepy-crawly monstrosities—hiding under the tent to escape the heat of the sun.

A heavy foot pressed down on the floor near Katie's left hand. Shouted instructions. She could feel the canvas sliding across her cheek. Could they see her heart pounding? the outline of her body under the floor?

The sleeping bag above her was swept to the side. Another sleeping bag slid across the floor to take its place. She closed her eyes, praying they wouldn't see her.

The weight by her hand shifted and then lifted altogether. The voices moved off to her right. Katie let out her breath with a gasp and sucked in a lungful of air. Another breath, another. Deep, silent breaths. *Thank you, God. . . . Thank you.* She breathed in and out to the cadence of her prayer. The burning in her lungs was starting to subside. She focused only on the words that filled her mind, letting the footsteps and shouting voices fade beyond the gentle rush of her breath.

Finally, she became aware of a shift in the sounds of the camp. The roar of the circling trucks had faded into the distance. The frantic shouts had softened into the murmur of focused conversation. The men were starting to congregate at the center of the compound. This was their chance to move—before the soldiers could transition to a new plan of action.

Katie reached over and poked Nick in the arm. Little by little she rolled onto her stomach and inched her way toward the back of the tent. There wasn't enough room to turn around; she'd have to back out. If anyone was behind the tents, they'd see her long before she'd be able to see them.

Her feet were out in the open now. She kept on going until her legs were clear, most of her back. Then, twisting herself around, she pulled her head and shoulders clear of the tent and looked around. Nobody was there—only the dim headlights of distant trucks. Everyone else was back in the camp. They seemed to be meeting around the table.

Katie reached under the tent and tugged on Nick's leg. The tent vibrated. Gradually, inch by inch, he backed out from under the rustling, swaying tent. He was making too much noise. She grabbed his arm and hoisted him the rest of the way out.

He scrambled onto his feet, sweeping the area with wild, darting eyes. "What do you think you're doing?" he hissed. "We could have been killed!"

She put her lips to his ear. "What do you think would happen if they put us in an Iraqi prison? Al-Jaza'iri brought three policemen—all the way from Baghdad. Think about it."

Nick shook his head and pressed his face into the palms of his hands. After a few seconds he looked up. His face had hardened with renewed resolve. He leaned in closer. "Okay, so what do we do?"

"We don't have a choice. We have to get out of here."

"But how? This place is crawling with soldiers."

"We have to get to Ahamed's truck. Hopefully it's still in the wadi."

Nick looked out across the desert and took a deep breath. Katie counted three sets of circling headlights. And those were just the trucks. Who knew how many soldiers were out there patrolling the area on foot.

"You have a better idea?" she asked.

Nick just stared.

"Then let's go."

Keeping the tent between her and the voices, Katie picked her way across the rocky ground. The strained rush of Nick's breathing sounded right behind her. So far so good. Katie broke into a slow trot. The voices behind them were getting louder. They seemed to be dispersing.

Katie started to run. Leaping over ditches, dodging to avoid rocks, they zigzagged their way across the desert plain. Nick's breath was coming in ragged pants now. They were making too much noise. The soldiers would hear them for sure.

A low rumble sounded just ahead of them. A truck turned toward them, sweeping its headlights across their path. Katie dove for the ground and rolled into a shallow gulley. A shower of pebbles rained down on her as Nick tumbled on top of her.

The truck roared past, leaving them in a cloud of dust and fine sand.

"Come on!" Nick lifted her onto her feet, and they took off across the plain. Two more trucks were coming. Katie ran harder. The trucks were moving too fast.

A dark chasm opened suddenly in front of her. Katie pushed off from the edge, leaping out into the void. Darkness swept by in a screaming, shrieking rush before she smashed shoulder-first into a steep, rocky wall. Her body went limp as she tipped back into nothingness and crashed into the ground.

Gasping for breath, Katie tried to fill her paralyzed lungs with air. A thud sounded next to her. Rumbling trucks. The flash of sweeping headlights. Unseen hands rolled her onto her back. A high-pitched tone rang in her ears. She needed oxygen. She still couldn't breathe. . . .

The bands compressing her chest suddenly loosened and her lungs filled with tingling air.

"You okay?" Nick whispered in her ear. "We've got to keep moving!"

Katie nodded and tried to sit up, but her ankle flashed out in sudden pain. "My ankle," she whispered through clenched teeth. "I must have landed on it wrong."

An arm circled around her shoulders and tipped her forward. Another arm pushed under her knees. She felt herself being lifted up, pressed against the warmth of Nick's broad chest. He carried her through the darkness, keeping to the murky shadows at the base of the deep erosion gulley.

"Let me try to walk," Katie whispered softly, but he didn't put her down. She flexed her leg muscles and tried rotating her ankle. It twinged a little bit, but not enough to prevent her from putting weight on it. "Seriously, put me down. I can walk."

"Are you sure?"

"I will be once you put me down."

Nick set her gently on her feet, keeping an arm around her as she took a few experimental steps. The ankle hurt worse than she'd expected, but she'd be okay until they reached the truck. It shouldn't be that far away now.

"It's okay. I'm fine," she whispered. Nick was holding her tighter now, lifting her weight as she stepped on her left foot.

"How much farther?"

Katie examined the slopes on either side of her. They were about the right size and shape. "I think we're almost there, but it's hard to know for sure without a GPS." She limped a few more steps. The wadi was getting broader. They were getting closer to its mouth.

A thorny shrub scraped past her leg. She'd seen that bush before. She was positive. "Don't move!" She pulled away from Nick and dropped onto the ground. Running her fingertips across the rocks and sand, she crawled forward on her hands and knees. There they were: sharp depressions in the sand. Tire tracks—the spot they'd parked their truck.

She opened her mouth, tried to tell Nick, but she couldn't find the words.

"Katie, what's wrong? Is this where we left the truck?"

She nodded without looking up. No shelter, no water, no transportation . . . She'd led them out into the desert to die.

Then the Lord said to Job, "Will the faultfinder contend with the Almighty? Let him who reproves God answer it."

Then Job answered the Lord and said, "Behold, I am insignificant; what can I reply to You? I lay my hand on my mouth. Once I have spoken, and I will not answer; even twice, and I will add nothing more."

Job 40:1-5, NASB

Part Four

Chapter 22

*Y*OU'RE HURT." Nick caught Katie around the waist as she stumbled over a loose rock. "Please . . . let me carry you."

Katie caught her breath and took another step. "I'm fine. We've got to get out of here."

Keeping his arm around her waist, Nick took her by the hand and pulled her arm around his neck to take more of her weight. He'd never in his life known anyone so stubborn. It was enough to make a fugitive scream. She'd been hobbling around all night on an ankle that looked like it had swallowed a tennis ball. Even with the soldiers closing in on them, she still refused to admit she needed help. He would have understood it from a guy, but she was a woman. She was supposed to have more sense.

"It'll be morning soon, but we're almost to the edge of their search zone. If we can just make it another half mile, things should get easier," Katie said.

"I thought we were getting closer to the camp."

"Right. But they're focusing their search around the area they found our truck. They won't expect us to make for a point a half mile east of camp. Once we get a little farther—" She sucked in her breath sharply.

That does it! Nick dropped her hand and swung her up into his arms.

"Nick!"

He started walking faster. No way was she going to be able to use speed as an excuse.

"Put me down. You're going to wear yourself out."

"I'm fine," he whispered between breaths. "It's easier this way."

"No, it isn't! We're out in the middle of the desert without any water. Start sweating now and you won't last half the day."

"If you'd stop squirming, I wouldn't be sweating."

Katie grew suddenly still. She wrapped her arms around his neck and pressed her head to his shoulder.

A lump formed in his throat. "Katie, I'm . . ." He swallowed hard and held her tighter. Did he really want to bring it all up again? "Look, there's something I need to say."

"What's that?"

"I was a total jerk yesterday. I'm really sorry. I was a jerk and an idiot. I know you'd never set me up—you'd never set anyone up."

"So what changed your mind?"

"I know what you're thinking, but it wasn't just the fact you saved my life—which I totally appreciate, by the way."

"You're welcome."

"It's just that . . . everything happened so fast. With me losing tenure and Thomas Woodburne and Max Weimmer saying he had proof . . . I couldn't help thinking back to that first night with Wayne. When he said you were a creationist, I'd been so sure he was wrong. . . ."

"Because I'd have to be an idiot to believe in God, right?"

"No! It's just . . . Okay, I admit it. You don't exactly fit my stereotypes."

"Stereotypes you developed scientifically from firsthand observation and controlled experimentation?"

"I'm admitting I was wrong, okay?" Nick clamped his mouth shut to keep from swearing. Why did he even bother?

"Sorry." Her tremulous whisper sent a shiver down his spine. Just like that, his anger was gone. She was driving him out of his mind.

A bang sounded in the distance. One of the trucks was getting closer. Nick set Katie on her feet and the two of them pressed themselves against the side of the gulley as the truck bore down on their position. Brakes squealed as heavy tires skidded across sand and rock. Arabic shouts. They were stopping.

Nick glanced at Katie. She nodded and started hobbling along the wadi. What was she nodding for? He hadn't been asking a question. They hadn't gone more than twenty feet before the truck revved its engine and moved off in the opposite direction.

"What was that all about?" Nick whispered.

Katie put a finger to her lips. She was walking faster now. Either her ankle wasn't bothering her or something else was bothering her more. He sidled up to her and tried to help support her weight, but she pulled away from him. Something was definitely wrong. Had the truck dropped off a patrol? He hadn't heard anything.

Katie stopped suddenly and raised a hand for silence. Nick strained his ears. Three or four trucks were moving in the distance, but that was all. When she started walking again, she was limping, but this time she was dragging her right foot. The edge of her boot cut a large gash through the sand. This was too much. She had to let him carry her. She was leaving a trail even he could follow.

He wrapped an arm around her and tried to lift her off her feet, but she twisted away and stalked out ahead of him. What was her problem? Sighing, he broke into a jog to catch up. If they ever got out of this alive, one thing was certain: he didn't need this kind of stress in his life. Even being with Cindy was better than this.

"Nick . . ." Katie stopped suddenly right before a bend in the wadi. She was so agitated she was practically jumping up and down.

"What's wrong?"

"I . . ." She looked around the narrow canyon. "Would you mind going on ahead without me—just a few hundred yards?"

"Why?"

She smiled and lowered her eyes. "I need to use the little girl's desert." More jumping up and down.

Nick didn't mean to laugh at her. It was just that . . . he'd been so worried. "Sure." He was still smiling as he turned and walked around the bend in the wadi. How long had she needed to go? No wonder she'd overreacted when he put his arm around her waist and squeezed. He walked around another bend in the canyon. The sky was getting rosy in the east. It was almost light enough to read by. How were they supposed to get across the plain once the sun was up?

The murmur of men's voices stopped Nick in his tracks. *Katie!* He turned and started running. More voices. Just around the corner. Leaping and hopping to avoid loose rocks, he made his way silently to the bend in the wadi and peered out from around a pile of scree.

Katie stood bare-legged next to the bank of the wadi, clutching her cargo pants in front of her like a shield. Two Iraqi soldiers stood facing her. One of them motioned toward her with his rifle and laughed. The other was leering at her, his eyes lit with a maniacal gleam. He swaggered toward her, murmuring in a low, guttural voice. The soldier with the drawn rifle followed close behind.

Nick's heart pounded in his throat. He took a step and stopped. If he showed himself now, he'd lose the only advantage he had. Crouching low to the ground, he picked up a heavy rock. He stood slowly, watching in horror as the soldiers drew closer and closer to their prey. Katie stood frozen in front of them with wide eyes. He could see her muscles trembling. Ten feet away. Five . . . The leering soldier was taunting her now, motioning toward her with lewd, suggestive gestures. A little closer. Just a little closer. Nick's muscles tensed. He leaned forward, ready to charge.

Katie suddenly spun in a blur of motion. She snapped the pants around, sweeping them in an arc at the armed soldier's face. The soldier crashed into his companion, knocking him off his feet. In another instant the pants swept around again, hitting him in the side of the head.

Nick charged across the wadi, gripping the rock in his hand. Katie had distracted them. Now was his chance to finish them off. He skidded to a stop at the prostrate soldiers, rock raised above his head. Why weren't they getting up? All she'd done was trip them up with her pants.

Hadn't she?

Then he saw the blood. A puffy gash across the first soldier's forehead. Both soldiers were deathly still. Nick looked to Katie for an explanation. It was too much. He couldn't even form the question.

"I'm really sorry." Tears were streaming down her cheeks. "I knew if I told you the truth . . ." She lifted up her pant leg and shook it. A rock the size of a large grapefruit tumbled out onto the ground.

"You gotta be kidding." Nick stared at the rock. She'd planned the whole thing out? sent him out of harm's way—like a little boy who needed . . . to be protected? He looked up at her in amazement.

"Please . . . I didn't mean anything by it." She frantically worked at the knot in her pant leg. "It's just that we used to play with bolas on the reservation. If you were here, they wouldn't have gotten close enough . . ."

Nick stepped toward her, but she jerked away like a frightened animal.

"What?" He studied her face, her wide, pleading eyes. "You think I'm . . . mad at you?" He shook his head in astonishment. "How could I be mad? You just saved our lives. You're the most amazing woman I've ever known."

A timid smile touched her lips. She looked down at the ground, hugging her pants to her chest. She looked so beautiful, so innocent. Like a little girl in her daddy's T-shirt.

A deep ache swelled in Nick's chest. She was squirming under his gaze, but he couldn't stop staring.

"Would you mind?" Her face puckered. She was looking around the bend he'd just come from.

Nick forced himself to look away, but he could still hear her squirming.

"Nick, what I said before . . . I wasn't lying. Would you mind waiting around the bend? I really do have to go."

Katie jogged toward the bend in the wadi, gritting her teeth against the pain flaring up from her ankle. Nick, dressed in the military fatigues and keffiyeh of one of the unconscious soldiers, was right ahead of her. The roar of an approaching truck sounded from the south. She pulled the excess fabric of her keffiyeh tighter across her face and tucked it into the collar of her oversize fatigues. Not only had the soldiers been good enough to provide them with uniforms, but they had also provided rifles and two canteens full of water. If they could just get out of the sun, they might have a decent chance of surviving. But Al-Jaza'iri's men were all over the place. Finding a shelter before they roasted to death wouldn't be easy.

A voice called out behind them. Katie hobbled forward to catch up with Nick. Another voice answered the first. They were getting closer. She started to run, but her ankle gave out, tipping her forward onto her face. Nick was there in an instant, lifting her off the ground, setting her back on her feet. He pulled her arm over his shoulder, but she jerked it away. "They're right behind us," she hissed. "Pull the keffiyeh over your face."

She could hear their footsteps now. They were approaching at a slow trot.

Nick pushed her back against the canyon wall and started to run. Before she could even react, he lifted his rifle to his shoulder and fired. What did he think he was doing? The soldiers were coming from the other direction. He fired again as a trio of shouting soldiers came running up behind him. Pointing wildly at the bend in the canyon far ahead of them, he charged forward, leading the soldiers on a mad dash through the wadi.

Katie stared after them as they disappeared around the corner. If they tried to talk to him . . . She pushed off the wall and limped after him. Already she could hear more trucks approaching. They were converging on Nick's position from every direction.

Shouting voices sounded around the bend. Unslinging the rifle, she switched off the safety and raised it to her shoulder. At least they weren't shooting yet. She broke into a run.

Suddenly a soldier came charging around the corner. Katie sighted down the rifle. He was running straight for her, keffiyeh flapping in the breeze. Olive skin, liquid brown eyes . . . Nick? She lowered her rifle and slowed to a stop. Whatever he was running from, it couldn't be good.

He hit her at full speed, scooping her legs out from under her.

Then she was bouncing up and down, swinging back and forth in his arms. Finally she managed to get an arm around his neck. She lifted herself up, pressed herself against his jolting chest.

"What happened back there?" Katie squirmed out of his arms as soon as they turned the first bend.

"I pretended to chase us until they caught up with me." Nick grabbed Katie's hand and pulled her up a rocky slope. "Then I tripped and fell flat on my face."

"And they kept on running?"

He turned a goofy grin on her. "I know. . . . Isn't it weird? It's like they've never watched Bugs Bunny before."

They topped the rise and ran out across the open plateau. A truck roared off to their left. Another one right behind them.

Then she saw it: a jagged gash in the rock only fifty yards away. The closer she got, the more familiar it looked. It was the wadi next to the shepherds' camp. Her shelter wasn't that far away! "Come on, Nick. Faster!" A burst of energy coursed through her body. Almost there. They were going to make it!

She threw herself over the edge of the canyon, sliding down the gravelly wall. Nick hit the bottom before she did and veered to the right.

"Left, left!" She rolled onto her feet and plunged up the gulley. This was definitely the place. She recognized a pile of scree, an exploratory hole she'd scraped the first day she was there. "There it is!" She hobbled over to a large mound of rocks and sand against the south wall. The bottom of an inverted wheelbarrow wheel was protruding from the top of the pile. The camp chairs were completely buried. She hoped that meant the trench was still empty.

"Quick, grab those rocks." Katie indicated a pile near the north wall of the gulley. "We need to cover up that wheel!"

"What wheel?" Nick walked up to the mound of sand.

"Not too close. You'll fall through." She grabbed his arm and pulled him back. "There's a shelter under there. That's how I stayed cool while I was looking for the whale." Katie limped across the wadi and grabbed an armload of flat rocks. Nick appeared at her side, carrying a small boulder. They arranged them around the top of the wheel. It didn't quite look natural, but hopefully the soldiers wouldn't be looking for unrealistic rock formations.

Voices sounded off in the distance. The soldiers had started spreading out. They were searching the area.

Katie dug her hands into the sand at the base of the mound. There it was. The buried camp chair. She pulled on the chair, sliding it toward her. Loose sand poured through the gap, falling down into the trench below. They reached into the trench, scooping the sand out frantically with their hands. The voices were getting closer.

"Quick. Get in!" Katie kept piling the sand on the chair while Nick struggled to squeeze his shoulders into the narrow opening. "There's a lot more room under the wheelbarrow part." She tried to sound confident. Why hadn't she dug a bigger trench?

Finally he was in. She wriggled her way feetfirst into the crowded hole. There was enough room for her legs, but the rest of her didn't seem to fit. She tried pushing harder. No use; she was stuck.

"Hnaa! Hnaa!" The shouts came from just around the bend.

Katie squirmed. She pushed against the end of the trench with all her might.

Strong hands clamped around her calves and pulled. Slowly, she started sliding back into the hole. Reaching out, she managed to grab the sand-covered chair just before her hips were dragged into the wider chamber beneath the wheelbarrow. Pulling the chair over the hole, she shook it to spread out the sand they'd piled on top.

A voice sounded right above her. She drew her hand back from the chair and held her breath. She could hear their footsteps. A group of soldiers were approaching their hiding place. If the chair was visible beneath the sand, they were dead.

Chapter 23

*N*ICK'S HEAD POUNDED to the beat of his racing heart. Muffled voices sounded through the rock and sand. The soldiers were getting closer. Had they seen Katie getting in? He stared back through the darkness, waiting for the crash, for that first stab of sunlight right before the men started shooting. What had he been thinking? Of course the soldiers would find them. The pile of rocks covering the wheel wouldn't fool anybody. It stuck out like a chimney on an igloo— an igloo made of sand with a folding-chair door.

Reaching around Katie's legs, he patted the ground until his hand closed around one of the rifles. *Beautiful!* The rifles were both pointing the wrong way. He was such a genius. Now when the soldiers broke through, he wouldn't even be able to make a show of defending himself. Not that he wanted to shoot anybody. But if they tried to hurt Katie, if they tried to . . . The throbbing in his head intensified. He could see the two soldiers back at the wadi, the way they'd looked at her. . . . If she hadn't knocked them out, he would have killed them. He'd never wanted to hurt anybody in his life, but he would have pummeled them both to death without the tiniest shred of regret.

His grip tightened around the barrel of his rifle. *Come on! Lift up the chair.* He was ready for them. He was tired of hiding!

Silence.

Nick raised his head off the ground and looked down at the entrance by his feet. What were they waiting for? Reinforcements? They couldn't have left. He would have heard them walking away.

He laid his head back on the sand and closed his eyes. *Relax. Deep, easy breaths.* He counted slowly to a hundred and back again. One more time . . . It was still quiet outside. The soldiers were gone. They had to be.

Katie suddenly started squirming. He tightened his grip on the barrel of the rifle. Little by little she was inching her way into the tiny space in front of his face. He pulled back his arm and felt her back. It felt like she was sitting up. He stretched his arm out above him. There was more room under the wheelbarrow than he'd thought. Almost three feet of head space. Suddenly he felt a lot less claustrophobic.

"You think they're gone?" he whispered as Katie continued to squirm.

"They could come back at any time."

"But it's okay to whisper, right?"

"Sure."

Something brushed past Nick's knees. He reached out a hand and felt an eye, a nose, the curve of soft lips. "Sorry." He jerked his hand back. Katie had flipped around and was lying down. If he leaned his head forward just a bit . . . The throb of his pulse beat against his brain. He felt lightheaded, dizzy, like he was going to pass out.

"I didn't take the fossil." Her voice sounded only inches away from him. "I promise."

"I know. You'd never do something like that. I trust you completely. I think I've always trusted you. That's why I've been fighting you so hard. My head's been trying to balance out the excesses of my . . . intuition."

There was a long pause. "So what do we do now?"

"We?" Nick's mind leaped to a thousand possibilities at once. "What do you mean?"

"At first I thought Al-Jaza'iri's men had stolen the fossil."

"You mean the soldiers?"

"Yeah, but now I'm not sure that makes any sense."

"Why not?"

"Either he's a brilliant actor, or he really didn't know it had been stolen. When I asked him if he wanted to see the fossil, he didn't react at all. I was watching him."

"Maybe his men hadn't told him yet," Nick suggested.

"If he'd ordered them to steal it, why post the guards? Wouldn't that just open himself to more suspicion? And why come here in person? It doesn't make any sense."

"But we know the soldiers are working for him. You saw how fast they reacted when we escaped." Nick was struck with a sudden thought. "And the soldiers have been following us since day one. Al-Jaza'iri tried to send guards with us, but when I refused to take them, I think he sent the soldiers instead."

"So maybe he was just trying to protect you."

"Like your guards protected you? The fossil and your so-called meteorite were stolen within a few weeks of each other. There has to be a connection."

"I'm almost positive the Sunni ministers hired our guards. And I get the impression Al-Jaza'iri and the Sunni ministers aren't exactly the best of friends."

"I got the same impression," Nick admitted. "But maybe he was more involved than they realized. Maybe he was trying to sabotage your expedition."

"Maybe . . . but I'm still not buying it. Something doesn't feel right."

"Like me suddenly being denied tenure? Or our paper suddenly getting unaccepted? Oh, and let's not forget Thomas Woodburne. I'm sure he just forgot to tell us he was planning to get fired. This is much bigger than the theft of the fossil."

"That was just science. Considering the nature of our data, we should have expected it."

"What are you talking about?" Nick said. "We reported exactly the results we got. It's not like we're making any unfounded claims."

"But the data doesn't square with any of our current models. And with us calling so many NAS members, I can see why they started checking up on us. Once they found out I was a Christian, it was all over. Everyone else was guilty by association."

"What do you mean, guilty? We haven't done anything wrong! And again, who is this 'they' you keep talking about?"

"Other paleontologists. Other scientists. You were almost one of them—or have you already forgotten your reaction to Brian's telephone call?"

"But that was different. I was reacting to his claims you'd tampered with the data. He made it sound like—"

"Hold on a second! How was that different? When the data didn't agree with your expectations, you automatically thought I'd rigged it. Think about it. You *know* me and you still jumped to conclusions. How can you think other scientists who don't know me wouldn't do the same thing?"

"But to fire someone—just for accepting a paper?"

"Not just any paper—a paper that doesn't square with the evolutionary model."

"So what? Nobody's going to get fired for that."

"Yeah, right. I know two scientists personally who would disagree with you—three if you count Thomas Woodburne. They were forced out of their jobs not because they'd done anything wrong—not even because they believe in God—but because they published something that was thought to be sympathetic to intelligent design."

Nick had heard stories—nutcases trying to twist science to support their own causes—but nothing like this. "Are you sure your friends weren't allowing their biases to corrupt their science?"

"Were you? Was Woodburne? Don't fool yourself; everybody's biased. The scientists who fired Woodburne—you think they don't have a cause? They're so confident in their beliefs they're willing to vilify anyone who disagrees with them. What do you think they do when they get data that doesn't agree with their model? I'll tell you what. They drop it like a hot potato."

"Yeah, but it's different when your cause is good science."

"The only difference is that once you buy into the majority bias, you get to be smug and self-righteous and laugh at everyone who disagrees with you. You can brand them 'the enemy' and run them out of their jobs if you want. You no longer need data to support your rhetoric; you can appeal to common belief, make ad hominem attacks, assume guilt by association. . . ."

Nick felt suddenly uncomfortable. There was something about Katie's tone—was it bitterness, resentment? "So did something happen to you? Did someone in science . . . hurt you?"

"What are you talking about?" She sounded angry now. "Our paper was rejected, and our editor was fired—just because someone didn't like our data. You were just denied tenure!"

"I mean before that. Was it hard getting through grad school? being a postdoc in Fischer's lab?"

A scrape sounded in the darkness. Katie was changing positions. "The hardest part about grad school was my demophobia. Sure, there was the occasional joke, the assumption that if you were intelligent at all you thought Christians were idiots, but you get used to that pretty fast. You just learn to keep your mouth shut and go about the business of science."

"But what about working for Fischer? You sound like you're . . . I don't know, mad. Mad at science."

"Mad at being fired when the chairman found out I was a Christian? Mad at being forced to agree to a gag order? at having the lead of the expedition taken away from me? Why would that make me mad?"

"I see. . . ." Nick lowered his voice. "I'm really sorry."

"Don't get me wrong. I'm not mad at science. I love science. And I understand why it has to be materialistic. If we were allowed to invoke divine intervention every time something didn't make sense, we'd never get anywhere. We never would have developed medicine. The workings of the human body, life itself—they would still be considered God's domain, a miracle that defies human understanding. Science *has* to be materialistic. It has to be blind to God."

"So what's the problem?"

"There's no problem. It's just frustrating; that's all. Science is a great tool, but because it's not allowed to see God, it can't be used to answer any of life's most important questions—like our ultimate origins or the existence of God. And then there's that vocal handful of popularizers who try to say that because science doesn't see God, there must not be a God—as if that somehow proves anything. Of course science is going to come up with a naturalistic explanation. It's the only kind of explanation it's *allowed* to come up with."

"But you have to admit, most Christians—"

"I'm not most Christians! I'm a scientist and most Christians aren't. Most Christians genuinely think they're showing their faith by taking a stand on these issues—whether or not the Bible is clear about them. The main difference between me and most other scientists is I'm willing to keep an open mind. Sure, I believe that if life did evolve God had to be behind it, but how does that bias my science? It's the only thing that makes sense. Forget the evolution of a bacterial flagellum. You want to talk about an unanswered question, tell me how life got started in the first place. Until an organism has the ability to reproduce itself, until a mechanism exists to let it pass down changes to its offspring, the principles of evolution don't even apply. Do you have any idea how many thousands of systems would have had to come together at once to get a primitive cell to the point it could reproduce? Even postulating a million universes isn't enough to bail you out on that one. Crick worked on the problem for years and the best he could come up with was the suggestion that life on this planet was seeded by life from another planet. Talk about begging the question. It's all because of the aliens! Yet I'm the one who's branded as unscientific. I'm the one who's antiscience."

"And now, apparently, so am I. Whether it's guilt by association or not, it's not just you anymore. We're both in the same boat."

"In the same hole, you mean."

Nick nodded. "I never thought what it would be like—"

"Shhh!"

He could hear voices. Approaching footsteps. He went suddenly rigid, holding his breath as the steps approached their hiding place. Closer and closer. It sounded like a whole mob of them. They were right on top of them!

Gradually the noise passed them by and receded into the distance. He let out his breath in a long sigh. "What do we do now? We can't stay here forever."

"The way I see it, there are only two reasonable possibilities. Either the Sunni ministers had the fossil stolen or Al-Jaza'iri did," Katie said. "But if Al-Jaza'iri stole it, why are his soldiers still searching for us? Once we ran, he had all the proof he needed to convince the courts of our guilt."

"Maybe he wants to silence us. Maybe he wants to make our silence permanent."

Katie was quiet for several seconds. "I guess I can buy that. But let's say he didn't steal it. Let's say the Sunnis stole it. If that's the case, then Al-Jaza'iri is chasing us because he thinks we stole it, and he wants it back."

"Either way makes sense. We're back to where we started."

"Except now we know what we have to do." Katie's voice rang with finality. "If Al-Jaza'iri catches us, he's either going to kill us or he's going to throw us in jail until we tell him where the fossil is. Either way we're dead. We have to get back to Baghdad. If Al-Jaza'iri stole the fossil, the Sunni ministers will have no reason to doubt our word and every political reason in the world to help us pin the theft on him."

"But if the Sunnis stole it?"

"Then they'll have to pretend they don't know anything about it. They'll still have to take us at our word, and they'll still have political reasons for helping us pin the theft on Al-Jaza'iri."

Katie scraped a gritty hand across her forehead. The trench was a bake oven. She could only imagine how hot it must be outside in the sun. A stream of sweat trickled across her eyelids as she rolled over onto her side. Nick lay next to her, breathing in a series of short, gasping pants. She reached out and touched his face. He was hot, but at least his skin was still moist. He'd be okay for now, but as soon as it cooled off outside, she was going out to find some water. Hopefully the soldiers were still searching for them. If they had packed up and left the desert with Dietrich and the others, she and Nick were up the creek without a creek. She flopped back against the side of the trench and drifted off to sleep.

»

A soft hum rumbled through Katie's brain. She took a deep breath and shifted on the hard, rocky ground. The trench felt so much better. She wanted to lie there forever, soaking in the coolness, drinking it in like a long sip of cold water.

The hum gradually became a distant roar. It buzzed through her brain, teasing her out of her lethargy. A burning pain in the back of her throat brought her to reality. Had she swallowed a mouthful of sand? She sat up and brushed the grit from her eyes. The humming noise—it was a truck. The soldiers were still searching for them.

She reached out and clutched at a sandy shoulder. Following the shoulder back to Nick's neck, she checked his pulse. Strong and regular. His skin was cool and dry. She ran a hand across his face, felt his forehead. He was going to be fine. All he needed was some water. They both needed water.

"How are you feeling?" A gravelly voice sounded in the darkness.

Katie jerked her hand away from his face. "I'm fine." Her voice felt as dry and scratchy as Nick's sounded. "I just heard a truck drive by. We've got to get to them before they leave. If we can catch a few soldiers away from the main group, they should have enough water to last us another day."

Nick groaned. The floor scraped next to her. He was pushing himself back against the side wall. "Okay. . . . Ladies first."

Katie flipped over onto her stomach and squirmed her way back to the foot of the trench. "Shhh." She stopped struggling and listened at the chair for several seconds. Nothing that she could hear. She pushed back on the chair and a stream of sand rained down on her neck, spilling soft light into the trench. The moon was almost directly above them. It was later than she thought. Katie pushed the chair all the way back and climbed out of the hole. Other than the hum of a distant truck, the wadi was perfectly still.

"Pass the rifles and canteens out first." Her ankle twinged as she put weight on it, but all things considered, it wasn't so bad.

Scanning the rim of the wadi, she reached down into the hole and pulled out their supplies. Then, raising one of the rifles to her shoulder, she covered the area while Nick scraped and grunted his way out of the hole.

"Our next house is going to have a bigger front door." He climbed to his feet and started brushing the sand from his fatigues. "For a minute there I was starting to worry. I was afraid Rabbit would have to use my legs as towel racks."

Katie smiled at the allusion. First Bugs Bunny and now Winnie the Pooh . . . It was a rare paleontologist who was so well-versed in the classics. She glanced shyly up at him, allowing her eyes to linger on his as he returned her gaze. "We really need to get some water."

He nodded and picked up the canteens and rifle with a sigh. "Which way?"

"A lot of trucks have been coming and going from over there." Katie pointed to the east—the direction opposite their camp. "If they have some kind of camp there, it might not be guarded." Scooting the chair back over the hole with her good foot, she turned and started following the path of the wadi.

Nick caught up and fell in step beside her. "Listen, do you like spicy food? It doesn't have to be burn-your-head-off spicy, but you know . . . Do you like other spices besides salt, pepper, and ketchup?"

"Why?" Katie studied his face. He looked way too serious.

"I was thinking . . . If we ever get out of this mess, maybe we could go get dinner together? I've been wanting to visit New Mexico forever."

Katie's stomach did a double-twisting front one-and-a-half. "Sure, I guess . . ." It was just dinner. They'd been eating dinner together for weeks back at the camp.

"Do you like to ski? I hear skiing is great in Taos." Nick's eyes sparkled. This wasn't just dinner he was talking about.

"I've only been twice. I'm not very good." Katie looked down at the floor of the wadi. "It was fun, but . . ."

"So, want to go skiing when we get back? After all this heat, we're going to need a little cold weather, don't you think?"

"Nick, I . . ." Katie stopped and searched the area around them. A truck somewhere off to their right was getting closer. This wasn't the time for this conversation. It would just lead to an argument.

"What's wrong?" She could already hear the wariness in his voice.

"Nothing. This just isn't the time." She broke away from him and climbed up the slope of the wadi. A truck was making for a point several hundred yards behind them—not too far from their shelter.

Nick scrambled up the slope and crouched down beside her. "Did you put the chair back?"

"Kind of," she whispered. "I wish now I'd been more careful." She watched as a group of soldiers spilled out of the truck and swarmed their wadi. "If they find the shelter, this place will be crawling with soldiers. Come on." Katie started to climb back down into the gulley, but a hand closed around her shoulder.

"Wait a second. I think that may be their camp."

Katie searched in the direction Nick was pointing. A faint smudge of orange-red light glowed softly in the distance, almost a mile and a half away from them. It looked like a fire or a lantern hidden behind one or two large tents. "I think you're right. What do you want to do? Keep following the wadi or set off across the plain?"

"Think they'll notice our tracks?"

"Probably."

"Then let's take the high road." Nick slung the rifle over his shoulder and climbed out of the gulley.

Katie considered doubling back to leave a false trail but decided against it. No point making their presence any more obvious. She hurried after Nick and fell into step at his side, adopting the quick, determined stride of a soldier on a mission.

They walked in silence for several minutes. The wadi behind them was perfectly still. Maybe the soldiers had gone the wrong way. Most of the footprints covering the floor of the wadi *did* lead back to their camp.

"We don't have to go skiing." Nick's whisper sounded like a shout against the stillness of the desert. "Isn't Carlsbad Caverns in New Mexico? I've always wanted to go there, too."

Katie stared down at the path in front of her. She was going to have to tell him. It wasn't fair to him or her. "Nick, I . . . please don't take this wrong. I really like you. . . ."

He let out a sigh. "That's never good."

"No, I'm serious. I really like you. I like you a lot."

"But . . ."

"I like you, but we're just not compatible—not where it matters most."

Nick didn't say anything for several steps. "I respect your decision, so please don't take this as argument, but I have to be honest. I've never in my life met anyone *more* compatible. I mean, how many people actually enjoy looking for bones out in the middle of a sweltering desert? traveling through dangerous countries? camping out in sand-filled tents?"

"I know what you're saying, and I feel it too, but . . . those are just the trappings of life. They're not the essentials."

"This is going back to the religion thing, isn't it?"

Katie nodded.

"Listen, I'm sorry I overreacted. I really didn't mean it. I'm totally fine with your faith. I really am."

"But I'm not fine . . . with yours."

Nick's head jerked back like he'd been slapped. His mouth hung open in a silent question as he searched her eyes for hope.

"Nick, I'm sorry; I really am. But our worldviews are so different. Do you want a relationship with a woman you can't respect? someone who bases her life on something you think is completely ridiculous?"

"You're putting words in my mouth. I never said your faith was ridiculous."

"But you think I'm wrong."

"Maybe. Or maybe I'm wrong. I'm willing to keep an open mind."

"I appreciate that, but I still want more. I want someone who loves me with more than the levels of oxytocin and vasopressin in his brain. I want to be more than just the product of a series of random chemical processes. I want someone who believes there's a purpose to life."

"So now you're saying just because I'm a biologist I'm incapable of love?"

"Of course not. You're a very loving person; anyone can see that. But what does your worldview tell you love is? What's the theoretical basis for your love?"

"Just because I understand some of the biochemical processes—"

Katie grabbed Nick's arm. Far behind them the truck had started up again. The soldiers were climbing out of the wadi and piling into the truck. They weren't running, but they weren't dawdling either. Had they found their shelter? She and Nick were only a quarter mile from the soldiers' camp. They needed a plan.

"When we get to the camp, I'll circle around the tents and try to get behind the sentries, if there are any. Once I'm in position, you walk up to the sentries with the rifle over your shoulder, and I'll surprise them from behind."

Nick nodded. "If they have trucks, we'll have to find the keys."

"Leave that to me. You stand guard over the sentries. Try to look like a sentry yourself."

"And if they don't have trucks?"

"We take as much water as we can carry. Maybe some canvas for a shelter. We can't risk going back to the wheelbarrow. Not now."

Nick shook his head and looked back at the truck. "I can't believe we're actually going to do this. Part of me just wants to turn myself in and get it over with."

"Which part is that?"

"The irrational part that doesn't think Al-Jaza'iri stole the bone."

"And what does the rational part think?"

"That you should go skiing with me in Taos."

Katie raised her finger to her lips to disguise her smile. She'd have to let that one slide. They were way too close to the camp for another argument. She reached out and pulled back on Nick's arm to slow him down. The truck had started moving. It was heading their way.

Nick pointed to a clump of rocks, his eyebrows raised in a silent question.

She shook her head. The sentries would be able to see them. She slung the rifle over her shoulder. "We're soldiers," she mouthed and raised herself to her full height.

Light from the truck's headlights swept across them and the roar of the engine jumped an octave in response. The soldiers were bearing down on them fast.

Katie forced herself to relax. She slowed her pace, taking a meandering path toward the closest tent. "Relax; don't look back," she hissed as the headlights caught them in a blast of blinding light. Their shadows were thrown against the tent, Nick's looking way too stiff and hers looking way too small.

She trudged toward the tent, an exhausted soldier coming back from patrol. The truck skidded to a stop not more than twenty feet behind them. A jumble of shouting voices sounded behind closed windows. Katie flopped an exhausted arm at them and turned to crouch down in front of the entrance of the tent. Nick was right next to her, looking far too awake. She unzipped the zipper and crawled inside. Her hand brushed against a bare foot. She pulled back and her knee landed on a blanket-covered lump.

"*Hamar!*" A bleary voice grumbled from inside the tent. "*Sid el bab!*"

Nick stood frozen halfway through the entrance. Katie pulled him all the way inside and yanked down on the zipper. Shouts sounded from the truck. Running footsteps. The tent shuddered. One of the soldiers outside was pounding against the canvas, calling out orders in Arabic.

A shadow moved in front of her. Someone's elbow bumped into her face. Katie crawled toward the back of the tent, ducking and dodging to avoid the struggling men. When she finally reached the back, she dropped to the floor and curled up into a loose ball. A large shadowy figure approached her from the side. She tried to calm her breathing, prayed it was only Nick. He knew enough to make for the back of the tent. It had to be him.

The zipper opened and the light of a distant lantern angled into the tent. Katie peeked out through her eyelashes as a line of groggy men shuffled out into the camp. Shouts arose from the nearby tents. The men from the truck didn't seem to be waiting at the door.

The last man to leave the tent turned and looked back inside. Katie held her breath and waited. She could hear something moving. Why wasn't he raising the alarm? Finally she cracked open her eyes. The man was gone.

"We should move now," Katie whispered to the figure next to her. "This may be our only chance."

Nick lifted his head and looked around the tent. "Are you sure? It sounds like they're going out on patrol."

"Exactly!" Katie climbed onto her knees and crawled over to the open door. Three soldiers were climbing into the backseat of one of the trucks that stood at the perimeter of the camp. Five more soldiers were shuffling toward the truck right beside it. The engine of the first truck turned over. Headlights stabbed the surrounding darkness.

"Nick, come on!" She waved for Nick to follow her and plunged out into the bustling camp, letting her head droop forward so that the fabric on both sides of her keffiyeh hid her face. Footsteps sounded right behind her. It had better be Nick. She cut across to the edge of the camp and circled around the perimeter, keeping to the heaviest shadows. One of the trucks stood off by itself, all but lost in the darkness.

Katie made for the truck and pulled back on the handle of the passenger door. It was open! Her eyes sought the ignition as she climbed through the door. It was almost too easy. Two keys dangled from the switch on the steering column. All Nick had to do was climb inside and drive away. But what was taking him so long? She slumped forward in her seat, fighting the urge to turn around. Finally she saw his reflection in the rearview mirror. He pulled open the door and slid behind the wheel.

"We've got company," he whispered and started up the truck.

The back doors flew open. Katie glanced at the rearview mirror in time to see three soldiers slide into the backseat. They were holding their rifles barrel up in front of them. Taking them by surprise wasn't going to be easy.

Nick found the headlights and pulled the truck forward. They rode several minutes in silence before the eyes of the middle soldier drifted to the rearview mirror. Katie slouched forward and looked out her window. *Come on, Nick, get us out of here!* She could hear the middle soldier stirring. He said something in Arabic. None of his friends responded. He repeated himself. It sounded like a question. Katie reached back and pulled the seat belt around her. She fumbled with the buckle, tapping the metal tongue loudly against the buckle before jamming it in place with a metallic snap.

The soldier jabbered something again, louder this time. Katie flipped the safety switch on her rifle and pulled it tight against her stomach. The man was yelling now. He leaned forward and grabbed Katie by the shoulder.

Crunch! Katie slammed against her seat belt as the truck plowed into a wall of rock and sand. Releasing her seat belt, she twisted around in her seat and covered the dazed soldiers with her rifle. "Nobody move!"

The middle soldier lunged for the floor of the truck.

Swinging her rifle over the seat, she brought the stock down on the back of his head, and he slumped to the floor. The soldier directly in front of her grabbed her rifle and tried to wrench it from her hands, but Nick was already out of the truck. The barrel of his rifle crashed through the back window, covering them in a spray of glass.

For a brief second, while her opponent's attention was on the broken window, Katie reversed the direction of her pull and smashed the rifle into his face. She twisted it out of his grasp and jammed its barrel into the side of his head.

"I've got them. Get their rifles!" Nick's rifle moved back and forth between the two conscious soldiers.

Katie pulled the rifle back and set it on the seat in front of her knees. The soldier in front of her slumped back in his seat, his eyes watery and unfocused. The other soldier stared wide-eyed at Nick. Both of his hands were raised in the air. He obviously had more sense than his two friends. She leaned cautiously over the seat and gathered up the rifles. Then, once their rifles were safely stowed in the front of the truck, she collected their radios and three deliciously heavy canteens.

"Okay, Nick. Open the door, and I'll herd them outside." Katie dug through the pile of rifles and brought her gun up. "I'm pretty sure all the fight's gone out of them, but call out if they give you any trouble."

Nick reached through the broken window and unlocked the door. Then, swinging the door wide open, he backed away from the truck and covered the men with his rifle.

"Out you go!" Katie motioned with her rifle, but the men just sat there. "Too bad you two don't understand English," she said. "Because the last one out gets a new hole in his head."

Both men scrambled for the door.

"I thought as much." She waited until they were both outside lying facedown on the sand before climbing out of the truck and dragging the unconscious soldier out onto the ground. Then, sweeping the cubes of glass off the backseat of the truck, she crawled across the seat and aimed her rifle through the broken window. "Okay, I've got them. Let's go."

"Pray the truck starts." Nick climbed behind the wheel and turned the key. Nothing but a clicking noise.

"Don't move!" Katie sighted down the rifle as one of the soldiers raised his head. "Don't even tempt me when I'm mad!" The man lowered his head.

Nick tried the truck again, and this time it roared to life. He backed the truck away from the sandy bank while Katie covered the men with her rifle. The truck lurched forward and they were off, bouncing and rattling over the uneven, rocky ground. She leaned her head out the window and looked behind them before climbing over the front seat. The men were still lying facedown on the ground.

They drove in silence for a long time, searching the desert ahead of them to find the best pathway through the network of forking wadis. Every mile they traveled was another two minutes of safety. If only they could get to the highway . . .

"How much time do you think we have before they come after us?" Nick finally broke the silence.

"Ten to twenty minutes, maybe less if our friends are smarter than they look."

"Beautiful!"

"You realize they'll probably call ahead. There could be a whole army waiting for us at the main road."

"Still, it gives us plenty of time." Nick grinned eagerly at Katie. His eyes burned with sudden intensity.

"Plenty of time for what?" Katie wasn't sure she liked where this was going.

"Plenty of time for a good stiff drink." He broke into a broad smile. "Hand me one of those canteens!"

Chapter 24

*N*ICK SLAMMED ON THE BRAKES and flipped the truck into reverse. Just ahead of him, not more than five feet from his front wheels, the ground opened into a deep ravine. Pierced by twin beams of light, a rolling dust cloud drifted over the chasm, plunging in slow motion into the dark depths below.

"That was close." He backed the truck several yards before putting it in drive and following the wadi around to the left.

"Are you getting sleepy? I could drive for a while." Katie turned down the volume on the squawking two-way radio she'd been playing with for the last half hour.

"I'm fine. We were climbing a hill and I just didn't see it."

"If you're sure . . ." Katie turned the volume on the radio back up. A deep voice was jabbering away in Arabic, barking out orders neither of them could understand.

Nick followed the wadi for almost a mile before it got shallow enough to cross. Then turning the truck back toward the east, he sped out across a flat and relatively smooth plain.

"So, have you taught yourself Arabic yet?" He glanced over at Katie, who was staring down at the radio, her brow furrowed in concentration.

"I'm beginning to piece a few things together."

"Oh, really?" He smiled. "What are they saying?"

"Deep Voice was telling his men to hurry up and find us, but one of the men, I think his name is Hakim, told Deep Voice not to worry because we were just going to fall into a wadi anyway."

"Hakim always was a dreamer. What else did he say?"

"The rest was kind of hard to make out. I'm pretty sure he was talking with his mouth full of Doritos—maybe Fritos. Those two sound alike to me."

"Maybe you should turn the radio off. We need to figure out what we're going to do when we get to Baghdad."

"Just a few more minutes. I really am picking up a few things."

"Such as?"

"Such as the fact that there are at least five different groups of men, three of them driving in trucks and two of them stationary. So far I've identified seven different voices and five different names of soldiers on the search team. And most important of all, they've mentioned Al-Jaza'iri's name eight or nine times, but they've never once mentioned the names of the Sunni ministers."

"Can you tell how close they are?" Nick swerved to avoid a particularly large rock. Off to his left he saw what looked like a strip of smooth sand.

"The signal's been getting fainter and fainter. I think we're losing them."

"Good. Let me know if that changes." He veered to the left and pulled onto what felt like a primitive dirt road. "I think we're getting close to the highway."

A loud, clear voice squawked out over the radio. Nick jammed his foot on the gas. One of them was catching up fast!

"Stop!" Katie cried out. "Turn right. We've got to get out of here!"

"But they're right behind us!"

"Not behind. In front. Turn right now!"

Nick yanked hard on the wheel, sending the truck careening over the rocky terrain. He fought to control the bouncing, rolling vehicle. A rock to the left. The mouth of a shallow wadi to the right.

"What makes you think they were in front of us?" He hit the brakes, slowing the truck to a more controllable speed.

"The voice was getting louder, but there wasn't any background noise. They were one of the stationary teams."

"Think they set up a roadblock on the main road?"

"Probably."

"So why go south? Won't we have to go north eventually to get to Baghdad?"

"They're expecting us to head north to get around the roadblocks. They'll be patrolling the strip of desert by the road for sure."

"So . . ."

"So what if we cut south and then cross over the main road? They won't be expecting us to skirt the roadblocks on the other side."

"Nobody will ever accuse you of being predictable." Nick flashed Katie a smile.

They drove several miles in silence, listening to Iraqi voices on the radio. Finally, the voices were starting to sound more faint.

"Okay. That should be far enough."

Nick angled the truck toward the pink-tinged glow in the eastern sky. "What if there's another roadblock?"

"I'm pretty sure there is, but it's probably much farther to the north." Katie turned up the volume on the radio. Nick was just beginning to distinguish between the voices when they came to the main road.

He turned south onto the highway and drove several minutes before finally coming to a gap in the concrete dividers separating north- and southbound traffic. Cutting through the gap, he headed out into the desert on the other side.

"I've been thinking," he said after they'd finally deemed it safe to turn and follow the highway to the north. "Dr. Littman invited us to stop by their place any time. I'm pretty sure I'll be able to find their apartment again."

"I'm not so sure that's a good idea."

"Why not?" Nick shot her a look.

"Remember what your friend said about a creationist having a motive to perpetrate a hoax? Well, what if Littman tampered with the soft tissue samples? I think I might have set the thermos down in his lab. What if he switched them?"

"You're saying Littman stole the fossil?"

"No, but what if the fossil was stolen because of his sequence? Remember? Right after we learned the date, the fossil was stolen—before we ever had a chance to send out another sample for confirmation. What if that wasn't a coincidence?"

"While we're being paranoid, maybe Dietrich stole the fossil, or Wayne, or Hooman, or Ahamed. . . . Or maybe I stole it. Have you ever thought of that?"

Katie shook her head. "None of you have motives—at least not that I can think of."

"And Dr. Littman has a motive? He wants to turn it into earrings for his wife?"

"I already told you. There's a good chance he's a creationist."

"Why? Because he likes fossil earrings?"

"No, because . . ." She looked over at him and seemed to falter. "I know you're going to think I'm crazy, but you have to trust me. He's a Christian. I can tell. I don't know what flavor he is—young earther, old earther, directed evolutionist, intelligent designer—but I know he's a Christian."

"Why? Because he's a nice guy? I've got news for you. Christians haven't cornered the market on nice."

"He's way more than nice. He has a cause, a purpose bigger than himself. Or don't you think it's strange he's still in Iraq—even with everything that's going on? And how many professors do you know who invite their students to dinner more than once or twice a year? And did you notice he's taken the time to learn Arabic? He even speaks Arabic with his students. And he spoke to Ahamed in Urdu. He noticed him—even though he's not a scientist."

Nick shook his head. "Okay, let's say he *is* a creationist—which I'm still not saying he is—but aren't you just doing the same thing to him you complained I was doing to you?"

"All I'm saying is he might have had a motive. I'm not saying he's guilty. I just want us to be careful; that's all. He had the opportunity too."

"Sorry," Nick said. "Still not buying it. I say we stay at Littman's place while we're in Baghdad."

"Okay . . . but I bet you a nickel he's a Christian."

"A whole nickel, huh?" Nick flashed her a smile. "I'll tell you what. Let's make this more interesting. How about a ski trip in Taos?"

»

Katie and Nick peered out from behind a low brick wall. Across the street, the Littmans' apartment building sprawled like a minimum security prison. Brick walls, metal gates, brown-shuttered windows . . . The flower boxes on their tiny second-story balcony provided the only color to be found on the entire street.

"See anything?" Nick leaned in close and whispered in her ear.

"Just that truck." Katie pointed to a white pickup parked at the end of the street. "But it's been there for days."

"Are you sure?"

"Positive. See that pile of trash behind its back wheel?"

"Okay, let's go." Nick stood up and crept across the street. In his torn keffiyeh and dusty fatigues, he looked completely out of place in this quiet city neighborhood, but they'd decided two soldiers would attract less attention than two filthy Americans in ragged clothes.

Katie waited until he'd gotten all the way across before limping after him. They couldn't afford to let their guard down for a second. The Iraqis were sparing no expense to find them. They had set up not two but three roadblocks along the road to Baghdad. Two they'd skirted around easily by driving cross-country through the desert, but they'd almost missed the third. If Nick hadn't noticed brake lights off in the distance and pulled off the road when he did, they would have been trapped for sure.

She followed Nick up the brick steps and stood next to him on the landing. "Aren't you going to knock?"

Nick backed away from the door. "We don't want to scare them. Maybe you should stand in front. I look rough enough to scare my own mom."

"Maybe if we yelled 'trick or treat.'" Katie stepped forward and knocked gently on the door. No answer. She waited a few more seconds and knocked louder.

The door cracked open and Mrs. Littman peered out with wide eyes. "Oh my goodness! Katie James? What are you doing in that getup?"

"May we come in, Mrs. Littman? We'll explain everything, but it's not safe for us to be outside."

"Of course!" She pulled the door open and stepped back to let them in. "I'm so sorry. I thought at first . . . when I saw those uniforms . . ."

Nick followed Katie inside and bolted the door behind them. "You should know up front we're in a great deal of trouble," he said. "The police are looking for us and maybe even an Iraqi militia. If you'd rather we go somewhere else, we'll both understand."

"You poor dears. Of course we want you to stay. But the police! What happened? Is it okay for me to ask?" She took Katie by the arm and guided her to a blue and white striped sofa. "Let me call Jerry. He'll know what to do."

"Mrs. Littman?" Katie stood awkwardly in front of the light-colored sofa. "Before you call your husband, could I ask you a personal question?"

Mrs. Littman looked back and forth between Nick and Katie with wide, astonished eyes. "Certainly, please, but I can't imagine how I'll be any help."

"Are you and your husband Christians?"

Mrs. Littman's face lit with a warm smile. "Yes, we are. How did you know?"

Katie shot Nick a smug look. Nick just shrugged.

"Are you Christians too?" She lowered her voice conspiratorially. "Is that what this is all about?"

"Not really. I'm a Christian, but Nick's—"

"I'm not a Christian yet, but I'm definitely open to the idea," Nick interjected.

Katie shot Nick another look. This wasn't the time for any more ski trip lobbying. "Your husband's a molecular biologist, right? Would you consider him a young earth creationist?"

Mrs. Littman frowned. "You should know Jerry's one of the strongest Christians I've ever met. He loves God, God's Word, everybody who comes across his path. . . ."

"It's okay," Katie soothed. "I'm not judging him. I'm totally okay with old earth. I just needed to know where he was coming from. We're in serious trouble and we had to rule out the possibility that he might have had a motive for tampering with our samples."

"Jerry would never . . ."

"We know that." Nick stepped forward. "That's why we're here. If we thought he had anything to do with this, we never would have come asking for help. Katie's just being . . . thorough." He glared at Katie as soon as Mrs. Littman looked away.

"So how can we help? You never told me." Mrs. Littman drifted across the room to hover over the phone.

"Mainly we just need a place to rest and hide," Katie said. "We've been running through the desert for two days."

"You poor dears. Please, sit down. Are you hungry? Let me get you something to eat." Mrs. Littman started toward the kitchen.

"Actually . . ." Katie looked from her dust-covered clothes to the white stripes on the sofa. "Would you mind if I took a shower? I'm afraid even by standing close to your sofa, I'm going to get it dirty."

"All right. Thanks, Mike." Nick followed the phone cord back to the old-fashioned telephone base. "Call me as soon as you hear back from Brian, okay?"

"Kay-kay. Later, dude."

"Bye." Nick hung up the phone and slumped against the wall. He pressed the palms of his hands into his eyes and took a deep breath. He couldn't keep going like this. The walls were already starting to spin. Maybe he should just forget about the other phone calls and go to bed. Mike would figure things out.

When he opened his eyes, Dr. Littman was watching him with a concerned frown. "Bad news about your tenure vote?" Littman reached out and put a hand on his shoulder.

For a second Nick was a little boy, running to his dad after tripping over the patio steps in the backyard. He blinked hard and forced his eyes open wide. He had to wake up or he was going to embarrass himself. "It looks like the president of the NAS talked to our department chair about the results of our tests. According to a couple of my friends, he made it sound like Katie had turned me to the 'dark side.'"

"I'm sorry. That was totally unfair. I'd be happy to register a formal protest, but coming from me, it would probably do more harm than good. The NAS would take it as a confirmation of your so-called guilt."

Nick shrugged. "Is that why you had to come here? To get funding for your research?"

"I was doing fine in the States." A mysterious smile lit Littman's features. "I came here for the students. The Iraqis are an extraordinary people. They've been through so many horrors, yet they've remained so warm and hospitable. They're amazingly kind."

Nick had to look away. Maybe they were kind to him—but then who wouldn't be? So far Nick hadn't seen much about the Iraqis to like. Littman's students were the only Iraqis he'd seen really smiling since he'd entered this country.

A burst of laughter came from the other room.

"Which reminds me . . ." Littman guided Nick into the living room, where Katie and Mrs. Littman were huddled next to each other on the sofa. "We were planning to have a few students over tonight, but I'd certainly understand if you'd be uncomfortable with that."

Katie laughed again. Nick stopped to drink in her smile. He'd never seen this side of her. After a shower and a meal, with no pressure from her boss and nobody trying to kill her, she was a completely different person. He could get used to this new Katie.

"Nick? Is something wrong?" Littman's worried face appeared in front of his eyes.

"Me? I'm fine. Just a little tired, that's all."

"Then I'll definitely cancel. You and Katie should get some rest."

"No, please. Don't cancel on my account." He replayed the conversation in his mind. "I'd love to meet your students. I'm sure I won't be uncomfortable at all." He pictured the church service he'd been to with one of his middle school friends. More likely he'd be too comfortable. The service had been mind-numbingly boring. He hoped he could stay awake.

Littman frowned as if he'd just read his thoughts.

"Seriously, I'll be fine."

"I just remembered." Littman's brow creased in concentration. "Tonight is bridge night. With you and Katie here, we'll need two more people. If I ask Mahdi and Karim, Shirzad will want to come too. Then I'll have to find three more people."

"Nick!" Katie's voice rang out from the corner of the room. "A truck full of soldiers. Right outside!"

Nick ran for the window as she pressed herself flat against the wall on the other side.

"They're getting out of the truck!" Katie hissed. "At least four of them. Make that five!"

"Is there a back door?" Nick turned to Littman.

Littman shook his head. "There's a window in the bedroom, but we're on the second floor."

Nick grabbed Katie's hand and pulled her into the bedroom.

"Wait; my shoes!" She ran back to the door and grabbed her shoes. Footsteps were tramping up the stairs.

Nick ran to the window and slid it to the side. A flat patio roof stood off to the left—only six feet down.

"Wait." Katie pushed her way in front of him and poked her head outside. She twisted herself around until she was looking up at the roof. "I think we can make it. Hold on. Make sure I don't fall."

He grabbed her by the belt as she climbed out onto the ledge and grasped the edge of the roof.

Shouting voices sounded from the front of the apartment, then a calmer voice. Littman was talking to them in Arabic.

Katie's feet slipped off the ledge. For a dizzying moment, she swung out over the two-story drop. Nick grabbed her around the legs and hoisted her up as high as he could reach. Then, leaping onto the ledge, he pushed up on her good foot until it disappeared over the edge of the roof.

Running footsteps pounded across the living room floor.

Nick stretched out, grabbed the edge of the roof, and swung himself away from the window. A pair of hands clamped onto his wrists as he hung dangling over the swimming void.

A shout came from inside the bedroom. Clomping footsteps approached the window.

He tried to pull up, but his arms were too tired. He swung farther away from the window. Hand by hand, inch by inch, he walked himself toward the corner of the roof.

More clomping inside the room. The chatter of excited voices. A soldier's head poked through the window, his face obscured by the hanging fabric of his keffiyeh.

Nick froze. His hands were starting to slip. The more Katie's grip tightened around his wrists, the weaker his hands were becoming. Finally the head disappeared back into the room. More shouts. Running footsteps. They were running around to check the back of the building. He had to get up now!

Pushing off the side of the brick wall with his feet, he threw an elbow over the eaves. Katie tugged on his arm as his feet scrabbled up the side of the wall. His shoulder was over, his right arm . . . Finally he got his left foot over the edge and rolled onto the blistering rooftop.

Katie hauled him onto his feet and pulled him to the center of the flat roof. "There's a stairway leading up here." Katie pointed to a set of metal stairs opening out onto the roof. "It won't take them long to find us."

Nick took a few more gulps of air. The soldiers had probably already called in the rest of the troops. He and Katie needed to get as far away from there as possible. "Maybe there's another way down." He led her across the rooftop to the far side of the building. Peeking over the edge, he searched the street below for signs of movement. "See anything?"

Katie appeared at his side. "I think they're searching the other end." A fresh fruity scent hung around her like a veil.

Nick had already leaned in closer before he could stop himself. He pulled away and forced his eyes to the street. What was he thinking? It wasn't even her shampoo. It was Mrs. Littman's.

"See that porch—with the barred window just above it?" Katie was leaning out over the edge of the roof. "We could slide down the bars and drop to the porch below."

Nick crept toward the window, studying it from above. If the soldiers walked around the corner while they were climbing down . . .

A shout rang out from the back of the building. The soldiers had discovered the stairs! Nick swung out over the edge of the roof and let go to land with a smack on the brick and cement porch. Stumbling back on tingling feet, he barely managed to catch Katie under the arms as she smacked down right in front of him.

"Ow!" She crumbled forward onto the porch, grasping at her ankle with both hands.

"Come on. There's no time." He picked her up and pounded down the stairs. Darting across the street, he made for a narrow alley on the other side.

Somewhere behind him a car engine roared. Or was it a truck? Nick set Katie down behind an adobe wall. The vehicle rumbled down the street. It sounded like a truck, but was it full of soldiers? He didn't dare look.

As soon as the truck passed their hiding place, Katie climbed to her feet and limped down the alley. Nick followed her around the corner of a decaying concrete building. The alley dead-ended at an old metal gate. Beyond the gate was a ramp leading down into darkness. It was the perfect hiding place, if they could just get inside.

Nick climbed over a pile of trash and pushed on the rusty metal bars. The gate didn't budge. They'd have to find another way.

Suddenly Katie gripped his arm. Another truck was driving down the road. He searched for a place to hide as it slowed to a stop close to the entrance into their alley.

"Quick, dig down under this pile of trash," he whispered.

Katie's eyes went wide. Her head whipped around. She was searching for a better hiding place?

"Come on. Start digging." He grabbed an armful of garbage and pulled it on top of himself. Katie still hadn't moved. "Katie!"

She stared down at the trash, her forehead wrinkled in disgust. "But I just took a shower!"

Chapter 25

NICK, PLEASE. I can't do this!" Katie pressed her face against Nick's arm as he guided her down the crowded sidewalk. Footsteps clacked all around her. Muffled voices. The rush of moving cars.

"It's okay. Just a few more minutes. We're almost there." He pulled her to the side and stopped as a herd of high-pitched voices stampeded by. Something brushed her arm. She could feel the rush of moving bodies all around her. "It's okay, Katie. It's just a few boys. They're not going to hurt you."

Katie tensed as something touched the back of her head. It was Nick. He was stroking her hair. Something stirred in her memory, tightening her stomach into knots.

"It's okay," Nick's voice soothed in her ear. "I'm right here with you."

She tried to focus on his voice, the gentle fingers combing through her hair. Gradually her trembling muscles began to relax. She loosened her grip on his arm. He wasn't going to leave her. Somehow he understood.

"Are you ready to start walking now? How's your ankle?"

"It's fine." Katie rocked her forehead against his arm.

"Okay, slow steps." His arm wrapped protectively around her shoulders, snuggling her against his chest.

Katie knew she should protest; she should pull away. Wasn't he crossing some kind of line? But she was so tired. They'd been walking all morning and most of the night. And there were so many people.

The later it got, the more people crowded out onto the streets. She needed him. The thought brought a sharp pang. She needed him to help her find the Sunni ministers. To help clear her name. But he wasn't a believer, and she had to remember that.

Taking a deep breath, she slipped out from under Nick's arm and opened her eyes. A dozen staring faces closed in on her, forcing her eyes to the ground. She clung to his arm as a wave of dizziness crashed over her. No, she could do this. Armed soldiers were chasing her. She couldn't let a handful of Iraqi grandmothers get into her head.

Squeezing her eyes shut, she concentrated on the texture of Nick's sleeve, the earthy smell of garbage and detergent and sweat. He'd been so kind to her, so considerate. . . . Letting her sleep in the pile of trash at the end of the alley while he stayed awake and kept watch. They'd wandered aimlessly through the city most of the night until they finally stumbled across a familiar street. Nick had insisted on going into the museum alone. The ministers hadn't been there, but at least he'd gotten the receptionist to write down the address of the government building they had their offices in.

"Okay, little step down." Nick's voice broke through her thoughts.

Katie peeked down at her feet and stepped off the curb. A long, black dress swept past her. Shoes scraped against the asphalt close behind. She tightened her grip on Nick's arm. "How much farther?" Her voice was shaking. She couldn't control it.

"Two more blocks. Maybe even—"

The squeal of brakes sliced through the air. Katie spun toward the sound. A white pickup rocked to a stop only inches away from her. A wide-eyed driver. Cloaked women, shouting men . . .

Her legs buckled beneath her. Hot asphalt burned into her skin. She was on her knees, retching into the rising heat. A sea of faces closed around her. Shouting voices. Reaching hands. She squeezed her eyes shut, tried to focus on her breathing. But all the voices . . .

A vivid image pushed into her brain: A twisted figure, lying still across a painted white line. Blood. So much blood. Rusty red against a sea green purse. The faces crowded against her. Shouted questions, grasping hands. She was fine. Why couldn't they understand? It was her mother's blood, not hers. It was her mother who needed the help.

»

"Please, stand back. She needs some room!" Nick stretched out his arms, pushing back against the crowding onlookers. "Katie, can you hear me? Everybody's okay. The truck didn't touch us. Nobody's hurt."

He kneeled down and put a hand on her back. Her whole body was shuddering with the force of her sobs. His heart twisted in his chest as her tears puddled onto the blacktop. "Katie, it's okay. I . . ." His throat swelled shut. "What's wrong? What do you need me to do?"

The wail of a distant siren rose above the din of the crowd. Was it an ambulance or the police? He had let her stay there way too long.

"Katie, this is Nick. I'm going to pick you up, okay? We're just going for a little walk."

She didn't give any indication she'd heard him.

Getting down on his knees, he reached around her and tipped her back into his arms. Her trembling frame was rigid as a board. "Shhh . . . Easy. Everything's fine." Shifting his weight onto his right knee, he managed to get his left foot under him and rose to his feet. "She's okay, everybody. Thanks for your concern."

The onlookers parted as he carried her across the street and stepped onto the curb. The siren was getting louder. He broke into a slow jog, turning and dodging through the gradually thinning crowd.

Katie's sobs were starting to subside now. Her rigid, shaking body slowly melted into his arms. She turned toward him and pressed her face against his chest.

Nick slowed to a fast walk. "Katie?"

She shifted in his arms. Her left arm came up and circled around his neck.

"Are you going to be all right?"

She nodded. "I'm really sorry. I didn't mean to cause a scene."

"No harm done." He hesitated before asking, "Would it help to talk about it?"

A fresh tear ran down the side of her face. He was such an idiot. Why hadn't he left well enough alone?

She took a deep breath. "My mother died when I was six. We were in San Francisco. It was her first time off the reservation. . . ." A hiccuping sob caught at her voice.

"It's okay. You don't have to talk about it."

"No, it's supposed to help." She cracked open her eyes and looked up at him with a vacant, faraway expression. "She and I had never been in such a big city. So many tall buildings. Cars were everywhere. She never even saw the traffic light. I'm not even sure she knew what it meant." Tears flooded her eyes. She pressed her face back against his chest. "So many people . . . They were just trying to help, but I—"

"Shhh . . . Don't talk. It's okay." Nick leaned over her, stroked her hair with his cheek. "It's going to be okay. I won't let anything hurt you. Never, ever again."

He quickened his pace, searching the street ahead of them. The government building was just a block and a half away.

A commotion behind them caught his attention. Running footsteps. A woman's surprised yelp.

Nick lumbered forward. The footsteps behind him were getting closer. He started to run, but his arms were going to give out soon.

"What's happening?" Katie pushed away from him, twisting in his arms.

He swung her onto her feet, keeping an arm around her waist until she'd recovered her balance enough to run. "A half block behind," he whispered. "Someone's following us."

Grabbing Katie by the hand, he pulled her through the crowd. *Come on, Katie. Focus on the bad guys.* If she freaked out now, they'd be ancient history.

The bank of shops to their left opened into a narrow street lined with carts and covered stalls. Nick pulled Katie into the dark alley and ran, searching the vacant stalls for a hiding place.

A canvas-draped counter stood in front of a jumble of carts and wagons. It would have to do. He signaled to Katie and they ducked behind it.

Lifting up the canvas, he helped her crawl underneath the counter. "Are you sure?" Her whisper was barely audible above the noise of the siren.

"Shhh . . ." He ducked in after her. There wasn't enough room for the canvas to cover them all the way. They needed to find a better—

Running feet scraped to a stop at the end of the alley. Someone was walking their way. Heavy footsteps. Deep, rasping breaths.

The man stopped right across from their hiding place. Nick raised his hands above his head until they rested on the underside of the counter. It didn't feel very heavy. If he could just get his feet under him, he might be able to throw it before the man had a chance to fire his weapon.

Somewhere back on the main street, the siren stopped. The man shuffled his feet. Then, letting out a rumbling sigh, he walked back in the direction he had come. Nick lowered his arms and put a finger to his lips. Katie smiled. They'd dodged yet another bullet. He wondered if she'd been praying. This God thing she had going was starting to get suspicious.

"Ten minutes." He held up the fingers of both hands as he mouthed the words. Katie nodded and slumped forward to rest her chin on her hands. He rolled his shoulders and tried to rub the fatigue out of his arms. He couldn't take much more of this. Katie was right. If they could just get to the other two ministers, all their problems would be solved. The Sunnis would be able to bring the whole thing out into the open. Then, after Al-Jaza'iri and his men were safely behind bars, he and Katie could fly back to the United States and focus on clearing themselves of the accusations there as well.

The sound of thudding feet echoed through the alley. A stern voice barked out orders in Arabic. Before Nick could even come up with a decent plan, he and Katie were surrounded. Two men stepped forward and swept the canvas off the counter. Four guns were thrust toward their faces as two dark sacks were pulled over their heads execution style. He didn't get a very good look at the men, but they looked like the Iraqi police.

Katie sat up slowly, blinking against the grit that crusted her eyes. Something had moved. She stared into the darkness, listening for a repeat of the sound. There it was again. The faint scrape of stealthy movement across the dusty floor. She scooted back against the cold cement wall of her prison and drew her legs up in front of her, supporting her throbbing handcuffed wrist with her free hand. She could hear the soft wheeze of Nick's breathing to her left. He was still asleep. Should she wake him? Or should she let him enjoy the last escape from suffering he was likely to ever know?

Their captors had been wearing uniforms, but Katie held out no hope that they were actually police officers. So far everything had played out just like one of those Middle East hostage stories on the news. Armed men throwing sacks over their victims' heads, dragging them off in front of silent witnesses, dumping them into a dark make-shift dungeon. And then, after months of futile demands, the hostages would be executed, probably on videotape so their relatives could be made to suffer even more.

Katie worked the cuff back onto her wrist and tried to rub life into her numb, swollen hand. The men hadn't spoken one word she could understand. They'd just chained them to a pipe and left them to scream themselves hoarse. How many hours had it been? Twelve? Twenty-four? It was impossible to tell. The only thing she knew for certain was that they wouldn't last much longer without food and water.

Bang! Katie jerked backward, knocking her head against the wall. *Thump . . . thump . . .* Heavy footsteps echoed through the building, descending the stairs at an impossibly slow pace. The pace of the drumbeat leading up to an execution.

"Nick!" She reached out with her free hand and shook his dangling arm. "Wake up. Someone's coming."

"Wha—?" His words dissolved in a fit of coughing.

"Someone's coming!"

The footsteps reached their level and stopped. Katie strained her ears, waiting for something to happen. Anything would be better than not knowing.

A metallic clank rang out like a chime. A soft, fluttering whir, then the roar of an engine. It sounded like a generator. For the video camera? It was the only thing she could think of that made sense.

Something brushed her side. A large hand closed around her arm. "I love you, Katie." Nick's voice was a hoarse whisper. "A lot more than oxytocin levels could ever account for."

Katie's mouth dropped open. "I . . ." The words stuck in her throat. Why couldn't she say it? This might be her only chance.

Hinges groaned as a door swung open. Slow, heavy footsteps. Deep, rasping breathing. A metallic scrape echoed in the empty chamber. The whoosh of air being forced from a vinyl cushion.

Nick's chain rattled. He was sliding forward to get in front of her. "Who are you? What do you want with us?"

No answer. Just the wheeze of heavy breathing.

"You can't hold us without a charge. We're American citizens."

Katie reached out and put a hand on his shoulder. Their status as Americans wasn't likely to earn them any special privileges.

Silence. They waited in the darkness for what seemed like hours. Whoever it was, Katie could hear him breathing. Great sighing gasps that seemed to suck all the air out of the room.

Suddenly a light snapped on. Katie squinted into the blinding brightness, shading her eyes with her hand.

"I'm going to ask three questions. Choose now whether you wish to live or die." The voice behind the light was cold and lifeless. Katie was sure she'd never heard it before, but the accent sounded vaguely European. She waited for the first question. No matter what she said, she knew it wasn't going to be the right answer.

"What are your names?"

"I'm Dr. Nicolas Aydin Murad." Nick paused a few seconds, waiting for her to speak. "My associate is Dr. Katie James from the University of New Mexico. I'm a professor at the University of Michigan. We're here—"

Katie tapped him in the back with her foot.

"We were here in Iraq to do research," he finished lamely.

The man was silent for several minutes. As far as Katie could tell, he wasn't taking notes. He obviously knew their names. The rest of the questions were probably a formality too.

"Where are your passports?" Again the cold, detached voice.

Katie spoke up before Nick could say anything. "They're in the middle of the Al Muthanna desert." She pressed her toe into Nick's back and waited. Either their interrogator cared about their answers or he didn't. She intended to find out.

She counted out 150 alligators before the next question.

"And why are your passports in the Al Muthanna desert?"

Katie smiled. The man had just told her what she needed to know. "Is that your third question?"

"Why are your passports in the Al Muthanna desert?" The man sounded angry now.

"It's a long story," she said. "I work with a paleontologist named Dietrich Fischer. Khaleed Talibani and Ameen Hamady, two of the ministers who run the Department of Antiquities and Heritage, invited us into Iraq to recover the fossilized remains of an extinct whale." She paused and squinted into the light. Apparently he was going to let her continue. She ran quickly through their whole story, focusing on the disappearance of the hominid fossil, the arrival of Al-Jaza'iri, and their subsequent escape. She hesitated when she got to the part about the Littmans taking them in but decided it wouldn't hurt. The soldiers had already been there. He probably already knew. When she reached the point of their capture, she fell silent and waited.

For a long time the hum of the generator was the only sound in the room. Finally there was a groan, the sound of a chair scraping against the floor. "You're lying! We know for a fact you are smugglers, defrauding Iraq of its national heritage. If you choose to continue protecting the insurgents you work with, you won't be of any use to anybody."

The light snapped off, leaving Katie and Nick in total darkness.

"Please. We need some water!" Katie called after the man as his footsteps clomped out of the room and up the stairs.

>>

"What did he mean—that part about us being smugglers? Was he just trying to sound like the police?" Nick rammed his shoulder into the metal pipe. One of the brackets was starting to give. If he could just hit it hard enough . . . get it to bend away from the wall . . . He rammed it again. One more time.

"It doesn't make any sense." Katie's voice came from closer to the floor. "If they wanted to sound like the police, why bring in a European?"

"I thought he sounded American."

"It still doesn't make sense. None of it does. What does Al-Jaza'iri gain by toying with us?"

"Time!" Nick knew as soon as he'd said it that he was on to something. "See? It makes total sense. Al-Jaza'iri knows we don't have the fossil because he's the one who stole it. But he needed to get us out of the way to give him time to frame the Sunnis. That's why he had to go down there. To set up the frame!"

"Sounds like a lousy frame to me. He was there but the Sunnis weren't."

Blinding light struck Nick full in the face. He threw up his hands and turned away, smacking his head into the wall.

"Tell me about the Sunnis!" The voice thundered from inside their cell. "Tell me everything. I want the name of every Iraqi you've encountered since you've been here."

Nick squinted into the light. How long had he been there? Surely not the whole time. They'd been talking for hours.

"We were talking about Talibani and Hamady, two ministers at the Department of Antiquities," Katie spoke up right away. She didn't sound that rattled.

"Who else? Start listing."

"Assistant minister Abdur Rashid, Adiba, a guide named Hassan—"

"Tell me who they are! I want names *and* relationship."

"Abdur Rashid is an assistant minister under Talibani and Hamady. Adiba is the receptionist at the museum. Hassan was the guide and translator the ministers hired for us. He worked with three Iraqi guards. I think two of their names were Nasser and Kamel; I'm not sure about the third. The guards and Hassan ended up stealing from us and abandoning us in the desert. After that my boss, Dietrich Fischer—"

"Stealing? What did they steal?"

The chain of Katie's handcuff rattled behind Nick. "They stole our trucks and all our equipment—in addition to something they thought was a priceless meteorite."

"A meteorite?"

"Actually it was just a chunk of basalt. I started getting suspicious and wanted to see what they'd do if we found something valuable."

"Basalt!" Something heavy skidded across the floor. "Was it dark gray? about the size of a soccer ball?"

"Actually, it was a little bit bigger . . . ," Katie answered cautiously.

"Out of the frying pan, baby!" The shout reverberated throughout the room. "I am so out of here!" The light flipped up to point at the ceiling, and an obese man lumbered toward them. Nick stepped in front of Katie and braced himself for the charge, balling his left hand into a fist.

"Whoa! Take it easy!" The man skidded to a stop, raising his hands palms outward. "I'm Big Bill, and I'm your new best friend." He mugged a cheesy smile, reached into his pocket, and pulled out a set of keys. "You going to let me unlock those cuffs or not?"

Nick glared at the man. "Who are you and why did you bring us here?"

"Like I said, I'm Big Bill, and I brought you here because Zerelda over there—that's her middle name, in case you didn't know—was seen packing into the desert with a known Iraqi smuggler."

"So you're with the police?" Nick stood aside and held out his cuffed hand.

"Something like that." Bill leaned over Katie with a groan and fitted a key into the cuffs. As soon as her hand was free, Nick reached down and helped her to her feet.

"I should probably mention we could have avoided all this fun if you two had been carrying your passports like good, law-abiding science nerds." He unlocked Nick's cuff and stepped back as Nick rubbed his wrist. "If you'd been carrying IDs, I could have confirmed your stories in five minutes. You have any idea how hard it is to set up a convincing interrogation cell?"

Katie looked suddenly concerned. "I assume you confirmed our stories. . . . You didn't say anything to my father, did you?"

Bill shook his head. "Ray Chappell at UNM, Stanley Roberts at Michigan, Jerry Littman here in Baghdad—"

"Dr. Littman?" Nick stepped forward. "Are he and his wife okay?"

"*They're* fine . . . but I'd hate to be their maid. The militiamen turned their whole apartment upside-down."

Katie aimed a look at Nick. If the soldiers had been searching for the fossil . . .

"If Al-Jaza'iri didn't steal the fossil, who did?" Nick asked the obvious question.

Bill flashed them a jowly smile and turned toward Katie. "That fake meteorite of yours—think you could pick it out of a lineup?"

"Absolutely." Her eyes flashed. "You caught the men who stole it?"

"Not yet, but I'm about to catch the man who hired them."

"The man, not the men . . ." Nick turned to Katie. Al-Jaza'iri's men had searched the Littmans' apartment for the fossil, so it couldn't have been him.

Katie's eyes suddenly went wide. "Abdur Rashid? The ministers' assistant?"

"Bingo!" Bill grinned. "A few weeks ago I caught the assistant minister red-handed with the goods, but at the time I didn't know that lump of basalt was supposed to be a priceless meteorite. I should have figured something was whacked up. He claimed he was hauling the rock for Al-Jaza'iri—as if a Sunni was going to run errands for a Shiite."

Nick nodded. It was all starting to make sense. "So the Sunni ministers had the assistant hire guards for Katie, and then, when Dietrich arrived, Al-Jaza'iri had the assistant hire guards for him?"

"I'm sure that's what we'll find. And not only that, but his so-called guards have been stealing from every archaeological site in Iraq. I personally ID'd one of your guards as he was stealing from an excavation near Nippur. Not too long afterward I saw the same guard going into the ministry building to meet with the assistant minister."

"Did the guard have a bushy black beard and black squinty eyes?" Katie asked.

Bill nodded. "I take it he's a good friend of yours?"

"One of my very best."

"Don't worry. We'll get him. Once we chop off the head, the rest of the beast always bleeds out nicely." Bill pulled a flashlight from his pocket and led them up a dark cement staircase.

"The assistant minister stole a very important fossil from us," Nick said. "And now Al-Jaza'iri and his men think we did it. We have to get that fossil back."

"Cool your jets. Everything's good now," the big man said between breaths. "Testify against Rashid, help us get him locked up good and tight, and I'll make sure Al-Jaza'iri doesn't kill you too bad. Be real good and I may even get your little fossil back."

Chapter 26

"C OME IN! Come in quick and close the door!" Bill ushered Katie and Nick into a suite of empty offices with peeling beige paint, filthy walls, and scratched-up floors. He guided them around a jumble of electronic equipment to the only chair in the room. "Over here. I want you to meet my best friend in the world, the only thing that got me through this ordeal." He pushed them into the jets of a massive window AC unit. Ice-cold air blasted in Katie's face, whipping her hair into a tangled frenzy.

"Isn't she a beauty?" he called out behind her.

"I feel like I'm riding shotgun in Santa Claus's sleigh." Katie stepped out of the maelstrom and stood to the side to let Bill take her place. He sighed contentedly, swaying and raising his arms in the air like Sister Johanna at a worship service.

A buzz sounded above the roar. Bill pulled a phone out of his pocket. "Just a minute. I have to take this." He hurried away to the back room.

Katie turned to her reflection in the window and began running her fingers through her hair. Right across the street was the ministry building. And there, just a half block to the left, was the little alley she and Nick had tried to hide in. So that's how Bill had managed to track them down.

"You okay?" Nick came up behind her. For a second she thought he was going to put his arms around her, but then he shifted to stand next to her at the window.

"I think so. Bill seems pretty confident they'll be able to recover Eve, and once we have the fossil, we'll eventually be able to clear our names back in the States."

"And if they don't?"

"Recover Eve?" Katie considered the question. "As important as the fossil is, it's still just one piece of data. Even if the sequence and date were right, you can't throw out an entire body of research based on one data point. If it's real, further discoveries will bear it out. If not, it wouldn't have gone anywhere anyway. As long as we don't dismiss every piece of data or approach we don't agree with—"

"Intelligent design, you mean?"

"*Any* approach . . . As long as we're willing to keep an open mind, we'll eventually be able to make that next big leap toward the truth."

Nick sighed and shook his head.

"What?"

"I wasn't talking about science. I was talking about you. Are *you* going to be okay?"

"Me?" Katie shrugged. "Even if they found her, we wouldn't be able to sort things out fast enough to save Dietrich's grant. But I think I'm okay with that. It'll do me good to live in the present for a while. I've been living in the Cenozoic era far too long."

"You're not seriously considering giving up on paleontology?"

"It's only a job. And it's not like my colleagues are going to miss me. They've made it perfectly clear how they feel."

"So that's it? You're going to let them win without a fight? I never saw you as a quitter."

"I'm not quitting. After all these years, I'm finally beginning. There's a lot more to life than reconstructing the past. I need to start thinking about constructing a future. My father needs me now. I can't take him away from his church and all his friends just because I want to keep working in science. It's time for me to move on."

"I could put you on one of my grants. Don't think of it as working for me. We'd be partners. You'll keep working from New Mexico, and I'll keep working in Michigan. It totally makes sense. You know how well we work together. We'll be unstoppable!"

Katie looked up into Nick's earnest face. As tempting as his offer was, it wasn't worth the risk. It wasn't going to work. Even after all they'd been through together, they still lived in two different worlds. He was living for this world; she was living for the next. A barrier far more profound than the K-T extinction layer would always separate them. She bit her lip as the hope slowly melted from his eyes. "I'm sorry, Nick. I really like you . . . probably more than I should. I just don't think that kind of partnership would be wise. Not right now."

"Okay . . ." He looked out the window for a couple of seconds and looked right back. "How about now?"

Katie laughed. It was good to see him smiling again. He was going to be fine.

"I'm serious." His features were stern, but his eyes were still smiling. "Don't give up on me yet. I've been through a lot lately. I may see the light at any minute."

"Woo-hoo!" A shout sounded from the back office. Bill clomped into the room and stationed himself in front of the air conditioner. "They just arrested our little assistant minister. Caught him at home with a cellar full of stolen artifacts. He's already confessed to stealing the meteorite. It's only a matter of time before he confesses to everything else."

A tangle of dusty cars jammed the sizzling Baghdad street, filling the air with shouts and honks and choleric fumes. Nick stepped onto the sidewalk and stared out into the roiling chaos. He felt like he was walking on a superheated frying pan full of snapping, popping bacon. A grease fire could break out at any second. And once the fire started, it would be impossible to extinguish all the flames.

He leaned back against the wall of Bill's office building and looked out at the barricaded government offices across the street. Armed guards plugged the gaps between the fifteen-foot-high walls. Pieces of machine gun–toting spinach caught between giant cement teeth.

Katie and Bill stepped from the shade of the entryway and onto the sidewalk. She was laughing—as if the last four weeks had never even happened. Her clothes were dirty and torn, and blood had soaked though the bandage around her wrist, but she was still laughing. Nick tried to imagine Cindy going through even one hour of what they'd just been through. She would have broken down after five minutes, but Katie . . . she was impregnable, an impenetrable fortress. Nothing could touch her—especially not him. He'd had four weeks, and he hadn't even scratched the surface.

A military truck rumbled down the side street to their left. Nick jerked away from the building, then stopped. Bill had already talked to Al-Jaza'iri on the phone. The manhunt was over. All they had to do was identify the fake meteorite, and then they would be escorted out of the country—whether Bill's people were able to recover the fossil or not. Ramadan started in three days. That's all the time they were being given.

Nick looked down at the littered sidewalk. Bill had offered to get them rooms at a Baghdad hotel, but Nick had insisted on calling the Littmans. He said he felt responsible and wanted to help them clean up their apartment, but most of all he wanted a chance to talk to them about Katie. If anyone could understand what Katie wanted, he felt certain it would be them. He only had two more days with her, and he wanted to make them count.

He looked at his watch. Where were they? Dr. Littman had said they'd be there in fifteen minutes. Fifteen minutes was fifteen minutes ago.

Finally the Littmans' car pulled up to the curb. "Sorry we're late!" Dr. Littman ran around the front of the car and surprised Nick with a bone-crunching hug. "Are you okay? We've been worried sick!"

Nick barely had a chance to get out a quick "I'm fine" before Mrs. Littman was hugging him and asking about his bandaged wrist.

"I'm fine, really. I just feel bad about your apartment getting trashed. Believe me, if we'd had any idea they'd be able to find us—"

"Nonsense. No harm done at all. It's already cleaned up." She took Nick by the arm and led him back to the car. "You sit in the front seat. Those long legs of yours will never fit in the back."

Nick slid into the car and shut the door behind him. He waited awkwardly as Dr. Littman slid behind the wheel. Mrs. Littman and Katie were already gabbling away in the back.

"If this is in any way inconvenient for you, the police have already offered to put us up at a hotel."

Littman laughed before pulling out into traffic. "Inconvenient. Does Judy sound inconvenienced? She's already got a lamb stew going in the Crock-Pot. That's part of the reason it took us so long. She would have baked you a cake if I hadn't insisted we get going."

Nick grinned. Lamb stew sounded fantastic. With or without cake.

"So what happened? How'd you get away from those soldiers? And what happened with the police?"

Nick told him the story, starting with their escape through the window. When he got to the part where they were walking to the ministry building, he turned and looked behind him. Katie was slumped to the side with her head resting in the crook of Mrs. Littman's neck. The older woman had her arm around Katie and was gently stroking her hair. A lump rose in Nick's throat. Katie's face radiated happiness. She looked so beautiful, so vulnerable. How could he ever think she couldn't be touched? The problem wasn't her. It was all him.

He turned to face the front and slashed an arm across his eyes.

"So what happened then? Did you make it to the police?"

Nick swallowed and stared out the window. They'd already reached the Littmans' street. "I heard running footsteps behind us and . . ."

An empty truck sat in the shade of a scrubby tree about three blocks ahead of them. Nick looked up at the Littmans' apartment. The curtains in the window were swaying.

"Keep on driving. Don't slow down!" Nick shouted. "Someone's in the apartment. Keep on going. Faster!"

Katie leaned forward over the seat. "Bill said they called off the soldiers."

"Maybe some of them haven't checked their e-mail." Nick turned and looked back down the street. Two soldiers were running down the apartment steps. "Faster; they see us!"

"Turn right here—*left* here!" Katie called out from the backseat.

Nick braced himself against the dash as the car squealed around the corner.

"This is the university!" Littman straightened out the car and stepped on the gas. "Where are we going?"

"The big parking lot on the far side of campus." Katie leaned over the seat. "I need you to take Judy to the embassy. Try to contact a man named Big Bill—he never gave us his last name. Let him know what happened."

"What are you trying to do?" Nick turned and almost bumped heads with Katie. "You don't think the truck is still there?"

"It has to be. The soldiers couldn't have found us by discovering the truck. They knew right where to look for us."

"Al-Jaza'iri?"

Katie nodded. "Dietrich said someone was following him after he mailed the samples. If Al-Jaza'iri had men watching the post offices . . ."

"But why?"

"That's what we need to figure out. We need to talk to him."

"Over there!" Nick pointed to the truck at the far end of the lot. Katie was right. The truck hadn't been touched. He jammed his hand into his pocket and dug out the keys.

Littman cut across the lot and pulled up next to the truck. "Shouldn't we all go to the embassy?"

"They'll be looking for us," Katie said. "But you and Judy should be safe. They didn't bother you before."

"Okay, but I want you to take this." Littman pulled out his cell phone and pushed it into Nick's hand. "We'll call you as soon as we get to the embassy. If anything looks suspicious, we'll let you know."

"Thanks." Nick put the phone in his pocket. "And sorry again about all the trouble." He got out of the car and opened the door for Katie. Mrs. Littman gave her one last tearful hug while Dr. Littman pressed a wad of cash into her hand.

"Thank you—for everything." Katie's voice was so faint Nick could barely hear. "I . . . don't know what to say. . . . I love you." She slid out of the car and closed the door.

Nick reached out to put an arm around her but hesitated. He waved awkwardly as Littman backed the car out of the parking space. He stopped the car and looked out through the window a few seconds before driving away. Mrs. Littman never even glanced to the side. Her eyes were closed and her lips were moving.

»

Katie jumped into the pickup as the Littmans' car pulled out of the parking lot. Why wouldn't it end? Every time, just when she was starting to let her guard down, something always happened. She slammed the door behind her as Nick backed out of the space.

"Okay, let's end this thing." She had to raise her voice to be heard over the roar of the air conditioner. "Do you know Al-Jaza'iri's number?"

"My administrative assistant does." Nick skidded the truck around a tight corner. "Here." He handed her the phone and called out a Michigan number, waiting as she punched it into the phone.

"Grand Central station." A weary voice sounded over the phone.

"Listen, this is Katie James. I'm here with Nick and we need Minister Al-Jaza'iri's number at his Baghdad office. This is an emergency."

"What's going on out there? Yesterday this guy called. Wanted a description of Nick. He sounded like a hit man or something."

"Did you tell him anything?"

"Heck no. Told him to call back when he could show me a badge."

"Thanks. I'll let Nick know. Now about that number."

She licked her finger and wrote the number on the inside of her window as Mike called it out. "Okay, thanks."

"No problemo. Tell Nick he owes me one."

She hung up the phone and dialed the number on the window. A man answered the phone in Arabic. It took a full minute to convince him to transfer the call to Al-Jaza'iri's office.

"Hello, Katie James." Al-Jaza'iri's smooth voice finally came on the line. "So good to be hearing from you. Our last visit was cut unfortunately short."

"You need to tell your men to back off," Katie blurted out. "Didn't the police talk to you? They've already arrested the thief."

"A good try on your part, but you and I both know Abdur Rashid didn't steal the human fossil."

"The assistant minister? What are you talking about? He already confessed!"

"To stealing the objects they found in his cellar, yes, but to everything else, no. As certainly as he was involved in the museum robbery back in 2003, I am just the same certain he could not have stolen the fossil."

"Why not?"

"Because you stole it. You and your associate."

Katie didn't know what to say. If the minister wouldn't listen to reason . . .

"Here is the deal I will give to you," Al-Jaza'iri continued. "We will meet face-to-face at the museum to discuss this—you, Nick Murad, and myself. Come alone. If you are, as you say, innocent, you will have nothing to fear. If not, then simply return the fossil to me and all will be forgiven. You will be free to leave the country, never again to return."

"Why should we trust you? If you're not willing to listen to reason now, why would you listen to reason at the museum?"

"It is you who do not listen to reason." The minister's voice hardened. "You expect me to believe a Sunni assistant knowing nothing of this fossil stole it from a distance of hundreds of miles?"

"The guards Dietrich brought down were working for him—just like the first set of guards that—"

"The guards work for me! You think me a fool? They are good Shiite soldiers, loyal only to me. I had men guarding the entire region—all of them loyal. They would die before stealing for Sunnis!"

Katie stared out the windshield as a row of disheveled buildings flashed by. The guards worked for Al-Jaza'iri? The guards *and* the soldiers? Something was wrong.

"If you do not agree to a meeting, I will tell to the police. They too will be searching. You cannot hope to leave the country. You must meet me at the museum. Nine o'clock tonight!"

"I'll talk to Nick. We'll discuss it and get back to you." Katie hung up the phone and looked at Nick.

He was watching her with a worried frown. "What happened?"

"He doesn't think the assistant minister stole the fossil. He said the guards were all working for him. The guards *and* the soldiers."

Nick shook his head. "He's lying. It's just a ploy to . . ." He shook his head again and studied the road ahead.

"I know. It doesn't make sense. Why would he lie? If he stole the fossil, wouldn't he be happy for a Sunni to take the blame? I think he's telling the truth."

"So what do we do?" Nick turned down a side street and pulled the truck over to the side of the road.

"Someone stole the fossil," Katie said. "We just have to figure out who."

"We've been over this a million times. Dietrich, Wayne, Hooman, Ahamed . . . It doesn't make sense. What's their motive? Jealousy? Trying to Wayne on your parade?"

Katie rolled her eyes. "We're still missing something. I can feel it. It has something to do with the sequence not matching the date. That can't be a coincidence."

"What? You think the president of the NAS stole it?" Nick threw his hands in the air. "I know! The NAS put out a contract on your life because they were afraid you'd disprove evolution. That's why that mummy was trying to assassinate you. The evil empire was trying to suppress Piltdown Junior."

"That's it!" Katie turned in her seat to face Nick. "You're a genius!"

"It was just a joke. A *stupid* joke." Nick looked suddenly worried.

"Piltdown Junior! Don't you get it? What if Eve is a fake? Everything suddenly makes sense then. We've got motive; we've got opportunity. . . ."

"But it wasn't a fake. We did the work ourselves. The matrix was real. The soft tissue was real. Nobody could have faked that."

"Not the fossil. The fossil was real enough. But what if the date was faked?"

"What? You think Brian did it? Just because he tried to warn me about you . . ."

"Not Brian. Remember? Until we got to Littman's lab, you and I were the only ones to handle the samples."

"Not back to Littman again. That's crazy."

"Of course not. What would his motive be? A 3-million-year-old *Homo sapiens* doesn't make any sense for a directed evolutionist. Come to think of it, a 3-million-year-old *Homo sapiens* doesn't make sense for a creationist either."

"It would if all he wanted to do is discredit Western science. What if Al-Jaza'iri somehow managed to switch the sample? He's as antiscience as they come."

"Al-Jaza'iri never had the opportunity." Katie shook her head. "Just listen, okay? Dietrich was the only one who could have switched the samples. Didn't you notice how eager he was to mail them? He practically ran out the door with them."

Nick shook his head. "And why would he want it? You think he's a closet creationist?"

"He didn't want a 3-million-year-old *Homo sapiens*. He wanted a 3-million-year-old *hominid*. Think about it. He couldn't have known we'd actually end up getting a sequence. Did you think we'd get a sequence? I sure didn't. DNA is way too fragile. The chances were one in a billion."

"I don't know. . . ."

"It's the only thing that fits! Dietrich switched the samples because he needed to convince the world Eve was a significant find. He needed something significant enough to get his grant renewed."

"And after we got a DNA sequence, you think he stole the fossil to cover his tracks? So we couldn't rerun the tests?"

"It makes sense, doesn't it? He had motive *and* opportunity. And we don't have to throw out the whole evolutionary framework."

"I don't know. I was kind of getting tired of the old framework. What happened to that bias thing we've been talking about? I've been thinking. What if God created the world with the *appearance* of age . . . ?"

"Would you stop it? This is serious!"

Nick sighed and turned to look out the window. "There's only one problem with your theory. In order for it to work, Dietrich needed to have a sample of 3-million-year-old volcanic ash sitting around in his backpack."

"He could have brought it with him from South Africa. He was at the Transvaal Museum."

"But you didn't find the fossil until after he got here, remember? He wouldn't have known to bring a sample."

"Wouldn't he?" Katie squirmed in her seat. This was the solution. It resonated with truth. "You were the one who commented about the fossil being right there out in the open for me to find. The color of the matrix didn't even match the other rocks. What if he got the fossil from the museum too?"

"That's ridiculous."

"You don't know Dietrich. He's desperate to save his grant. His self-respect is on the line. He'd do almost anything. And you know how museum vaults are. If he pulled it from a locker with hundreds of samples, the curators wouldn't notice for years—if ever."

Nick bit his lip and tapped out a slow beat on the steering wheel.

Katie waited, going over and over the evidence in her mind. Everything fit. Dietrich's telling her to search the deeper strata, his being so hands-off with the find. He didn't even get involved when they were calling other scientists for support. Normally he'd never stay in the background on such an important find. He would have been right there in the thick of things, grasping for as much of the credit as he could get.

"Okay . . ." Nick turned toward her, resolve hardening his features. "Let's say you're right. Dietrich could have hidden the fossil anywhere. How are we going to find it? Do we just confront him with our theory and hope he confesses?"

"Right." Katie laughed. "You don't know Dietrich. He'd never confess to anything—even if he was caught red-handed. Not even to save his life. He's way too proud."

"Are you sure? A man will do almost anything to save his life. And we have rifles. . . ."

"He knows we'd never use them. Besides, we need more than just the fossil. If we return it to Al-Jaza'iri now, he'll still think we stole it. He's never going to believe . . ." Katie followed the thought to its logical conclusion. "I think I have something. I think I know how to kill three finches with one stone!" She grabbed the phone and hit redial.

"What? Who are you calling? Al-Jaza'iri?"

Katie nodded. "He probably won't go along with it, but it's worth a shot."

"He won't go along with what? What's the plan?"

The same Iraqi man answered the phone. This time Katie was able to convince him to transfer her call right away. A few seconds later, Al-Jaza'iri's voice came on the line.

"Katie James. I assume you are willing to listen to reason?"

"Just listen to me, Mohammed. We know who stole the fossil. It was my boss, Dietrich Fischer." She ran quickly through her reasoning, starting with Dietrich's grant trouble and ending with his motives.

"A very interesting and elaborate explanation," the minister said when she was finally finished. "And yet fifteen minutes ago you blamed Abdur Rashid."

"We just figured it out. Once we knew it had to be someone at the camp, it started us thinking in a completely different direction."

"So I see. Very reasonable. And yet Dr. Fischer did not run from the police. He remains still working in the camp."

"We ran because we thought *you* had stolen the fossil. I thought you were trying to blame the theft on Nick."

"And you suggest the tip I received was from Dietrich? Your explanation does seem reasonable. We should meet face-to-face to discuss the possibilities. Nine o'clock at the museum."

"I have a better idea," Katie said. "Meet us down at our camp in the desert. All you have to do is threaten Dietrich, force him to tell you where the fossil is. Better yet, threaten to kill me. There's a chance he'd rather die than admit his guilt, but I don't think he'd stand by and watch me get hurt."

"An excellent suggestion," Al-Jaza'iri said smoothly. "I have experience with such things. You and your associate will meet me at the museum at nine o'clock. We will drive down to the desert in the morning."

"Dietrich would never believe it if we arrived together. We'll drive down now, and you can have your soldiers capture us in the morning. We'll be hiding in Dietrich's tent. Don't leave Baghdad until you hear from your soldiers. It would be too suspicious if you showed up for no reason."

"Of course. We will drive together, and I will wait in the desert for your capture."

"No, we'll get down there on our own, but you need to call off your soldiers, okay? They need to let us get through to the camp."

"Of course."

"And make sure you're angry. Dietrich has to believe you're a killer."

"This will be no problem." The minister already sounded angry. "As I said, I have experience in these matters."

"Okay . . ." Katie ran through the plan in her head. Everything seemed to be covered. "So we're agreed?"

"Agreed. But I insist we meet first at the museum. We must plan out the details."

"There's not enough time. We'll see you tomorrow afternoon. And remember, call off your soldiers!" She hung up the phone.

"He actually went for that?" Nick was watching her with wide eyes.

"Sure, why not? What does he have to lose? If Dietrich doesn't confess, he'll have all three of us."

"So what happens if we mess it up? What if Dietrich doesn't confess?"

"We can't let that happen. Dietrich *has* to confess."

Chapter 27

NICK YANKED THE STEERING WHEEL hard to the right. The left side of the truck bucked as the front wheel clipped the edge of a shadowy rock.

"Slow down!" Katie called out from the passenger seat. "This isn't a race. We're supposed to make it look like we're sneaking."

"I *am* sneaking." Nick leaned forward and searched the uneven terrain ahead of him. Sometime during their long drive down from Baghdad, one of the headlights had gone out, making it almost impossible to see the rocks on the driver's side of the truck. "The slower we go, the more likely one of those patrols will catch up to us."

"But they're not going to do anything. Al-Jaza'iri said he would call them off."

"I know what he *said*."

"Come on, Nick." Katie huffed. "You already agreed. We have to trust him. We don't have a choice."

"Trusting him when we're surrounded by witnesses is one thing." Nick veered left to avoid a narrow ditch. "But all alone out in the middle of the desert—that's completely different. Especially since nobody knows we're here."

He glanced up at the rearview mirror. Good, nobody was following them. Seeing all those military trucks on patrol by the road had really bothered him. And that wasn't the only thing. Just after Katie had finished talking to Al-Jaza'iri, they'd seen two trucks full of soldiers speeding down the Littmans' street. Maybe they were on their way home or maybe they weren't even working for Al-Jaza'iri, but he couldn't help wondering if they might be heading south toward the desert. To make matters worse, they'd tried all afternoon to call the minister, but he wasn't in his office.

Headlights suddenly appeared in the distance. Whatever it was, it was bearing down on them fast.

Nick stepped on the gas and veered away from the approaching vehicle, but it turned to follow them.

"Nick, slow down!" Katie shouted. "You're going to run us into a ravine."

"Good idea." He made for a distant shadow. It looked like one of the deeper ones. Cutting suddenly to the left, he drove them around the mouth of the canyon and turned to follow its winding path.

The other vehicle was still coming right at them. If the wadi gave out now, he'd be in big trouble. Nick yanked on the steering wheel, skidding the truck into a sharp turn. The approaching truck was behind them now. "Come on. Keep following!" He looked at his rearview mirror. Brake lights backlit the skidding truck of their pursuers. A huge cloud of dust enveloped it just as it slid to a stop inches from the edge of the ravine.

"Nice!" Katie called out. "Slow down and turn off your headlights. We're going to have company real soon."

Nick switched off his headlight, plunging them into darkness. He slammed on the brakes and waited for his eyes to adjust.

"Come on! Take a right. We've got to get out of here."

"Won't that take us closer to the camp?"

"That's where we're going, remember?"

"You're sure that's a good idea?" He eased them forward, straining to see in the dim light.

"You have a better idea?"

He shrugged and swung the truck in a wide turn. Gradually, as his eyes adjusted to the light, he picked up speed. The truck behind him was racing back along the wadi. Another truck was approaching from the top of the ridge. "Still think he called his men off?"

Katie didn't respond.

Nick picked up speed, angling away from the approaching trucks. "We've gone about fifty miles. How much farther to the camp?"

"Just a few more minutes. See that ridge?" She pointed to a spot behind the second truck. "That's not too far from our hidey-hole."

Nick nodded and turned toward the top of the ridge. "Be on the lookout for a place to hide. We're not going to be able to drive much farther."

"Okay. Watch out for eight o'clock."

Two more sets of headlights had appeared back to their left. How many soldiers did the minister have working for him? It was a small army.

"Over there!" Katie said. "A little more to the right."

Nick angled the truck in the direction she was pointing. At first he didn't see it. Then, as he got closer, a dark band became distinguishable against the lighter slope. It was a broad wadi, running almost parallel to their course. "Hold on!" He angled the truck into the gulley, sending it careening over the edge and down the side of the bank. He turned sharply as they slammed into the bottom. The truck bounced several yards before grinding to a stop.

Grabbing their canteens and rifles, they abandoned their truck and set out on foot along the wide gulley. The clatter of tumbling rocks sounded somewhere off in the distance. They crept stealthily around a bend in the wadi, pausing at every step to listen for sounds of pursuit.

After ten or twenty minutes of silence, Nick finally relaxed. "What do you think is going on with all the soldiers?" he asked in a whisper.

"I don't know." Katie swung the rifle she was carrying over her shoulder. "But you're right about not wanting to get caught out here. When we finally confront Al-Jaza'iri, I want to be surrounded by as many witnesses as possible."

They followed the gulley another quarter mile and climbed out onto the plain. Peeking over the rim, they watched as three sets of headlights circled a large camp. At first Nick didn't recognize it as their own; then he noticed the familiar line of tents to the left. The cluster of tents to the right was new. The soldiers had set up a base right next to Fischer's camp.

He crouched down and whispered into Katie's ear. "Are you sure about this?"

She nodded solemnly. "The trucks are moving slow enough we should be able to make it through."

"Okay, but we're not hiding in Dietrich's tent. That part of the plan has to change."

"Good idea." She climbed out onto the plateau and started walking toward the camp. Suddenly she stopped and pointed at the ground.

Nick scrambled after her and whispered, "What's wrong?"

"Fish fossil. It looks like another *Nursallia*."

He bent closer to the ground and smiled. Sure enough. The caudal section of a *Nursallia* fish protruded just above the sandstone. He straightened and placed a hand on her shoulder. "You sure you don't want to be partners?"

She smiled and kept walking. It was dark, but there was something about the look in her eyes. Was she actually considering it? He caught up to her and the two of them set out across the plain. Aside from the trucks circling in the distance, the night was calm and still. Almost too calm, considering the number of patrolling trucks.

"*Oogaf!*" Two figures rose from the ground just thirty feet in front of them.

Nick spun around. Three more soldiers were running up from behind. Gunshots rang out all around him. The twang of ricocheting bullets. Nick put his hands in the air and looked back at Katie. "Don't do it, Katie. There's five of them!"

She tossed her rifle on the ground. The men were shouting at them. Nick didn't know whether he was supposed to drop his gun or leave his hands in the air. What if—

A heavy body hit him from behind, driving him face-first into the biting sandstone. Red-hot pain stabbed down his arms as a knee smashed against the back of his neck. The rifle was ripped from his back. The knee bore down harder. His neck felt like it was going to snap. He tried to cry out, but he couldn't make a sound. *God, if you're really there, please do something. Keep Katie safe.*

The pressure eased off his neck as his arms were yanked behind his back. A thin band cut into his wrists. The men were laughing now. *Katie!* He twisted his head around. Katie was lying facedown on the ground, her hands crossed behind her back. They'd taken away her canteen.

"Al-Jaza'iri's not going to be happy about this." She spat out the words. "You were supposed to let us reach the camp!"

Two sets of hands dragged Nick roughly onto his feet. A rifle barrel jabbed into his back, shoving him forward with vertebrae-cracking force. "Katie? You okay?" He turned to look back at her, but a rifle barrel smacked into the side of his head. A pulsing red and blue cloud rose before his eyes. He stumbled forward, staggering to stay on his feet.

"I'm fine. How about you?" Her words were thick and slurred. She sounded anything but fine.

"I've been better." He forced a hollow laugh. "Still think Al's following the plan?"

"He won't have a choice. We don't have the fossil to give him. He'll have to get it from Dietrich."

Nick kept his mouth shut. The last thing she needed was for a joy-leech like him to drain her last drop of optimism. He marched on in silence, stumbling through the darkness for what seemed like hours. Trying not to fall down. Facing straight ahead. Keeping one step ahead of the hollow steel goad.

Finally they arrived at a ring of tents and trucks. The soldiers' camp. A mob of jabbering men closed around them. Shouts and movement. Faces and shoving hands. A commotion at the corner of his eye caught his attention. Katie was rolling on the ground.

"Get back! Get away from her! She can't handle so many people." He shouldered his way over to Katie, pushing the men out of his way. "Katie, it's okay. Focus on my—"

A starburst of pain exploded in his head, blinding red light shrinking to a tiny point. And then there was darkness.

❯❯

Katie froze as a sentry tramped across the darkened camp. As soon as he was past, she strained against her bonds, pulling herself off the ground until the thin nylon zip ties cut deep into her wrists. The soldiers had tied their hands to two cinch rings on the side of one of their trucks. She sawed her bonds back and forth across the metal rings until her arms burned with fatigue. She wouldn't be able to take much more of this. Her back and shoulders already ached from holding her hands above her head. Al-Jaza'iri wouldn't be there for another five hours. If they didn't manage to escape soon, she and Nick were going to be in for some serious agony.

"Nick? Are you still with me?" she whispered into the darkness.

"Yeah, I thought about going for a stroll, but I decided I like it here." His groggy voice sounded right beside her.

"How's your head? Feel any pressure? dizziness?"

"I can't tell. It still hurts too much."

Seething anger boiled up inside her. Al-Jaza'iri's soldiers had gone way over the line. As soon as the minister got there, heads were going to roll. Before, when she'd knocked the other soldiers out, it had been in self-defense. She'd had no other choice. But what they'd done to Nick was totally uncalled-for. Dietrich hadn't even been there to see it.

She yanked down on her arms, wondering whether the change in plans had been the soldiers' idea or Al-Jaza'iri's. Whichever it was, she was going to give the minister an earful when he finally got there.

"Katie . . ." Nick's dull voice sounded in the shadow. "Something's been bothering me, but I've been . . . hesitant to bring it up."

"What?" Her mind raced through a hundred possibilities: she was too overbearing, too headstrong, too competitive, too lacking in social graces. . . . It was her fault they were in this situation.

"Remember when I was talking about us going skiing in Taos?"

Incredible. He's still thinking about skiing? "Yeah."

"What I meant was . . . I hope you didn't think . . ." There was a long pause. "My expectation all along was that we'd be staying in separate rooms. I hope you didn't think . . ."

Katie couldn't help laughing. He'd been beaten up, knocked unconscious, and tied to a truck with his hands above his head—all because of her stupidity. But what was he worried about? He was afraid she'd think he was a womanizer?

"I know you don't have much of an opinion of me, but I hope you know I'd never do anything to hurt you."

"Nick . . . of course you wouldn't. I . . ." Katie's throat was starting to constrict. "I think you're one of the kindest, most sensitive, smartest . . . guys I've ever known." Her mind went totally blank. She could feel her face glowing through the darkness. "You're a really great guy. I mean *really* great. I don't know how anybody could ever think otherwise."

"I know—you don't have to say it. But we're incompatible, right? I'm a heathen and you're a . . . nonheathen."

"Look, I'm not trying to make myself out to be any better than you. I just believe—"

"I'm not a bigot, you know. I'm not a skeptic out of choice. I just don't see any evidence for the existence of God. Belief isn't a light switch I can turn on and off."

"So do you believe parallel universes can interact? Do you believe in loop quantum gravity?"

"I don't know. I'd have to . . ." There was a long pause. "I get what you're saying. I can't believe in something until I've actually investigated it. And I'm willing to give it a shot. I really am."

"But?"

"But if science is so blind to God—and I understand why it has to be—where am I supposed to look for evidence? Art? History?"

"That's a good start. Or maybe you could try reading the manual. It's—"

A shout broke the silence. Floodlights snapped on above the center tent. Soldiers hurried across the clearing, dusting off their uniforms as they ran. More voices. A truck was approaching from the east. She listened as it squealed to a stop at the edge of camp. Doors squawked and slammed. Loud voices were coming their way.

Katie tried to climb to her feet, but her bonds were too tight.

She sat back down and waited as a group of silhouetted men strode toward her from the other side of the camp. Al-Jaza'iri had arrived—five hours too early.

"Your soldiers are way out of line!" Katie hissed as soon as he was close enough to hear. "They almost killed Nick. He was unconscious for almost a minute."

"Katie James and Nick Murad. How good it is to finally see you again." The minister's voice ran thick with genuine Iraqi crude. "I believe you have something for me?"

Katie looked through the group of men to the empty camp beyond. "Dietrich's not here!" she whispered. "We can do this tomorrow morning. You aren't even supposed to be here yet. Untie our hands before they fall off!"

"No more lies!" Al-Jaza'iri bellowed. "Where is the human fossil?"

"Dietrich has it! This is pointless. If you'd just go get him and bring him back here . . ."

"Dr. Fischer didn't run when the police came! Dr. Fischer hasn't left the camp since the bone disappeared!"

"He could have hidden it—"

"I am finished with these games! Either tell me where is the fossil now, or . . ." He drew a large handgun from the holster at his side and pointed it at Katie's face. "Tell me where is the fossil *now*!"

Katie looked him straight in the eye. "We don't have it."

The gun jerked to the side with a deafening shot. The ground by Katie's leg erupted in a spray of pelting sand. Another shot rang out. An explosion only inches from her other leg.

"She already told you—we don't have it!" Nick called out from the shadows. "You want to shoot someone, shoot me! But we can't give you what we don't have!"

Al-Jaza'iri leveled the gun at Nick and turned back to face Katie. "You see? I am following your most excellent plan. Tell me what I need to know. *Now!*"

"Nick!" An accented voice came from across the camp. Running footsteps.

"Ahamed!" Nick shouted. "Over here!"

The soldiers behind Al-Jaza'iri turned and charged across the camp. The minister shouted something in Arabic. A shot was fired. Two more.

Al-Jaza'iri barked another order, and a bristling group of soldiers pushed forward, herding Ahamed, Hooman, and Dietrich toward the truck. Only three of them? Where was Wayne?

Dietrich, Hooman, and Ahamed started talking at once.

"Katie, are you all right?"

"We have all been worrying for you."

Another set of armed soldiers came up behind them. They were all watching her. Staring . . .

Katie closed her eyes and took a deep breath. Now wasn't the time. Too many lives were depending on her.

"I'm okay." She took another deep breath. "They hit Nick on the—"

"Enough!" Al-Jaza'iri shouted. "Look at me!" He shoved the gun in her face. "I have three more of your friends now. Even better for your plan. How many must I shoot? Where is the fossil?"

"Leave her alone!" Dietrich thundered. "This has gone too far enough!"

"Quiet!" The minister turned back to Katie. "I give you three seconds. *One!*"

"She doesn't know," Dietrich called out. "The guards—"

"*Two!*"

"Would you just listen to—?"

"*Three!*" Al-Jaza'iri wheeled around and fired the gun point-blank into Nick's chest.

"No!" Katie screamed as Nick's body jerked and shuddered. He went rigid for an agonizing second and then, with a long, gasping sigh, his body went limp.

"No!" Screams and shouts battered against Katie's senses. Ahamed was running, flying through the air. There was a sickening thud as he was crushed to the ground. A struggling mass of arms and legs and hands.

"Where is the fossil?" A gun was thrust in front of her face. "Final warning!"

Katie couldn't control her voice. She was trembling from head to foot.

"One!"

"Halt!" Dietrich's voice cut through the confusion. *"I have the fossil."*

"You lie!" The minister pressed the gun against Katie's head. "She knew you would lie to save her. She thought to frame you with big, complicated plan."

"No. I can show you!"

Al-Jaza'iri shouted a command in Arabic and a group of soldiers surrounded Katie. Cold blades jabbed against her wrists and her arms dropped lifelessly to her sides. Grasping hands lifted her onto her feet. She was dragged toward the minister. Made to stand by his side.

"Show me now," Al-Jaza'iri called out to her trembling mentor. "Quickly, or she dies."

Dietrich stumbled across the camp, surrounded by a small cluster of soldiers. Katie sagged in the soldier's arms, watching as the bobbing flashlights disappeared behind the tents. He'd told her he loved her. Why hadn't she said something? Would it have been so wrong? The men dragged her through the camp and out into the desert. They were moving toward the excavation site, past the site, onto the path leading to the latrine.

"Let this be a warning to you," Al-Jaza'iri called to Dietrich. "I know what it looks like. I've seen pictures." He waved a flashlight in Katie's face, staring at her with a leering smile. "Move!"

Dietrich stopped next to a rocky outcropping and pointed at a pile of rocks on the ground. "It is here, buried in the ground. Now, please . . ." A sob choked off his voice. "Please let her go."

A half dozen splashes of jittering light were focused on the ground. The minister barked an order and a soldier started clearing away the rocks. Digging down a few inches in the sand, he came to a white towel.

Katie watched in a daze as the man unrolled the towel and pulled out a large rock sealed in a ziplock bag.

The minister pushed toward Dietrich, got up in his face. "You know the penalty for stealing a national treasure from the people of Iraq?"

"Is not from Iraq. I swear!" Dietrich whined. "I took it from South Africa—from the vaults of the Transvaal Museum. It was among a bin of ape fossils. I swear! The fools didn't even know what they had!"

"Good! That solves a problem for everybody." Al-Jaza'iri turned his back on Dietrich and sauntered up to Katie. "So . . . how did I do?"

The soldiers gripped her arms tighter, but Katie could only stare.

"I trust I was convincing enough?" His mouth lifted in a self-satisfied smirk. "It was a most brilliant plan—most brilliantly executed." He spoke a few words in Arabic and one of the soldiers took off running toward the camp.

"I must apologize for the behavior of my men. It seems they were much humiliated to be beaten by two eggheaded scientists. I assure you. They will be severely punished." His eyes wandered. He was looking over her head.

Running footsteps pounded up the trail behind her. Deep, steady breaths.

"Did it work? Did he actually have it?"

Katie gasped as Nick burst into the group of soldiers. The minister held up the bag containing the fossil and Nick let out a loud whoop. He flashed Katie a big smile and clapped a hand on Al-Jaza'iri's back.

"Okay! *Now* you may release her!" The grinning minister motioned to the soldiers and turned back to Katie. "As I tell you before, I am most experienced in these things."

The soldiers dropped her arms and melted into the shadows.

"So, the gun . . . You knew?" Katie took an unsteady step toward Nick. "The third shot was a blank?"

Nick shook his head. "I had no idea. For a second, I thought he'd actually killed me."

She took two more steps and launched herself into his arms. "When I get through with you, you're going to wish he had."

Epilogue

*K*ATIE LEANED HER HEAD against the Land Rover's window, watching the blur of umbrellas, canopies, and markets race inexorably by. Everything was happening so fast. Too fast. Only yesterday she'd been on the run with Nick. She and Nick together, working shoulder to shoulder, they'd actually managed to recover the fossil. Would it have hurt so much to let them have a few days to celebrate?

Sure, there had been the ride back to Baghdad. For a few glorious hours she'd been a hero. Checking into the best hotel in the city, taking the world's longest shower, sleeping on real sheets without bugs or rocks or even the tiniest grain of sand . . .

And then nothing.

Just like that, they were done. *Thank you very much. Ramadan starts tomorrow; you all have to go home now.* No debriefing, no handoff to the museum. All she got for a send-off was an overweight diplomat hammering on her door at eight o'clock in the morning. Big Bill had only given her forty-five minutes to pack up her things, and then he'd bustled her out the door. He hadn't even let her call up to Nick's room to say good-bye.

A clutch of shrouded women stepped out into the narrow street. "For the love of—" Bill slammed on the brakes. "Would you look at that? It's like they want to get hit." He drummed his fingers on the steering wheel and checked his watch. "I guess if I had to live here, I'd throw myself in front of a car too." As soon as the last woman was clear, he stepped on the gas.

"So . . . when does the flight leave?"

"What?"

"When does the flight leave?" Katie had to shout to be heard over the roar of the blasting air conditioner.

"Don't worry. We're fine." The big man spun the wheel, skidding the car onto a busy street.

Katie braced a hand against the dash as a row of ornate buildings rushed past her. "This isn't the way to the airport."

"What?"

"Isn't this the street the museum is on?"

"I still need you to identify that rock." Bill swerved around a slow bus and whipped his car back into his lane. "Once you give me a signed statement, I'm out of here for good."

"You're leaving? Before they catch the guards? I thought you still had to find some artifacts."

"Done and done." He flashed her a smile. "Caught two of them this morning. The assistant minister led us right to them."

"And the artifacts?"

"Sewn into sacks of rice and barley in the basement of a bombed-out building. We got about a third of what they stole from Nippur. Everything else is probably long gone."

He hit the brakes and turned left into the museum compound, circling around the visitor lot to park in front of the main entrance. "As far as I'm concerned, this job is a wrap. The assistant minister is singing like a songbird, and your boss is awaiting extradition back to South Africa. He's already confessed to planting the fossil and stealing it back again after it started generating so much bad press."

"What about the radiometric dating? Did he say anything about switching the samples?"

"He says he didn't touch the samples, but you'll have to sort that out on your own. As soon as you identify your chunk of rock, I'm on a plane to Reykjavík!"

"Iceland? That's going to be a shock."

"I know. It's going to be glorious! And if I play my cards right, I may be able to stay there all winter."

"Right." Katie climbed out of the car and turned, maybe for the last time, toward the blistering sun. The heat beat against her like a physical being. So intense, so brutal. In a strange, twisted sort of way, she was going to miss it. She might never in her life get to experience such savage ferocity in nature again.

A clank sounded behind her. Big Bill had already gone inside. Turning reluctantly, she jogged across the sidewalk and pushed through the door into the museum. The place was deserted. Even the reception-ist was gone. She followed Bill through the artifact exhibits, their foot-steps echoing soft and lonely against the silence of the large hall. In a few more days she wouldn't have to worry about crowds anymore. No more airports, no more university students, no more . . . Nick Murad. Just her and her father and a quiet, tame, emasculated sort of desert.

Bill led her down a hall to a conference room, the conference room where she'd first met Talibani and Hamady. Bill opened the door and she stepped into the room. A row of rocks was laid out on the conference table. One of them, her fake meteorite, was disguised behind a black beard and a pair of dark glasses.

"Okay, who's the wise guy?" Bill called out. "I find the person who did this, and I'm going to rip his eyes out."

"Our apologies . . ." Minister Talibani, his face lit with a mischie-vous smile, burst through the door at the other end of the room. "We could not resist."

"Katie James! *Hamdu lillaah!* So good to see you again!" Hamady and Al-Jaza'iri were behind the short minister. In their hands were glass trays filled with some kind of sugared fruit.

"Congratulations, boss!" Hooman was right behind them. Then came the Littmans, the receptionist, Ahamed, and Wayne.

"What are you guys—?" Katie could barely take it in. They were setting out pastries, drinks, salads; Mrs. Littman was carrying a huge chocolate cake on a crystal pedestal.

"Way to go!"

"Were you surprised?"

"We couldn't let you go without saying good-bye."

They were all talking at once. Watching her. Waiting . . . Her chest tightened. The room was tilting. Twisting. She was supposed to say something. They were all waiting.

"Congratulations, Katie." Nick's voice broke through the tumult.

Katie looked up and all she could do was stare. With his hair washed and combed, his face freshly shaven, he looked like an after-shave commercial. Where was the scruffy scientist she'd worked with out in the desert?

"Are you okay?" he asked in a gentle voice. "If this is too much, we can go outside. We can come in a few at a time."

"No, it's . . . I'll be fine." She turned to smile at her friends, but her eyes kept gravitating back to Nick.

Minister Talibani's voice broke the awkward silence. "Katie James, I have heard from everyone such stories. We are all eager to hear of your adventures. From the beginning to the end. Especially the part where my good friend Al-Jaza'iri shoots Dr. Murad with blanks!" The short minister reached up and slapped the Shiite on the shoulder.

Al-Jaza'iri glared at him fiercely.

"And of course your remarkable escape." The short minister jerked his hand away. "Did you really overpower armed soldiers with your . . . *ahem* . . . outer garments? It is all so amazing."

"But first we should eat." Al-Jaza'iri stepped away from the Sunnis. "This is a celebration, not a news conference. Congratulations, Katie James!"

"Congratulations?" Katie glanced over at Nick. "Why congratulate me? It was a group effort."

Eyes darted about the room. Knowing looks. Dr. Littman turned to Nick and nodded.

"Congratulations on your new job."

"My new what?"

Nick smiled and took out his satellite phone. "Last night I called your department chairman and explained the whole situation. He told me to tell you that when Dietrich resigns, they'll need a new paleontologist. You're the only candidate they're considering."

"But Max Weimmer . . . the NAS . . . I thought I was public enemy number one."

"Enjoy the notoriety while it lasts." Dr. Littman chuckled and looked over at Nick. "It won't last long—not once Nick goes public."

Katie turned to Nick for an explanation.

"After the truth comes out, nobody in their right mind will accuse you of cooking the data again. You're the one who kept pushing to report the facts—whether anyone was willing to publish them or not. Max Weimmer will have a lot of explaining to do. He was using his position to run a smear campaign against us while we were running for our lives in the desert. People in my department are furious."

"Your department?"

"They've reversed their tenure vote. I leave for Pakistan this afternoon." Nick's eyes sparkled mysteriously. There was still something he wasn't telling her.

"But you're going to help with our whale paper, right? Your team did most of the work."

"I doubt you'll have time to work on the whale for quite a while."

"Why not?"

Again the mysterious smile. "Have you already forgotten about Eve? You have soft tissue from an ancient hominid. Even at a scant hundred thousand years, Eve will be the hottest babe to hit the cover of *Science* since Lucy."

"But she belongs to the Transvaal Museum. They're going to want her back—like yesterday."

Nick punched a few buttons on his satellite phone and handed it to Katie.

"What are you doing? I don't want to talk—" She put the phone to her ear. It was ringing. "Nick!"

A click cut the ringing short. "Hello, Kruger speaking." A man with a soft accent.

"I'm sorry, this is Katie James, and my friend—"

"Dr. James. Very good. Thank you so much for calling. I take it Dr. Murad explained our situation to you?"

"Nick didn't explain *anything* to me. He just dialed and handed me the phone." She glared up at Nick.

"Well, I'll tell you what I told Murad. The hominid fossil Dr. Fischer stole was mixed in with a collection of ape fossils collected by a graduate student, Murray Cherry, in 1939. Dr. Cherry's been dead for eighteen years. Since we don't have the resources to study the fossil ourselves, we'd like you to finish the analysis you already started."

"That's . . . I'd love to!" Katie looked up at Nick. He was grinning from ear to ear. "We've already got a partial sequence for several markers. We'll just need to do another round of radiometric dating and we'll have a paper."

"Ah yes," Kruger said. "They were able to get an excellent date for those fossils. Three and a half million years, I believe."

"Three and a half million years?" Katie lowered the phone and covered the mouthpiece with her hand. "He says the fossil is three and a half million years old."

"No way . . ." Nick grinned. "Those intelligent design people are everywhere."

Katie shook her head and sighed. It wasn't going to end. No matter what they did, they'd never be able to make the controversy go away. She thanked Kruger again and hung up the phone. The room was totally silent.

"Katie, it's okay. This time will be different." Nick's soothing voice. "This time you've got the fossil. You can take all the time you want."

You? Katie's heart sank into her stomach. "Don't you mean *we?*"

Nick just stood there, shifting miserably on his feet. Surely he wasn't going to bail on her. Not now, after everything they'd been through together.

"I . . ." He cast a desperate look at Dr. Littman. "I talked to Jerry about why we can't work together. It's okay. I get it now. I told Kruger Eve was all yours."

"But I never meant . . ." Katie felt the room closing in on her. "We already agreed. We already started. . . ."

"You'll be fine." Jerry Littman stepped forward and placed a hand on her shoulder. "You'll take some flak for a while, but you've got the fossil now. Eventually the other scientists will be able to confirm your results."

"But . . ."

"Meanwhile, Judy and I just learned we'll be in New Mexico over Christmas, doing a Bible study with a very good friend of ours."

Katie turned to Mrs. Littman.

"I don't suppose you'd be able to come out to visit us?"

"Sure, I guess. . . . Where will you be?"

"At a ski resort in Taos. It's supposed to be quite spectacular."

"Taos?" Katie's breath caught in her throat. A *Bible study* in Taos? Whirling around, she looked at Nick. He was watching her with intense, hope-filled eyes.

"I'd . . . love to," she said. "Maybe while we're there, we can discuss setting up a new collaboration?"

Nick's face lit with a radiant smile. "Beautiful."

A Note from the Author

*T*HE INTELLIGENT DESIGN MOVEMENT isn't new. For thousands of years man has looked at the world around him and wondered whether somehow, somewhere there might not have been an intelligent designer behind it all. Not only is the question obvious, but its ramifications are profound in the extreme.

Considering the importance of the answer, one would think the world of science would encourage this direction of inquiry. But in reality, nothing could be further from the truth. The search for evidence for an intelligent designer, they say, isn't science. It doesn't belong in the research labs, let alone the classrooms. Anyone who engages in such a search is viewed with derision and suspicion—or even worse.

It's tempting for intelligent design advocates to vilify the scientific establishment for this type of narrow-mindedness, but scientists have had very good reason to be suspicious. More than a century ago, Christian creationists began to engage in a pitched battle against the theory of evolution. The majority of these Christians, however, weren't trained as research scientists. No matter how earnest and well-meaning their intentions may have been, many of their techniques and assertions were seriously flawed. Because they were already convinced of the rightness of their conclusions, they tended to cherry-pick the data, including only the snippets that seemed to support their view and rejecting as propaganda everything that argued against it. It's little wonder that in most scientists' minds both creationism and intelligent design have come to be almost synonymous with bad science.

So how can we help to bring resolution to this situation? In my mind, both sides of the debate would do well to consider the oldest book in the Bible. In the book of Job, God sets forth the tone for our investigations. When he asks Job, "Where were you when I laid the foundation of the earth?" he wasn't looking for a pat, scientific-sounding answer backed with persuasive rhetoric. As he continued to ask Job question after question about the expanse of heaven and death and Leviathan, it wasn't because he expected Job to have all the answers. Just the opposite; God wanted to show Job that he *didn't* have all the answers.

The study of science shouldn't make us more arrogant; it should make us more humble. When it comes to the details of creation, we could all take a lesson from Job. Sometimes the best, most profound answer is to say we don't know and put our hands over our mouths. Some things really are too wonderful for us to understand.

John B. Olson

About the Author

JOHN B. OLSON is a novelist and computational biochemist who lives with his wife, Amy, and children, Peter and Arianna, in San Leandro, California. John earned a PhD in biochemistry from the University of Wisconsin at Madison, and did postdoctoral research at the University of California at San Francisco. After almost eight years as a director and principal scientist at a scientific software company, John now devotes himself full-time to a ministry of writing and speaking. He is the author of *Adrenaline* and, with Randall Ingermanson, the Christy Award–winning *Oxygen* and its sequel, *The Fifth Man*. See John's Web site at www.litany.com.

INTELLIGENT DESIGN?